Praise for *Akhmed and the Atomic Matzo Balls*

"This book is very sick. Highly recommended."
— J. Maarten Troost, author of *The Sex Lives of Cannibals,*
Getting Stoned with Savages, and *Lost on Planet China*

"*Akhmed* is the *Dr. Strangelove* for our times."
— Marcy Gordon, editor of *Leave the Lipstick,*
Take the Iguana

"I'm ashamed to say I loved this book. It's demented, deranged, and offensive...but hysterically funny."
— Lavinia Spalding, author of *Writing Away: A Guide to Au~~~~~ Traveler*

"Delectably despicable. W~~~~~~~~~~~~~~~~~~~~~~~~qa."
— Kir~~~~~~~~~~~~~~~~~~~~~~~~~ in Moscow: A Brat in the USSR

"Buslik will throw anyone under the bus for a cheap laugh. Frankly, we're sick of it."
— Rabbi T. Canarish

"Patients like Buslik are the reason I got into this business... and why I quit."
— Daniel P. Luce, psychotherapist

"The world's funniest book outside of North Korea."
— Supreme Leader, name withheld

"Wackier than a bus plunge!"
— Hugo C., prominent Venezuelan

"You'll wet your Depends! Trust me!"
— Fidel C., prominent Cuban

AKHMED

AND THE ATOMIC
MATZO BALLS

AKHMED
AND THE ATOMIC MATZO BALLS

A Novel of International Intrigue,
Pork-Crazed Termites,
and Motherhood

Gary Buslik

Solas House Fiction
Palo Alto

Travelers' Tales and Solas House are trademarks of Solas House, Inc., 853 Alma Street, Palo Alto, California 94301. www.travelerstales.com

Cover Design: Kimberly N. Coombs
Page Layout: Cynthia Lamb, using the fonts Bembo and TheMixBold
Production: Christy Quinto

Distributed by Publishers Group West, 1700 Fourth Street, Berkeley, California 94710.

Library of Congress Cataloging-in-Publication Data

Buslik, Gary.
 Akhmed and the atomic matzo balls : a novel of international intrigue, pork-crazed termites, and motherhood / Gary Buslik.
    p. cm.
 Summary: "Iranian president Akhmed teams up with the leaders of Venezuela and Cuba and their American intelligence agents to smuggle radioactive matzo balls into Miami Beach. But intelligence being as slippery a concept to these nincompoops as chicken fat on linoleum, when each member of the gang decides to ladle out his own personal nuke soup, holy terror Akhmed is left steaming. Will his plan to destroy America float like a fly or sink like a lead dumpling? Star-crossed lovers, conniving academics, and blustery social climbers collide with ravenous termites, international do-badders, and multi-level marketing in a plot as fast-paced and hilarious as a runaway mountain bus. Radioactivity has never been so much fun." — Provided by publisher.
 ISBN 978-1-60952-069-4 (pbk.) — ISBN 978-1-60952-070-0 (ebook)
 1. Presidents—Iran—Fiction. 2. International relations—Fiction. 3. Nuclear terrorism—Fiction. 4. Satire. I. Title.
 PS3552.U82335A46 2012
 813'.54—dc23

                                2011047346

First Edition
Printed in the United States
10 9 8 7 6 5 4 3 2 1

For everyone who is kind to animals.

PART I

One

"They're killing me, Hazeem," whined the Iranian president, Akhmed, as he lay in his jammies, tucked into the sheets of his ornately carved, gold-plated bed in the master bedroom wing of his Tehran palace. "Hand me the thermometer again, will you?"

"But you just finished taking your temperature, Your Greatness, and it was perfectly normal. A little below, in fact."

"Don't you turn on me, too, Hazeem," the president moaned. "I couldn't bear it. Everyone around here wants to see me dead—don't deny it. I thought I could depend on you, at least."

"Of course you can."

"Then hand me the damn thermometer. I feel feverish."

Hazeem complied.

"Shake it down for me, will you?"

Hazeem shook it down.

The president opened his mouth and lifted his tongue. Hazeem guided the thermometer in gingerly. Akhmed gestured for his friend, interpreter, and confidant to hand him the *Popular Mechanics* magazine that, along with *People*, *Marie Claire*, and *House Beautiful*, littered the foot of the bed. He leafed through it, found a dog-eared page, and, pointing at his mouth to indicate he didn't want to talk with the thermometer under his tongue, handed the magazine to Hazeem.

The interpreter glanced at the article, "How Terrorists Could Make a Suitcase Atomic Bomb." There were some nice graphics—very detailed illustrations—and even without reading the article, Hazeem could see they had researched the topic. Even at a glance he got the feeling that any rogue knucklehead could slap the thing together in the back of his carpet stall on weekends, between hits of his hookah. They not only made it look easy but fun. Even Hazeem—a peace-loving fellow if ever there was one—felt the urge to run out to Omar's Hardware and round himself up some nuclear weapons parts.

He handed the magazine back to his president. "Nice."

"Nice!" Akhmed exploded, apparently forgetting the thermometer. It did a little pirouette at the tip of his tongue, and as he inhaled for another shout, it slid down his esophagus and got stuck.

He gasped for breath and began to turn blue. He pointed desperately to his throat, but Hazeem pretended not to understand. He knew he'd rescue the little bugger but wanted to screw with his head for a minute—although he did consider breaking for lunch, which he was fully entitled to do, as there was nothing in his contract that stipulated Heimliching his boss back to planet earth. Finally, though, he reached into his president's mouth and, with two fingers, fished out the thermometer.

"What the hell were you waiting for?!" the president gasped.

"I didn't understand what you were saying."

"You're an interpreter!"

"No harm done, Most High One." He held the thermometer at the angle where he could read the mercury. "Still just short."

Akhmed shot him a glare.

"I assure you," Hazeem said, displaying the thermometer, "I was not referring to height. I meant you'll be happy to know you're a little below normal."

"Well, guess what? I'm not happy, okay? Don't think for a second I don't know they're slipping me some funky thermometers made in China by six-year-olds who wouldn't know the right temperature if they stuck their heads up their scrawny butts. I'm telling you, they're trying to kill me around here." He hurled the thermometer against the wall. "I don't care what it says! I have a fever!" He pounded his ankles against the mattress. "Fever! Fever! Fever!"

"But the doctor said he suspects only an ulcer. It's not going to kill you at all. When you get your X-ray tomorrow, you'll see. Once you know you're not dying, you'll automatically feel better. That's the way the mind works."

"So now you're a mind expert? Spare me, Einstein."

"I think you mean Freud."

"Who cares? They're all Jews. It's me we're talking about. Stick to the subject."

"All I'm saying is, a simple change of diet, and you'll be your old lovable self. Soft foods, that's the ticket."

The president grabbed *Popular Mechanics* and shook it stupid. "It's not my diet, Hazeem. It's our so-called scientists. You see for yourself: every mope on the planet knows how to make a nuclear bomb except us. Look at the Pakis. When Persia was ruling the world, Pakis were eating grubs out of tree stumps—not that they're still not. When we were opening merchant trade routes throughout Europe and Africa, they were telling bedtime stories to their goats. But do they have the bomb? You bet! While we were conquering the entire Middle East, the Chinese were still blowing off their fingers with firecrackers! While they were stuffing fortunes into cookies, our people were inventing aqueducts! But do *they* have the bomb? Naturally. It's maddening! And now North fricking Korea!!! Pyong freaking Yang. Was there ever a more root-eating people? That little simian Kim Jong! Talk about no fashion sense!"

"Perhaps he doesn't want to appear too contemporary while the rest of his people are dying in gutters."

"Hasn't he heard of the Internet? Doesn't he know you can buy the coolest threads online at deep discount? The latest stuff. Slim cut, smart colors, all the latest outerwear? And don't even get me started on shoes."

"Maybe he doesn't have a credit card."

"Oh, I don't doubt that. Even Visa isn't dumb enough to give that deadbeat a line. All right, so he doesn't have plastic. I'll grant you that." He paused dramatically, then hissed, "But he does have something else, doesn't he, Hazeem?"

"I see what you're getting at."

"And, pray tell, what would that be?"

"Do you really want me to say it?"

"Yes, yes I do. I want you to say it. Right here, right now. Tell me what that squat little midget freak has that we don't."

"The bomb," Hazeem whispered.

"I can't heeaar you."

"The bomb," he said, louder.

"What kind of bomb?"

Hazeem cleared his throat.

"Go on, say it. I promise not to hurt you."

"Atomic bomb, Your Tallness."

"Atomic bomb!! Nuclear bomb!! Radiation!! WMD! Mass destruction! Mayhem!! Geno-frigging-cide!!"

"Your ulcer—"

Akhmed's knees bucked broncolike under the sheet. "Even that Korean turd has the bomb!" Again he waved *Popular Mechanics*. "Oh, sure, the mighty Iranians—we have oil and television and the Internet and plenty of stinking credit cards. But we can't even read simple instructions on how to make a goddamn bomb!! What are we, chopped liver??!"

"Your Mightiness—"

"I can't be very mighty if I can't even get my brain trust to figure out what every other jerkwater race has already filed under 'Been There, Done That.' I can't even *torture* my scientists into making me a bomb. I'm telling you, Hazeem, my self-esteem has never been lower. I'm emotionally fragile!"

"I see your point, I do. But we have to believe that Allah has a plan."

"With all due respect to the Almighty, I'd like to see some results already. What's the matter, we're not theocratic *enough*?"

"Perhaps it's His way of testing your patience?"

"He's pushing it, that's all I'm saying." He cast his eyes skyward. "How about cutting me a little break? Get me one teensy-weensy scientist with half a fricking brain?"

"It's obvious He's got something special in mind for you. The trials of martyrdom, after all."

The president plopped back, exhausted. He heaved for breath, sweating profusely. His sheet was heaped on the floor in a pile roughly the shape of Mount Ararat. His Dr. Denton jammies were all askew—back flap twisted to the side, his toe poking through left bootie. Magazines were scattered all over the room. Feathers began squirting out of his pillow. He stretched his arms at his side, Christlike. When at last he caught his breath, he panted, "Martyrdom? You think?"

"If not you, who?"

"Not those pains-in-the-ass mullahs, that's for sure."

"Indeed not."

"You always know what to say to me, don't you, Hazeem?"

"I try."

"We're sort of soul mates, you and I." The toe sticking out of his bootie hole wiggled. "You always manage to make me feel better about myself."

"I like you."

"I'm a good person."

"Firm but fair."

"Could you find *People*?" he asked, casting an eye floor-ward. "It's down there somewhere."

Crunching broken thermometer, Hazeem searched for and found the magazine and picked up the sheet, too. He draped both over his president's knees.

"Allah's will aside," Akhmed said plaintively, "I do wish our scientists would quit screwing around already. Sometimes I think we'd be better off with a few Zionists ourselves."

"I'll get one of the women to sweep up the broken glass."

"How about Sahala?"

"Yes, she's a pretty one." He caught himself. "That is, under the fabric. I'm only guessing."

"It's all right, Hazeem. Man does not live by falafel alone."

"Sahala, then."

"And could you do me another favor?"

"Any…almost anything."

"You know that bar refrigerator in the gym? The one no one is allowed to open but me?"

Hazeem pretended to search his memory.

"In the freezer compartment is a plastic container with a blue top. It's the matzo ball soup one of our agents sneaks out to me every month from Tel Aviv. Would you heat me a bowl? Nice and hot? Put it in the microwave on high for six full minutes."

"Matzo ball?"

"Come, come, Hazeem. You needn't seem surprised. You've heard the rumors, and they happen to be true. Yes, I do like Jew food. It's my one weakness."

"You need not tell me this—"

"The plain truth is, deli makes me feel better. It's like having my own sweet mother again before I had her killed. Alas, I always feel sturdier after a good brisket au jus. Always peppier after an apple-cinnamon rugelach."

"I dare say, chicken soup will soothe your ulcer."

The president cast him an accusatory gaze.

"I'm merely conjecturing, I assure you. I have absolutely no personal experience in the matter."

Akhmed broke into a grin. "Relax, my friend. I'm only tugging your chain. I wouldn't mind if you too were to experience the pleasures of deli. Why should I keep the *joi* to myself?"

"You're very generous," Hazeem confirmed with a bow.

"And, don't forget, a good interior designer!"

Hazeem began to back out of the room.

"And a splendid dancer!" the president called after his interpreter. "And I have fashion sense! I know eyewear!"

But Hazeem was already gone—sprinting down the hallway as if being chased by a scimitar-wielding maniac.

The next morning, the Iranian leader, feeling a bit mellower, waved to an admiring throng as his bodyguards ushered him into Khomeini General Hospital. A couple of nurses, clad in white burqas, wanted to put him in a wheelchair, but he brushed them aside. "I walk in, I walk out," he blustered, swaggering to the X-ray department. Since he was preregistered (Hazeem), he had only to flash his Blue Star/Blue Crescent insurance card before being whisked to a locker cubicle, where he was to store his clothes and don an examination robe. First, of course, the bodyguards checked the locker for explosives—planted by Mossad agents, posing as hospital accountants, presumably—and after the all-clear, he slipped in and got undressed. Before stowing his clothes, he plucked out his wallet and, still feeling warm and fuzzy from last night's steaming matzo ball soup, leafed sentimentally through his photos. There was a picture of Nazar, his late cockatiel, the best little friend a fellow could have, and of his idol, Josef

Stalin, who knew how to deal with lazy, stupid scientists. Oh, if only he, himself, hadn't been cursed with such a soft heart; if only he'd had Uncle Joe's executive temperament. He sighed wistfully and flipped to the next two photos: the black-and-white of Gordon MacRae that had come with the wallet, and a color shot of Rosie O'Donnell, scowling—perhaps mocking Donald Trump. Now there was a woman! Oh, what Akhmed wouldn't do to claim her for his stable! How she would give it to those insufferable mullahs! Look at the way she got into The Donald's face! And that mousy Hasselbeck's! Yes, sure, she was a little on the hefty side, but he happened to like plump on a woman. What was wrong with a bit of blubber? You didn't see that kind of self-assured shape on Iranian women—assuming you could see their shape, which you could not, but he had a pretty good idea what was going on under those threads. He had heard stories. He closed his eyes and imagined the lusty fullness of Rosie's burqa as it waddled around Tehran's narrow streets, trundling from one sidewalk to the other. Mmm, mmm.

"We are ready for you, Your Excellency," head nurse Fafoola called.

Akhmed stowed his things and slipped into the hospital gown. It was dreadful! Despite the recent matzo ball soup, his trip down cockatiel lane, and his wishful fantasies about Rosie, the moment he laid eyes on the robe, he fell into gloom. He recalled depictions of Persian Empire merchants and noblemen, with their ornate, flowing garments, their magnificent turbans, their sumptuous silk scarves and opulent slippers, woven with silver and gold threads. Yet where was that resplendent Persia now? He fingered the hideously frumpy hospital gown. Here, that's where.

Schmatas made in India and a so-called nuclear program without a frigging bomb! "Did you forget something, Dr. Nuclear-Bomb Scientist?" he mocked. "Oh, yes, now that you mention it, I think I forgot a nuclear bomb!"

"Your Excellency? Are you all right in there?" called the nurse, tapping.

"Of course I'm all right," he snapped. "Get me marking pens."

"Marking pens?"

"As many different colors as you can find. Red, blue, green, black. Quickly!"

"I'm not sure we have—"

Oh, great. We don't have a nuclear bomb, and we don't have marking pens. He remembered his wallet photo of Uncle Joe. "Do you happen to know where Siberia is, Nurse Fafoola?"

"Siberia?"

"Yes, you know: frozen tundra, man-eating wolves, eleven-month nights? If you don't give me red, blue, green, and black marking pens within five minutes, I am going to send you there on an extended holiday—say, the rest of your life—but only after boiling you in camel spit."

"I'm on it."

"Purple, too, if you can manage. That one is optional."

In a couple of minutes, red, blue, green, and black felt-tipped pens came rolling under the dressing room door. He had done Uncle Joe proud. He took off the gown and got to work, stretching it over the bench and tattooing it with multicolored designs—curlicues and fleurs-de-lis and butterflies and bluebirds and swirls and spirals and miscellaneous amorphous flights of graphic fancies. "There, that's better," he declared, holding the robe at arm's length and feeling glad for his people that they were blessed with such a creative despot.

When, finally, he emerged from the cubicle, six or seven of the hospital staff were semicircled around the dressing area waiting for him with grave expressions. But as soon as they laid eyeballs on his handcrafted design, they broke into spontaneous and heartfelt applause.

After having the X-rays taken and being given a Tootsie Roll Pop, the president, dressed again and with his folded gown on his lap, waited in a private lounge for an internist to discuss the results. Since his matzo ball soup, he hadn't experienced any of the sharp duodenal pain that had made him call the physician in the first place, so he felt pretty upbeat. Maybe Hazeem was right; maybe he wasn't going to croak.

But the instant the doctor entered, and Akhmed spotted that look on his face, he knew something was very wrong. His throat thickened, and his Tootsie Pop drooped. The doctor looked around to make sure they were alone. He closed the door behind him and, holding the X-rays, sat next to the president.

"I'm going to die, aren't I doctor? It's all right, you can level with me. I've lived a good life. My only regret is never having hooked up with Rosie O'Donnell, but it's too late for that now."

The doctor held up an X-ray. Akhmed's eye immediately spotted the problem. There, smack dab in his stomach were three half-roundish black spots.

"It is like no cancer pathology I have ever seen," the M.D. said glumly. "It must be very grave. But we want another opinion before losing hope. I suggest we send the films to the best clinic in the world. Unfortunately"—the doctor braced himself—"it happens to be in Tel Aviv."

The president broke out in robust laughter.

"Your Excellency," consoled the doctor, perhaps assuming his patient had gone berserk from the shock, "we need not become hysterical with fear yet."

Akhmed shoved his Tootsie Roll Pop back into his cheek. "That's not pathology, you blithering idiot."

"Your Supremeness, calm yourself. It need not mean the worst and—"

"Where the hell did you get your medical degree—Greece?!" He shook his head. "No wonder we can't make a stinking bomb!" His laugh sputtered. "I'm telling you that's not cancer. Sheesh!"

"It's not?"

"Of course not, you bloody quack. It's matzo balls."

The doctor cast a glance at the door, in case he had to make a quick getaway.

"It's matzo balls, I'm telling you. Nuked on high setting for six minutes."

"Nuked?"

"Microwaved, you knucklenuts. Get with the twenty-first century."

"Microwaved," repeated the internist, holding the film up to the light. "Yes, yes, I see it now. Matzo balls." He tittered, "How could I have missed it before?"

"Don't patronize me, you butcher. I'm telling you, I ate a bowl of soup before fasting last night. Ask Hazeem—he's the one who brought it for me. I was so hungry I swallowed without much chewing. Please don't lecture me about chewing before swallowing. I'm not in the mood. And, *pssst*, if you ever tell anyone I ate Jew food, you'll be sucking Siberian tubers with Nurse Fafoola."

"But if it's true—"

The tyrant cut him a death glare.

"What I mean is, why are the…matzo balls, you say?…"

"Go on," Akhmed growled.

"Why did the matzo balls absorb all this radiation?"

The president peered at the X-ray again. "What do you mean?"

"They shouldn't be black like this, Excellency. Not unless they were made of base-mineral ore. And even then…"

Akhmed filliped the sucker stick with his pinky.

"There is simply no way any food would show up on this X-ray," insisted the doctor. "None."

"The explanation is simple."

"It is, Great One?"

"Of course. It's obvious your X-ray machine was made in Iran by Iranian scientists. They can't do anything else right, may as well make defective diagnostic equipment."

"The machine was made by Mitsubishi, I believe."

"Say 'honest.'"

The doctor semicircled his smock. "Crescent my heart."

"Japanese, you say?" The president scratched his stubble. He snatched back the X-ray film and held it up once more. "Then what *does* it mean? Is it ominous? Did they try to poison me? I must say, I feel fine. Ore, you say?"

"Have you any more of these matzo balls, Supreme One?"

"I never let myself run out."

"I suggest lab testing at once. We should get to the bottom of it without delay."

Akhmed was concerned. "All right. I'll have Hazeem bring you a jar. Would you like it frozen or thawed?"

"You say you heated the soup in your microwave oven?"

"Not me. Hazeem."

"Perhaps we ought to test the oven as well."

"All right. I'll have him bring that, too."

The doctor hesitated.

"What?"

"Maybe it would be prudent to have another party bring the items, Your Good and Plentyness."

"Another party? What's wrong with—" He stopped. He cast the doctor a stunned look. "Hazeem? You don't think… You can't mean…"

"It's simply a matter of protecting the experiment from contamination," the physician said tactfully. "I can send someone around right away with the necessary protective gear."

"Hazeem?" the president wheezed. "No, no, I refuse to believe—"

The doctor whispered, "These are perilous times, Enormous One."

But Akhmed hardly heard him. He just lowered his head and, shaking it, kept muttering, "Not Hazeem… By the grace of Allah, not Hazeem…"

"Great news, Mr. President," Hazeem chirped on the phone the next morning. "I think you'd better pop right over."

"Right over where?" the leader asked suspiciously, mindful of the doctor's implied accusation against the president's so-called friend. Akhmed had not slept a wink imagining Hazeem cornering him in the sauna and beating him to death with a hot rock; locking him inside and turning the temperature to two hundred (he had seen that once in a Matt Helm movie); secretly replacing his baby oil with battery acid.

"To Facility Six-A."

What was this? Facility Six-A? That was code, of course, for one of the underground nuclear laboratories. Were they in on the assassination plot, too? Traitorous bastards!

"Why there?"

"You'll see. It's very exciting. A surprise!"

I'll bet, the despot sneered silently.

"An early birthday present," Hazeem pressed.

We'll just see about that. Akhmed was starting to get a little miffed. Hadn't he trusted Hazeem with his life? Hadn't he confided all kinds of personal matters, including his profound love for his cockatiel? Hadn't he shown him his wallet photos? *So this is how the dirty rat repays me. Yes, we'll just see who is more cunning than whom. You'll have to get up a lot earlier than this to get the drop on yours truly.*

He decided to play along. "Can you give me a hint, my *trusted* friend?"

"Not over the phone, Your Fullness—not even the cell phone."

"Convenient."

"Sir?"

"And I suppose you want me to ditch the bodyguards? Or are they in on it, too?"

"In on what?"

"All right, Hazeem. I'll bite. But I think there is something you should know first."

"Yes?"

"Your young niece…the one who attends university in the United States…"

"Samreen?" Hazeem said, his voice rising. "What about her? Is she all right? Nothing has happened—"

"Nothing yet, my *trusted* friend."

"*Yet?* Good heavens, this is no topic for riddles."

"Quite so. I know how fond of her you are. And vice versa. I know how much she depends on you—as do we all. And I'm sure she and all of her…activities, shall we say, will remain under cloak to assure her continued safety."

"Activities? What activities? What the blazes are you talking about? Don't joke about Samreen. I won't have it."

"Never mind. God willing, she will be safe and sound, snug as a bug."

"She does her studies, that's her only activity. She is a straight-A student. I see her grade reports."

"And you never need worry about monkey business, if you know what I mean."

"I have no idea what you mean."

"Naturally, we have people in strategic places everywhere to protect our interests. Something could easily be arranged."

"Samreen is my interest only, no one else's."

"To make sure she doesn't get seduced by the wrong element, you know? America is not a safe place for young

Muslim women—with all their drugs and alcohol and young black men, heaven forbid."

"Are you suggesting having her followed? I won't stand for it. She is pure and innocent. She has nothing to do with geopolitics."

"I take you at your word. It is only something to consider for the future, which, Allah be praised, will be long and blessed. Perhaps we could discuss the matter further after meeting at the Facility?"

Agitated, Hazeem spluttered, "There is nothing to discuss, Mr. President. The matter is closed."

"Ah, I thought you might see it that way. Do you still have a 'surprise' for me, then?"

"Here," Hazeem bristled, handing the phone to someone. "You deal with him."

"Your Eminence?" said a new voice. "It is I, Tahir."

"Tahir? You mean, Hazeem really is calling from Facility Six-A?"

"You'd better come see for yourself, Your Prominence. We have made a wondrous discovery."

Akhmed leapt out of bed. His covers went flying. "What?! A breakthrough?!"

"This is a momentous occasion."

"OMG! Why the bloody hell didn't Hazeem say so?! What's wrong with that man? You're not yanking my cord, now, are you? Because if you're screwing around, I'll reupholster my minibus with your children's flesh. Baby Tahir will be the steering wheel cover."

"Congratulations to you and all Iran, Your Heightness!"

"I knew you could do it! Never a doubt in my mind! Break out the Tab. You can make a toast to me."

"As you request, Your Eminence."
"I'm on my way down!"

Down was right. Nine floors below a location so secret that even he didn't know where the heck he was (design was his thing, not directions), the president sat sipping a diet soda and listening with wide-eye, rapt attention as Tahir stood at a control panel in front of a thick-glass observation window, explaining what was about to happen. Next to him sat a lab-coated (he wished he could work his marking-pen magic on that puppy) assistant, and next to the president Hazeem rested against the edge of a counter.

Behind the observation window, marked with several yellow-and-black international radioactivity symbols, a robot arm hovered over a stainless-steel table on which sat one of Akhmed's matzo balls. Well, he presumed it was his, not imagining anyone else in the country having any. Seeing it made his tummy growl.

"We bombarded this food item"—the scientist couldn't bring himself to utter a Jewish epicurean term—"with enough rads of enriched uranium to kill an entire harem of goats. When we pass the Geiger counter over it, it should click like a sky filled with locusts, and the needle should bend like the Strait of Hormuz."

"Very literary," the despot said, slurping. "But may I remind you, you're paid to be a man of science, not Kahlil Gibran?"

"Watch." Tahir nodded to his assistant, who flicked a switch and, with two fingertips, tickled a joystick. The console speaker whirred, and beyond the glass the robot arm swung to a countertop, grasped a Geiger counter, arced over the table, and floated the radiation detector within an inch of the Zionist food item.

The device clicked lethargically.

"Some uranium," the president scoffed. Did he have *stupid* written on his forehead? Was this puny demonstration how they intended to save their incompetent hides?

"You don't understand, Your Greatbigness. I assure you, that dough ball is radioactive enough to fell a camel at a thousand meters. But for some reason it's clutching those rads like a collapsed star's gravity field. I've never seen anything like it. It's a scientific wonder. We haven't the slightest notion why on an atomic level it's behaving this way. It could be the texture of the dough—very moist and absorbent—possibly neutronically mutated by some fortuitous outside agent. Or its properties: a certain kind of chicken used in the production of fat, or a method of distilling its grease."

"Outside agent?" Akhmed hissed, gazing accusatorially at Hazeem.

"Not a person agent," clarified Tahir. "A circumstantial agent."

"Speak Farsi, man."

"Perhaps a serendipitous confluence of forces, each benign in itself, creating an effect greater than the sum of its parts. That microwave oven of yours, for instance: did it emit electromagnetic energy at an aberrant frequency? Or said chicken: what did it eat the day it was slaughtered to produce the fat in the doughy mixture? Or the cracker meal: was it somehow affected by an unusual blast of solar gamma rays—from intense sunspot activity, perhaps? Or…" He hesitated.

"What?" the president demanded.

Tahir cleared his throat. He lowered his voice. "Or possibly the hospital's X-ray machine."

"I knew it!"

"Not to say it's defective, Momentous One," he clarified. "Only to suggest a possible unexpected influence on the unstable Zionist product, which, as you are well aware, is made with the blood of Christian children."

"Your point being?"

"We are taking a close look at the X-ray apparatus and also testing the microwave as we speak. Perhaps an examination of the food itself may reveal answers."

"All mildly interesting, but what does it have to do with our atomic bomb, and"—he glared at Hazeem—"how is it an early birthday present? Are you telling me that this matzo ball will detonate a nuclear device?"

Tahir looked down. "Not precisely, Your Tremendousness."

"Then I suggest you precisely tell me why you dragged me out of bed."

The scientist poked the air. "Observe, please."

As the assistant worked the joystick, the robot arm placed the Geiger counter next to the matzo ball and picked up a nearby hammer, with which it gave the ball a sound thump. The Jewish delicacy split open and scattered in mushy fragments. The radiation detector went wild, its languorous clicking erupting into a plague-like clamor.

"Allah be great!" the president gasped, leaping off his chair and launching his can of pop into the air, soda splattering on the window. Immediately sensing the significance of what had taken place before his very eyes, he exclaimed, "We've split our atom! And it's Jew food!"

"Again, Your Fullness—not exactly. But we've done the next best thing. And I quite believe it's not only as good as an actual nuclear bomb, but in practical respects, even better."

Akhmed's eyes narrowed. "Better than the *bomb*?"

"Please sit again, and I will explain. Would you care for another Tab? And possibly another pair of pants?"

Tahir did explain, and it was magnificent. While his highly competent scientists (Tahir's words) were assiduously developing a controlled nuclear reaction—a true atomic bomb—the president had lurched into a substitute so stunningly insidious, so ingeniously nefarious, so understatedly efficacious, regarding His Eminence's brilliance and killing Jews, that the chances of sneaking a nuclear-type explosive into the United States and wreaking havoc on its life and economic well-being had increased manyfold.

"What the devil do you mean 'nuclear-*type*'?" the Iranian leader asked with healthy skepticism.

"No, no," Tahir assured him. "It's nuclear, certainly, but not in the normal"—he splayed his hands—"*ka-boom!* sense of the word…. More in the brilliantly creatively ingenious sense of the word. You see, developing a conventional atomic bomb is difficult enough, but miniaturizing it to be able to stand even half a chance of smuggling it into the U.S.—well, who knows how long that might take, despite our tireless, dedicated, patriotic, religious, and completely loyal work ethic? But sneaking in a suitcase full of spherical Zionist food items that won't even appear on low-level airport or, better yet, seaport radiation X-ray scanners into a Jewish-dominated American urban center of depravity would be a slam-dunk, if I understand the expression correctly. The beauty of your discovery—that is to say, your *invention*—is that it will require only a small amount of conventional detonation to impose maximum death and destruction, not to mention commercial disruption and chaos."

"I like where this is going," admitted the president.

"As you yourself witnessed, for some mysterious chemo-molecular-subatomic reason, the radioactive dough balls appear completely inert—indeed *are* radioactively entropic—until violently agitated, at which time they release their stupendous stored energy like a tiger, devouring every coolie on the riverbank, so to speak."

"Yes, I see," Akhmed said, rubbing his hands in glee. "That Zionist-loving city won't be fit for habitation for months. What a boon to civilization!"

"Months?" said Tahir, glancing twinkle-eyed at his assistant. "Try *years*."

"Years!"

"Thousands will die painful, gruesome, agonizing deaths."

"You're right! A regular atomic bomb would be quick and painless—too good for the infidels! But this...slow and...gruesome, you say?"

"Excruciating."

"Oh, if only I could be there to take a video!"

Tahir considered. "Perhaps you could arrange it."

The president screwed him a glare. "I'm speaking rhetorically, you traitorous imbecile."

"Traitorous? Me? Oh, no, Your Stubbleness. Ask anyone here. They will all vouch for my complete devotion to your health and well-being. Why, just the other day I was telling Faizal—"

But the president was no longer paying attention to the head scientist. He was standing with his face pressed to the observation glass, gazing at his smashed matzo ball as if it were a pound puppy. He loved the little guy more than ever. The runt had given its all-too-brief life in full devotion to its master. There it lay, broken and alone in a melting ring of chicken fat, crackling rads in dying fealty to its nation and faith. Well, not faith, to be sure, for the brave little fellow was a Hebrew heretic, though in the end he had given himself to the one true belief, and there was no doubt, no doubt at all, that there awaited him in paradise seventy-two potato latkes.

He turned to Hazeem with tears trickling down his cheeks. "Life is good, my friend," he whimpered. "I did you an injustice this morning, and I am sorry. May I give you a hug of contrition?"

Hazeem hesitated. Tahir and his assistant watched the leader and interpreter with more than passing curiosity. Hazeem's glance darted from one scientist to the other. "Perhaps a heartfelt handshake would suffice," he suggested to his president.

"No, no, nothing short of an apologetic embrace will do," Akhmed replied, crossing the floor, clasping his interpreter, and burying his wet face in the crook of Hazeem's neck, as his friend-interpreter squirmed with embarrassment.

"There," the tyrant exclaimed, letting go and wiping his cheeks with the back of his wrists. "All forgiven?"

"Of course," Hazeem assured him.

"Then all is well." The president glanced back at the observation window. "And this is indeed an early birthday present." He turned to Tahir. "Tell me, would you all mind leaving me alone for a minute?"

"Of course," the scientist agreed, ushering out his assistant and Hazeem.

When he was alone with his matzo ball, Akhmed considered the fragility of life, the transience of happiness, the injustices of this world, the capriciousness of fate. He decided that, apart from devotion to God, the noblest existence was in service to one's people, but that, as there were many who were self-serving, ungrateful, and carnal, the true martyrs had to be eternally vigilant. Was not essential loneliness, silent suffering, the fate of all great men?

Perhaps, he decided as he gazed blurrily through the observation window, he had been too sentimental for his own good. Perhaps in letting down his guard, his sensitivity had been mistaken as weakness. Perhaps he had let his loyalty to Hazeem cloud his judgment. Did the rascal think his veiled comments about Akhmed's height did not register? Did he think his repeatedly turning down his president's invitation to join him in the sauna went unnoticed? Did Hazeem really believe he could cop an attitude with his great leader the way he had regarding his niece Samreen? That he could speak to Akhmed so snippily about a what…a female?

Blinking teary-eyed at his matzo ball, Akhmed was suddenly very aware that by having taken Hazeem into his confidence, he had exposed his own vulnerability…

not only of feelings but, apparently, of life and limb. This morning's fright had perhaps been a wake-up call in more ways than one.

Kissing his fingertips and pressing his palm to the glass, he bade his matzo ball farewell and decided that, yes, he had trustingly revealed too much of his sensitive side to Hazeem—what a fool he had been!—and that a plan of remedial action was most assuredly in order.

He would pick his time and place. There was no hurry. He would toy with Hazeem as it pleased him before administering justice. Before lowering the blade.

Two

O N E   Y E A R   L A T E R

"It's not you," Leslie Fenwich exclaimed, springing from his desk at DePewe State University in Chicago. He offered his hand, politically correct-wise, even though the last time he saw Diane they were both as naked as mole rats. "Tell me it's not literally you."

"In the flesh. More flesh than ever." She glanced around his messy office, ran her eyes over his rumpled corduroy blazer, threadbare polo shirt, crinkled Dockers. His still-thick reddish mane now sported distinguished gray streaks over his ears. She shook his hand politically correct-wise back, hoping he couldn't detect her nervousness. He pumped it once and dropped it quickly, as if afraid of a sexual-harassment lawsuit, and nudged his half-reading glasses back from the tip of his nose.

"So," she said, not quite sure what to do with her cantilevered arm. "Head of the English Department. Big-time scholar. I'm not the least bit surprised."

He motioned for her to sit. "How long has it been?"

"Twenty-seven years, five months, three weeks—roughly."

He plopped into his high-backed chair. He cleared his throat. "I moved back to Florida," he bumbled, apparently referring to his having sneaked out in the middle of the night, twenty-seven years, five months, three weeks before, leaving her a note saying he'd call her later that day. "I had a superlative job offer. Tenure track position at—"

"It's okay, Les. I forgave you a long time ago. I'm cool with it."

"You did? You are?"

"We were both young. I didn't take it personally."

"I was peripatetic. In the Aristotelian sense of the word."

"I moved on, too."

"Think of me as Auguste Rodin, in a manner." He spoke more formally than she had recalled, more carefully. And where did he get that Cary Grant faux-British accent? "I saw my future in this giant block of academic marble, and it was my calling to chisel it out. As the German philosophers would say, *gesamtkunstwerk*. I speak metaphorically, of course."

"I'm not going to sue you."

He stared at her worriedly, his thumb stabbing his chin cleft. If he had smoked a pipe, he would be puffing like mad. But when she broke into a smile, he relaxed—a little. On his credenza, his CD player was spinning Wagner's *Der Ring des Nibelungen*. He reached over, brushed aside some administrative detritus, and turned down the volume.

"In the old days, it would have been the Beatles," she said.

"And rusted-out VWs and love beads," he sniggered. "Well, some of us grew up."

She pictured him stark naked, except for his Viking horned warrior helmet and fringed vest, running around the motel room role-playing Leif Ericsson discovering Newfoundland.

"Please, have a seat. Care for some tea?"

Instead of sitting, though, she padded in her Birkenstocks to the window. She gazed down at the campus triangle, its budding maple trees, newly green grass, and the DePewe State student center casting a rhomboid shadow over the lily pond, from which two maintenance men were dragging off plywood sheeting.

"Carl is still here," she said, nodding at the older janitor. "Everything's the same." She nodded at the student union building. "Is the bowling alley still here? The 'balling' alley?"

"Diane, I—"

"I'm not here to blackmail you, Les. You know me better than that…don't you? Students and professors did it all the time."

"Times are different, trust me."

"Those days were groovy."

"It meant a lot to me, too," he added, unconvincingly. "I'll never be sorry about what we had." He gazed at her dreamily, batting his lashes. Cynics might have taken his rapid blinking as a sign of deception, but for Diane it was a look that transported her back to the sensitive poetry-class lecturer she had fallen head-over-heels for all those years ago, and suddenly she was embarrassed by her own wrinkles, neck flesh, too-wide, middle-aged hips.

What torture it had been to contact him, although she promised herself to show nothing of her torment. She would be thoroughly decent. After all, it had been her choice not to have come forward sooner—and, for that matter, her choice not to do…certain things…in the first place.

And, as she had feared, now that she saw him again—officially, anyhow, for she had watched him several times from behind sunglasses in back seats of lecture halls—she fell in love with him all over again. He was still handsome and brilliant and thin and, though his writing had morphed from poetry to literary theory—whatever that was—when he spoke, he was hypnotizing. His long, complex sentences, stitched with discursive subordinate clauses, phrase slathered upon phrase, digression after digression, turned on themselves like eddying pools, only to eventually emerge into grammatical Valhalla—the syntactical equivalent of rapids rushing over a waterfall before settling into a placid alpine lake. She adored the way he used compound adjectives, convoluted modifiers that precariously dangled, metaphysical tropes, and Latinate roots with Anglo-Saxon appendages. She swooned at the way his nose twitched when he pronounced mellifluous four-syllable, hyphenated French verbs and manly, guttural German nouns. Her heart tangoed when he wielded obscure Middle-English words like a halberd, at his fearless defiance of verbal simplicity, his swashbuckling abstractions, protracted introductory gerund phrases, arcane predicate-nominatives. Her eyes rolled into her forehead when he fell into his dreamy—some would say monotonous, tedious, and wearying, but, then, they weren't in love with him—professorial cadence. She melted when he would say things like "variegated" instead of "different," "perambulate" instead of "walk," "*Homo erectus*" instead of "dude," "matrix of reproductivity" instead of "crotch."

And even though one part of her—the brain part—suspected he was now saying nice things only because he was terrified she had come back to shake him down, another part—the heart (or as Les would say, the "cardio-muscular, arterial-vascular exchange") part—tantalized her with the notion that he was sincerely glad to see her. In his deer-in-headlights way, he was darn cute. Maybe, just maybe, despite her fleshy neck, she turned him on again too, after all these years.

"So what have you been up to?" he asked, rocking squeakily. "Still writing poetry?"

"You remember."

"Of course I remember. You were damned good, too. I had high hopes for you."

"I haven't written much lately—over the past, oh, twenty-seven years or so."

"Why not? You have talent."

She sighed. "But lack artistic courage."

He puffed out his chest. "It certainly does require more than a soupçon of self-affirmation."

"Maybe I'll take it up again sometime."

"I'd be delighted to render my opinion."

"So," she said, finally sitting, tapping her thighs with her fingertips. "Corner office and everything."

"A superficial homage to bourgeois hegemony. An insult to the intelligence. They give us this instead of practical emoluments. Still, all these windows are somewhat salubrious."

"They don't teach actual literature anymore, I hear."

"It's far more enlightened this way, really." He had slipped again into his Cary Grant accent. "No dead white males dictating our syllabi."

"I know. I read your last book."

"*Shakesqueer*? Marvelous! You always were more perspicacious than your peers."

"You gave me an A," she reminded him saucily.

"Yes, well," he stammered. "Say, how about that tea? I can get Margie to run down—"

"I brought my own tips and strainer."

He intercommed his secretary, even though her desk was ten feet away through an open door. "Can you bring Ms."—he turned to Diane—"I assume it's not 'Doctor'?"

"No, but I did get my M.A. at night school."

While they waited, they quickly brought each other up to date on their personal lives, with Les, rocking hobby-horselike, apparently trying hard to stay interested. Diane still lived in Rogers Park, had a grown daughter, Karma, the love of her life, who was going to be married this June. Les had given up his Wicker Park two-flat to his parasitic, unimaginative, flaccid, passive-aggressive ex-wife during their ugly divorce (she having felt threatened by his success, having let herself get flabby, and having had low self-esteem—though he couldn't imagine why). Thank heavens they'd had no kids. "I say 'heavens' metaphorically, of course—being a proud atheist. Nothing's changed there, all right."

His secretary came in and handed Diane a cup of steaming water and a napkin. On her way out, she left the door ajar. Diane plucked a strainer and an envelope of chai buds from her purse, tapped out about half into the little colander, and poured the steaming water. She blew on it, whiffed deeply, and sipped. For several minutes, neither she nor Les spoke.

Finally, swiveling, his knee whacking the desk, he coughed, "So, what brings you back to DePewe after all these years?"

She took another sip, got up, and closed the door, testing it to make sure it was latched.

"We need to talk, Les."

He turned white—even paler than he already was.

She sat again. "This wasn't easy, I want you to know that. I've been thinking about it for a very long time. Twenty-seven years, five months, three weeks, to be exact. Even as recently as this morning I wondered if I'm doing the right thing."

He peered over his glasses. "Really, Diane, if there's something—"

She exhaled. "You know when you said thank heavens you don't have any kids?"

The glasses slipped off his nose.

"Well," she whispered, "that thing about not having kids isn't exactly true. I hope the 'thank heavens' part too."

He fumbled with his glasses, trying to flip them back on but poking himself in the eye.

"Remember that night after the Paul Simon concert, when we went back to your office to toke and get wild? Remember how you put your reserve condom next to the ashtray, and your joint fell and burned the package? How you thought it would be all right because foil doesn't burn? Well…foil does burn, apparently."

"Good goddamn God."

"Karma's *your* daughter, too. She's a cool young woman, Les, and I think you'll dig her."

"You're not kidding, are you?" His knee thudded against the desk. "This isn't a joke."

"I'm so sorry to intrude on your life, I truly am. Truly, truly. But something's come up, and I think I should tell you so you'll be prepared."

He shot a look at the door, making sure it was closed. Still, he lowered his voice. "You mean something besides *this*?" He sprang up and paced. The office began to smell of sweat and toxic exhalations. Every few seconds he dinged her a glance and bleated, "You aren't kidding, are you?" and she shook her head glumly, and he resumed pacing and looking at the door. He yanked open a desk drawer, found a gnarled pack of Kool cigarettes and a lighter, torched himself a smoke, and finally collapsed back into his chair, raking his fingers over his scalp.

"I knew in those days you didn't like kids, and after you stopped calling me, I—"

"How can you be sure she's mine?"

"You're the only guy I was getting it on with."

"Yes, yes, but what I mean is—"

She put her cup on the edge of his desk and took her wallet from her purse. "For one thing, look." She handed over Karma's picture. "Recognize anyone?"

He studied the picture. "Oh, God. *God*."

"It's her real hair color, too," she said of her daughter's flaming red mop, glancing at Les's own rusty lid.

"God, God."

"I'm not here to hassle you," she repeated. "Only to let you know."

He wasn't listening. He was deep into his panic. "Twenty-seven, you say?"

"No financial support required or sought." Despite Diane's renewed crush on him, she was getting a little vexed. "Les, listen up for a second. She doesn't need money from either of us." She grimaced. "She'll soon have plenty. I mean *plenty*."

"You mean I actually have a child? A daughter, you say?"

"Karma. And she's a good, devoted daughter, even though sometimes she's…misunderstood."

"God, God, God, *God*."

"Les, something happened. I was always afraid it might come up. When she was little I told her her father was a brilliant man whom I loved and who loved me, but that he had another life now, and she understood. She never asked about you. She's always been very mature and basically a decent person, even though some people might get the wrong impression." She took a sharp breath and let out a gurgle. "But now that she's getting married, something"— tea spilled into her napkin—"changed. I know how middle class it is, how utterly bourgeois, but"—she winced—"she wants her father to walk her down the aisle."

Autistically he rocked and swiveled, swiveled and rocked.

"She's become obsessed with the idea, and I can't seem to talk her out of it. She says it's a 'family values' thing."

He slathered her a basset-hound look. "Family values?"

She lowered her head. "I'm so ashamed."

He tugged his dewlap, scratched one ear, then the other. He licked his lips. He rubbed his nostril red. He seemed to swirl into a mental abyss, as if trying to translate Marcel Proust. Finally, he said, "You told her who I am?"

"Absolutely not," Diane assured him. "But if she's determined to find out, she will. Karma can be very…focused. Anyhow, she's now got the"—she paused—"resources to find out whatever she wants."

"Why not tell her I was a one-night stand?" he offered frantically. "You know, a hippie passing through? Or that I'm dead? That's it, I'm dead."

"Because, for one thing, I don't lie to my daughter. And she'd find you anyway, trust me."

He returned to rocking.

"I thought I should prepare you, that's all. It seemed the right thing to do."

He bellowed his shirt to circulate air.

"In the name of full disclosure," she stuttered, "there's something else I need to tell you. Could you please sit still for a second?"

He stopped, and, before putting out the first, lit another cigarette.

"I did my best to bring her up with good values," she went on, wiping her palms on her jeans. "When she was a teenager she was a strict vegan—totally organic. Never wore leather, let alone fur. Wouldn't step on an ant. Volunteered at hospitals, was a big sister to underprivileged kids, helped out at a nursing home. She was a totally far-out, out-of-sight chick. Wore Earth Shoes, recycled, shunned Styrofoam, always chose paper over plastic—"

He started slapping his head.

"—refused to spray fluorocarbons, rode her bike instead of depleting earth's unrenewable resources, worked the phones for PBS, passed out fliers for Bill Clinton and—" She sighed. "Then something happened, Les. Something weird, and I don't know what to do. I did my best with

her. I thought she was going to be all right. But now—"
She began to cry. She pulled a wad of recycled tissue from
her purse and covered her face. "Oh, Les," she sobbed,
"we'll need all your brain power now."

He raced around with his box of Puffs, handed her a
half-dozen with which to smother her hysteria, all the
while glancing nervously at the door. "Diane, listen to me,"
he whispered. "Please. Control yourself. Listen, listen." He
paused until she nodded. He knelt in front of her. "The fact
is," he said measuredly, "I'm currently dating the chancellor, and any hint of a scandal would destroy—" He shook
his head and started over. "What I mean is, I've worked
assiduously to advance in the department and, hopefully,
beyond. I have a chance of becoming dean of Liberal Arts,
and it all depends on her, the chancellor, Leona Beebe."

Diane peered up, dark-faced, from the tissue.

"I know, I know. I used to belittle the whole administrative infrastructure," he said. "But practicality being what
it is, I—"

"He's a Republican," she whimpered.

He looked around, as if to be sure no one was in earshot
of such language. "Please, Diane, you're distraught—"

"Karma's fiancé. Angus." She choked back a sob. "A *conservative. And now she's one, too*." She pulled the tissues from
her face, squeezed them into an even tighter ball, drew a
mournful breath, and moaned, "They're *both* Republicans!"

He reeled as if shot. He tried to get up, staggered, collapsed into a lump of corduroy blazer.

"Karma's become one of *them*!"

"Have mercy."

"Now she's working *their* phones! Passing out *Newt
Gingrich* fliers! Volunteering for the Republican National

Committee! Oh, Les, Les. Maybe if she'd had a father in her life—"

But Professor Fenwich wasn't even pretending to listen anymore. He returned to his desk, buried his ears under his elbows, and curled into himself like a dying spider, kicking his desk rhythmically, possibly to the beat of an old Peter, Paul, and Mary song. Kick, kick, kick.

"She watches conservative TV," Diane stammered. "*Sean Hannity...The O'Reilly Factor...Mad Money with Jim Cramer...*Tucker Carlson...Joe Scarborough.... She reads Charles Krauthammer, George Will..." She gulped dryly and reburied her face in the tissue. "Michelle Malkin!"

Kick, kick, kick.

"Oh Les, Les, *Les...*"

Kick, kick, kick, kick, kick. "Oh God, God, *God...*"

Three

Henri Charbonnay, commerce minister of Haiti, thrust his kisser at his island's western shoreline three thousand feet below the Cessna and, as if he had never experienced glass before, whacked his face and made his nose bleed.

"You quite all right, there, Mr. Minister?" shouted Alex Gleason, chapter head of the British West Indies Benevolence Club, over the propeller roar. Gleason was convinced that the commerce minister was a cretin and probably a danger to others as well as himself.

"*Byen, byen,*" the minister, bleeding into an airsickness bag, assured him.

Gleason had let the imbecile talk him into taking the plane to view the country's catastrophic erosion. As if Gleason's file folder crammed with UN environmental reports, Red Cross disaster records, UNESCO health, nutritional, and mortality crisis bulletins, and U.S. Geodetic satellite photos—which even more dramatically showed the vast delta of Haitian topsoil dissolving into the leeward sea—were somehow not enough to convince the Benevolences to name Haiti its donee of the year. Gleason strongly suspected that the commerce minister was so bored out of his skull—Haiti having had no real commerce for the last, oh, two hundred years—that almost any diversion, including breaking his nose, was more appealing than sitting in his office swatting flies. Besides, Charbonnay, like his ministerial colleagues, knew graft opportunity when he smelled it—said sense of smell being as highly developed in Haitian olfactory membranes as hearing is to Haitian tympanic bones when voodoo drums thump over hill and dale—and, in order to make damn well sure that Henri Charbonnay and only Henri Charbonnay would be the legitimate beneficiary of any illegitimate remittances, he wished to impress on Gleason his power and importance by pretending that this was his personal airplane at his ministerial beck and call, a charade that would have been hilarious if it hadn't been so pathetic, because evidently Henri thought you could smash your face against an airplane window and people with money to hand out would not think of you as an incompetent moron.

"I've seen quite enough," Gleason shouted over the din of the engine, which had been sputtering anyhow, so it was probably a good idea to get back to terra firma. "No sense dying before the check clears."

"Quite so, quite so," the minister agreed, grinning complicitly. He tapped the pilot on the shoulder, lifted his right headphone, and yelled, "*Desann!*"

An hour later, in the foothills overlooking Port-au-Prince and the sea, the minister and Gleason sat at a white wicker table on Charbonnay's fretworked veranda, sipping rum punches and munching conch fritters. Unfurled between them, a satellite map of Hispaniola's western sea shockingly confirmed the massive, Rasputin-beardlike estuary of topsoil runoff the men had observed from the plane.

The minister's yard was lush with flowering shrubs, a bougainvillea-woven picket fence, yellow-hibiscus hedges, stands of flaming poinsettia, lavender plumbago, and trumpeting morning glories. Iridescent hummingbirds zipped between clusters of oleander and lantana, yellow bananaquits and red-winged bullfinches flitted from railing to sugar bowl, and a nimbus of bees hovered over a koi-speckled lily pond.

"Look here," scolded the BWI Benevolence head, "after our frightful experience with your previous great-hope-of-the-common-man president, why the devil shouldn't we be reluctant? We sent all those fat pink pigs to replace your scrawny black ones to start a pork colony for starving people, and when I came back a year later to see how it's doing, what do you think I saw on the president's bloody front lawn?"

"All your bloody pink pigs," confirmed the commerce minister, jutting his lower lip. "The man was a miscreant. A damned thief."

"Like the bloody rest of you."

"True, but look how arrogant he was about it. No humility, that one. When we ran him out, do you think he was even good enough to leave the pigs for our next president? They say his girlfriend accidentally left the gate open, but my own theory is that the spiteful cur deliberately released them into the hills! If he couldn't have them, no one could!"

"A man of the people," Gleason snorted.

"Still—decorum, you know."

"Decorum, my foot. I suppose—" But Gleason stopped talking when the servant girl glided out with another plate of fritters.

"*Pa gen pwoblèm*," the minister assured him, patting the girl's rump, which pleasantly bulged in pinkish-beige stretch pants. "Cléo has no ears for politics." He winked at Gleason. "Only a tail for her employer." He turned again to the young woman. "*Wi, cheri?*"

"Only legs for my purse," she replied.

The minister laughed and spanked her bottom. "Later, you naughty girl," he called as she slipped back into the house. "For the time being, more drink!"

The sun bumped the crown of a distant hill, spilling shadows across the sprawling city, draining its color. A fretwork outline stretched onto Gleason's map. He set his drink on the border between Haiti and the D.R. "Look here, Henri, this erosion business has to stop. It's going to kill you all. There, now my conscience is clear."

The minister shrugged. "These are a very ignorant people. Perhaps it would be nature's way of—what's the expression?—thinning the herd?"

"I don't doubt you're right, but in the meantime we can't very well send you another fifty thousand saplings, only to have the peasants keep cutting them down and burning them for fuel. Good heavens, man, can't someone teach them the concept of foregoing immediate gratification for longer-term good? It's not bloody brain surgery."

The minister pouted. "They care more for having babies and eating."

"It's not like the first batch came without training. We bloody well explained it takes ten years to reforest. That's not so long in the scheme of things."

"The ungrateful wretches claim it's a lifetime when you're starving."

Gleason tapped the photograph. "Look at this mess. There's barely an inch of topsoil left on this whole side of the island. You can't keep cutting down trees and expect to keep your blasted dirt, man. One more hurricane like Oscar, and what's left of your agriculture will be completely done for. Then all the Benevolence trees in the world won't save your damn black hides."

"But I can promise you—"

Gleason gazed around the minister's lush garden. No shortage of topsoil here. "*Promise* me?!"

Ignoring the insult, Charbonnay, sipping his punch, went on: "The problem was in giving them trees directly, you see." He gazed at a deforested range of southern hills, where barren streaks of gray runoff made it look like God had wiped his shoes.

"How the devil are we supposed to save your damned ecosystem if we don't plant trees?"

"What I mean is," Henri said, slurping, "you should give the trees to the government, and we will sell them the trees."

"*Sell* them?! Good grief."

"You don't understand the Haitian peasant brain, my good friend. If they purchase a sapling, even for a lowly centime, they will never cut it down until it stops growing. Every year they will come out and stare at their investment and measure how much it has grown from one month to the next. Only when the 'interest' stops compounding will they cut it down for fuel or to sell for furniture."

Gleason crunched an ice cube. "You know, Henri, your wormy mind might have crawled into the truth."

The minister raised his tumbler. "*Mèsi*, my friend. To our mutual health."

"But how can we be sure the farmers will want to buy the trees—even on credit?" Gleason asked.

"Wanting has nothing to do with it," Henri snorted. "We will merely pass a new law. How many would you like them to buy? Five, ten each?"

Gleason raised his glass. "Your lack of conscience is an inspiration."

"Thank you once again. But it's for their own good, dear friend. You see how avaricious they are, without any appreciation for your kindness. They are like infants. We have a responsibility to teach them the value of money, do we not? Teach them that money doesn't grow on trees." He coughed with laughter at his own pun, and the hack knotted into a gasping choke. He motioned for Gleason to slap him on his back.

But something strange had caught Gleason's eye, and he was no longer paying attention to the commerce minister. A denuded oval, perhaps a half-mile wide, scabbed a southern mountainside. This patch of eroded earth was different from the surrounding washed-out land, a more ghostly gray, mounded like a grave. If the mountainside resembled a dying man's waxy pate, this was a basal-cell carcinoma, a ceraceous mole, a malignant hatchery feasting on its victim's scalp, gathering strength to metastasize.

Gleason stared at the spot with a terrible premonition. Clouds congealed on the mountain's brow. A premature chill rose zombie-like from the veranda floorboards. He shivered, and his ice cubes crackled. When the city fell completely into shadow, and distant voodoo drums began their twilight rumblings, the chapter head of the BWI

Benevolence Club snapped out of his waking nightmare to glance over at his host, face down on the table, passed out from his pun-guffawing lack of oxygen. Gleason bolted up, frightened. "Cléo!" he yelled into the house. "Come help! Help!"

"I feel like such a failure," Diane told Les, as she swirled an asparagus spear around a dollop of Hollandaise sauce. A week after she had dropped the bomb on him in his office and his catatonic meltdown, they sat in a cozy booth at Chez le Pitre just west of Chicago's Gold Coast, Les apparently recovered.

"We wanted to change the world, remember?" she went on. "We were going to, too." She self-consciously paused, wondering if it was ungrammatical to juxtapose two homophones. But since Les didn't cast a disapproving look, she assumed that, its awkward (and ill-conceived, to be sure) construction aside, it was probably kosher. "You did your part," she went on, "ridding literature of all those oppressive European males—Shakespeare and Hemingway and Dickens—but me, what have I done? Matzo balls, that's what."

"Matzo balls?" he asked, nibbling his Moët (true champagne, having been produced in France, not that ersatz California excretion, and also containing a French *tréma* diacritical accent mark over the *e*).

"I've become my mother, plain and simple. No, I mean it. It's not funny. Remember how I used to mock her?

How she would call me to make sure I had enough clean underwear and Tide, how she'd send me all those chocolate coins for Passover? The time she sent that two-pound block of halvah that I didn't pick up from the post office for a few months, so that by the time I did, it was an ant farm?"

Diane wouldn't mention how comforting the tiny, industrious pets had been after Les had stopped calling. "It was a good joke at her expense…and now I'm sure *my* daughter is laughing at me. It's true, I call her every night for no rational reason. 'Hello. Fine. Goodbye.' I'm even starting to talk Yiddish to her. '*Nu? Vus machst du? Zay gezunt.*' Once a month I send her a jar of matzo ball soup. Can you believe it? Me, bell-bottomed, love-beaded, toe-ringed, hippie-Diane, sweating over a stove, boiling matzo balls?"

"It's not morphing into your matronly progenitor that's bothering you," he offered. "It's having become"—he crinkled his nose—"middle class."

She sighed. "What happened, Les? I was going to join the Peace Corps, feed the hungry, build houses in Africa. Instead, I'm rolling matzo meal."

"But you produced a female progeny. That's something. The world needs more women. If only women ran the world. Progressive-thinking women," he hastened to add, "not Margaret Thatchers or, heaven knows, Michele Bachmanns. Again, I use the word *heaven* in its secular sense."

"I was sure she would grow up to be everything I wasn't. Until…this."

"One door *se ferme* and another *s'ouvrit*," Les assured her.

"Isn't that just like you."

"When you told me, I admit the first thing I thought of was my relationship with Chancellor Beebe—how my career was going to be completely deconstructed. Don't get me wrong. I'd like to be dean. I certainly deserve to be, and, for all its faults, DePewe deserves to have me. Liberal Arts and Sciences could definitely use my superior intelligence and administrative hyper-competence. But it got me cogitating. I've been kissing Leona's posterior for almost three years now, and *regardez-moi*—I'm still only head of the English Department. After seeing you, I faced the inescapable realization that she's *never* going to give up that power over me. Power never gives itself up voluntarily, does it?" he sneered. "There's your so-called democracy for you. It's enough to make you want to join forces with—"

He stopped. He pierced her a look. Had he said too much? But no, her eyes were still focused on some faraway galaxy, where couples were always in love.

He cleared his throat. "So," he said, steering himself back on message, "my realization turned out to be positively epiphanous. It got me to thinking even more globally—figuratively globally, that is. I actually have a daughter now, an heir, a child who wants me in her life, in addition to which I have a former girlfriend who doesn't despise me—"

"Despise you? Oh, Les, you couldn't be more—"

"No, please, let me get it off my chest. It's been swirling around my *région d'intérieur* for too long. All right, I ratiocinated, so what if I never become dean? So what if I never see Leona socially again? So what if I'm reduced to persona non grata, career-wise—if I'm professionally nihilized? The important thing is, now I have you and Karma and…"

"Angus."

He studied her again for any sign that she wasn't buying this. But she just continued to gaze fatuously at her distant galaxy.

"I've been given a second chance, Diane, if you'll pardon the passive construction. How many people can say that? I mean the second-chance part, not the passive-construction part. In any event, you can't imagine"—he secretly winced—"how much I'm looking forward to meeting her and, um…"

"Angus."

"The Four Seasons restaurant, you say?"

"Thursday night."

"I'm fervently anticipatory."

She smiled at him over entwined fingers. "You're a mensch, Leslie Fenwich."

"Who knows, maybe menschdom's been in here the whole time, subcutaneously. But now, thanks to you, it's risen to the dermis."

"And you know what? I still adore your dermis." She glanced around at the other patrons and felt herself blush. "Maybe that's the champagne talking."

He reached over and took her hand. "Truth is nectar of the soul."

"Who said that? Shakespeare? I mean, Shakes*queer*?"

He shook his head. "Fenwich." He wrist-flicked the sommelier. "I don't mean *immortal* soul, of course," he hastened to add. Thumb in bottle punt, the wine waiter topped off their bubbly. Les tongued the liquid. "So, tell me a little about our future son-in-law."

"Angus Culvertdale, heir to Global Boffo."

"A Republican."

She made a face as if snapping into a jalapeño.

"No social conscience at all?"

"That's the heck of it, Les. He's got a heart of gold. He set up his own charitable trust—"

"Tax dodge."

"—that gives gobs of money to causes we could only dream about. Plus, he treats Karma like a queen—"

"Cunning!"

"Takes her on trips around the world, introduces her to celebrities, buys her expensive jewelry. He bought her a new Mercedes SUV, and they're not even married yet. A gas-guzzler. Twelve miles to the gallon."

"Capitalist skullduggery. You won't fall for it, of course."

"That's the worst part of it. I *like* him. I mean, really *like* him. He's sweet and thoughtful and never says a harsh word about anyone. He's offered to take me to Switzerland with them in November, and I'm embarrassed to say I'm considering it. He's funny and optimistic and cheerful and completely supportive of everything Karma wants to do, and I just want to squeeze his cheeks to death. I'm so confused."

"It so happens, I do have one of my brilliant suggestions. It wouldn't be an entire solution to the problem—more a palliative than a cure—but it would be a start." He swished bubbly around his molars and swallowed contemplatively. "You know the state is insolvent, and, naturally, this being such a brutally plutocratic country, the universities are always the first to suffer. If the governor would raise income taxes again, fine, but the malefactor is more concerned about not offending wealthy landowners than nurturing our wombs of intellectualism."

She clung to his every word, trying desperately to hold on, as he dragged her around by his linguistic ankle.

"The department hasn't hired anyone in five years, and the faculty haven't gotten a raise in three. It's abominable, unconscionable, and disgraceful. How do they expect us to attract superior theorists? The best we'd ever be able to snare are *literature* people. Now, if your…*our* future son-in-law…"

"Angus."

"…could be persuaded to include the English Department on his list of foundation recipients? Oh, I know it's ill-gotten money—no doubt profiting off the poor—but if you, let's say, could persuade him to add the department to his charitable trust, or however those things work, to the tune of, oh, as much as humanly possible, I believe he could depend on his future father-in-law's blessing, in terms of walking down the aisle?"

She frowned. "Does it mean that if he won't—"

He squeezed her hand. "You know me better than that. Of course I will. It's within the framework of my moral cadre"—he pronounced it *cahd-ray*. "I'll walk my daughter down the aisle irregardless—or regardless, if you believe *irregardless* is a tautology, which I don't happen to—pardon ending my clause with a preposition. I hope to meet her beforehand too."

She smiled again.

"That'll be our little secret for now—leverage, you know? If you make the presentation the correct way—you know, don't actually conjoin the ideas formally, no ultimatums per se, he'll undoubtedly seize the opportunity to display his so-called generosity to his prospective in-laws—assuming he's as self-centeredly charitable as you portray."

"Brilliant!"

"*Précisément.* I do feel we have to give him some guidance, in terms of amount? He surely has no idea what dire straits DePewe State is in. Probably never bothered himself with the exigencies of higher callings. I haven't the faintest idea how much he'd be inclined to contribute. A chair is only a million dollars. Quite spectacular recognition, though. Probably name the cafeteria meatloaf after him. Unless he's a vegetarian, and then he'll get the cauliflower."

"A million dollars?!"

"They arrange payment plans, I'm told."

"A million dollars," she murmured, deflatedly.

"Or for the less committed, a hundred thousand could secure an endowment. A family endowment, for that matter. Maybe he'd get the mashed potatoes."

"A family endowment! Far out!"

"Something the grandchildren would be proud of."

"Grandchildren! Oy!"

"Then you'd…*we* would certainly never have to worry about them getting into DePewe. I mean, in the unlikely event their high school grades aren't stellar."

"Oh, I'm sure they'll be brilliant grandchildren."

"Consider it a safety net, then." He raised his flute. "To Angus."

"To Angus."

"To…"

"Karma."

"To Karma. And to genius grandchildren."

She pressed her hands to her cheeks. "*Kinders!* From your mouth to God's ears!"

They clinked glasses. Sipping, he muttered, "Whatever."

The captain of Elysium Cruise Line's newest and grandest ship, *Countess of the Sea*, currently docked at the Port of Miami, received an e-mail from his marketing director and sent this reply:

> Dear Miss Bjornson:
> Let me see if I understand you correctly. A certain apparently very wealthy young woman…the future Mrs. Culvertdale, you say?…has chosen to *charter*, for her and her bridegroom's *exclusive* use, our magnificent new ship, in order to grace us with her wedding ceremony and subsequent honeymoon, during which bride and groom will ply the Eastern Caribbean with a complement of two hundred crew—all because she believes *Countess of the Sea* resembles a *giant wedding cake*? Do I have, then, a full understanding of the situation?

To which the marketing director replied:

> Dear Captain Pfeffing: This is an outstanding opportunity for us, it being off-season.

To which the captain responded:

> Dear Miss Bjornson:
> I understood the line to be doing well. The

bonuses were certainly generous—which, needless to say, we appreciate.

The marketing director wrote:

Dear Captain Pfeffing: Times aren't always so wonderful. The industry is just now recovering from the recession, barely, and another economic slowdown seems always around the corner. The business cycle, you know. It's simply prudent to bury your nuts for the winter.

The captain wrote back:

Dear Miss Bjornson:
Bury my nuts?

The marketing director clarified:

Dear Captain Pfeffing: Not *your* nuts. Not anyone's nuts per se. Not any *man's* nuts, certainly. We simply see this as an unexpected profit source—a windfall, if you will.

The captain explained:

Dear Miss Bjornson:
The staff works hard all season. Most work twelve, fourteen-hour shifts—very little sleep from December through May. They look forward to relaxing in between. It's vital to restoring body and soul. I believe I speak for the crew in saying

there are more important things than unexpected profit sources. Of course, it's your prerogative to poll them yourself. Do your own market study, as it were.

The marketing director explained in return:

Dear Captain Pfeffing: Sorry to say, we can't pick and choose our opportunities. We simply seize them or not, and I dare say, the cruise-line boneyard is littered with skeletons not designed to flex.

The captain replied:

Dear Miss Bjornson:
You're lecturing me on ship design?

The marketing director replied in return:

Captain: Don't you think you're putting the worst possible spin on this? *Of course* I'm not lecturing you on ship design. Surely you know I didn't mean that literally. What do I know about ship design? They float, that's good enough for me. I haven't the faintest idea how they float, and, frankly, I don't care. As long as our passengers don't drown, so we have a chance to sell them cruises in the future, that's all I'm concerned with. The rest isn't my business. I don't even like water, to be honest. And I'm not that crazy about fresh air and sunshine. I've grown accustomed to doing

without either. But this I do know: we, both you
and I, have an obligation not only to ourselves and
our staff but to our investors, who pay our salaries
whether we like it or not.

I really think you're letting your pride get in
the way.

The captain summed up:

Marketing Director:
Now at last I do understand. Pride ought have
nothing to do with it. I'll be sure to pass that
along to my crew.

The marketing director bristled:

Capt.: You know that's not how I meant it.
Threats aren't productive. Technically it's not *your*
crew, you know? You don't sign their paychecks.

The captain bristled back:

Mkt. Dir.:
I'll pass that along as well.

The marketing director shot:

I was hoping this might go more rationally.

To which there came no reply.
To which the marketing director suggested:

Dear Captain Pfeffing: Perhaps a short phone call might clear up this little misunderstanding.

To which there still came no reply.

To which the marketing director slammed her fist on her keyboard, demolishing the numeric keys. Oh, how she despised that haughty Karma Weinberg. How she wished "the imminent Mrs. Angus Culvertdale" would be tanning herself on the ship's deck when a giant intergalactic-alien-squid tentacle would pull her into the Bermuda Triangle and force her to breed to freshen its gene pool.

Just not before her honeymoon-cruise check cleared the bank.

Four

IN THE RESTAURANT LOBBY OF THE CHICAGO FOUR SEASONS Hotel, Diane nudged Les (and herself) toward their daughter. "Les, meet Karma." Diane shifted her weight, wiped her palms on her dress, and cleared her throat. "Karma, allow me to introduce you to your, um, well, uh…"

"Father," Karma said, completing Diane's sentence with a baleful glance. She turned to Professor Fenwich and offered her hand. "Glad to finally meet you, Popsie."

Les detected something vaguely sarcastic there. Nevertheless, girding himself, he opened his arms in a well-rehearsed, completely insincere gesture of paternal affability. "Please, call me Les."

Karma, refusing to step into his embrace, withdrew her hand. "I'll stick with Popsie."

He looked her over in the dimness of the elegant eatery, this Gold Coast gastronomical temple to *nouveau riche* epicurean gluttony (as if you could tell the difference when it came out the other end). Sure enough, even in the *impuissant* light, he could (unfortunately) see Karma's resemblance to her picture in Diane's purse and, necessarily by extension, to himself. Popsie and daughter, mother and future son-in-law—one big happy family.

After shaking his future father-in-law's hand on behalf of himself and his betrothed, Angus whispered something to the maître d' and, (despite the languorous lighting) visibly enough for all to see, slipped him a folded hundred-dollar bill, whereupon Karma snapped her fingers for her little tribe to follow him to their window table.

Snapped her fingers.

So right off the bat Little Lord Fauntleroy Culvertdale and his future *femme* confirmed the impression they had precursorily made on Popsie (being Republicans was abominable enough, but chartering a giant cruise ship for their exclusive use as a bridal suite was beyond the solar system in over-consumptive insufferability).

Nevertheless, Leslie Fenwich, Ph.D.—*Professor* Leslie Fenwich—had always wondered what it would be like to have dinner at a decadent bourgeois trough like Seasons, overlooking this boulevardian emblem of conspicuous self-indulgence (until now he had dared not try the experiment; aside from the cost, there was always the risk that someone from the university, perhaps sightseeing on Michigan Avenue after having had a properly proletarian Gino's pizza, would connoiter him leaving said decadent bourgeois trough, imperiling his reputation as a committed proponent of wealth redistribution and dashing his pedagogical ambitions), so Angus's invitation had held a certain fascination. If anyone from the English Department did happen to spot him, he had only to tell the truth—that he was enduring the unendurable as a sacrifice to the welfare of the university; that to attract big money, you sometimes had to jump into slop with swine. It was disgusting, and average college administrators wouldn't do it, but, of course, Leslie Fenwich wasn't average. Whatever he did, he did to perfection—with, as he would sniff to chancellor Beebe, while scrubbing her back in the shower, "full devotion to the cause."

In preparation for this dinner, he'd had his blazer cleaned and pressed—menial work that marginalized and degraded Third World subalterns, who had immigrated to America hoping to find freedom, only to be forced into a life of unfulfilling labor and subservience to middle-class, white-customer oppressors, forced to adhere to historically Eurocentric, repressive standards of commerce, such as competitive pricing, guarantee of quality, an unblocked fire exit, and rat-free premises; not only did they have to touch their so-called superiors' personal garments (sometimes of a most metonymically demeaning nature—e.g., pantyhose), they were forced to call them "Mr." and "Mrs." (in Les's case, "Dr.") and actually thank them for their business, as if they were serfs thanking their feudal lords for not pillorying them in the public square or strapping them to a tree to be eaten alive by hounds. What's more, also in preparation for this meet-up, having discovered that he had no shirts without secretion stains in the nipple areas, Les had rushed out to Marshall Field's to buy a new button-down-collar long-sleeve, only to discover that the beloved emporium was no longer Field's but—get this—Macy's, the flagship brand of the national corporate behemoth, Federated Department Stores, which unsentimentally devoured venerable regional treasures the way barracuda devour shrimp.

Which was precisely the menu item—shrimp, not barracuda—the Professor now screwed his eyes into on the

Season's appetizer list. North Atlantic jumbo shrimp, detailed and shucked, served on shaved ice with Thousand
Island-cilantro dressing and wedge of lemon. Yum. His
glance minueting to the right side of the menu, he began
to salivate at the description of the various steak dishes.
At first he thought he might select the Delmonico New
York sirloin *au poivre* with cognac sauce, but that city reminded him of Macy's, which was not only the standard
bearer of the aforesaid Federated corporate monster but
which sponsored the Fifth Avenue Christmas Day parade.
Sponsoring anything remotely to do with religion he
found so repulsive that his salivary glands immediately
shut down, his throat closed up, and he had to quell his
gag reflex. What's more, he recalled his recent shirt-buying excursion, in which, instead of nostalgically finding
the cozy and comforting—despite its annual Christmas
tree—Marshall Field's, he had come face to face with
the conglomerate-spawned Macy's, and further in which,
being thus forced to suffer the grim truth that nothing
was more sacred in corporate America than the almighty
bottom line, he had dejectedly shuffled over to Carson
Pirie Scott, where instead of *that* hometown favorite, he
found only a boarded-up former department store, now
ententacled in construction scaffolding at the bottom of
which a gargantuan sign announced the coming of luxury
condominiums, starting at "only" $750,000! Good God,
who made that kind of money? Not anyone in the damn
English Department.

Which was why, despite its come-hither delineation, he
now decided to take a pass on the New York pepper steak
and order the house specialty instead. That description was
no slouch: "Two-inch thick prime Kobe beef, brushed

with a light honey glaze, nestled in caramelized onions and knighted with cross-swords of asparagus." Who wrote this stuff, anyway? Starving linguistics majors?

Unlike the Delmonico, this Kobe meat sat well with Les's conscience. Kobe was Japanese beef, from Japanese cows that had been fed only the finest grains, never force-fed, never rushed to market. True, at a gazillion dollars a pound (this he knew from listening to National Public Radio, not from the menu, because, in fact, his had no prices listed, Angus having made self-aggrandizingly sure the waiter knew that he was host), the meat did seem a bit pricey, but didn't we owe them that? Didn't we racistly and cruelly intern Japanese-Americans at the start of World War II? Didn't we murder, maim, and genetically deform thousands of their civilians—the elderly, women, children, handicapped—by dropping atomic bombs on Hiroshima and Nagasaki—vile, unnecessary, barbarous acts whose only true motive was a show of force that would ensure the supremacy of the American military-industrial complex? Not to mention that sickening newsreel footage of the mushroom cloud rising behind the *Enola Gay*, shown in every theater in the United States, reducing unspeakable and gratuitous human suffering to petty bourgeois entertainment? *See melting flesh, pop a licorice.* Not that anyone could ever make up for that savagery or the hundreds of thousands, perhaps millions, of innocent lives America had destroyed in its wars of military occupation, cultural hegemony, and economic imperialism, but didn't the collectively and historically culpable have the responsibility to at least try? Wouldn't ordering Japanese meat be the least Professor Leslie Fenwich could do? Not that Les himself, personally, was guilty, of course. Anyone who knew him would understand that he was thinking synecdochically—which he liked to do.

So he was all set to order the Kobe, his salivary glands once more in full shock and awe, his fingernails scraping the silk-lined menu in happy and (after his department-store running-around, shirt-buying ordeal) ravenous anticipation, his throat again as wide and wet as Tokyo Bay, when Diane furtively leaned over to him and whispered, "Don't forget, strictly vegetarian."

A blinding flash of light. Reflexively, he looked up from his menu to the other side of the table, but it was only Angus smiling fatuously at his soon-to-be bride, who was gulping her Dom P. with one hand and pointing at her dinner roll with the other, indicating to soon-to-be Mr. Karma to butter her a morsel.

"What?" Leslie whispered back.

"Don't order any meat." Diane nodded at their daughter. "We have to set a good example."

And so, trembling with Kobe-anticipation-deficiency—a term he immediately coined and about which he might write a scholarly article for *Verbatim: The Language Bi-Quarterly*, either from his office or, if he failed to finish dinner without murdering all three of these horrible creatures, his prison cell—he wound up ordering the pasta Olivia with broccoli and pigeon peas with a side of potatoes au gratin, holding the cheese because cheese comes from cows, and it's not enough not to eat the goddamn cows, no ma'am, you also can't eat their goddamn cheese—like they even care. Like it's not a tad too late for Democrat Mom to be setting a good example for Republican daughter—the same daughter who currently wouldn't stop complaining, loudly enough for the entire restaurant to hear, about everything in sight, including but not limited to the awful service, the stink of the waiter, his unpolished fingernails, the anemic shrimp, wilted lettuce, dry tomatoes, tasteless carrots, unabsorbent napkin, cheap perfume of the "low-class bitch" sitting two tables over, inadequate leg room, inane Muzak, clanking dishes, streaked windows, dusty chandelier, tarnished silverware, thin salad dressing, hard rolls, tasteless tie on the "appliance salesman" sitting at the next table, improperly deflected air conditioning, and rancid breath of said daughter's fiancé.

In the meantime, lovesick, puppy-eyed, obsequious Angus—butter-spreading-for-his-betrothed, humongous-blood-diamond-ring-giving, *O'Reilly Factor*-watching, Armani-tie-wearing, Polo-argyle-sock-wearing, Bruno-Magli-loafer-tapping, snort-laughing, chewing-with-mouth-open-eating, calling-in-trades-to-his-Hong-Kong-exchange-cell-phoning Angus—ordered a guess what? Correct. Flaccid-cheeked, Alfred E. Newman-eared Angus Culvertdale ordered the son-of-a-bitching Delmonico New York sirloin *au poivre* in cognac sauce—with a called-in-advance side order of macaroni and fucking *cheese*.

As Professor Leslie Fenwich—Popsie—sat nibbling his disgusting broccoli and trying to figure out how he might familiacide this threesome, in view of the fact that, even though he was philosophically opposed to capital punishment if for no other reason than that it included the word *capital*, if he himself had to go to the electric chair, it might be worth it, he watched his biological daughter eat so much of her future groom's *steak au poivre* off his plate, mopping it in his cognac sauce (complaining about it the whole time), that Angus himself got very little of it down his own materialistic gullet and so ordered a second, this time Kobe (!) steak for himself and polished off the last of this follow-up cut while Popsie was sucking his final sprig of parsley.

On the outskirts of Havana, Cuba, on the rooftop of an eighteenth-century former mansion, Akhmed, his translator Hazeem, and the leaders of two other countries sat eating a splendid parador lunch of grilled sea bass, creole shrimp, olive oil-braised chicken, honeyed ham, spicy rice and beans, steaming potatoes, and mixed salad with pepper-mayonnaise dressing. The president of Venezuela washed down a mouthful of meat with a sip of Heineken from a straw and belched, accidentally launching a shard of ham onto the Iranian president's forehead. The Venezuelan apologized to the Iranian's translator. Interlingual babble was exchanged, Akhmed speaking with his mouth full. He flicked the meat off his face onto the concrete floor, where a scrawny blackbird pounced on it and hobbled away behind a vine-threaded trellis. Hazeem assured the South American leader that no harm had been done, either to feelings or international relations. Akhmed washed down his own mouthful of lunch with a swig of Tab, a supply of which he had brought from Tehran, turned and, again through Hazeem, complimented their host, the president of Cuba, on such a magnificent meal—considering that other products and services in his country were total shit. "Do I use the term correctly?" the Iranian president asked.

When they had first arranged this meeting, they had considered speaking English, which they all managed pretty well, but decided against it on principle. Hazeem used the word *wonderful* instead of *shit*.

"Pork makes you stupid," said Akhmed, with an air of superiority. He plucked his napkin-bib from his shirt, crumpled it into a pile next to his plate, and, turning to the Cuban president, said, "Now, shall we discuss our business, El Maximo?"

But his host pretended not to hear.

"El Maximo?"

"Code names," the Venezuelan whispered urgently, glancing around, focusing narrow-eyed on the blackbird. "American spies are everywhere."

"Code names," Hazeem repeated in Farsi.

Akhmed sighed forbearingly. He turned again to the Cuban president. "Okay. I mean...Lovey."

El Presidente clapped his hands and giggled with joy.

In addition to having agreed not to speak English, they had also decided to always use their code names. This was the Cuban leader's idea, as were the names themselves. The Venezuelan went along with it because he so admired his revolutionary mentor, and Akhmed thought it was infantile and moronic but acceded anyway because it seemed a harmless enough way to humor these nitwits. And so the Venezuelan president became "Thurston," the Cuban leader "Lovey," and the Iranian "Little Buddy." The Cuban had written these names on slips of paper, distributed them for memorization, reclaimed the scraps, counted all three to make sure none were missing, basted them with a smidge of sofrito sauce, and then, for obvious reasons, swallowed them.

"Business?" Akhmed reminded them, squeezing his crumpled napkin like a tension ball. "Lovey? Thurston?"

"The Yanquis misuse their pigs," Lovey declared, swishing Havana Club rum around his cheeks, gargling, and, not sure what to do next, turning to Thurston.

"Swallow," said the Venezuelan.

The Cuban complied. He wiped a trickle from his beard with the back of his hand. "They feed them massive amounts of grain that could feed the starving children of the world. Look at us: our pigs are thin and hungry—good socialist pigs."

Thurston belched percussively.

"Our *plan*?" said Akhmed—Little Buddy—squeezing his napkin harder.

"Fine, thank you," answered the Cuban.

"The Americans are cruel to their animals," Thurston pointed out. "They fry their chickens without making them fight and kill each other first." He raised his finger. "Undignified."

"Our chickens we choke," Lovey added proudly.

The waitress came with another tray of food.

Akhmed asked if it was safe to talk with her nearby.

"Cecilia is one of us," the Cuban president declared. He reached over to pinch her buttock, but she scooted out of range, so he pinched his own buttock instead. "A loyal socialist. Her mother is head of her local CDR, and the parador is fully licensed. Yes so, Cecilia?"

"Yes, Maximum Leader, all paperwork up to date. We accept only Yanqui dollars and give change only in Cuban pesos."

"You see," he told his guests, "she is completely trustworthy. Her own grandfather was among the forces defending our nation against the imperialists at the Bay of Pigs, for which I awarded him a…" He searched his memory.

"Medal?" Akhmed suggested.

"No, a goat. That's it, I awarded him a goat. For a moment I couldn't recall which farm animals we were working with in those days, until I remembered that we have never given out anything other than goats and chickens, and in those glorious days we actually still had goats, so by deduction, I realized there was a better than fifty-fifty chance we awarded his bravery with a goat. Quite maximum of me, no?"

"A goat is worth far more than a medal," the Venezuelan president said, picking his teeth with a fingernail. "Only the Americans give useless medals."

"You can't eat a medal!" Akhmed agreed.

"More drinks, Cecilia," Lovey called through the doorway.

"She's a looker," said the Venezuelan, sucking his teeth. "I wonder if she screams out manifesto in the throes of passion."

"I might have been married to her mother," the Cuban leader replied. "I don't quite recall, but I'm sure it's written down somewhere. I'll ask my brother."

Growing impatient with the nonsensical ramblings of these Hispanic nincompoops, Akhmed sought once again to get the conversation on track. "So, our plan is almost one hundred percent operational, is it not?" he asked his co-conspirators.

"They have just now poured the foundation," Lovey answered, nodding over the roof's railing at a construction site next door. He waved his cigar to the security guard, who was sitting in front of the fresh cement to make sure no children came to deface it with seditious slogans like RESCUE US FROM THIS MARXIST HELL. "The concrete is still wet, if you would like to engrave your initials. Especially you"—he momentarily forgot the Venezuelan's code name—"since it is your donation with which we are building this magnificent new Museum of the Revolution."

"I'm not talking about *those* plans," Akhmed sniped. "I'm talking about the reason I came. You know…killing the Great Satan, bringing the imperialist dogs to their knees, destroying capitalism and Western-style democracy. Draining that Zionist swamp."

"Israel must be destroyed," the South American dictator agreed.

"No, you imbeciles. Not Israel!" Akhmed shouted, stomping his foot. "Miami Beach! Doesn't anyone listen to me? Is it because I'm short? Good things come in small packages. My own mother told me that before I had her beaten to death! Look at Napoleon! Hitler was no circus giant, I assure you. I know on good authority that he wore lifts in his boots and a contraption in his cap that gave his head an extra couple of inches. What's wrong with you people? We can't destroy Israel. We need Israel!" He turned to Thurston with a torching glare. "Who do you think caters our stonings?! It's Miami we don't need! Miami Beach! Remember our *plan*? *My* plan!"

"Mellow out, my tiny friend," the Venezuelan suggested.

"I don't want to mellow out! I want to destroy America! I'm not tiny! In my country, I'm average, maybe even a little taller than average! What do you want from me?!

How come you nicknamed me 'Little Buddy' unless you think I'm short?"

"Would you rather be 'Ginger'?" suggested El Max. "That would be all right with me."

"Me too," agreed the Venezuelan. "Ginger it is."

"No!" Akhmed blared. "Not Ginger! What's wrong with you people?! Do I look even vaguely like Ginger?"

"How about 'Minnow,' then?"

Akhmed cut the Cuban a withering stare.

"Minnow would be good," agreed the Venezuelan.

"Okay, okay, I'll be Little Buddy."

"Whichever you prefer."

"Either or."

Cecilia brought a fresh round.

"Too much caffeine in his soda, perhaps," the Cuban suggested to his fellow Latin American tyrant. Not recalling what the ashtray in front of him was for, he extinguished his cigar on his knee, sipped his new rum and, with a sigh, said, "All right, my dear…Little Buddy?…let's talk about the plan."

"*My* plan!"

"All right, *your* plan."

"I'm sorry I lost my temper," Akhmed said. "Look, you're the one who wants to obliterate those expatriate Cubans before you die."

"My legacy," Lovey agreed. "Personally, I have nothing against Jews, though. I like them, if you want to know."

"Well, I don't want to know, all right? I want to kill them without adversely affecting our catering needs, and you want to kill Miami Cubans, and Thurston wants to shut down the oil refinery operations off the Florida coast. Win-win-win. Do we have a plan, or don't we?"

"Eat more beans," the Cuban president said. "Don't you like our beans?"

"I like your beans fine! Where are we with our plan?!"

Thurston farted—a long bass note. "You try it," he told the Iranian leader.

"I don't want to fart. I want to destroy the Great Satan."

"Don't be ashamed," Lovey said. "It's a compliment to our beans."

The Venezuelan president leaned over to his Cuban comrade and, ruffling his own shirt, whispered, "Does this make me look fat?"

Akhmed sighed. "All right, all right. Tell me where we are with our plan, and I promise to fart."

The Latinos' glances locked. They weren't sure they could trust the little cockroach. "You go first," Thurston said.

Akhmed rolled his eyeballs. "I flew all the way from Tehran to discuss the mission. You think it was a picnic? Iranian Air isn't exactly Funjet. You can't even make out what the flight attendants are saying behind those burqas. Did she say 'your vest is under the seat' or 'your testes smell worse than my feet'? 'Yank the string to inflate' or 'spank your wang and gyrate'? It's maddening. Are you supposed to ask for a pillow or throw her out of the plane? And *you* try flying on an airline that has beaded curtains for lavatory doors and sand for toilet paper."

"That's nothing," the Venezuelan leader protested with a wave. "Try flying out of San Juan sometime! Screaming Puerto Rican kids running up and down the aisles, squirting you with water pistols. One time we had to make an emergency landing, and they found one of the little brats wedged behind the altimeter."

"I like to fly," the Cuban piped. "My feet swell and get stuck in my combat boots, so I have a good excuse for never taking them off. I also go crazy for pedal cabs. When I was in Vietnam, I hired a girl to take me around for days, just so I could stare at her rump."

"What about Caracas women? They have good rumps."

"I'm not saying they don't."

"Stop!" Akhmed wailed. "Why do you have to always do me one better? Is it because I'm short?"

Their host called to Cecilia, "Get Little Buddy a nice bowl of three-bean soup."

"I don't want soup! I want to discuss the mission! I've already proven my goodwill. I'll fart only after we discuss the mission!"

Lovey, puckering, and Thurston, running his tongue around the inside of his lip, passed each other nods. "All right, my friend," said the Cuban leader. "We'll discuss the mission first. But at least cross your heart about the fart."

Akhmed gazed dementedly at his co-tyrants, as if wanting to impale them on his fork. Instead, he sighed, lowered the utensil, and crossed his heart.

"You have to say it," the Venezuelan insisted.

"Okay! I cross my heart!"

"I'm satisfied."

"Me too."

"Then let's get on with business," Akhmed barked.

"I like business!" exclaimed Lovey.

"The mission," Thurston agreed, sucking a garbanzo.

Akhmed's glance careened from one cohort to the other. "Was that so hard?"

"I guess not," the Venezuelan admitted.

"The instrument of devastation is almost ready," Akhmed said. "Any day now. All we are waiting for is your martyr."

His colleagues fidgeted.

"What?" Akhmed, smelling a rat, demanded.

"There's a slight glitch in the martyr department," Thurston explained. "Face it, these people are basically Christians. Sad to say, they'd rather sit around praying to Jesus all day than strap explosives to themselves and blow up civilians. Go figure."

"It's not possible."

"'Fraid so," added Lovey. "Plus, they like music."

"Music!"

"We have no churches," the Cuban clarified. "So they listen to music."

"How are we supposed to destroy Western civilization if they listen to music?! Martyrs hate music!"

"Look," the Venezuelan reassured him, "we're working on it. We'll figure something out. We'll contact the Professor in Chicago. He's a jackass, but at least he's a Ph.D. jackass."

"A brilliant jackass," Lovey said, choking back a laugh.

"I never liked the blundering fool," Akhmed reminded them. "He's a buttocks-kissing toady."

"Precisely. Plus, he was raised in Miami," Thurston reminded him in return, "so he may know someone of our particular mindset. Which is why Skipper suggested we bring him onboard as a standby. That, and the fact that he despises America as much as we do. If not an actual martyr per se, he may know of at least a reliable…courier, shall we say?"

Akhmed puckered, unconvinced.

"Meanwhile," Thurston went on, "our engineers are working on the satellite signal transducer. They're arranging a final experiment as we speak. It should only be a matter of days."

Akhmed's eyes narrowed. "Days?"

"Chill out, my man. Cecilia! Bring Little Buddy a dish of ice cream."

"Ice cream? Well, yes, I do like ice cream. What flavor, may I ask?"

"We have a complete variety," Cecilia said, without a hint of sarcasm.

"You're joking?"

"Name a flavor."

Akhmed rubbed his hands. "Spumoni!"

"Spumoni it is. Also, we're testing a new flavor of the month—Mango Schmango. Would you like to try some?"

He licked his lips. "Mango Schmango? Sounds intriguing. Yes, yes, I believe I would."

"By itself or with spumoni?"

"I can have both. Really?"

"Of course. We Cubanos are nothing if not good hosts."

"I can see that."

"Besides, you are the president of Iran."

Akhmed puffed his cheeks. "Then, yes, I believe I will have them both. When in Rome—"

"Spumoni and Mango Schmango, coming up." She winked furtively at her own president, who swallowed a giggle. "Would you like whipped cream?" she asked the Iranian.

"You're kidding."

"How about a nice cherry?"

"I'm not a cherry man, but I do love whipped cream! Whipped is good! And I'm crazy about nuts."

"And a little hot fudge?" Lovey asked. "Quite the thing."

"Fudge! Oh, this is wonderful!" Akhmed exclaimed. "I feel completely relaxed now. I'm sorry I got upset before, my good comrades."

"No problema. Cecilia, bring the man his dessert."

She glided into the house.

Akhmed smacked his lips. "Hot fudge!"

"Aren't you forgetting something?" Lovey asked.

"Your promise," Thurston, blowing bubbles with his straw, reminded him.

"Really, gentlemen—"

"Now, Little Buddy," the Cuban leader scolded. "I won't have you going back on your promise. It's a matter of trust—international goodwill."

"Well, if you put it like that." And just as Cecilia stepped back out with a drooping, unadorned, mostly melted glob of vanilla ice cream, Akhmed let out a pipsqueak peep of intestinal gas. Cecilia gazed at Lovey; Lovey gazed at Thurston; Thurston gazed at Cecilia, and they all burst out in a collective, doubled-over, gasping guffaw.

Not Hazeem, though. He knew better.

In truth, Hazeem was uneasy having sat in on the meetings with those three witless troublemakers, bearing witness to the mischief percolating in their ninny brains. He had not asked for this assignment but, as usual, had been conscripted by the head ninny, Akhmed. True, back in Iran and other venues supportive of Akhmed's various zany schemes and antics, Hazeem had been present during many meetings in which various bizarre and asinine ideas were exchanged to drive Israel into the sea, wipe Christianity off the map of Europe, reestablish the continent to pre-Crusades demography, and other-such lunatic notions.

But while this cabal's lame-brained scheme, which they had goofily named "Operation Castaways' Revenge," was in a class of nuttiness by itself, the truth was, it was tinged with just enough real danger to give Hazeem a vague premonition of disaster. They weren't in the Middle East anymore—they were in the Western Hemisphere, where even before 9/11 the United States did not put up with anti-American mischief, and post-9/11 had, as the Venezuelan dictator pointed out, spies everywhere.

So, yes, it was easy for Hazeem himself to chuckle at the loony ambitiousness of their plan: how they were going to find some poor sucker to carry Akhmed's radioactive matzo balls into Miami and detonate them with conventional explosives from afar by radio transmitter, to kill many Jews and former Cubans and wreak havoc on American gasoline prices and create economic chaos and ensure the destruction of imperialist bullies and lay the groundwork for a rise of the oppressed and, not coincidentally, Muslims, and be El Maximo's parting gift to the nation that had rejected him as a baseball pitcher. Easy for Hazeem to giggle at because he knew the degree to which these three so-called national leaders were such bungling boobs, and that their plan for international upheaval would eventually amount to nothing more destructive than Akhmed's retarded little fart.

On the other hand, he also knew that America, not appreciating the inevitability of these three stooges running into one another and knocking themselves out cold, would, once it caught wind of Castaways' Revenge, not find Little Buddy's, Thurston's, and Lovey's bumbling incompetence the least bit funny.

There was something else that disturbed Hazeem, something ominous. When, as Cecilia was clearing off their table, the smirking Venezuelan greaseball, deliberately in plain view of everyone, stuck a five-hundred-peso bill down her bodice, his fingers attempting to massage her breasts (there could not be enough hot water in all of Cuba to wash away his filth), Hazeem for an instant had a dark premonition that perhaps at least one of these seeming nincompoops was not quite as incompetent as he appeared—that there was more cunning, calculating evil here than met the eye. A shiver ran through him. He feared for the innocent parador owner, who had overheard much—perhaps too much—and he feared for other unwitting witnesses and for innocent Americans.

And, yes, he feared for himself.

Five

A few years earlier, Hurricane Oscar had ravaged Haiti. It was a strange storm—obeah practitioners believed it to be not the work of Shango, god of weather, but of Damballah-Wedo, the serpent Loa enraged by man's ecological folly. It had spawned in November, late in the hurricane season, had come out of nowhere, and had moved, oddly, from northwest to southeast. Most unsettling of all, unlike other Northern-Hemisphere storms, it spiraled clockwise. No one could recall a hurricane ever doing that, although an old *houngan*, consulting cowry shells, claimed there had been one on the eve of Napoleon's betrayal of Toussaint L'Ouverture.

Also unlike most hurricanes, which skitter across the Caribbean scorpion-like, Oscar hunted like a crocodile—crawling, lunging, feasting, fattening itself in the sun. And whereas normal storms soon lose force on land, this hellish beast grew more ferocious. First ravaging Port-de-Paix, then, clawing its way past Anse-Rouge and Gonaïves and tearing into the Artibonite valley, Dessalines, Saint-Marc, and Montrouis, it grew bolder as it mutilated the Haitian hills behind Port-au-Prince and Pétionville, devouring what was left of the tropical forest, rearing demonically on the mountaintops before retracing its murderous path.

Weakened from decades of deforestation, the overplanting of shallow-rooted tubers, and other desperate, short-sighted agricultural practices, what remained of Haiti's topsoil was no match for the two-hundred-mile-an-hour fiend. Muddy torrents roiled down ghauts and gullies, hurling cows and pigs and goats, snapping palm trees, heaving tamarind trunks and banyan roots over washed-out ridges and ancient volcanic folds. When, five days later, Oscar, finally sated, slithered back to the underworld, the western half of Hispaniola resembled Hiroshima in September 1945. In satellite photos it was difficult to tell where land ended and ocean began, so murky was the coastal sea.

Over millennia, in most of the Caribbean, ecology had learned to deal with hurricanes. Trees, leaves, roots, branches, and fronds had evolved to spill fierce winds, to roll up, lean away, bear down. Birds and frogs and mongooses were born knowing how to burrow and deflect, hunker down and seek out, dig in and cover up. And when the storms passed, the land blossomed greener and more fecund than before, more melodious finches plumed brighter yellow, mammals emerged from their mothers' wombs more lustrous and stout. Nature had destroyed the weak to make room for the strong.

Even months after Oscar, though, no finch-chirring or mockingbird-guffawing or grackle-cawing filled Haiti's bruised skies. No mongoose-scurrying skipped through underbrush. No cooing of Zenaida Dove lullabied from low branches, no crowing of rooster pealed over dawn's first yawns. No whistling of tree frog, braying of donkey, naying of goat, buzzing of crepuscular bug, burbling of rufous-throated solitaire, warbling of forest thrush, hooing of vervet monkey. In Haiti, nature, like politics, had never been allowed to evolve fruitfully. For two hundred years it had been a sick and dying addict, so weakened from self-abuse, it hardly had the will to curl up under Oscar's demented beating, let alone strength to restore itself. The nutrients that nature had taken millions of years to give, the desperately poor Haitians had depleted in decades. Now when farmers gazed down at their fields, what they saw were endless stretches of glistening clay, exposed volcanic boulders, pointy stumps of truncated trees—rotting teeth and pyorrheaic gums. Without a healthy immune system, now when the land mutated it did so malignantly.

Which is what happened to a certain colony of termites.

Ordinarily the most adaptable of mandibled marauders, termites are hardy little brutes who, reproducing quickly and prodigiously and displaying adaptations of natural selection within a few brief generations, have survived almost since eels grew knuckles and crawled out of primordial slime. Yet even Haitian termites had struggled mightily during the decades the Duvaliers had kleptocrated the public treasury, forcing ordinary Haitians to chop down topsoil-retaining trees for fuel. With rich dirt washed to the sea, organic and mineral nutrients vanished. Those remaining plants whose fruits, fronds, marrow, and flesh the termites had depended on to feed their queens withered and fell. Turning their mandibles' attention to roots, the gnawing little critters found those also leached of life—for, indeed, farmers had cut mere saplings for fuel, to peddle in Port-au-Prince for pennies a pound. Millions of termites—thousands of colonies—starved to death.

But a third of the way up the south slope of the mountains behind Plaine de Cul-de-Sac, one desperate termite population found salvation in the poop of runaway pink pigs. A unique alchemy of unusual waste matter—decaying non-indigenous pink-pig excrement, dead-root detritus, ultra-violet-bombarded prehistoric diluvial clay—the sudden disappearance of natural predators, and whatever supernatural forces the mysterious Oscar had brought to bear, visited a fortuitous mutation on this colony's queen. Many worker termites died from the unholy enzymes and unique deprivations, as did their queen herself, but not before she had spawned a voracious, bloodthirsty brood of genetically altered offspring.

The first thing the brood did was eat alive those of the previous generation. They bypassed the carcasses of the already dead workers and went right for the living, separating individuals from the colony like skilled lionesses, hunting them down, ripping them limb from limb—not only to kill but kill with cruelty. These were infants hardwired in hell. Only Damballah-Wedo knew what a collective monster this unholy tribe would soon become.

Holy crap, Professor Leslie Fenwich thought as he sat on his toilet, thesaurus on lap, insufflating a joint and gazing out the window at South Loop rooftops. How was it possible? Diane seemed like a decent, if stupidly credulous, example of contemporary muliebrity. Sensitive, loving, committed to society and the planet. Member of PETA and the ACLU. Supported unions and Michael Moore and Greenpeace. Detested big business. Believed in taxing corporations to the hilt but denying them the vote. Protested against Guantanamo, Abu Ghraib, waterboarding, identity stops of Hispanic-looking drivers. Wanted full amnesty for undocumented workers, open borders, automatic citizenship for babies born in the U.S.

He took an airy drag, held his breath, ingurgitated, exhaled a limp thread of happy smoke. Not that he was happy.

He strained and strained but only managed a baby-size poop. He was seldom at a loss for either brilliant ideas or words (although getting stoned did tend to degrade his otherwise prodigious and astucious vocabulary), but this Karma beast had him mentally constipated to full blockage. Diane was a reasonably lucid woman. Not in his league of lucidity, of course, but not altogether obtuse. How could she not have seen the patently obvious? How could she possibly think her daughter was in the same cosmos as "basically good"? How could even a mother be so myopic, even if Karma was her only offspring and apparently raised under the burden of pathological guilt?

The sun was setting, and the rooftops were the color of tomato juice. They gave Leslie appetence for a bloody Mary. He assumed it was the broccoli he'd had for dinner at the Seasons that was binding him. A bit of vodka might help. Couldn't a reasonably intelligent progenitor tell that she had given birth to the Antichrist? That her daughter was the most self-centered, loathsome, bullying, condescending, arrogant, narcissistic, piggish, materialistic, solipsistic, acquisitive, shallow, callous, and, in general, miserable wretch on the face of the earth?

He shivered thinking about his meeting last night with Diane, Karma, and the future Mr. Karma. He winced with the recollection of having pretended to be enjoying their company. His viscera knotted at the prospect of having to continue the charade—though persist he would (having often assured Chancellor Beebe, while massaging her feet, that when it comes to raising funds to perpetuate their progressive curriculum, as the great Lenin said, "the end always justifies the means").

How was it possible that he, and even Diane for that matter, could have spawned that ogress, Charon, Chimera, satyr, Minotaur, griffon, gargoyle, flying monkey? In his bathroom overlooking Mr. & Mrs. T-colored roofs, as he tried to squeeze out another broccoli-bound poop while lighting a fresh kiff (unlike most English Ph.D.s, he could actually do more than one task at the same time), Professor Fenwich pondered this terrifying question. It was not a rhetorical question, for Diane had assured him that—strictly to test for any latent genetic diseases—after Karma's birth she had lab-tested the baby's spit relative to Les's own drool, a dried sample of which Diane had kept solely as a wistful memento of their love affair (unlike Monica Lewinsky, who had kept that crusty dress spooge as legal evidence), and Les believed her. If he was anything, it was a judge of character, and Diane was simply too idealistic, flower-childish, and simple-minded to be disingenuous, devious, and deceitful. Although he did suggest having a look-see at that lab report.

It was nature's cruelty, that's what. Although in considering what might have gone wrong with Karma, Les couldn't help but think of those examples in English literature in which Beelzebub reigns—*Faust, The Inferno, Paradise Lost, The Exorcist*—he was too much of a secular pansophist to actually believe in such nonsense. But how else to explain this demon, apparently born of his loins? He thought and thought, hoping the marijuana would start expanding his mind, offspring-wise. He recalled having gone to high school with a fellow named Eric Shapiro, who resembled a Neanderthal. He had a wide, sloping cranium, prognathous jawbone, heavy brow bones, thick, muscular, densely forested thorax. He walked slumped over, as if permanently deformed from dragging saber-toothed tigers back to his cave (on the plus side, no one could bowl like Eric; he knocked down pins in midair). So even before Leslie had ever heard the word *atavistic*, he realized that sometimes nature just plain screws up. It was nobody's fault. Eric's parents had looked normal enough—two regular-size Miami Jews whose genes seemed to have originated in the post-Paleozoic Era—and his younger sister had seemed more *Homo sapiens* than not, despite the fact that she diddled high-school boys with the promiscuity of a Precambrian mud fish.

So Professor F. had no choice but to conclude that his shallow, acquisitive, demanding, egocentric, avaricious, rotten bitch of a daughter was, like Eric Shapiro, an unfortunate freak of nature and certainly no fault of his own. Some might have considered her an incarnation of the liturgical Mephistopheles, Diabolus, or Lucifer, but hylotheistic Dr. Fenwich preferred to simply think of her as biology turning on itself. A walking, talking cancer cell, as it were. A virus that, like genital herpes, might be made to go dormant but never actually succumb to necrosis. Which, of course, was the problem. How to make the bitch and her turgid-headed entourage permanently go away—ideally before word got out to the public about her wretchedly prodigal honeymoon cruise—while unburdening Little Lord Angus of some of the Culvertdale millions for the benefit of the DePewe State English Department and, not coincidentally, Fenwich's own professional ambitions; i.e., a well-earned (think Leona Beebe) promotion to Liberal Arts and Sciences deanship.

Finally, giving up on pooping anything bigger than a poppy seed, Les reluctantly debouched his bathroom and, continuing to suckle his doobie, wandered mostly naked through his apartment, trying to figure out how to prevent Chancellor Beebe from finding out about this horrible product of an indifferent, godless universe, this infuriating and potentially disastrous intrusion on his otherwise well-planned career path, this malefic blight on his heretofore impressive résumé. In short, preventing her from finding out about Karma and—certainly, certainly, *certainly*—her obscenely solipsistic honeymoon voyage.

He imagined the university board of trustees, considering his deanship appointment, perusing his curriculum vitae:

Leslie Fenwich, B.A., M.A., Ph.D.

ELEMENTARY/HIGH SCHOOL EDUCATION
Frequently beat up by playground bullies for ruining
  the grade curve

UNDERGRADUATE EDUCATION
Read Proust in unannotated French

GRADUATE EDUCATION

Ph.D. Johns Hopkins University, *summa cum laude*,
  English Literature, specialty in Linguistic Theory of
  French Suffixes

M.A. University of Florida at Miami, *summa cum laude*,
  French Literature, specialty in Linguistic Theory of
  English Prefixes

DISSERTATIONS

The Handshake as Hegemonic Masculine Predation:
  Where Have Those Fingers Just Been? (Johns Hopkins
  University)

Marx and Engels: Who Pitched, Who Caught? (University
  of Florida at Miami)

PROFESSIONAL EXPERIENCE

Head, Department of English, DePewe State at Chicago

Visiting Director, Office of Counteraction to the
  Subliminal Deleterious Literature of the Military-
  Industrial Complex (OCSDLMIC), Fuega College,
  Nicaragua

Co-Organizer, Forum for Research on the Literature
  of Food Labeling in Industrialized Countries as an
  Effect on Lower-Income Persons, Especially Persons
  of Color (FRLFLICELIPEPC), University of the
  Revolution, Havana

Designed Progressive Graduate-Level Courses:
  Amorphous Transfiguration in Seventeenth-Century
    Metaphysical Poetry
  How to Talk and Write Like an English Ph.D. to
    Impress Strangers
  The Literature of Confusion

PUBLICATIONS
Books

Shakesqueer: What Fairies These Mortals Be

The Word "Putz": A Temporal-Socio-Sexual Study of Textual Transmodification

Syllabation as Mediation (nominated for the prestigious Institute of Higher Learning Filbert Frobish Prize)

The Literature of Atlantis If There Had Actually Been One

Unequal Doctors: Why Are University Professors' Incomes Disproportionately Low Compared to Those of Pulmonary Surgeons'?

Articles

"Tea as Sexuality in *Turn of the Screw*: Subtextual Gender-Role Meanings of the Word *Cup*"

"Somerset Maugham's Secret Trip to the Wisconsin Dells"

"The Brontë Sisters: Why They Wrote Instead of Sang"

"'To His Coy Mistress': Argument for 'Winged' Being One Syllable"

"Why Capitalist Society Wants the Words *Entomological* and *Etymological* To Be Virtually Indistinguishable to the Human Ear"

"Small-Minded America: The Literature and Politics of Dwarfism"

"*Unequal Doctors* Revisited: I Still Don't Understand Why English Ph.D.s Don't Make As Much Money As Medical Doctors"

ACADEMIC SERVICE

President, University Chapter of Illinois Nuclear-Free Zone (UCINFZ)

Director, United Tenured English Professors
  for Increased Benefits and Even More Paid
  Time Off Than the Rest of Civilization
  (UTEPIBEMPTOTRC)
Team Leader, Copy Machines Ink Cartridge
  Replacement Volunteers (CMICRV)

NOTEWORTHY MISCELLANY
Between-the-Legs Frisbee-Throwing Champion, 1981
Spawned Satan **(But it wasn't my fault!)**

He lay on his sofa and, contemplating the electrical out-
let cover where a ceiling fan had probably once hung and
which had always reminded him of one of the chancellor's
nipples, tried to think this through. He knew the giddy
was starting to work because on the ceiling appeared,
slideshow-like, Daguerre's diorama of the Civil War, followed by Picasso's *Guernica*, then Rembrandt's *Night Watch*.
Before long, details began to leap from scene to scene, so
that, for instance, the bearer of the Dutch flag, a reefer
dangling from his lips, was leading a two-headed horse,
each head also working a spliff, across a Gettysburg wheat
field. He felt his subconscious bursting from the corporeal
extrémité of his hippocampus, trying to communicate with
his limbic nerve bundle. The ceiling was no longer white
plaster but a museum-size canvas oozing arterial blood.

Suddenly the flag bearer wasn't a Dutch soldier but
Leona Beebe, the parakeet-faced chancellor, his ersatz girlfriend, his ticket to deanland. On the ceiling she wasn't half
as parakeet-looking as she was in person, and carrying the
flag like that into the maw of cannon fire gave her a heroic
countenance, especially with her electrical-outlet nipple

bared like a painting of the Revolutionary Lady Liberty.
He recalled the time they had first made love—such as it
was—in her office on the top floor of the administration
building. He had turned off the lights so he wouldn't have
to look at her, and in the hot summer night—the state
having again cut DePewe's budget, the building's air-con-
ditioning had automatically shut off at nine—they heaved
and sweated and squirmed and writhed, and finally he slid
off her and lay exhausted in a swamp of marijuana-reeking
perspiration, and on the ceiling in his own apartment now,
in his pothead's eye, the chancellor morphed into George
Washington crossing the Delaware, the Dutch flag became
the New Hampshire state flag with a severed snake and
the motto "Live Free or Die," and its pole a tightly-rolled
doobie.

His subconscious was trying to tell him something. But
what? Death and destruction, that's what. Blood and guts
and mayhem and war, but what did it all mean, and how
was it helping him prevent his plague of a daughter from
completely destroying his career?

Popsie.

Oh, Les thought, if only there could be a god, even
in the classic Greek *deus ex machina* sense of the term: a
mechanical device for dropping an angel onto the stage
to non-causally resolve the entanglements of the plot.
God from a machine, a crane-delivered solution to all his
problems. Oh, how he wished he had never laid eyes or
any other part of him on or in Diane Weinberg. How he
wished he didn't have to tell Chancellor Beebe, while he
was grinding her doggy style, how much he loved her
Chronicle of Higher Education article series, "Interfacing
Online Course Assimilation with Tactile Classroom

Capillarity." In truth, she was a mediocre writer, her ideas and prose postulations nothing close to the brilliance of his own. Yet there he was, servilely thwopping away at her bottom, she commanding him to go faster or slower as she liked, he obeying; she the engine, he the caboose. And still, *still*, she would not make him dean, claiming one fallacious excuse after another, month after month, year after year, as he continued his interminable compliments to the Botticellian slope of her bosom, the Raphaelian proportions of her thighs, the pleasant Velázquezian roundness of her buttocks; as he fawned and flattered ad nauseam about the aphrodisiac effects of her ambrosial perfumes, the genius of her linguistic stylings, her managerial acuity, her agile and perspicacious intellect.

All right, fine. The university wasn't an intellectual meritocracy; he understood that. But don't tell him he hadn't been providing the chancellor the best goddamn *shtupping* she'd ever had in her Jabba-assed life. If nothing else in the system of higher education, wasn't that supposed to be the path to advancement, the hierarchal *élan vital*?

There were your bitching gods for you. Laughing as men wept. Still, would it have killed them to crane in an angel just once? Put him out of his head-of-department misery? *I deserve better than having to suck the chancellor's big toe to make her come.*

One thing was for damn sure. If Professor Les Fenwich's *new* friends—his very special new friends (true, he hadn't actually met Lovey yet, but he could hope, hope, hope)— ever did turn out to need him, Leona Beebe could suck her own big toe to make herself come.

He must have dozed off, because he jolted awake to the sound of gunfire. His heart thumped like a Pete

Townshend riff. His feet vibrated. It took him a second to realize where he was and that the sound wasn't a cannon or AK-47 or firing squad or even a bass guitar. It was his phone.

Whoever was calling was determined. It took Les a minute to collect his thoughts, and still the phone wouldn't stop tintinnabulating. Finally, clearing his throat to sound head-of-departmentish, deep-throated and calm, he answered.

"Dr. Fenwich here." The phone had stopped ringing—obviously—yet his tympanic membranes still reverberated, as the Isthmus of Panama must have continued to reverberate long after those gigantic American earth grinders had stopped gnawing their imperialist way from one ocean to the other.

No answer.

"Hallo. Fenwich speaking."

There was still no voice, but he recognized the low, miasmic breathing. He could almost smell its poisonous vapors. He glanced down and noticed that while he had been dozing his penis had slipped out of his underwear, but he was so gripped by the caller's audible breath—exhalations from the underworld—that he was too paralyzed to adjust himself.

"Skipper?" Les whispered. He turned his caller ID out of the glare, but it was blank. "*The* Skipper?"

Silence.

"The *Skipper*?" Les repeated. "Yes, yes, its…*the Professor* here."

"Is the weather fair?" the caller whispered cryptically.

"It's sunny and clear," the Professor cryptoed back, sort of.

Pause. "Is it fucking *fair*?" the Skipper growled.

Les sat up, gasping oxygen into his brain. "Oh, *fair*. Yes, yes, the weather is indubitably *fair*, in the sense that—"

"Shut your trap for once and listen," the Skipper rasped. "You know anyone we can trust in southern Florida as a courier?"

Les, alert enough now to realize this was no social call, but pure, glorious business, replied, "Courier?"

"Martyr, courier, who gives a fuck? You know what I mean. Cut the bullshit."

"Hm, let me see," the Professor mumbled, more to himself than to his caller. "There might be—"

"What're you, fucking stoned? Not on the phone, numnuts. I'll get back to you."

The Skipper hung up. Leslie held the receiver to his ear for another minute and in the air a minute more. He shook his head, trying to clear the last of the fog. Was he really awake, or was this another part of his bad ceiling trip?

He whiffed something fowl, glanced down and saw that his roach had burned a hole in the carpet. He poured a glass of water from his kitchen faucet, doused the smoldering dub, and guzzled the rest of the water. His throat was desiccated and sore. He had never had a dream in which it was uncomfortable inhaling good biff, so he was convinced he was no longer sleeping. He sat on his couch and considered the phone call. He looked up at the ceiling, but it was as white again as Leona Beebe's knees.

He glanced out the window. It was nighttime now, and two old warehouse buildings bookended a skimpy spine of Lake Michigan, encyclopedias squeezing a poetry chapbook. A garland of lights drifted across the narrow gap, bulbs festooning a sightseeing boat.

It hit him. He jumped up and began pacing in front of the window, forgetting that his penis was still dangling *à la region d'extérieur* of his fly. He began to put two and two together. The weather was becoming fair indeed. Yes, indeedy, fair indeed. Fair skies, calm seas. Low seas, *perfect for honeymoon cruising.* No high waves to upset Princess Bride Karma's delicate tum-tum. Yes, indeedy. Calm seas. Calm cruising all the way.

Did he happen to know anyone in Florida they could trust? Not exactly. But he knew someone better. *Much* better. In fact, *more* than one.

Again he gazed at the ceiling. But now he saw there not blood and guts but a heavenly parting of clouds, God touching Adam's fingertip, trumpeting angels, archangels, sunbeams and flowing robes, naked cherubs, stars, feathery wings, and heavenly splendor.

Dean, my foot. Leona Beebe, my foot. DePewe State or anywhere the goddamn else in America, my stinking foot.

Professor Fenwich realized he had been knocking his brains out, chancellor-wise, for nothing. Nothing, nada, bupkis. He didn't need Leona Beebe. He didn't need her parakeet beak, her flabby tuchas, her yogurty nipples. He didn't need to be crummy dean of Liberal Arts. Fate had something much greater in store for *the* Professor Les Fenwich. For *the* Professor, Fate had chosen not run-of-the-mill ambition, not garden-variety ass-kissing, not commonplace curve-ruining. For him, Fate had chosen *glory.* Glory on an historical scale. Glory on a biblical scale (as an atheist, of course, he used the term strictly as a trope).

Let's see what those playground bullies will think of little Leslie now.

Six

"I want to go dancing!" Akhmed told Hazeem, in the lobby lounge of the Parque Central in Habana Vieja, two evenings after their parador lunch with Thurston and Lovey.

"But I beg you to be reasonable," Hazeem replied. "I've been up for the past twenty hours, following you around Havana like a puppy, this way and that, never stopping. I can't keep my eyes open."

Akhmed stomped his foot. "I don't care! I want to say I danced with Cuban girls!"

"But why? They are no different than Iranian girls. Except that"—desperate times called for desperate measures—"they are taller."

"What are you saying?"

"Only to take that into consideration."

"That they won't dance with me because I'm short? I'll make them bend their knees! I'm president of Iran! I'm a player! I have mojo!"

"But what if word gets out, Your Bigness? The imams might not construe you as holy." He shook his head and clicked his tongue. "Scripture strictly prohibits dancing with infidels."

"It does?"

"Chapter fifteen, verse twenty-three," Hazeem fibbed— for, indeed, he had never read the book, preferring lighter fare, such as Rex Stout mysteries.

Fortunately, his president had apparently not read the holy book either. "It's something to think about, isn't it?" Akhmed agreed. "The Zionist oppressors have their noses everywhere, and they control all the media."

"Wouldn't want to be seen in the *National Enquirer*, Excellency. Especially in the section on bad fashion." He made a sour face. "Or next to those drawings in which you have to find ten slight differences."

"Indeed, no." Akhmed thought for a second, then snapped his fingers. "I've got it! I'll wear a disguise! That's it! I'll dress up as a…a…woman!"

"But then girls will not want to dance with you."

The president frowned. "Yes, you're right! You see, Hazeem, why I need you?" (*You'd like to think so, wouldn't you?* Akhmed thought. *Well, we'll just see about that.*)

"Perhaps we are both overtired, Superior One. Perhaps a good night's sleep—"

"I know! Girls everywhere love strong male role models. I'll dress up as Adolf Hitler! I can stuff my shoes with toilet paper to make myself taller."

"The toilet paper here is very thin."

"Coincidentally, I brought an armband and field marshal's cap with me. Come on, Hazeem. Don't be a poop.

Let's go dancing!" He grabbed Hazeem's hands and twirled him in front of a sofa. "Find a nightclub. I want to practice my samba!"

Hazeem sighed. He knew it would be useless to argue. Besides, now that he thought about it, he could use a bit of fun. Not only his lack of sleep, but his worry about bearing witness to the Castaways' sinister plotting had left him mentally exhausted. Heaven knew, he was ready for some womanly company, perhaps even a little affection. Who knew, maybe he would even get lucky with a *señorita*. The closest he had ever come to kissing a woman's lips in Iran had been through polyester.

So at nine-thirty Hazeem and his president hailed a "lemon" taxi, one of those round, yellow, two-seater, scooter-powered intercity cabs that had tickled Akhmed's fancy, and they wound through the narrow streets of the Old City, Hazeem dressed as himself, the president as der Führer, saluting young woman and believing they secretly wished to dance with him and brush their lips across his mustache. True, it wasn't a mustache per se. Because he already had a bristly beard—the type that tall men, especially strong, muscular American athletes, grew—and certainly had no intentions of shaving off that bad boy, what he did instead was denude a postage-stamp-size square under his nose, so that in the exact place where the actual Führer had grown his dinky little stein-duster, the Iranian president now had a sexy smooth spot, a romantic clearing in his meadow of stubbly mug, a converse image to the rather (forgive him for thinking so) unimaginative, Third-Reich, hirsute version. Akhmed's, on the other hand (face), being bare-skinned, had an edgily lusty look and was even, he was convinced, a little arty.

Near Obropia and Bernaza Streets, across from El
Floridita restaurant and bar, whose daiquiris Hemingway
had made famous, they pressed into Caliente, a singles
club their hotel concierge had recommended. It was
crowded and cacophonous, inside and out, and Hazeem
and Akhmed had to squeeze through the throng sideways
(it was a good time to be small), holding their ears. Inside,
no one seemed to notice or care that Adolf Hitler was
among them. Del Shannon's "Runaway" blared from two
elephantine speakers hanging over the dance floor. The
president glanced at Hazeem and grinned. His eyes twinkled in disco-ball reflection. "Decadent, no?!" he shouted.

Hazeem looked around at the girls, long and languid
in their platform shoes and capri slacks, shallow-breathing
in their skinny-waisted spandex tops, their lustrous Latin
bosoms shimmering in the close heat. He was no longer
tired. A dark-skinned waitress, her hair cornrowed, her ear
studded silver, leaned so close to him to ask for his order
that his cochlea tingled under her sweet, hot breath, and
his Eustachian tube became rigid. He had heard marvelous
things about these Afro-Latina beauties but heretofore had
resigned himself to dying without ever having the pleasure
of partaking of one himself.

"Go on, Hazeem," said Akhmed, "order a mojito!"

"Your Excellency!"

"As far as I know, there is nothing specifically in
Scripture prohibiting cane distillates."

"True, true," Hazeem guessed. "Very well," he shouted
to the beauty. "A mojito it will be!"

Akhmed ordered one for himself, too. He leaned into
Hazeem's other ear and said that if he ever snitched to
anyone back home, his tongue would be torn from his

mouth, his eyes would be gouged out with a hot poker, his male organs would be lopped off, a wood screw would be drilled under his kneecap and worked up through his body and out through his nostril with a giant magnet, he would be skinned alive in one-inch strips, which would then be woven into a woman's menstruation pad, a large jar of spaghetti sauce would be inserted into his rectum sideways, and he would be beheaded with a spoon.

Hazeem gave him a thumbs-up. "No problemo." He zipped his lips. "What happens in the Western Hemisphere stays in the Western Hemisphere."

"Wonderful," the president said. "Now let's have a good time!"

You think you know a person, but until you see him on the dance floor, you really have no idea. To Hazeem's amazement, Akhmed was quite a rug-cutter. At first a couple of girls demurred, gazing in stupefaction at his Führer armband and nonmustache, but after the speakers broke into a salsa, Akhmed, frustrated, grabbed someone's hand and dragged her to the parquet—now that was the confidence Hazeem liked to see! Akhmed danced like a Latin Fred Astaire, hips swiveling rhythmically, feet gliding flying-carpet-like, hands flitting, arms undulating, shoulders thrusting and retreating, knees dipping and wriggling like gummy worms.

It was only minutes before everyone moved back to give the despot more room and then stopped dancing to watch. The women were now fighting over who would be Adolf's next partner, and the moment one song finished, he discarded his current girl with a flick and grasped the next breathless Latina. It didn't matter what kind of song they played; he knew how to dance to everything—

jitterbug, twist, tango, mashed potatoes. The crowd moved back to give him even more room, fluttering at the edges of the parquet like shower curtains in steam. Strangers, knowing he was der Führer's friend, slapped Hazeem on his back admiringly. But, truly, he felt sorry for his president. How many hours must Akhmed have spent alone in his room secretly practicing all these magnificent steps to evil Western music?

"He is something," whispered the black waitress, who had stopped serving to watch. She turned to Hazeem. "You are not Cuban."

"Here on business."

"Much longer?"

Her voice had changed. He eyed her curiously. "Not… much."

"A shame. If you had the time, I would show you some of the sights."

"Really? How much time?"

"Perhaps if we got started right away. I finish working at one o'clock."

"Tonight? You and I?"

"Maybe you could take me home, and I could point out some things along the way."

"One o'clock you say?"

"My name is Jacobita."

He offered his hand. "Hazeem. Pleased to meet you."

"Aren't you the gentleman." She ignored his hand and kissed his cheek. "Hazeem. Hazeem. Very poetic-sounding name. Like leaves in the breeze, rustling palms."

His own palm rustled. His flesh sizzled. "Leaves? Breeze?"

"*Hot, tropical* breeze."

His crotch plumped like a puffer fish.

"I'll bet you're not always such a gentleman," she said saucily. "I bet sometimes you're a rascal."

A black girl! An erotic, passionate, sultry libertine! An amorous, equatorial Negress! A cocktail waitress! Hazeem had all he could do not to squeeze his eyes shut and pop them open to make sure he wasn't hallucinating.

"Can you stay until I'm finished working, then?" she asked. "I can slip you a couple of free drinks."

He glanced at Akhmed pirouetting around the parquet. He tried to flush the weariness from his head. "I would have to accompany, um, Adolf back to the hotel."

"And return for me?"

"Yes, I think I could manage that. Perhaps. Yes. Definitely yes."

"One o'clock? You won't disappoint me? This is the gentleman speaking and not the rascal?"

"No. I positively promise. Word of honor."

She leaned over her tray and kissed his cheek again, this time brushing her bosom against his arm. "See you, then, Señor Rustling Palm Leaves."

She disappeared into the sweaty mass of nightclubbers, leaving him with a throbbing fish in his pants. He gazed at his gliding president and wondered what to do. On the one hand, it wasn't likely the little madman would settle for Hazeem going home with a girl if he, the leader of Iran, did not at least appear to make a score—Akhmed, like his costume counterpart, being much too mean-spirited and selfish. On the other hand, if the bonehead had been a halfway normal human being, he obviously could have his pick among this crowd of hot-to-trots—if Hazeem was recalling the term correctly. The problem being that Hazeem had always suspected his president of not liking girls all that much.

He glanced around anxiously, as if just *thinking* this blasphemy would get him reworked into a maxi pad. He had to watch himself. The Iranian president had eyes and ears in every country. Akhmed would never admit it publicly, but he very much admired the American CIA and Israeli Mossad and was a bit of a James Bond wannabe. He secretly watched old Matt Helm movies starring Dean Martin and for a while even took to smoking unfiltered cigarettes and sipping Johnny Walker Red in front of a mirror. He had tried putting some Italian curl into his hair but found it stubbornly straight, for which his barber paid with his life. All Akhmed's heterosexual dancing seemed to Hazeem to be a case of, to paraphrase Shakespeare, the queen protesting too much. For, indeed, he had never seen the tyrant at ease with the ladies, certainly not one-on-one. What's more, the president had a great flair for decorating, his taste leaning toward pastels and natural light. The Tehran palace, formerly closed-in and stuffily traditional with its arabesque curlicues, ponderous columns, gold-leafed, trayed ceilings, and dreary torture dungeons, the president had opened up to skylights and tropical palette. Once he had the new prison built, he converted the basement of the central palace, formerly a labyrinth of cells and oubliettes, to a wine cellar, fabrics studio, and personal health club, complete with sauna and a dozen Nautilus machines. He had invited Hazeem to join him a few times in the gym, and although the interpreter complied, he made sure never to turn his back on his leader. No mischief ever occurred, thankfully, but Hazeem still always made one excuse after another for not joining Akhmed in the sauna.

It had been difficult not to feel sorry for the man, as he flexed his puny biceps in the full-length exercise mirror and kept asking Hazeem if he could see any difference in muscle mass since his last visit. And it was hard not to feel sorry for him now, at Caliente, as he twirled around the dance floor, knowing Akhmed was going to return to his room to watch Cuban TV, such as it was, well into the night, all alone, just him and his fashion magazines.

Still, Hazeem had to figure out some way to ditch the little cocksucker. He had to think of something. There was simply no way in hell he was going to let that luscious black waitress leave without him.

The club closed at midnight, the last customers trickling out a half-hour later. Outside, Adolf adjusted his armband, wiped sweat from the inside of his Führer cap, and yawned. "I have to admit it, Hazeem. I'm fagged."

"Your Excellency?"

"Worn out, tired. What the devil do you think I mean? Why are you looking at me like that?"

Hazeem exhaled. "Worn out? But surely not you, Wholesome One. A man of such…virility."

"That stooge Thurston and his even-bigger-stooge Lovey took it out of me. Would you be terribly disappointed if we head back to the hotel?"

Hazeem glanced at his watch. "In truth, those two dunces took it out of me too."

"I brought a couple of decadent Western videotapes with me from home, if you would like to join me. I had the hotel install a VCR in my suite. Have you ever seen *Captain Ron*, with Kurt Russell and Martin Short? I've watched it a dozen times and wet my pants each time. You understand, of course, you're not to repeat that." He lifted his cap to let in air. "Martin Short is probably a Jew, and Russell is definitely a Jew, but sometimes you have to overlook principle for the sake of a few good yuks. One thing you can say about Zionist dogs is, they know how to tickle the old funny bone, and I can use a good chuckle now and then. Demagoguery is a strenuous business, I don't have to tell you."

"No, indeed."

"I heard that der Führer himself read *The Katzenjammer Kids* in his bunker."

Hazeem knew that Akhmed was asking him to his suite only as a matter of form, that the president knew full well his friend would never take him up on the offer. Still, Hazeem played along with the little charade. "Perhaps I'll see the movie some other time, Excellency," he said. "We have a full day tomorrow, and I don't have your stamina."

"As you wish. Well, maybe I'll save it too. Perhaps I'll do some fashion sketches instead."

"Let's head back, then, shall we? Here is a taxi."

"Let's take a lemon!"

"There are none in sight."

"Please, oh please?"

Hazeem sighed. "Very well. I'll walk around the block to see if I can find any."

Akhmed clapped. "I'll wait here. Hurry!"

The lemons having apparently all retired for the evening, the Iranians wound up taking a regular sedan cab back after all. They said goodnight to each other and double-locked their hotel room doors. But a few minutes later, Hazeem peeked out of his room, up and down the hall, and finding no sign of his president or other life, eased open the door, latched it behind him stealthily, and, carrying his ice bucket as an alibi, tiptoed toward the stairway.

He ducked into a waiting taxi, a dusty 1955 Chevrolet, and headed back to Caliente, imploring the driver to quicken his pace. As it was, he would be a few minutes late. The Chevy and his teeth clacked over the cobblestones. The cab screeched around corners, jouncing him like a pinball. He was absolutely sure Jacobita would not be there.

But—glory of glories, Allah be praised!—there she stood, outside the club, leaning against a lamp post, her brown, thoroughbred legs gleaming, her breasts resting perkily on her folded arms, her elbow wrapped sensually around her purse strap. On her other shoulder hung a canvas sack, on which her scarlet fingernails scratched a silent tango. Bliss!

But even then Hazeem was certain she could not be waiting for *him*. Why, she must have a hundred suitors, he thought—a thousand! She might not remember him from even an hour ago. He had to be careful not to make a fool of himself. The taxi squealed to a stop half a block away. Instead of jumping out and holding the door open for her, he slipped out insouciantly and strolled in Jacobita's direction, resisting the urge to make eye contact with her.

"Oh, hello," he said, acting surprised, pretending to try to recall where he had seen her before.

She grabbed his hand. "Hazeem. Rustling leaves."

Great, merciful God! What were seventy-two virgins on paper compared to one slender-legged Negress in the flesh?!

He waved the Chevy forward and now did open the door for her.

"What's this?" she asked inside, fingernail-drumming a beat on the ice bucket.

He fumbled for an explanation. Fortunately, working as Akhmed's translator had made him a quick and accomplished liar. "I thought we could find someplace to buy a bottle of wine and—"

"Buy? Now?" she laughed. "Silly man. This is Cuba. Here the workers have to go to bed early so they can get up at the crack of dawn to sit on their front stairs all day to dream about what they would do if only they had jobs." She put the bucket aside, reached into her canvas sack, and pulled out a bottle of Bacardi Gold. "One hundred fifty proof," she declared.

The driver raised his eyebrows in the rearview mirror.

"I live with my mother and brother, so we can't go to my apartment," she explained. "But we can lie on the Malecón and listen to the sea." She plucked out three plastic Caliente glasses from the sack. Hazeem held two as she poured. She handed the third glass and bottle over the front seat.

"*Muchas gracias, señorita.*"

"Just by San Lázaro," she instructed the driver, as he happily gulped, then handed the bottle back. She turned again to Hazeem. "It's a perfect evening for love under the stars, *sí?*"

Sí, Hazeem thought, as the overproofed rum ignited his gullet, its fumes searing his sinuses and eddying in his brain. *Sí, sí, sí, sí, sí, sí, sí, sí, sí, sí, sí, sí, sí, sí, sí, sí, sí, sí, sí, sí, sí, sí, sí, sí, sí, sí, sí, sí, sí, sí, sí, sí, sí, sí, sí, sí, sí, sí, sí, sí, sí, sí, sí, sí, sí, sí, sí, sí, sí, sí, sí, sí, sí, sí, sí, sí, sí, sí, sí, sí, sí, sí,*

*sí, sí, sí, sí, sí, sí, sí, sí, sí, sí, sí, sí, sí, sí, sí, sí, sí, sí, sí, sí, sí, sí,
sí, sí, sí, sí, sí, sí, sí, sí, sí, sí, sí, sí, sí, sí, sí, sí, sí.*

A thousand yards off the Malecón shore, a twenty-five-foot Ranger mini-trawler, *Key Stroke,* heaved and yawed in jagged surf, groaning as if in great pain, choking for breath, struggling against a homicidal tide that ached to smash it to shards on the Malecón's looming concrete blocks. Except for street lamps—which, when the boat pitched skyward from a crest, appeared only in ghostly flashes behind atomized surf—the shoreline was as black as hell. If the engine failed, it would be only a matter of minutes before the boat, sturdy though she was, would vaporize on the rocks, toothpicks for sharks.

With one hand on his throttle, the other on the helm, the captain, code-named "the Skipper," heavy and miserable in his drenched canvas pants and windbreaker, wrestled the bow close-wind. With whitecaps detonating over the prow, *Key Stroke* stalled above each crest, her propeller clawing for water but finding only air, her engine gasping for air but finding only water. Hanging between heaven and hell, her hull twisted and torqued and twanged like a tortured soul, before being sucked down the leviathan's throat.

The Skipper constantly gazed over his shoulder, squinting into the briny haze, to make sure he was no closer to the Malecón's bite and to try to spot the signal. He shot a glance at the pilothouse's starboard hold, its padlock open and smashing against the fiberglass. The pounding was driving him crazy. It was like a voice that wouldn't shut up. With every bang the voice got louder. He wished to hell the signal would come. *Dirty fucking bastards.*

The old Chevrolet swung from Avenue de Italia onto the Malecón, hurling Hazeem into Jacobita's bosom. She enveloped him in her arms, so that even as the taxi rebalanced, he was a willing prisoner. He accidentally spilled some of his rum into her lap, but it only made her giggle. She smelled wonderful, her perfume freshly applied, a tangy hint of womanly perspiration wafting from her cleavage. He sucked his drink and let the vapors permeate his palate before swallowing.

There was no traffic this time of night, even here, on the city's coastal highway. The driver didn't rush. He mentioned that he had been working since early morning, and his lips were exceedingly dry. Hazeem reached between Jacobita's ankles for the rum bottle, but when he brushed her purse, she stiffened and shoved him away, alarming him.

"It's nothing," she apologized, grabbing the bottle, tucking her purse more snuggly behind her legs. She handed the rum to the driver, who poured himself a refill.

Hazeem was back on the other side of the seat. Jacobita slid over, planted her feet firmly between her purse and the car's differential hump, and leaned on his shoulder. She took his arm and draped it around her neck and nuzzled him. Her other hand fell onto his thigh, and with a fingernail she began scrolling spirals onto his pants.

"Hurry," he called to the driver.

The Chevy gasped and lurched, and the side streets jounced by faster.

At the far end of the Malecón, at Calzada de Infanta, Jacobita tapped the driver's shoulder. "There," she said, pointing to a section of the great breakwater where two street lights had burned out, a gap in the skyline's rotted smile. "Turn into this street, here."

The Chevy took a rust-squeaking left and squealed to a stop in front of a disintegrating apartment building with a gaping hole in its side.

"Wait here," she told Hazeem. "I want to make sure we'll be alone."

"Where?" he asked, gazing into the darkness.

Jacobita dragged her fingernails across his thigh and into his crotch.

That was the only reply he needed. "I'll wait," he assured her.

"I'll be right back." She snatched her canvas sack, stepped over her purse and out of the cab.

He watched out the back window as she dashed across the highway. He didn't quite know what to say to the driver. Instead, he groped around the floor for the bottle. It leaned against Jacobita's purse. Grasping, he nicked his fingernail against the purse clasp. Something was strange. He lifted up the purse, feeling guilty about prying, and saw something odd. Very odd.

Dodging geysers roaring up through fissures in the asphalt, Jacobita sprinted across the highway to the rock wall. Below, surf exploded thunderously, drenching her. She gazed across the whitecaps but saw nothing except a pulsing lighthouse beacon, which seemed to be rolling like a ship. She saw no real boats. Despite the deluge, she climbed down from the top row of stone blocks to the slick, deeply shadowed course below. From her sack she took a flashlight, dropping the empty bag and not caring that it vortexed into the wind. She pointed the beam toward the horizon forty-five degrees from the lighthouse and flashed it in five quick blinks, followed by a pause, followed by five slower blinks. She repeated the signal seven times and wondered what was taking the son of a bitch so long, while she was risking life and limb. This surf wasn't exactly *rustling leaves*.

Rustling leaves. That was a good one. She thought of her purse and the bottle of rum she had left with the men in the cab.

Well, at least they would die happy.

Despite being preoccupied keeping *Key Stroke* close-hauled and at a safe distance from the rocks, the Skipper, with a percussive sigh of relief, spotted the signal. But the worst was far from over. The worst was coming. With one hand fighting the helm, he stretched to unhasp the starboard hold. The lock fell with a splattering thud. He flipped open the lid, let go of the helm momentarily, and with both hands reached in and grabbed a plastic bag. The mini-trawler, liberated, tumbled and spun on three axes, knocking him to the deck, smashing his knee, detonating his optic nerves. He bellowed and swore but managed to hold the bag fast. The boat tossed like Styrofoam. He sat up and, with the plastic bag in his lap, looped his wrist around the helm, steadying the rudder. With his other hand, he took a device from the bag, peeled back even more plastic, and exposed an electronic transmitter, holding it away from him so he wouldn't drip on it.

The boat bucked and tried to throw him out of the pilothouse but only succeeded in flipping him atop the hold, from where he could see the shore. He only had moments before the surf would overturn the trawler or tear it apart. Cursing, he extended the transmitter's antenna and flicked a toggle switch. A meter needle flickered feebly. "Damn, damn," he groaned. He realized there was no avoiding it. With his knee throbbing, he limped and staggered out of the pilothouse onto the heaving deck, and in the maw of exploding breakers pointed the antenna toward the rocks. *Key Stroke* spun like a roulette wheel, knocking him down again and hurling him starboard to port. But this time the needle jumped to life. A red LED blinked. He flicked another toggle, and the LED became steady. He hauled himself to his good knee, held a cleat for dear life, and pointed the antenna at the signaling flashlight.

Hazeem saw that for some strange reason Jacobita's purse had been fitted with a small padlock, barely bigger than a thumbnail but enough to prevent casual prying. It was a large, well-used, imitation-snakeskin handbag, badly cracked, straps frayed. A six-inch patch of dirty duct tape, curled at the corners, bandaged one end. Its zipper was fastened to a strap hook by a loop of lamp chain, secured with the mini-lock. Odd indeed, for what could there be in this junky old bag so valuable as to have to keep out curious eyes? It wasn't money, surely; a thief could easily steal the purse or break the flimsy lock. Hazeem took an extra-long sip of rum and handed the bottle to the driver.

"Cuba still has the finest, don't you think, señor?" the cabby said, raising the bottle to the rearview mirror.

"Yes, yes, quite good," Hazeem said distractedly, for he was thinking about the padlocked purse. If something inside was so valuable, why then wouldn't Jacobita have taken the purse with her? Why only the canvas sack? It didn't make sense.

Gazing over the vicious surf towards the Malecón, the Skipper positioned his thumb above a red button next to the toggle switches and took a deep breath. He pressed the red button hard. A second later, an orange flash lit up venerable Spanish facades. Shadows of dripping corbels and gap-toothed balconies tattooed his retinas. Then came the blast, duller than he had expected but longer-lasting, like distant thunder, pealing over cobblestone, rumbling through narrow streets, reverberating off ancient stucco, ricocheting off whitecaps. Bricks collapsed, metal tore, glass shattered, and four-hundred-year-old dust billowed over the noble seaside thoroughfare.

He crawled back into the pilothouse and tossed the device into the hold without rewrapping it, grabbed his helm with both hands, shoved the throttle full ahead, and made a beeline for the Florida Keys, which, with any luck, he'd reach before McDonald's stopped serving breakfast. Man, how blowing up people made him crave Egg McMuffins.

PART II

Seven

HAVING FORAGED ON PINK-PIG-MANURED, SOLAR-SPOT-bombarded, topsoil-depleted, atmospheric-disturbed, machete-truncated sapling roots, one post-Hurricane Oscar termite colony in the foothills southeast of Port-au-Prince mutated into an army of marauding predators with an insatiable craving for the "other" white meat. You didn't have to dig deep to unearth their provenance.

The well-meaning British West Indies Benevolence Club had donated dozens of fat blond swine to the half-island nation as a husbandry starter kit meant to produce enough chubby, nutritious pale hogs to eventually replace the scrawny black ones that had been the staple of the local diet since the days before Dessalines declared himself emperor. But in the great tradition of backfiring democratic-industrial-nation generosity, the effort failed twice. First, in the equally great tradition of formerly-colonized-island-nation-ruling-party-hopelessly-entrenched corruption, the oinkers found their way not to the breeding farms which the BWI Bennies had intended but to the front yard of the presidential palace, where they lazed away their days under salubrious sunshine and congenial tropical breezes, until such time as Haiti's then-president, yet another post-Baby Doc reformer, decided he had a taste for ham sandwich, pickled pig foot, roasted snout, spiced sow hock, barbecued rib tip, jerked squealer ear, braised curlicue tail, fried chitterlings, batter-dipped oinker dick, bacon cheeseburger, marinated maw, pork-fried rice, pulled pork, pork roast, boiled pig brain, pork tenderloin, pork and beans, pork chop, eggs and pork sausage, pork patty, pork tamale, pork patty links, or pork surprise, when said lawn swine would be rudely dragged screaming for their miserable pink lives across presidential lawn to presidential basement, where Pierre the drunken cook would chop off their pork heads with much animosity and nasty language.

So it was no wonder the reformer-president had conveniently forgotten to distribute the delicious donated oinkers to the common man, whose unevolved digestive systems he figured would have been shocked to death by the sweet meat anyhow, and the absolute last thing he wanted to do was injure the common man, the very people who had, more or less, voted him into office. As for husbandrying the brutes (four-legged)—they seemed to be doing quite well on their own, *mesi*, plopping screeching piglets all over nook and cranny of presidential lawn, so that soon the neighborhood sounded like a microphone had been lowered into the deepest circle of hell, and one of those campaign vans with loudspeakers on top was driving around making aforesaid common man listen to what his soul would sound like if he didn't voluntarily and enthusiastically vote for the reformer-president again in the upcoming election.

The second time the Benevolences' generosity had backfired was the day (according to rumor) the president's girlfriend, Viola, snuck into the palace through a back service gate, as was her custom, but this time forgot to secure the latch. Among the livestock, in whatever porcine language they communicate these things to one another, word had gotten around that life on the lawn was not only salubrious sunshine and congenial tropical breezes but also Pierre's nasty language and dull hatchet. So, pigs being the smartest four-legged land mammal—slightly more intelligent than the reformer president role-playing Seabiscuit as Viola spanked him to the finish line—the oinkers and affiliated oinklets, spotting the unlatched service gate, saw their chance and sprinted to the foothills like Boukman and his band of Maroons.

Meanwhile, many of the island's termites, having run out of both good topsoil with which to build their colossal mounds and, to add insult to injury, good tree roots to feed themselves and their queen—what deforestation had started, Hurricane Oscar finished—died by the millions. But a few adapted, and when unwary, erstwhile-presidential-palace-lawned, now freedom-loving pink pigs would rut their mounds, the mutated termites thought they had died and gone to entomologic heaven. There would be no happiness with black hog thereafter, brudda. Not only did blond meat fill them with orgasmic epicurean ecstasy, the molecular structure of pink-oinker fat—slobbering, inert, indolent, drooling, belching, farting, mud-plopping pink fatness—invigorated and intensified the atomic structure of the insects' mutated voracity—so that when pink snor-fer meat depleted, the mutated termites went nearly wild with being pissed off (or whatever is the scientific term for insect disgruntlement).

They spilled from the hills as a marauding phalanx, de-vouring every hovel, ravaging every rum shop, ambushing every farmer's donkey and farmer too, blitzkrieging inno-cent gal waiting on roadside for minibus, pouncing upon naked pickney, searching in vain for true pink meat, even if it momentarily resided inside said farmer, roadside gal, or naked pickney.

On their onslaught to Port-au-Prince—which any reasonable flesh-eating termite could see from the heights was a place likely to be chock full of entrée—the man-dibled army happened on a certain home a thousand feet above the valley. A plump young human stood at a bar sink mixing rum punches, her back to the window. Because she was charcoal-colored, the termites first thought to give her wide berth. They stopped en masse and were about to reverse course when something caught their attention. While the woman was fixing drinks, her corpulent rump was jiggling to the beat of a calypso song blaring from a tape player. The termites were famished, and although her skin was very black, her stretch pants were pinkish-beige and reminded them of you-know-what. Their little bug eyes darted back and forth, following her swaying pink derrière. Those soldiers in the rear of the phalanx no doubt wondered what the hang-up was, until they too climbed onto the windowsill and their own bug eyes were hypnotically seized by the undulating beige batty. Finally, as if through instantaneous electro-chemical signal trans-fer, a synchronetic jolt ran through the tiny legion, and it lurched as a single unit toward the sink, leapt from the tile floor onto the roly-poly, bouncing stretch pants, and before the young woman either realized what had hit her or could scream in terror, she was smothered by the malevolent buzzing brutes.

There was commotion on the veranda—someone shouting "Cléo! Come help! Help! Henri is out cold!" in a voice unlike those the termites ever heard among mountainside farmer and pickney. Another jolt electrified the phalanx. A man ran into the room, waving his arms— and, *Jezi*, he was pure, *pure* pink. Not stretch-polyester pink—*flesh* pink. The real deal. When he looked down and saw what was left of the Cléo woman, his skin turned even more scrumptious-looking white. His mistake was to hesitate, to try to make sense of it, before fear and self-preservation kicked in. That instant was good enough for the insects to have at him.

He ran away screaming, his legs covered with white-meat-tearing, bloody pincers. He fell down the veranda stairs, flailing in pain and terror, giving the rest of the phalanx time to join the feast. He tried lurching away on all fours, but the ravenous bugs had already entered his BWI Benevolence Club orifices, and he was doomed. His throat filled with mucous membrane-peeling warriors, smothering his cries.

But not before the minister of commerce, Henri Charbonnay, stirred awake from his laughing, lack-of-air faint, lifted his head from his plate of conch fritters, rose shakily from the veranda table, followed what, unless he had been having a terrible nightmare, sounded like a muffled wail. He stood at the top of the stairs, clutching the railing. In the dimness he saw an undulating shape on the ground—a writhing mass of *something*. A frenetic buzzing, screeching, shrieking rent the night air—at once, high and low pitched, oscillating at a hellish frequency. He did not have to know what he was looking at to sense that it was very bad. Still lightheaded, he snuck back into his house, saw Cléo's half-skeleton, was absolutely sure he was having a nightmare, but hid in his bedroom closet just in case.

He squatted there for two days and nights, not eating, not moving, hardly breathing. During the second night he dozed fitfully, waking up every few minutes in terror, imagining horrible things crawling on him.

Finally, on the third morning he crawled out, stood up creaking, and listened, listened. He tiptoed through the house, stepped over Cléo's exposed spine, steadied himself at the top of the veranda stairs, stared at Gleason's skeleton below, gazed at the city spilling effluviently to the sea, and knew he had to get off the island *now*. There was no time to warn anyone. Not his wives and children in the city, not his mistresses. Warning meant explaining, and there was no time for that.

Brandishing a clipboard in one fist and shaking the other, Karma Weinberg, back-dropped by Miami Beach skyline, stood on the Lido deck of the *Countess of the Sea*, screaming her head off at the chief purser, a diminutive East Indian. He wore a sharply creased white uniform and stood at colonial attention, leaning forward from his ankles at an eight-degree angle, his cap tucked under his left elbow, his eyes half-closed, as spittle, blasphemy, deprecation, ad hominem epithet, ethnic degradation, scorching threats, and dragon-fire breath blasted his subaltern kisser and vortexed around his hamster-brown ears.

"Don't you patronize me, you dot-headed asswipe!"

"Yes, madam."

"Quit it!"

"Quite right, madam."

"I'll 'yes, madam' you, you cable-ready bootlick! If you spent half as much time doing what you're told as nodding your fly-eating head, I wouldn't have to spend most of *my* time doing your do-nothing job, you reeking little turd!"

"Yes—"

She shook her fist a centimeter from his nose. "Shut up!"

He nodded.

She swung her fist toward a davit. "What color is that lifeboat?"

"White, mad—"

"Don't say it! I can see it's fucking white, you insolent, curry-eating pygmy. You think I can't see with my own eyes?!"

"Ye—"

"You think I'm fucking color blind?!"

"No, ma—"

She raised her finger and drew a long breath. In a calmer tone—an evenness steadied with the underpinnings of a gangland hit—she cooed, "And you know what else I don't see?"

"No, missus."

"Go on, take a guess."

He began to open his mouth, but before he could utter a peep, she offered, "I don't see any of your overpaid union assholes painting them, that's what." She paused a beat for him to open his mouth, then piped, "You know, the color they're supposed to be for my *wedding*?"

"Hazel," he confirmed.

"To match my eyes?"

"Eyes, yes, madam. Hazel-colored eyes, hazel-colored lifeboats."

"So I wasn't imagining it, then?" she asked serenely. "I really did contract to pay five times your cost to paint them hazel and repaint them white after the wedding? Five times?"

"I believe that's correct, missus."

"I'm not crazy, then?"

He hesitated.

"I didn't dream it?"

"No dream, no madam lady."

She drew another measured breath. She torqued at the waist and shrieked, "Then why the *fuck* aren't they hazel?!!"

He shut his eyes and stiffened against a new furnace-blast of derogation, castigation, malediction, and imprecation.

Reading from her clipboard, she bellowed, "The vodka hasn't been dyed yet, the slot machines *still* don't have my picture in place of the cherries, I *still* haven't seen a clay model of the Michelangelo's *David* ice sculpture with my fiancé's head on David's shoulders, and where the *hell* is the contract for renting St. John? Do I have to do every goddamn thing myself?! What the fuck do *you* do around here! I'll tell you what you're *going* to do: you're going to be my personal human paintbrush!"

"Yes, well, you see, madam," he whimpered, his Adam's apple scampering up his throat like a gecko chased by a mongoose, "there was a slight problem renting the entire island. You see—"

"A *what?!*"

The lizard tumbled to the ground.

She raised her clipboard to brain him. He braced. But at heart he was a Brit and refused to flinch.

As the clipboard was about to split open his skull, her attention was miraculously drawn to a cargo hoist, swinging a crate from the dock to an aft deck.

"What the fuck is that?"

His gaze followed hers. "Provisions, madam," he replied, seeming not to find anything wrong there, at least. "We're quite on schedule, missus lady."

Her eyeballs elongated. On the side of the crate was stenciled the word HAM. Her corneas pulsed. Her cheeks quavered. Her molars ground. She flicked off her sunglasses and stared even harder, but the crate still said HAM.

"What's going on?" she stammered.

He wasn't quite sure what she meant. Couldn't she see for herself? In addition to being evil, was she also blind and/or illiterate? Had her wickedness corroded her eyeballs, casting her into literal, as well as moral, darkness?

"Ham?" he muttered.

"For *my* wedding? For my *kosher* wedding?"

He felt immensely relieved. He smiled. "Oh, no, madam, not for your wedding at all. For staff and crew only. For the captain and—"

"The *captain*?"

He exhaled. "Yes, indeed. Captain's favorite snack is ham sandwich. Some captains love to sit with the passengers and eat rich foods, you know, but not our good Captain Pfeffing, no madam lady. Captain Pfeffing is a fellow of simple tastes, a common man at heart, and—"

"Get that fucking crate off this boat *now*! And every fucking crate like it!"

His Adam's apple recommenced scampering. "Missus?"

"Captain Pfeffing, huh? Common man, huh? Where is the son of a bitch?!"

The chief purser cleared his throat. He patted his pants. "Son of a bitch, missus?"

"Never mind, you useless guttersnipe. I'll find him myself. I'll ruin him, his career, and his ability to have kids." She knocked the purser aside. Without turning around, she snarled, "That goyish shit better be off this ship in an hour."

"Goyish shit?" he mumbled. He wasn't sure what it meant, but he knew he'd better warn the captain—pronto.

Soon-to-be-former Haiti commerce minister Henri Charbonnay, having been scared mulatto, didn't even bother driving down the hillside road, for fear the demon insects might be waiting for him in his car's backseat—a version of which he had seen in the movie *The Godfather*, where mafia hit men sprung up from behind and garroted to death unsuspecting brothers-in-law, whose feet would break out the windshield. That was a horrible way to go but could not be half as bad as being nibbled to death by exoskeletal fiends. The minister had once had his big toe bitten by a sand crab, and he hobbled around the beach trying to shake the brute from his foot, and he was quite humiliated because people knew who he was, and although the adults knew enough to keep their mouths shut, a pack of brats followed him down the beach, pointing and jeering and shrieking with laughter. He couldn't shake the damn thing off and only got rid of it when Renée Fouillard's mongrel leapt from under her bar deck and attacked the clinging crab and not only ferociously mauled the crustacean but also the minister's foot. Ever since, his subconscious mind had associated nonvertebrates with deep and prolonged bodily pain, so that, on top of remembering *The Godfather*, there was no way he was going to get into his car, plain and simple.

Not bothering to follow the rutted road, he sprinted down the hillside, through brush and bramble, in what he reckoned was the straightest path to the seashore. He tumbled and rolled, banged his shins, scraped his flesh, nearly poked out his eyes on woodsy stalk and daggery thorn. By the time, almost an hour later, he reached the outskirts of Port-au-Prince, he looked not much different from his loyal constituents—the ragged beggars and waifs who littered doorways, draped out of windows, clogged gutters, and foraged garbage bins. A few people, not recognizing him in this dilapidated state, even nodded *bonjou* to him, but he had no time for such nonsense. He was in a hurry to save his sorry ass.

He was pretty sure where he could thieve a reliable fishing skiff. There would be too many prying eyes at the deepwater dock, and if he scoured a fishing settlement, he'd find only engineless rowboats—less than worthless. But his brother-in-law, that scoundrel François, ran a rum shop next to a god-awful, rat-infested ghaut, across the road from a rocky spit, a couple of miles north of town. The rogue owned a yellow skiff with the double-entendre name *Fat Banana* that had a hefty and durable Evinrude outboard engine, with which François often zipped over the channel to Île de la Gonâve to visit his mistress and her daughter. With a great deal of satisfaction, Henri Charbonnay imagined the look on François's face as, with the marauding insects bearing down on the rum shop, he ran for his life to his boat, which, like his mistress and her daughter, had always served him so faithfully, only to find it had been thieved—and the even more splendid look on François's kisser when, in sheer panic, he turned to see the flock of bloodthirsty devils leap from the shore rocks onto his scoundrely eyeballs.

As usual, *Fat Banana* was tied to a rickety pier within sight of the rum shop. From behind a coconut palm, the minister cast an eye at the clapboard shack and saw the back of François's head silhouetted against rows of bottles. He slunk to the boat, never taking an eye off the rum shop. He already knew that the engine required a key to start, because of the many times he had joined François on his jaunts to Gonâve. He also recalled that François, being one of those irritating individuals who went through life not trusting his fellow man, never left the key in the ignition but kept it hanging on a hook in a cabinet under his bar counter. On the plus side, François never locked the cabinet, since that would have required yet another key to hide from potential thieves (no one had ever accused François of being a Sorbonne scholar—one reason Henri had appointed him head of his district reelection committee).

As Henri had expected, the key was nowhere in the boat. Well, he had to try. His mental propeller spinning, he sauntered across the road and strolled into the rum shop as if he had nothing else to do in the wide world—such as, oh, save his miserable skin.

"Henri?" said François, startled to see his brother-in-law looking so disheveled. "Is that you?"

"*Se mwen*," he answered, insouciantly.

The rum shop owner ran his murky eyes over the murky politician. "What the devil happened to you?"

"What do you mean?" Henri replied in the same accusatorial, the-best-defense-is-an-offense tone as when the national comptroller once asked him if he knew why airport departure tax funds were nowhere to be found.

"You look like you rolled down a gully."

"It's been that kind of day. You've had them, I'm sure."

"Not *that* bad."

"Let's not dwell on it, shall we? I didn't come here to be maligned."

"It's a long way for a rum punch."

The minister looked around cautiously. Though they were alone, he lowered his voice. "I've had a rough day, François."

"Obviously."

"I'm desperate for a bit of"—he shifted his eyes toward Gonâve—"you know, this and that."

"Come again?" the rum shop owner asked, cupping his ear.

"This and that."

"This *and* that?"

"Go on, have your fun. Mock me. But I'm telling you, if I don't get either one—this *or* that—I'm going to go mad."

"It's too late to be setting out, Henri. We'll catch sundown, and I don't like crossing after dark."

"You do it all the time, you villain. You're talking to me, for Christ's sake." He looked around. "And it's not like you're packing in customers, exactly. Come on, old friend. Let's make it a short one."

"Jeanette expects me home for supper."

The minister huffed. "Fine. How much do you want to let me use the damn boat?"

François shrugged. "It's not a question of money. Neither *this* nor *that* will accommodate *you* without *me*."

"A thousand dollars."

"What?"

"A thousand U.S. And I'll take a chance with this and that."

"Good God. It must have been some day."

"You have no idea."

"Tell you what. Give me the thousand, throw in an extra two hundred for the business I'll lose by closing early, and I'll go along. No problem with this, that, or their husband and father, respectively."

"What will you tell Jeanette?"

"To hell with her."

"Deal."

They paused for a moment, each waiting for something to happen. "Well?" asked François.

"Well what? It's not getting any earlier, man, and two hundred for loss of business is sounding more and more insulting."

"Well, the twelve hundred, that's well what."

Henri had run out of his house without having emptied the wall safe behind the pope's portrait. He had to give a convincing reason. "You think I'm dumb enough to carry that kind of cash with all these cutthroat socialists around? These are perilous times, my friend."

François deflated. "That's a lot of credit you're suggesting."

"What're you saying, I'm not good for it? After all I've done for you?"

"It's not your credit I'm questioning, Henri. It's your memory."

"That only happened once or twice, and I was drunk at the time. But I assure you, now I'm as sober as a lamb. Get me pen and paper. I'll give you my personal IOU."

The rum shop owner looked glum.

"Hurry up, will you?" Henri peeled off his watch. "Here, bandit. This is worth twenty times that much."

In a patch of orange sunlight François inspected the watch. He broke into a grin. "All right. Let's go." Through the open doorway, he spotted an old man hauling himself up the steps. "Sorry, Gustave. We're closed. Get out." He ran to the doorway and shoved Gustave whence he came.

"May as well bring a couple bottles of overproof, eh?" Henri suggested. "One for this and that, one to keep us company along the way."

François raced behind the counter again and found two dusty bottles of Rothschild—his very best—on an upper shelf. He placed them in front of Henri and bent down to reach for the Evinrude key.

As François was leaning over, the commerce minister whacked his skull with one of the bottles, shattering glass and rendering François facedown and lowing like a birthing cow, and, unfortunately, breaking a seventy-dollar bottle of rum. It was too much waste to bear. So Henri stepped around the counter, stood on his groaning in-law's back to reach the high shelf, and snatched a couple of Rémy Martins.

With bottles tucked under his arms and engine key nestled in his pocket, he headed for the skiff, thinking, What a buzz those insects are going to get on François's liver.

The Evinrude started like a champ. He hefted the two spare tanks of gas to make sure they were full—they were—untied *Fat Banana*, engaged the throttle, and gunned away from his accursed homeland.

He had planned on not opening his first bottle until Port-au-Prince disappeared under the horizon, and the sea and evening sky engulfed him in unsettling blackness. It would be a long journey to the Turks and Caicos, and he wished to pace himself, physically and mentally. But he had thumped northward for only fifteen minutes when he changed his mind and uncorked the Rémy Martin. The problem was that ever since he had gotten into the skiff, he had felt a dull pain, a tightness, in his windpipe, and it wasn't getting any better. He was a little short of breath. So he gulped some R.M., thinking it might relax him a little.

It wasn't like any kind of pain he had ever felt before.

Eight

On her way to shove the captain's ham up his ass, Karma bumped into her fiancé in the elevator foyer.

"Something I need to talk to you about, cupkins," Angus puckered. He had a golf physique, short and plump, and he was slurping a piña colada without a straw, the tip of the parasol poking up a nostril. He wore burgundy Keen sandals, palm-tree Tommy Bahama shorts, and a brass-buttoned navy blazer over an untucked, white NIKE T-shirt on which you could only see, between blazer lapels, the letters IK. He also wore, for the time being, a creamy white mustache.

"Not now," Karma panted. "I'm putting out fires."

"Everything all right, puppy?"

"Will be shortly—soon as I kick in the captain's testicles."

"The captain, really? Don't we need him for the cruise?"

"Out of my way."

"I think we need a little talk, pumpky."

The elevator door opened, and she was about to step in. A cabin maid was inside with her cleaning cart. When she laid eyes on Karma, she shrank into a corner, making herself as small a target as possible.

"Daddo is waiting for us in the Lido Lounge," Angus cooed.

Karma held the elevator door open with her clipboard. She turned to him with narrowed eyes. "Your father? What the hell is he doing here?"

"Had a little time to kill before testing out the new Lear."

"You're lying."

"Yes, I am. Not about the new jet, but about, well, you see—"

"Cut the bullshit. I'm on a mission."

The elevator bell started to complain.

"Uh, um," he slurped, "he and mother thought they'd like to see the ship and all—"

"Wait a second. Your *mother* is here, too? The *tightass*?"

"Yes, sweet thing, and they're dying to see you." When he nodded, the parasol went farther up his nose.

She turned to the maid, self-mashed into the elevator's corner. "What are *you* looking at, you whore?"

"*Nada, nada, señora.*"

She turned back to Angus. "You're not telling me something."

"I think they think it's time for a little prenuptial chat, that's all," he said, smothering the word *nuptial* in a slurp. "Shouldn't take long. Couple minutes. Then we'll all have a nice nap in prep for an expensive dinner in town."

Her pupils morphed into the shape of fortress gun holes. "A what kind of chat, did you say? Quit mumbling."

"Come on, pup. We'll be cordial to them and get it over with. They are paying for everything, so why not make them feel good about themselves? Generosity of spirit as well as purse, that's my motto. Who knows, maybe we can even weasel out of going to dinner with them. Just spend the evening with ourselves and…you know. We haven't done it in a while now, you've been so distracted and all, and—"

She turned to the maid. "Get out."

"*¿Señora?*"

"Get out! Don't you understand fucking English?"

"*No, por favor.*"

"Maybe this will help." She strode into the elevator, pulled the door hold-open button, and, with the bell screaming for mercy, grabbed the maid's cleaning cart and, with her back against the hand rail, kick-launched it out of the cab with such velocity that it flew across the foyer and down the opposite stairway, where it crashed into a huge oil portrait of Queen Beatrix and her Border Terrier, Chip. Suspecting what might be coming, Angus had stepped aside at the last nanosecond, fortunately without losing a drop of colada.

The queen's nose dripped with Windex, so that it appeared for all the world as if she had a touch of blue flu, and Chip foamed at the mouth with Scrubbing Bubbles. Karma seared the maid a glare. "YOU," she enunciated, pointing first at her, then at her cart, wrecked and strewn over the stairway landing, "YOU…NEXT!"

The maid bolted from the elevator, clutching her heart.

"Funny how they understand when they want to," Karma said, calmly. She turned to Angus. "Maybe I should have been a translator."

"They're waiting, kitten. The sooner we get this over with, the sooner we can get on with normality."

"I'm warning you. This fucking better be good, or you're off my anal sex list for a month."

He winced. "Don't talk like that, mittens—not even in jest."

It was not good, not good at all. Eddward and Marybethlehem Culvertdale sat tucked into a window-side booth in *Countess of the Sea*'s observation lounge, far above the frenetic hoi polloi crashing into itself on the quay, human worker ants feeding, preening, and sacrificing themselves to their queen. Eddward, dressed in a blue blazer identical to Angus's, except that it was four sizes taller and slimmer, blue-striped shirt, white linen tie, white slacks, and blue wingtip loafers with no socks, sat erect and cross-legged at the knees, his shoe tip studiously avoiding the underside of the table so as not to touch old gum or whatnot. Mrs. Culvertdale, wearing a bleached-bone-white pants suit with a frilly, high-collar blouse, sat equally erect, but that might have been a function of her hair bun, pulled so tautly behind her elongated head that it not only fashionably eliminated her face, neck, and thorax wrinkles but forced her to arch her back and painfully half-smile. When he wasn't fiddling with his gold cufflinks, the Mr.

nursed a Glenlivet on one rock with a twist, whilst the Mrs. tapped her diamond-ring band on an austere glass of club soda—no ice, no garnish, no swizzle stick, no straw, no lipstick imprint, no wet ring on coaster, even condensation being afraid to show its drippy self.

There was so much white at that table that the Culvertdales reflected a large swath of sunlight onto the quay, causing stevedores to squint.

Karma entered, Angus followed. She led, he lagged. She bounded to the Culvertdale booth; his upper body lurched, his lower body lumbered. The Mr. sprung up and extended his buffed fingernails. "Hello, Karma, dear. It's good to see you," he said, his teeth newly enameled and fiberglass-hull-bright.

Karma returned his fingershake. "Eddward. Good to see you too. I only wish I had more time to spend with you two darlings. Maybe after the wedding." She wasn't about to take shit from these two. On the other hand, she had to tread lightly—for now. No sense getting ninety-nine percent up the hill only to let the Culvertdale boulder roll you back down. She turned to the Mrs. "Good to see you, too, Mary," she said, squeezing out the phrase like hard toothpaste and not extending her hand. No way was she going to call this pinch-assed, Presbyterian bitch Marybethlehem. Five-syllable names were not only unnatural, they were a goddamned imposition. Karma had more important things to do in life than waste time calling people by geographically biblical names. Plus, she had to establish pecking order early and reinforce it often.

The Mrs. didn't get up, also didn't extend her hand, barely breathed, hardly spoke, didn't blink, didn't dilate or attenuate her pupils. She only countered her unfortunately-soon-to-be daughter-in-law's impudence with impudence of her own. "Karmy," she sniffed.

"Have a seat, won't you?" said the Mr., gesturing to the booth next to his wife. "Why don't you have a drink?"

"Really, Eddward, ordinarily I'd love to chat up charities and so forth, but it so happens I'm on my way to the bridge to shove a hambone up the captain's rectum."

Finally, the Mrs.'s Presbyterian eyelids moved. Despite her life's work of response repression, some reactions were simply involuntary, which on occasion even caused her to doubt the perfection of the species—and by species, she meant, of course, the wealthy.

"You know how it is, I'm sure," Karma pressed.

The Mr. tittered, "I suppose I do."

"So what's up?"

He motioned again. "Please. We wouldn't bother you if it weren't important."

Karma sighed. By this time Angus had caught up to the powwow, and she indicated with an eye quiver for *him* to sit next to his squeeze-ass mommy. He slid in.

Karma squeaked in next to him. Angus cricked a finger at the waitress, ordered another colada. "About this much rum," he indicated with thumb and forefinger, "and yea coconut juice. Bacardi Gold, nothing else will do, and tell him to simultaneously pour the rum and juice. I know it gets blended anyway, but I like knowing that it comes with a certain symmetry. I'm funny that way. Not humorous funny but quirky funny. Top it off with five shakes of nutmeg, or, better yet, fresh-ground, in which case about five or six passes over the shaver. Hang a good-size wedge of fresh pineapple over one side of the rim and a half-orange slice over the other. Spear it with two—not one, two—cocktail cherries, leaving the stems on. Oh, and make sure the coconut is either fresh chopped—obviously preferred—or flash frozen. And, oh, I like those wide-mouth straws that bend. I only drink directly from the top third of the glass. And don't forget the umbrella. Green if you've got one."

Karma told the waitress, "Maybe as an infant he didn't receive an adequate stream of breast milk."

The waitress backed away.

Karma called after her, "Nothing for me, thanks." She turned to the Mr. "So, guys, what's so drop-dead urgent?"

Eddward swirled his ice cube. "I take it Angus didn't tell you, then?" He glanced at his son and sighed. "No, I suppose he wouldn't have."

"Tell me what?"

The Mr. sputtered.

"Oh, for heaven's sake," piped the Mrs., eyes skyward. "This must be what a truffle feels like in a forest of toadstools." She turned to Karma and, again barely firing a neuron, said, "We insist that you sign a prenuptial agreement." She turned back to her men. "There. Was that so difficult?"

A long pause followed. The Mr. stared at his ice. Angus stared at his empty glass. Karma glared at the Mrs. The Mrs. glared at Karma. From behind the bar came the clink of bottle neck against glass rim. From under the table came the soft thump of shoe heel against upholstery. From outside came the muffled cacophony of hoi polloi. From across the room came the sound of buzzing fly. From Angus's T-shirt came the sound of oozing sweat.

Finally, Karma said to the Mr., "May I borrow your pen, Eddward dear?"

"Of course." He whipped a Mount Blanc from his blazer. "Anything for my daughter-in-law." He uncapped the pen and handed it over.

From Angus she swiped a cocktail napkin. As she wrote, she muttered, "Add to shopping list: package of Q-Tips." She recapped and handed the Mount Blanc back to the Mr. "There, that should fix the problem." She chuckled. "The strangest thing just happened, which obviously has to do with my being so busy playing compensatory wet nurse to your son that I've temporarily neglected my personal hygiene and have let wax accumulate in my ear canals." She exhaled and began sliding out. "It's been terrific seeing you guys. Totally awesome. I look forward to bumping into you at the ceremony. Now, if you'll excuse me, I've got to see the captain about a certain shipment of pork—"

"Angus was supposed to have mentioned this months ago," tut-tutted the Mrs., frosting her boy a look. "He obviously was terrified."

Karma continued to get up. "Yes, well, you guys can work out your DNA deficiencies among yourselves. I've got real work to do. Ta-ta for now."

Marybethlehem slapped Angus on the back of his head. It was the first actual movement she had made. "Tell her."

With Karma's one knee still on the Naugahyde, he mumbled, "If you don't agree—"

"Louder," insisted the Mrs.

"—they're cutting us off."

"There's that ear wax thing again."

"Mother's right. I should have told you a long time ago. I never seemed to find the right moment."

"We trusted him," offered the Mrs. "We're very sorry you had to hear it at the eleventh hour…but it really wasn't our fault." A three-quarter smile broke through her hair-bun torque and just as quickly sprang back to half.

Karma teetered on the upholstery piping. "So let me get this straight," she said, examining her fingernails. "Angy should have given me this news, oh, many strap-on butt-fucks and dressing-him-up-as-Aunty-Mame-and-raising-welts-on-his-fat-ass-with-rolled-up-*Robb-Report*s ago? But for some strange reason he put off mentioning it? Hm. I wonder what that reason could be."

"I assure you," said the Mrs. with aplomb, "implied blackmail will get you nowhere."

"I know!" Karma offered, snapping her fingers. "It has to do with the fact that I'm…of the 'Hebrew persuasion,' as you time-warped, country-club martini suckers like to put it, yes?" She clicked her tongue at the Mr. "Shame on you, Eddward. I never took you for the type. Having all those illegals around the house and all."

"Nor implied threats," sniffed the Mrs.

A different waitress came with Angus's cocktail. He grabbed it and began to slurp like a water buffalo.

"If Angus wants to experiment with…alternative life forms, there's not much we can do about it," added Marybethlehem. "He's free, white, and twenty-one."

"I can see you've given this some thought—or whatever you want to call it."

"Not to throw cold water on an otherwise happy occasion," said the Mrs., "but, frankly, if it were up to me, I'd offer you a tidy sum to go away. But I know how these things work. Viruses never die, only go dormant. If you were to throw yourself overboard, that might be different—we'd never have to worry about Angus actually jumping in to save you—but then what good would all that tidy sum do you? And, anyway, a dock worker might fish you out of the water—no doubt someone you've also strapped it on for, in case you were wondering if I knew to what you were referring."

"It never occurred to me you wouldn't."

"How dare you."

"You're trying to provoke me, Mummsy, but I'm smarter than you. That's the Hebrew-persuasion part of me."

"That's not the only Hebrew part of you."

The Mr. finally interceded. "Not to worry," he assured Karma. "We're definitely not suggesting you won't fully live a lifestyle commensurate with your new status. As long as you're married to the family, you'll live like a princess, of that you may be certain—a life even the wealthiest and most glamorous movie stars could only dream of. Villas on the coast of France, in Nevis, on Kauai. A penthouse at the Kowloon Peninsula, your own wing at Raffles in Singapore, a chalet in Montreux—"

She pretended to yawn. "Tell me something I don't already know."

"You'll have more jewels than the Tower of London. Your luggage will be made from the skins of animals that went extinct millions of years ago. Your homes will be dripping with original Van Goghs"—he pronounced it *Goffs*—"and Rembrandts and Picassos—"

"Right," she interrupted. "Except they won't exactly be *my* homes, *my* animal pelts, *my* paintings. That's the point, isn't it? Let's cut the dog shit. Those diamonds and rubies I'll be wearing will be on loan."

He cleared his throat. "Of course, if it comes down to that, I suppose we could work something out on the jewelry—in regard to deed, I mean."

"Over my dead body," said the Mrs.

Karma plucked the cocktail parasol out of her fiancé's nose. "I suppose you have no comment about all this."

"Angus isn't the founder of the family empire," clarified Marybethlehem.

Karma puckered. "From what I hear, your half of the family wasn't exactly an empire builder itself."

The Mrs. throttled Angus a glare and quickly turned back to Karma. "What do you mean by that?"

"Oh, a little something I heard about drunks and pyromaniacs and insane asylums and incest and all that icky business with the maternal family sheep. Probably just vile rumor and innuendo."

"I should say so."

"You're not making this any easier," the Mr. scolded his wife.

"*Me?* What about *her?* Tell *her.*"

He turned to his future daughter-in-law. "Look, Karma. I, for one, like you. I like you an awful lot."

"I like you, too, Eddie. Awfully, too." She chopped Angus a look. "Often better than your son."

The Mr. tilted his head. "Really?"

Karma reached over and pinched Eddward's cheek. He blushed and stuttered, "Anyway, the point is, we have to be realistic about this thing. Face it: young people today aren't as committed to the drudgeries and daily tortures of marriage as"—he flashed his wife an appreciative smile— "say, Mother and I. I understand it's a generational thing… we old fogies taking on our burdens with a certain stoic aplomb. Grace under pressure and all…"

"Oh, for God's sake, Eddward!" his wife snapped. "Can't we wrap this up? And I'm not her damn mother!"

"I'm just trying to make the point," he told Karma, "that even if things don't work out between you and Angus—hard though it may be to imagine now—we'll still make sure you're well-provided for in the future. You see, it's not like we'd disown you...nothing so common as that."

"Promise-wommis?"

"We're not heartless."

"I could keep my wittle jewelry?"

"Of course!"

"Oh, Lord!" moaned the Mrs. "Can't you see she's mocking us? Are you that dense?"

"Tell you what," Karma said in adult again, "Why don't your son and I have a little chat about this in private? It has come on me so suddenly, owing to Angus being a weasel, and all. A few minutes alone? Just the two of us?"

Furtively, Angus shook his head *no* at his father.

"You bet!" said the Mr. "Sounds perfectly reasonable to me. Come on Marybethlehem. Let's leave the lovebirds to themselves." He turned to Karma. "We'll all meet"—he checked his Rolex—"say, for dinner? Ristorante Vesuvius? Seven o'clock?"

"It's a date," Karma agreed.

"Well done!"

The Culvertdales creaked to their feet, Eddward once again extending his manicure to his imminent daughter-in-law. "I'm so glad we had this tête-à-tête. I knew you'd handle it maturely, I just knew it. Marybethlehem was a bit skeptical, but I said no, I have a good feeling about that young woman of ours—"

"Will you shut up, Eddward. You're making me sick."

Karma shook his hand and held it longer than etiquette required. "I also feel we've bonded a little here, Eddward, you and I."

He sighed. When she finally released his hand, it remained cantilevered and twitching. The Mrs. grabbed his blazer and hauled him to the entrance.

When the soon-to-be newlyweds were alone, Karma said, "Call me crazy, but I don't think Mummsy likes me."

"Karma, sweetheart, puppy, kitty, puss. Before you go off the deep end—"

"I'm not going off the deep end, Angus."

"You're not?"

"Of course not. You've got me all wrong."

"I do?"

"Meeting with your parents like this has changed me as a person on a very fundamental level."

"It has?"

"They made me see an aspect of this enterprise I never saw before."

"They did?"

"I realize now I've been looking at this whole marriage concept in the wrong light."

"You do? You have?"

She looked around. "But you know, I do think we need to discuss this away from prying ears. Why don't we go up to the suite and finish the conversation…or, as Eddward might say, the tête-à-tête…between ourselves, in total private?" She slid out. "Come on, poopsie-woopsie. Don't be afraid. Take your drinky-winky with you. Really, it's going to be perfectly fine, absolutely safe, I promise."

"Cross your heart?"

She offered her hand to help him out. "Star of David my heart."

Clutching his drink, he squeaked over the Naugahyde, and, with his soon-to-be-bride nudging him, shuffled toward the elevator. Shuffled because, despite her assurances, it had all the feel of an imminent hanging.

My Dearest El Maximo:

I was only prepubescent when you liberated Cuba from the avaricious clutches of the U.S. military-industrial complex and its surrogate, the debauched and barbarous Batista, but I well recollect the jubilance I felt upon hearing news reports of your perambulating into Havana from the Sierra Maestra. Even as a juvenile I had prodigious aspirations for your country and your people—and still do, of course—but little could I have then surmised the extents to which the imperialistic *lusus naturae* would go to trample the *élan vital* crying out from the Antilles. From the Bay of Pigs to the corrupt Nicaraguan Contras, to Reagan's illicit and obliquitous invasion of Grenada; from Che's assassination, to Allende's murder, to Manley's and Bishop's abrogations, to trying to extirpate you (what, twenty-eight times?—Exploding cigars...ha!), U.S. interventionism (adventurism!) has been responsible for more anguish and subjugation than any imperialist aggression in history. And,

of course—with the Bush administration's
psychopathic war in Iraq, its pertinacious support
of the illegal Israeli occupation; its xenophobic
oppression of inculpable American Muslims
and undocumented Hispanic workers; its
repudiation of the Kyoto Treaty and the Geneva
Convention regarding treatment of prisoners of
war; its disproportionate waste of precious natural
resources; its scabrous tax breaks for the wealthy;
its union-undermining, fascist tactics against labor;
its pretermission of the indigent; its *apologia* of
big corporations, including tobacco and liquor
companies and those that sully the environment
with Augean abandon; its fattening the richest
one percent of the population at the expense of
the most indigent thirty percent; its pandering to
right-wing reactionary fanaticism; its declaring
the rights of women subsidiary to the rights
of amorphous *foeti*; its truculent refusal to ban
hunting; its blackguardian electoral process; its
opprobrious health-care system; its chauvinistic
disdain of the metric system and Spanish-language
road signs; its corrosive under-emolumentation
of public education and the arts; its unrestrained
and unabashed racism—it still is. I could go on
and on, of course, so heinous are the U.S.'s (only
the U.S refers to itself as "America," ignoring
the residuous of the hemisphere!) crimes against
humanity and the world, but I'm the type of
person who prefers not to dwell on the negatives.

My salient thesis is, ever since I was a stripling
I have venerated you and everything you
emblematize: your intrepidity in the face of great

personal risk, your Argus-eyed vision of the future,
your constancy to your people and cause, your
unwavering idealism, a utopianism that lesser men
have abandoned to impracticality—to paraphrase
Hamlet, "The native hue of resolution sicklying
o'er with the pale cast of thought, and enterprises
great with pitch and moment, in this regard
their currents turning awry and losing the name
of action." If, in my formative years, someone
would have told me that one day I would be in
the company of you, my idol, my personal deity,
I would have thought it impossible—although I
have reveried about such a meeting every day of
my life.

And yet, here I am, engaged in this
monumental undertaking, this sublime endeavor
so extrospective to future generations and the
future of the world. At every temporal juncture I
have to pinch myself (this is an English idiom—
don't know if there is a Spanish approximation)
to see if I am certifiably awake or still
phantasmagorifying.

I didn't want either of us to expire without
my having perlocuted my profoundest sentiments.
I want you to be percipient of how privileged,
how uniquely special I feel to be collaborating
with you to advance our mutual objective. I want
you to be unqualifiedly assured with every micro
fiber of your *soma* how dedicated I am to ensuring
our—again, to quote the Bard—"enterprise be
great with pitch and moment" (I'm not sure how
the subjunctive mood translates to Spanish, if at
all), i.e., complete *coup de mâitre*, and that I will do

everything within both my orbs of exteriority and interiority not to falter in any manner or form. As a matter of fact, I have already made what I believe are a few significant suggestions to "the Skipper," the efficacy of which I hope and entrust you will appreciate, and you can depend on me without reservation to continue to ruminate on ways to enrich the Mission, if possible, and to work propinquitously and with unswerving constancy to "the Skipper" and the others until such time as we emerge rapturously victorious over the forces of oligarchical oppression.

That would make me the most rhapsodic *Homo erectus* in the world.

Yours Eudaemonistically,
"The Professor"

P.S. For what it's worth, when I was a lad I was perpetually persecuted and even frequently corporally assaulted for defending your glorious revolution. Forgive my presumption, but in the name of comprehensive veracity, I must disclose to you that another part of my being-long dream is to someday see a statue of myself in a Havana park. It wouldn't be of monumental (pardon the pun!) consequence, of course, but the closer to the Plaza of the Revolution, the better.

T.P.

The Cuban president's assistant, a former army colonel, finished reading the letter to his *comandante* and, pen poised, waited for a reply. If, as happened often lately, the president forgot what the beginning of the letter said by the time the colonel got to the end, or forgot about the letter altogether, or simply fell asleep halfway through, or had to go to the bathroom, the colonel merely expedited the letter to El Maximo's brother, who was going to answer it for him anyhow.

On this occasion, though, the president couldn't doze because he was busy clutching his stomach with laughter at the way his assistant twisted and knotted and tripped over his tongue trying to read the letter, so that near its end he raised his hands for the colonel to stop and told him he had wee-weed his pants.

"You're making this whole thing up," the Cuban leader guffawed, grabbing the letter.

"I assure you, El Maximo, I read it faithfully."

The president couldn't catch his breath. "It's true," he wailed as he read, wiping tears of joy with his knuckles. "The *lunático* sounds like either an idiot or a university English teacher!"

"Would you like to reply when you come back from changing, *Comandante*?"

"Reply to what? I don't understand a word of it."

"Perhaps a translation?"

"I can't imagine why, Lieutenant. I haven't the faintest notion who this fellow is. Who the devil is he, and what in the world does he want?"

"'The Professor,'" the colonel reminded him.

"He wants to sell us chalk?" The president stroked his beard. "Do we have enough blackboards? I realize we are low on certain luxury items, such as electricity, but surely there is enough chalk in the country."

"*Sí, Comandante.*"

"Well, Sergeant, I suppose we should give him the courtesy of replying to that effect, no?"

"I believe 'the Professor' is a code name, *Comandante*."

"Impossible. I know very well what chalk is. Does he think I'm dotty?"

"I doubt that, Bearded One."

"There's too much of this going on lately. Do they think I don't keep up with current events? That I don't watch television? I happen to love television. Don't I watch *WWF Smackdown* and *Gilligan's Island* late at night from under my covers? I'm warning you, Major, this underestimating me has to stop."

"Yes, El Maximo. But I believe Thurston would care to see the letter."

"Not my yahoo of a brother?"

The colonel took back the letter and slapped it on his palm. "I believe this one should go directly to Venezuela. I believe the Professor has supplied a useful idea to further your…secret operation."

"I'm having another secret operation?"

"Not that kind of operation, *Comandante*. I mean Castaways' Revenge."

"Oh, *that* operation." He narrowed an eye. "You didn't tell my brother, did you?"

"Your secret is safe with me," the colonel lied.

The president chewed his lip. Nodding at the letter, he said, "A useful idea, the fellow claims? Does he say what, General?"

"It's hard to tell, but I don't think so, not here. I think he just wants you to know it's *his* idea."

The dictator rolled his eyes mischievously. "Bypass El Minimo, eh?"

"If you like."

"That would be like a bowel bypass," he said, howling.

"Quite amusing."

"Do it!"

"It will be our little secret, then?"

"My lips are sealed," said the president. "Seal-a-Meal! Isn't that amazing!? What would you pay for this amazing, money-saving, *revolutionary* food-storage device? Ninety-nine dollars? Not here, not now. With this special TV offer, this incredible invention won't cost you eighty-nine dollars. Not seventy-nine dollars. Not even sixty-nine dollars. If you call now, we will reserve your new Seal-a-Meal for the low, low investment of only…forty-nine ninety-five!"

The colonel backed out of the room.

"But wait…there's more!"

Nine

Former Haiti commerce minister Henri Charbonnay lay crumpled in the stolen fishing skiff *Fat Banana*, the tropical sun gnawing him awake. Sometime during the night the engine had broken down—curse that cheapskate François—and try after try of key-turning and button-pushing and cord-pulling had failed to turn it over. He had panicked, all right. The tub was at the mercy of the currents, the constellations spun around, and he could hear evil things under the hull, whispering, laughing, licking their chops. A crescent moon rose late and what small light it shed only illuminated vast, black emptiness. Physically and mentally exhausted, he had curled up in the bottom of the boat and prayed to Agwe, the voodoo spirit of the sea; to Olòrún, the absolute god; to Ayza, the protector; to Damballah-Wedo, the serpent spirit; and to every other blasted obeah deity he could think of to save his wretched hide.

Then came the nightmares. Nightmares as he had never suffered his whole life. Hallucinatory nightmares. Delirium nightmares. Nightmares he could not awake from because to wake would only remind him of where he was, which was an even worse nightmare. Nightmares that held him in a claw-grip, a pack of nightmares tearing at his viscera, sucking his brain, chewing his bones, masticating his arteries, ripping his heart. Then came the night chill, the sunless, hellish cold that seeped through his sea-soaked clothes like barbed parasites, burrowing through his flesh, composting sinew and bone. Rum was his only defense, and it was not enough. Rum only seemed to make the boat's rocking more violent, the slapping of the waves against the hull angrier. If only the sea would sleep. If only what was inside him would stop feasting on his guts. If only daylight would come once more. *Olòrún, beg you, make daylight come soon.*

Former commerce minister Charbonnay had temporarily forgotten the adage to be careful of what you pray for, because you might just get it.

He slept through dawn's first warming rays—vapors rising from his hair and clothes. Then, as sweat-mingled stink wormed up his nostrils and burrowed into his head bone, his conscious and subconscious minds began to wrestle. The sunrise's sweetness began to turn sour, her tender caress started to sting, her kiss became bite. His eyes shot open. Although the bottom of the skiff was still in shadow, his eyes snapped shut again in solar pain. The side of his face, his ear, arm, ribs, and leg were on fire. For an instant he believed *Fat Banana* was literally ablaze. He jolted up, shielding his eyes, preparing to jump into the water. In a moment, though, with relief, now almost fully awake, he realized the fire was not from below or behind but from above.

His relief didn't last long. Still cupping his eyes, he gazed at the sea, a cauldron of molten slag. He glanced up at an incinerator sky. Not a cloud in sight. Not a cloud nor land nor salvation from what he knew would be a hideous death. He glanced at the bottles of Rémy Martin and Rothschild and felt like throwing up. He searched for drinking water. Fishermen kept jugs of water in their boats at all times, but not that fool François. Still, the rum was mostly water and would keep him alive as long as it lasted. And it would ease his fear a little. He uncorked the Rothschild and held it under his nose. If only the thought of it didn't make him sick. What he wouldn't have done for a thimbleful of plain, cool, fresh water. François!

He held his nose, sipped, and gagged anyway. Something was wrong. His lungs felt like they were filled with sand. He tried starting the engine again—first with the key, then by cord, but neither worked. He realized it wouldn't have mattered anyhow. The most the dashboard compass would tell him was where he was heading, but who knew where he was? He was drifting east now, but for how long? Was he already in the Atlantic? Judging by the waves' frothiness and size, it was possible. The sea was still too fiery to tell its shade of blue, but if it emerged inky, the dark sea of fathomless abyss, he was finished.

He cursed every god he could think of: Oshun, Elegua, Mawu Lisa, Ogou Balamo, Jesus, Zeus, Thor, Vishnu, Buddha. And when he was out of gods, he cursed prophets and disciples and biblical kings and saviors and saints. Moses, Mary, Joseph, Jesus again, Abraham, Isaac, Eve, Adam, Isaiah, Judah, Esther, Gideon, Jonah, Mary again, Peter, Saul. And when he ran out of those, he cursed Satan and Beelzebub and Lucifer and Mephistopheles and the Prince of Darkness and the Beast.

Then, believing that eternity in hell would be better than this, he changed his mind and blessed Satan and Beelzebub and Lucifer and Mephistopheles and the Prince of Darkness and the Beast.

He raked his fingers over his steaming scalp. He could smell his hair burning. But he dare not take off his shirt or pants to cover his head. To expose much flesh to protect a little would be suicidal. Instead, he removed his slacks, wiggled off his underpants, put his trousers back on, and fitted his shorts over his skull, tucking the elastic under his ears.

By the time the sun was directly overhead, he had hunkered into the hull, pressing as much of himself under a seat plank as possible, but there was too much of him still exposed. He cursed his mother for having him. He cursed his father for screwing her. He cursed God for not making him a dwarf. A part of him was getting hungry, but another part of him was too ill to eat—sick with fear, but also sick in fact. It felt like someone was twisting his esophagus, the way women wrung out clothes in rivers. His lung pain wasn't dull anymore—it felt like ice picks chiseling their way out. His intestines gurgled and spasmed and cried for pity. He tried to perch himself on the gunwale to shit in the ocean but lost his balance and almost tumbled overboard. He changed his mind and crapped into the bottom of the boat. Now he sloshed up to his ankles in shit, but he didn't care. He drank more rum and threw up. He waded in a putrid bouillabaisse.

He cursed Haiti and Aristide and Dessalines and Boukman and L'Ouverture and Christophe and Napoleon and both Duvaliers and their whory wives. He cursed his own wives and mistresses, and this and that, and he cursed his children. He wasn't quite sure what he had against his children but, spitting over the side, cursed them anyway. He forgot a couple of their names, so he put out a generalized child-curse and worked up an extra-big glob of spit.

By sunset he was lying supine in his crap-and-vomit stew, his underpants a jellyfish-like bladder floating from his head, as much of himself submerged in the god-awful, putrid, but relatively cool muck as he could manage. Once in a while he would haul himself up with zombie-stiffness, peer out at the sea for signs of land and, seeing none, fall back with a splat. The intervals between lookouts were getting longer and longer. The last one saw the bottom of the sun touching the horizon. He became weaker and weaker. Even for the coming darkness he lacked the energy to be grateful.

Nothing between him and another predatory day but another predatory night.

"You know, Professor Fenwich," Diane cooed as Les topped their flutes with bubbly, "if I didn't know better, I'd say you're trying to be romantic."

"It's quasi-bioluminescence-like," Les said, gazing into the river, skyscraper lights shimmering.

"A fairyland," she agreed.

As their Wendella sightseeing boat glided beneath the Chicago high-rises, they clinked glasses, entwined forearms, and sipped first their own champagne (Moët 2004), then each other's.

"I feel like no time has passed," she whispered. "Like all the years in between have vanished."

He sighed. "To be honest, I feel pretty rotten about the way I handled things. Or, more germanely, didn't handle them."

"We have to live in the moment, you know? Life is so short."

She snuggled close, and he put his arm around her.

As the Wendella slid under Michigan Avenue, he said, "In Venice, it's good luck to kiss under the bridges."

She gazed up at him, and he brushed her mouth with his. "It's not exactly a gondola," he whispered, his eyelashes fluttering in that romantic way of his—the way that skeptics and body-language experts might have thought was a mark of calculating insincerity.

Diane, of course, knew better. "It'll do," she whispered, returning his kiss.

"You deserve a gondola." *Flutter.*

"Stop apologizing, Les. We're here now, that's what counts. Besides, Chicago is as beautiful as Venice any day. Think how lucky we are. A clear night, a gorgeous, twinkling city. Our daughter getting married…" Her voice trailed off.

"Go on, may as well say it. No sense ignoring our eight-hundred-pound gorilla."

She sighed. "As long as she's happy, I'm happy."

"I'm looking forward to it." *Flutter.* "Not just the wedding but…everything." *Flutter, flutter.* "Having an instant family. It sounds implausible, I know. I have a hard time accrediting it to myself, but there you are. For the first time, I feel…I'm not sure *happy* is the precise word. *Content*? I'm not positive that's the right term either. Not exactly *blithe*, certainly not *felicitous* or *jubilant*…" He fell into a professorial trance. "*Blissful*? Mm, not quite but on the right track. Not really *joyous*…" He thought some more. "*Gratified* comes closest but…"

She put her hand gently over his mouth. With her flute she pointed at the sliver of moon rising over the lake. She removed her hand and kissed him on the cheek. "Words are nice," she whispered, "but this is even nicer."

"*Eudaemonic*, that's it! This whole thing has made me feel positively *eudaemonic*."

As the Wendella wound its way to the lock gate and, engine gurgling, waited in line behind two other boats, Diane glanced behind her at the fairyland city, at once majestic and as delicate as lace, rising with a paternal sturdiness and motherly warmth. Les topped off her flute. A cool lake breeze washed over the deck. She sipped her champagne and snuggled closer. She was determined not to mention her real feelings about the imminent marriage—the feeling of impending doom she couldn't seem to shake no matter how many feel-good philosophies she tried to pestle into her brain. True, she believed in sharing fears with those you loved most, and if all continued to go well, there would soon be a time and place to express hers with Les, but not here, not now. Tonight was perfect, and she would do nothing to risk that. Tonight was about exquisite champagne and snuggling and the most beautiful city in the world, the river, the lake, the skyline, the moon. Tonight was about two parents and their only child and the future and, above all, the moment.

The Wendella nosed up to the lock gate. They were next.

"Don't get me wrong," he said, foaming up his Moët. "It's not like I don't have my trenchant anxieties. It's not as if I'm making a fortune or anything. I'm still only a pedagogue. You know I've never been into affectation. How can I hope to compete with Karma's in-laws, when it comes to that?"

"Do you think Karma would have wanted to find you if she cared about that? If you think about it, their being so rich does take a lot of pressure off us. They're in such a financial league of their own, there's no point trying to compete with them, even if we wanted to. Which, of course, we don't."

He gave her a squeeze. "You're the most percipient woman I know. You always did know how to assuage my restiveness."

"I could tell something's been on your mind. You can tell me anything, you know."

"I've been feeling so…eudaemonic, I guess I've also been apprehensive that I might do something so amentiferous, it will deconstruct my new"—he made quote marks with his fingers—"*happiness*, for lack of a more efficacious term. I know it sounds kind of solipsistic, but that's how I've been feeling recently. It's all such new territorial imperative, and although I've been eudaemonic, I've also been trepidatious…of losing again what it's taken me so long to rediscover."

"But it's not solipsistic at all, Les. It's completely humanistic. You are human, you know."

"At first I was cogitating what I could possibly give them for a wedding present—"

"Oh, Les, you don't have to—"

He held up his hand. "Please. I *do* have to, that's the point. If you don't want to ruminate about the past, fine, but I, I've got things for which to compensate. The unvarnished truth is, I'd give her everything I have if I thought it would recompense for my previous neglect. I've been feeling extremely self-reproachful about it all." *Flutter, flutter, flutter.* "But we both know that 'everything I have' would blanch compared to what Eddward and Marybethlehem Culvertdale can give them just by turning their pockets inside out. But then tonight, being with you, I came to a Joycean epiphany."

She snuggled even closer. "That's some company."

"Since there's nothing even remotely materialistic I could give them to make me feel adequate, I decided the thing to do is not try to compete with the Culvertdales but, rather, to do what I do best, which is to *metaphor*—if you can use *metaphor* as a verb, which I believe you can if you want to, even if you don't see it used frequently as such, certainly in formal writing, but, in any event, I'm using it here because this is, after all, an informal, conversational setting, and I'm comfortable with the knowledge that you know what I mean."

"Metaphor as a verb."

"Even if, technically, it isn't precise usage in the *pre*scriptive, rather than *de*scriptive, sense of the word. Anyhow, I decided to give her"—his eyebrows rose—"luggage." He watched her reaction, but she didn't offer much. "Oh, I know what you're thinking—how cliché-ish…luggage for a wedding present." He chuckled. "But give my imagination a little credit. I don't mean garden-variety wedding-present luggage."

"There's nothing wrong with…I mean, I never doubted your imagina—"

"I'm going to give her my old knapsack, one of the pair I bought—remember?—when we were going to go on that sojourn to Europe that we…" He glanced down, and his voice tapered off contritely.

"Never went on?" She sat up. She grinned. "Don't tell me you still have those? After all this time? Those canvas knapsacks you bought at the army surplus?"

"Before backpacks became de rigueur."

"I can't believe you kept them!"

"Positively. And I even kept my old fringed vest." *Flutter, flutter.* "You know, the one I wore with nothing else when we—"

"No! You kept that, too?"

"It meant a lot to me, Diane."

"I can't believe it." She squeezed his hand. "You sweet man, you."

"However…and this isn't easy for me to vocalize, Diane…but the sordid truth is, I gave one of the knapsacks away."

Her smile faded.

"No, no, it's not like that. I didn't *throw* it away, and I didn't give it to any *woman*. I'd never do that."

"You wouldn't?"

"*Never.* I gave it to the Lighthouse for the Blind." *Flutter, flutter, flutter, flutter.*

"Lighthouse for the Blind?"

"In your name."

Her smile sprang back. "Oh, Les! The *blind!*"

"I was a coward, Diane, I admit that now, but even back then I knew I owed you something. The gesture was…"

"Metaphoric."

"Yes, yes. Exactly. *Metaphoric.*"

She threw her arms around him. "You sweet, romantic professor."

"Wait, that was only my penultimate pronouncement. I'm not finished. I have a correlative idea."

She clasped her hands.

"You remember, the other day, when you were bemoaning the fact that 'you've become your own mother,' quote-unquote?"

"I am her."

"It occurred to me that we *both* have subconscious issues that need deconstructing—purging, if you will. See, you've been thinking of 'motherhood' in the traditional, bourgeois sense of the word—something very middle-class-valued, correct?"

"I suppose…yes, I guess so."

"The world of our parents. The world we rebelled against. So naturally, the thought of 'becoming your mother'—again, quote-unquote—makes you uncomfortable, in the pejorative sense of the word."

"Okay."

"So, here's my concept. I give the newlyweds one of our old knapsacks, and inside we put a container of your homemade matzo balls." Again he paused to watch her reaction.

None came.

"My gift is metonymic in the sense already elucidated, and your matzo balls are sublimely symbolic of passing along 'motherness' to the next iteration. Absolutely, totally cathartic, in both cases. Flairishly metaphoric."

Silence.

"Well, Diane?" he asked after a minute. "What do you think? Is it too insipient?"

"Insipient?"

"Too inerudite?"

"Inerudite?"

"Very well, all right…I just thought maybe—"

"It's totally, absolutely, supremely *brilliant!*"

He puffed out his chest. "You really think so?"

"Only you, Leslie Fenwich—*professor extraordinaire* Leslie Fenwich—could have thought of a subconsciously metonymic wedding present!"

"I assume you mean that nonironically."

She hugged his neck. "You bet I do! And noninsipiently and nonineruditely, too!"

"You're sort of choking me," he coughed.

"Let's not tell them the metaphor part right off the bat. You know, let them wonder what the heck it's all about—an old backpack with matzo balls!" She clapped her hands and giggled. "They'll talk about it their whole honeymoon!"

He shrugged. "What if she gets piqued about our reticence, not to mention our apparent parsimony?"

She waved off the notion. "Oh, she's been a little on edge lately, sure, but, trust me, in her heart Karma's a sweet, gentle soul." And then, elated and tipsy, she leaned over and gently kissed one of Les's fluttering eyelids.

"You fucking dirty fucking, motherfucking, weasel-fucking motherfucker!" Karma panted, wielding a rolled-up and battered *Miami Herald*, as Angus, fully naked, lay facedown, spread-eagle, his wrists and ankles cuffed to the bed frame, his butt a mound of rising welts, the bedspread under his face a swamp of tears, spittle, and snot.

"I think you're going a little overboard, bunny," he gurgled, his joyful-terrified pleas smothered in quilt.

"I'll overboard you, you tit-sucking mama's boy. Overboard? You want to see overboard?"

"Not really, sweetkins," he moaned. "I really think it's time to let me go."

She stormed into the suite's kitchen, flung open the refrigerator, yanked out a bottle of Dom Pérignon 1972, stormed back into the bedroom, and watched the terror on his face as she knelt at the edge of the bed and showed him the bottle.

"What are you going to do with that?" he stammered.

"So, the Culvertdale clan wants me to sign a prenup, huh? So, you superior Presbyterian fuckwads think you're better than the gutter-slime Weinbergs?"

"You're overreacting, cupcake. You're pure emotion right now and…What *are* you going to do with that?"

She peeled off the foil top and unscrewed the wire. Calmly she said, "I figure as long as you civic-leading rulers of us common people love and deserve all the finest things in life, including the best wine and caviar, why stop at just pampering your digestive track from the top down?"

"Oh, no. No, mumpkins, you can't—"

She grabbed the bottle by its throat and twisted the cork.

"No, lovemuff, you don't mean—"

She worked the cork loose but did not pull it out. Instead, she held the bottle where he could see it and gave it a good shake.

His eyes got big. "Oh, jeez."

"Jeez isn't going to help you now, you WASP son of a bitch."

She got up and moved out of his field of vision.

"Karma! Karma! Where are you? I need to see you. I'm having a stress issue!"

She got up on the bed and knelt between his legs. "So, Culvertdales only go for the very best?"

"Karma? Karma! Panic! Panic!"

"Okay, Richie Rich," she snarled, yanking out the cork with a window-quavering *pop!*, "treat yourself to a lower-intestinal vintage spa!"

And as she shoved the exploding bottle up his tuchas, she was already beyond Angus's joyful agony and was thinking of ways to shower Eddward and Marybethlehem with the finest of the fine.

The Wendella slipped into the lock. The rear gate thudded closed, and there came a tense pause, like the moment between a neck set in a guillotine and the releasing of the blade. Diane watched the score marks on the lock wall, but nothing was happening. She felt no rising motion. Then, a subtle jerk, and the bottom hash mark submerged. She wondered why she had thought of a guillotine just then. Why that image? Why tonight, when she was so happy?

The boat rose to quay level, and a chilling wind blustered the deck.

"Lake effect," Les said, shivering.

She slipped into her heretofore-tied-around-her-waist sweater and resumed her spot under his arm. The front lock gate opened, forming maelstroms in the dark water. The engine raced, and the boat slapped into the lake's first waves, spilling Leslie's champagne onto Diane's sweater sleeve. The bow chomped into the wind and thudded into the surf, spray exploding, foam raining down. They ducked and screamed but got drenched anyway.

They grabbed their belongings and careened below deck, where less sentimental but more clear-thinking sightseers sat warm and dry. They made a joke of the rough ride, although Diane was beginning to feel seasick. An attendant handed them a roll of paper towels, and Les blotted her and himself down. But it was too late; they were clammy to the bone. They curled up near a space heater, but she didn't want to snuggle into his soaked clothes.

As the boat headed out, the attendant passed around cups of coffee. It was weak and lukewarm and tasteless. Away from shore, the lake got even rougher, and the skyline pitched and heaved, dipped and yawed—no longer comforting or fairylike.

Les and Diane barely spoke another word.

Ten

FORMER HAITI COMMERCE MINISTER HENRI CHARBONNAY peeked out from thread gaps in his underpants and spotted a shadow on the fiery sea. He glanced up but saw no corresponding cloud. He slid the elastic to his forehead, shielded his eyes with his hand, and squinted, certain he was hallucinating.

But there it was…or seemed to be—a ship on the horizon. With ebbing strength, he swirled his hand around the boat-bottom muck and found one of the empty rum bottles he now used for bailing. He rinsed it out over the side, held the spout to his eyeball like a telescope, and, indeed, got a better look. If it was a hallucination, it was a dandy: a tall, glinting, triple-stacked, lapis-blue-hulled cruise ship, heading his way. He was almost sure it was a mirage because its iridescent, sparkling blue reminded him of Curaçao liqueur, an apéritif he liked very much, and its three smoke stacks resembled triplet bottles, side by side on the shelf behind Francois's bar.

For the next couple of hours he sat up in *Fat Banana*, enduring the savage midday sun, refusing to hunker into the slop, trying with all his waning might not to blink, while he watched the ship—or its illusion—get closer and closer, larger and larger, bluer and bluer, apéritifer and apéritifer. He was terrified that if he retreated to the boat bottom or even turned away momentarily, he would look again, and it would be gone.

It occurred to him that he was already dead and in hell, and that this was his eternal punishment. A cruise ship—with its magnificent buffet, splendid bars, prompt room service, cornucopian entrees, sumptuous desserts, delectable appetizers, crab Louies and shrimp cocktails, escargots in garlic butter, bisques and biscuits, fresh spiny lobsters, broiled groupers, beef Wellingtons, veal scaloppinis, angel hair pastas, spaghettis and meatballs, fettuccini alfredos, broiled *langoustes*, spinach-and-tomato salads, succulent papayas, juicy mangoes, creamy cheesecakes, cold lagers, frosty ales, tickly champagnes, mellow cabernets, smoky scotches—would get only so close, and he would blink, and it would suddenly appear on the distant horizon again, steaming toward him, only to repeat the Sisyphean torment over and over, forever.

He chuckled deliriously. He had to admit it was a very customized punishment, even well-deserved. It conceded him a bit of style, a little class—this was no dilapidated freighter but a sleek ocean-going work of art; no greasy beer mug but a snifter of expensive digestif—and for that, at least, he thanked the devil.

Still, forever was a long time.

Thurston and Lovey—both wearing trunks, unbuttoned guayaberas, and sunglasses—lounged on a Varadero beach, sipping mojitos. The Cuban dictator, his toes burrowing in the sand, gazed vacuously at the tourmaline surf, while the Venezuelan tyrant, working a calculator, added up this month's oil revenues.

"Tell me," El Maximo sighed, "have you ever thought about chucking our high-pressure, despot lifestyles, so we could blend into the crowd and be like everyone else?"

"Don't talk stupid," said the Venezuelan, jotting a nine-digit figure onto a legal pad. "Holy carambas!"

"I haven't built a sand castle since I was a little boy. Don't you sometimes just want to stop being the guy everyone else depends on and reclaim that child in your soul?"

"That child in my soul had no goddamn *clue* that the grownup in my pocket would be raking in this kind of dough. If I build anything on the beach, *hermano*, it's going to be another refinery."

"I took my grandson to the beach last year, and do you know what he made out of sand? An apartment complex for government workers. It's the kind of thing that sometimes makes me question my life's work. Did I make the right choices? How will history remember me? What about my family? I don't trust my brother as far as I can throw him, the sneaky little lizard."

But the Venezuelan president, furiously punching calculator keys, wouldn't look up from his numbers. "Let me finish this quarterly summary, and I'll wax philosophical with you, comrade-in-arms," he mumbled distractedly. "*Un momento.*"

The Cuban sighed ponderously.

Thurston caressed the number he had written on the pad. "Yes indeedy. Come to Papa."

"Maybe there is more to life than imposing our will," El Max wondered, wistfully.

That seemed to shake the Venezuelan from his arithmetic masturbation. Sporting a Cheshire-cat grin, he finally looked up at his host. He could see that his amigo needed some commiserating. "Don't ever think like that, my dear old friend."

"I never won the Nobel Prize," sighed Lovey. "It would've been nice. Would it have killed them? They gave it to Arafat. What am I, borscht?"

"I want to tell you a little story," said the Venezuelan leader, tucking his calculator into his guayabera pocket. "A true story. Maybe it will put things in perspective. Make you feel better."

The Cuban president sat up. He rubbed his hands together. "A story like 'Once upon a time there lived a handsome prince'?"

"No, not that kind of story, not today."

Lovey's smile fell.

"Okay, maybe later. After I tell you my true story."

"I love stories with castles…you know, like sand castles?"

The Venezuelan reached into his beach bag and pulled out two cigars. "Come on, amigo. You only live once. To hell with your doctors. To hell with your so-called limit. Who's the boss around here, anyhow? You've already out-lived nine U.S. presidents."

The Cuban leader glanced around for busybodies. But the authorities had cordoned off the beach, and the two autocrats were alone with the sand crabs. "Okay, I will, I will. You're right. Screw those *pendejos*. We keep telling the world what great doctors we have here, but the truth is, they're shit. They read medical books from the 1950s. What I wouldn't give for one filthy-rich Jewish internist."

"Now you're talking!"

"I'm glad I came to the beach with you today!" El Max exclaimed as he tugged the cellophane from the cigar. "You're my true pal!"

"Darn tootin'." Thurston reached over to light the Cuban's Cohiba, then lit his own with half-a-dozen lusty sucks.

"You're right," said Lovey, exhaling desultory exhaust, swizzling his mojito, and gazing at a cloud shaped like SpongeBob SquarePants's pet snail, Gary. "This is the life. Now, what about your story?"

"Strictly confidential, you understand?"

Lovey's toes samba-ed in the sand. "No problema, amigo."

"When I was a young man, driving that stupid bus through the mountains, bringing villagers in and out of Caracas—what a grind! The old women yapping, yapping, while I'm trying to concentrate—you try driving one of those contraptions along winding mountain roads…yikes!"

"No, thank you."

"No, thank you is right. Not to mention the chickens they bring on with them. Who wrote those rules, anyhow? Chickens! Yap, yap, yap, cluck, cluck, cluck. I'm telling you, it drove me nuts. And don't get me started on the brats. Running up and down the aisle, hanging out the windows, throwing things, screaming, babies crawling on my lap! And I'm trying desperately not to plunge!"

Lovey shook his head. "I'm glad I was in law school."

"I got news for you, kiddo. Remember when Batista locked you up in Moncada Barracks? *That* was better than driving a busload of peasants. Remember Che getting shot, what, like a hundred fifty times in the face? *That* was better than ten hours of clucking chickens!"

Lovey clapped. "This is a good story!"

"So, anyhow, one evening after dropping off my last villager, I'm heading back to town, enjoying the peace and quiet, digging the great scenery—you know, the valley three thousand feet below? It's starting to get dark, and I guess I wasn't paying much attention to the road—"

"Uh, oh."

"You know what I was thinking about, compadre?"

"Let me guess!"

"Forget it."

"Let me try!"

"All right, all right. Two guesses."

El Maximo pondered. He tilted his head back and puffed gray smoke like a factory stack. "*Señoritas*!"

"Nope."

The Bearded One frowned. "Give me two more."

"One more."

The Cuban screwed up his face. He scratched his whiskers. He twirled his cigar.

"While I'm young, comrade."

"I got it! Food! You were thinking of dinner!"

"Sorry, Charlie. Not even in the same solar system."

"Let me try one more. Please?"

"You're done."

"This is *my* country!"

"Do you want to hear the rest of the story or not?"

The Cuban leader sulked.

"All right, then, listen up. What I was thinking about was…dietary fiber." He paused for dramatic effect. But nothing seemed to register on Lovey's bristly kisser. "Vitamin supplements," the Venezuelan elaborated. "You know, with the rainforest being depleted, and minerals being leached out of the soil, and fruits and vegetables being frozen and canned? Exponential rise in colon polyps? Look at you, amigo: you had half your bowels removed. Maybe if *you* had been taking supplements all these years, they'd still be in there, nice and cozy, where nature intended."

Lovey, taking another puff, nodded agreement.

"But I wasn't thinking about just any dinky supplements. I was thinking big. I was thinking *Wow-tality* brand vits and mins."

"I see their ads in *TV Guide.*"

"Damn right you do. They're the largest distributor of health and beauty supplements in the known universe. Notice I didn't say 'manufacturer' but 'distributor.' That's the beauty of the sales structure. They don't actually *make* a blasted thing. It's all in MLM. Multilevel marketing, baby—the leveraged path to financial independence. If you flip through their catalog, you'll cream in your camos. So, anyhow, as I'm winding down the mountain, I'm thinking, My God, what a potential market I'm sitting on! Who eats nutritious meals anymore, especially in this jerkwater country? Not the rush–rush Caracas yuppies. Not the dimwit peasants, who eat the same wormy tubers year after year. And God knows, my people can use beauty supplements. You see where I'm going with this?"

"When does the prince come in?"

"I thought, here's an exclusive territory just waiting for a go-getter like me. These mopes need pep and plenty of it: renewed energy, facial glow, a fresh outlook on life—not only as end-users *but as subdistributors*. I looked down at the city, but I didn't just see buildings and streets and cars and trucks anymore. No sirree. What I saw was…*commissions*."

"Wow-tality!"

"All at once I knew my life's purpose. It became my longing, my obsession. Do you know how few people have purpose in the world, good friend?"

"Let me guess!"

"Never mind. Forget that."

"Four hundred twenty-five!"

"What I didn't know then was that you don't just wake up one day and say, 'Now I'm a Wow-tality distributor.'"

"How come?"

"You need to buy a small initial inventory, and I was flat broke."

"I would have loaned you money."

"We didn't know each other."

"Still."

"I was so desperate to follow my dream, I even stole pennies from the church offering plate. When the priest caught me, he threatened to beat me to death unless I rubbed his back."

"We shot all our priests."

"But nothing would deter me…*nothing*. I was absolutely determined to own my local distributorship, be my own boss, lock in Caracas, maybe even the whole northern coast. I was sure that no one who ever wanted something so much could fail." He squeezed out a cynical laugh. "I even believed God himself wanted me to be a great vit and min rep. That's what I was thinking as I was driving the bus that night."

"A spiritual awakening."

"Exactly."

"We killed those too."

"Yeah, well, unfortunately, my spirit was the only thing awake. The next thing I know, the road curved right, the bus went straight ahead, and God was telling me the only Wow-tality territory I'd ever control was in hell."

"Did you die?"

He cut Lovey a look. "Yes, my old friend. I died. I'm actually dead. This isn't me talking to you right now." He snorted. "Sheesh."

"This is going to be a sad story, isn't it?"

"This isn't me sitting next to you but my twin brother, Dwayne. But he knows the whole story, so you won't miss a thing."

"You were both on the bus?"

"Yes, both of us. Driving. At the same time. And as the bus teetered on a precipice, Dwayne prayed, 'Jesus, if you will not let this bus plunge into the gorge, my twin brother will be the best damn vit and min representative Wow-tality ever had.'"

"We don't believe in God."

"I don't anymore either."

"Because the bus plunged, and you died?"

"No, because if Jesus had wanted me to have my own territory, he conveniently forgot to mention it to Wow-tality corporate. The bastards rejected me cold. Never gave me a chance. Never even told me a reason, just sent back my application and photograph with a funky letter saying they were looking for someone more 'embedded in the company image.'"

When the Cuban seemed perplexed—more than usual—Thurston explained, "It's a euphemism if there ever was one, *mi amigo*, and don't you forget it. I'll tell you what they *really* meant. They meant I'm pudgy. Too plump for corporate's taste. I tried to tell them I'd be the hardest working distributor they ever had. But did they listen? I wrote follow-up letters, I phoned, I sent telegrams. I said I'm big-boned, not fat. Did they answer? No, no, and no. Did they give one squat about dashing an ambitious, idealistic young man's hopes and dreams? They did not. You know all they cared about?"

"Let me guess!"

The Venezuelan slapped his forehead. "Comrade?"

"Yes, Dwayne?"

"We're coming to a very sensitive part of the story. Very delicate. You need to be a good audience here."

"No clapping?"

"No clapping, no cheering, no cracking gum, no idiotic questions, *nada*. Just listen."

"Can I puff my Cohiba?"

"Quietly."

"Okel-dokel."

The Venezuelan president drew a deep breath. "*Image*, that's all they cared about. Not hopes and dreams. Not flesh and blood. How would it look to have a flab-ass at a Wow-tality convention?—that's what they were worried about. But tell me, how is it my fault? We're all born with certain DNA. And, anyhow, I'm not exactly obese." He pulled back his guayabera. "Look here. Am I fat? A little baby plump, that's all. Cherubic. I've always looked beefier in pictures than I really am. Chubby in a spot or two, that's it."

"Suck it in for a second."

He tightened his abs. "Okay, no six-pack, I admit. But driving a bus all day isn't exactly playing soccer for a living. Give a guy a break."

Lovey leaned over to inspect his friend's belly. "Ooo, an outie." He tugged down his elastic. "I have an innie."

"Trust me, you don't know how lucky you are being so emaciated and sickly looking. Me, I've been paying for other people's sins my whole life. My *madre* and *padre* were both big-cheekboned. Did they think about consequences? No, they just went ahead and did the nasty. They had their fun at my expense. My sister is even worse off. She looks exactly like me. If I weren't the sentimental type, I'd have my folks shot."

"I'll do it."

"Do you know who Wow-tality awarded the local franchise to?"

"Consuela Martinez?"

"Who the heck is she?"

"My fifth grade teacher."

Thurston paused to sip his mojito. "Lurleen Hopkins, that's who."

"I wouldn't have guessed her," Lovey admitted.

"Never heard of her, did you?"

He shrugged no.

"Don't feel bad."

"Okay!"

"Because no one else ever heard of her either—before or since. You know why? Because she was a big dud, that's why. A total fizzle. Couldn't sell fire to Eskimos. Didn't even speak Spanish! But she sure as hell was *thin*. Had a face like a kangaroo and an ass like dental floss. Couldn't tell the difference between a vit and a min in broad day-light at six inches. *But she sure did look svelte at the annual convention!* Plus, guess what else?"

"Um, she was the chairman's cousin-in-law?"

The Venezuelan president stopped, stunned. "How did you know that?"

"Lucky guess."

"I was traumatized. But I learned something from my heartbreak, yes sirree. I'd never set myself up to be disillu-sioned again—*never*. I felt the sting of capitalist corruption first hand, let me tell you."

"Another story!"

"No, compadre. Same story. I just told it to you. They cheated me. They robbed me of my hopes and dreams. But I didn't let them beat me, no no. You can't keep a good man down. I succeeded in spite of them. Look at where I am today. I'm somebody. I thumb my nose at America. I insult their president. I rant and rave at the United Nations. People fear me. They think I have a screw loose, that I'm capable of anything, and maybe I am. I canceled the electoral process, I nullified the constitution, I na-tionalized businesses. I have oil money squirreled away in Switzerland. It's a great gig. But you know the irony of it all? I still haven't given up on my dream to be a Wow-tality distributor." He slapped his solar plexus. "The fire still burns. It's the one thing in life I still long to do. Unfinished business. No one likes being told he *can't*, you understand? It makes him want it all the more."

"I wanted to nuke the United States in 1962, and Khrushchev wouldn't let me. I'm still a little put out about it."

"Exactly. But now you're going to get the next best thing. A nuclear dirty bomb on Miami. You've waited all these years, but you're going to die fulfilled."

"To be honest, Dwayne, I would have liked to learn to play the drums. Maybe draw a little bit…not fine art or anything like that…more like cartoons. Of course, you know about that baseball thing. I'm too old for that now, but I don't see why I still couldn't draw."

"You've got to put it in perspective, dear friend. We're about to destroy Florida, so you can't have strong regrets about not *drawing*. But me, what does killing Jews and Miami Cubans do for me? Where do I come out? A few more pennies at the pump? Well and good. But to die knowing they wouldn't let me be a Wow–tality distributor…" He wiped a tear with the back of his wrist. He shielded his eyes from the glare and gazed at a stone jetty. "See that old fisherman standing there?"

Lovey followed his gaze. "No, but I see an old guy with a fishing pole."

"Tell me, do you think that poor slob is happy waking up before dawn, seven days a week, 365 days a year, and dying from overwork and poverty and poor nutrition?"

The Cuban president rubbed his chin. "Give me a minute."

"Wouldn't you think he'd rather sleep late and have a few discretionary pesos under his mattress, nice clothes, and be a respected member of society? Wouldn't he rather have strong, white teeth, glowing cheeks, and vibrant hair than that catastrophe he now calls personal grooming?"

Lovey squinted toward the pier. "You can see that far?"

"Wouldn't he like to feel energetic and young again and free of the aches and pains that come with age? Live his

life with dignity and pride? Be around to see his grandchildren grow up strong and healthy and have distributor-
ships of their own? Tell me something, my old and trusted
friend. What if—and at this point I'm only being hypo-
thetical—what if you yourself could get aboard the Wow-
tality train…say, as one of my subdistributors? I don't mean
just for yourself but on behalf of all Cuba? Think of the
multilevel potential, man. All of Havana and Santiago and
Piña del Rey. The prospects are staggering."

"*Mucho dinero*."

"Enough to wipe out your trade deficit three times
over. Enough to tell the IMF to go IMF itself. But the
money's the least of it. Think of the health benefits to your
people. No offense, but if any country needs mins and vits,
it's yours. Universal health care is all well and good, but
wouldn't it be great if folks felt so good they didn't *want* to
go to the free clinic? Think of all the unused needles you
could melt down to make antiaircraft guns."

"It would be a great legacy," Lovey agreed. "That and
destroying Miami Cubans."

"You bet it would. You're thinking exactly the right
way."

"And I'd have my very own money to spend?"

"You'll never have to ask your brother for a centavo
again."

"Sign me up!"

"I can't…not yet," Thurston said. "But I've got a plan,
amigo. A big plan." His eyes twinkled. "Yes sirree, when
I'm done with them, I'll have those bastards crawling back,
begging me to be their regional franchisee. And when I say
regional, I'm not just talking the northern coast or even
all of Venezuela. Maybe not even all of South and Central

America and the Caribbean. No, *hermano*. The price of poker has gone up…*way* up."

"Help!" the former Haiti commerce minister cried, waving his arms feebly at the hands waving back at him from the cruise ship's railings. "Help!"

The captain and first mate of the lapis-blue-hulled cruise ship *Sterling Star* had long ago spotted the troubled skiff and, as maritime and human ethics dictated, sailed full speed toward the floundering vessel. Many of the passengers, coalescing on deck, began taking photos and videos of the quaint boatman, and a few threw him coins.

"What's that on his head?" asked one man, the treasurer of the Midwest Pork Producers Association of America (MPPAA), a group holding its annual convention on the *Star's* weeklong cruise. He pointed his cigarette at the native's head. "Looks like damn underpants."

"It is underpants!" exclaimed his wife, snapping pictures.

"Don't look!" demanded the treasurer.

"It must be some kind of local custom. Throw him a nickel!"

Her husband covered the viewfinder. "It's disgusting."

"Must be some kind of whad'yacallit, Carnival or one of them black deals," suggested a colleague. "Some kind of parade float."

"Help me," squeaked Charbonnay, trying to stand, tottering.

"What?!" demanded the MPPAA treasurer.

Henri fell, then stood teetering once more. "Help me, please."

"Sorry, brother," the treasurer guffawed, glancing around for the approval of his fellow MPPAAs, "I gave at the office!"

There followed hearty backslapping and robust drink-spilling, and drunken laughter pealed into midday heat and burled into the Caribbean breeze.

"Help."

Two *Star* hands wedged their way to the railing and tossed life preservers overboard. "Paddle over!" one shouted. "Grab hold!"

The former commerce minister sat back down and paddled like hell.

"We're coming down to get you!"

"He's coming on board?" one of the MPPAA wives demanded to know. "How come? Doesn't he have to pay like everyone else?"

"Shut up, Mill. Can't you see it's the beginning of some sort of show?"

"Show?" piped a guy with drywall-colored thighs. "Entertainment show?"

"I heard about them," answered another MPPAA. "It's called *folk-lor-eeks*, or some shit like that."

"Does it cost extra? I didn't agree to pay extra. What is it, some kind of rip-off?"

"It's not extra, you jerk. Can't you see it's free?"

"It's included?"

"Can't you see with your own two eyes? Everything's included."

"Tell that to my loose change department, pal. You know what we already spent on drinks and tips?"

"You're not supposed to tip until the end. Didn't you read the card they slipped under your door?"

"I didn't see no card. Milly!"

Five decks below, a service hatch opened, and a deck hand, held by his pants by two others, leaned out and tried several times to grapple-hook *Fat Banana*'s prow before connecting. They tugged the skiff to the hatch, where they tried hauling up the delirious Haitian. Too weak, the poor soul could offer no help, so one of the crew jumped into the boat, steadied the man, and pushed him up while the other hands pulled.

On board, Charbonnay collapsed and passed out and awoke with cold water trickling down his gullet and cheeks. His retinas having been seared by tropical sunlight, and the service hatch having been secured, the room was dim and funereal. He could vaguely make out the silhouettes of mourners standing over him.

"Am I dead?" he asked.

"You alive," came an Asian voice. "Not going die."

"Food," he whimpered.

"You get plenty food now, mister. Plenty, plenty."

"You sit up?" asked a different Asian.

They helped him sit. Someone stood behind him, propping him up. Henri's vision was starting to adjust; faces were emerging out of the darkness—almond-eyed angel faces.

"More water."

A uniformed officer, a white man, knelt beside him and held a bottle to his lips. Henri tried to grab it and guzzle, but the officer yanked it away. "Better go easy, there, old boy. Too much of a good thing and all."

Exhausted from the small struggle, Henri took the trickle and lay back, gasping.

"Dr. Cummings here," said the British officer. "We'll need to get you to the infirmary. Can you tell me your name?"

"Char…bon…"

"You think you can make it on your own, Mr. Bon, or would you prefer a lift?"

"Where am I?"

"I shouldn't think that would matter much, but if you insist, I'd say today's your lucky day, old bean."

The Asians laughed. "Nice ship. Bingo night. Health crub."

The doctor motioned for help getting the Haitian to his feet. "Take your time. No rush."

But Henri wobbled, and his legs gave way. With a whirl of his finger, the doctor called for a wheelchair, and one of the Asians scurried away.

"Food," Henri whimpered. The room was chilly and filled with strange, loud sounds. A crate scraped across the floor, and he jumped.

"Easy, man," said the doctor, calming him with a touch. Cummings cupped his palm, and a crew member gave him a chunk of meat. He tore off a morsel. "Any problem with pork?"

Henri shook his head and opened his mouth, tearing its corners.

"One never knows whom you might offend these days," the doctor said, plopping a sliver of meat onto Henri's tongue. "Then it's your lucky day indeed. Seems we're hosting the right convention this trip"—he glanced at the laughing Asians—"a whole boatload of prime pig parts."

A wheelchair rolled up, and they hauled Henri, shivering, into it. Cummings slipped off his smock and covered his patient. He told one of the hands to ask the captain to meet them in the infirmary.

Before they got there, Henri clutched his gut, let out a blood-curdling shriek, fell out of the wheelchair, wailed piteously, curled into himself, and, horror-eyed, died.

On a swampy spit of land on the west end of South Florida's Big Pine Key, sat a listing, unpainted clapboard shack, speckled with mold, mushy with rotted and worm-eaten siding, its tar-paper roof sagging and peeling, the corner of a filthy pillowcase curtain occasionally flapping out of a shattered window. Water-stained corrugated cardboard covered the insides of its other windows, dead houseflies sandwiched between the cardboard and glass. A sign hammered crookedly next to the mud driveway said KEEP OUT OR ELSE!!!, the sign bearing a hand-painted, fang-bearing snake.

Inside, a tall, broad-shouldered man with shoulder-length, gray-streaked hair and a long, angry, Seminole face sat on a rickety kitchen chair at an even more rickety, pink-and-black kitchen table, circa 1950s, on which he was browsing the Internet on his laptop. On one side of the computer, an ashtray overflowed with cigarette butts. On the other side, a gooseneck lamp, whose fiberglass shade was burned brown and brittle, provided the only usable light, despite the fact that outside the sun beat down on the mosquito-infested lowland. Under the lamp a half-eaten Hostess Twinkie oozed filling onto the Formica. On the floor around and under his chair, a dozen Twinkie wrappers lay strewn, waiting to stick to the bottom of the Skipper's bare feet.

He was bored and claustrophobic in this shithole, would much rather have been living aboard *Key Stroke*—just him, his laptop, Jack Daniels, and Marlboros—even if it meant kissing the asses of dilettante mainlanders jaunting to Key West for a day-outing of snorkeling or scuba diving. At least if he got antsy then—which he did often when in the migraine-inducing presence of those giggling, SPF-smeared, Coors-sucking dinks—he could head out to sea for some fresh air, away from the stink of customers and civilization. But now, even though his mini-trawler was a few dozen yards away—through a chink in the window cardboard he could barely make out her glorious mast, her pilothouse roof rack with glinting stainless ladder, her sweetly curved antenna, her navy blue Bimini top—he was stuck in this rotting cesspool of a cabin waiting for further instructions.

Said hiding out under thick, cypress-tree cover soon to be remedied, if only fucking Thurston would fucking show up with fucking instructions. *Where the fuck is that Venezuelan motherfucker?*

The Skipper navigated to Facebook, clicked on his homepage—this one registered under "John Gacy" (wanting to prove how desperately lonely and stupid Facebook users are, he also had "Jeff Dahmer," "Dick Speck," "Chuck Manson," and "Teddy Bundy" pages)—and checked his wall. He had set up this page only a week ago and already had 426 "friends." He scrolled down among them and, on a whim, clicked on a young black woman's avatar. Up popped Sondra Alexander's wall, which delighted the Skipper with its ignorant ramblings.

Sondra:

> I remember when I was in kindergarden and wanting so much to be white, I thought if I ate enough white crayolas this would happen and I remember seeing another dark skinned girl and thought she looked dirty. These issues need to be addressed in a serious way unlike a news broadcast with sound bites disguised as addressing the issue head on.

Sondra's friend:

> Yes, Sondra. I feel this is a topic for raising the awareness of the issue. However, this is only a symptom of a deeper social problem, if we are ever to overcome these circumstances, an in depth analysis must take place.

Another friend:

> I am a black man. In high school I liked this beautiful cheerleader. When I pointed her out to my (black) male peers and declared how attractive she was, one of them said, with a most disgusting look on his face, "that black ugly thing?!?" I promptly disagreed with his assessment, at which point the dude threatened me because he didn't

like my tone. Maybe what he really took issue
with was that I was upsetting his sorely limited
world view with my expression of interest in a
girl who fell outside the twisted parameters of
his European-inspired ideal of beauty. This light
skin preference in the black community is a skin
cancer that needs to be excised once and for all.

Another:

Whoah, brothers and sisters, I think black in
bautiful and in this countrie you do not even no
about skin shade until you meet a white person
and then they make you feel like you are like a
monkey or smothing. Be proud of your own race
we are the world.

Everyone's a fucking writer, thought the Skipper. He
took a long, thoughtful drag of Marlboro, blew a smoke ball
at the desk lamp, took another bite of Twinkie, squeegeed
some cream filling off the table with his finger and sucked
it clean. He wiped his hand on his T-shirt and typed:

Sondra: I can tell you are a bitter black woman,
or as you like to call yourselves these days,
"African-American," a term misappropriated
(look it up; I can't do everything for your lazy
ass) from the pre-European, aboriginal (look that
up, too, if you're not worn out already) American
inhabitants, who lived in harmony with the
land and who didn't bitch and moan about not
receiving enough welfare—if you get my drift.

Yours for online enlightenment,
John Wayne Gacy

P.S. Go ahead and sue me for racism. That's what
you're thinking right now, isn't it? You don't know
what racism is, baby. Try being a *Native* American.
Regards to Cornel West.

He finished his Twinkie, put out and lit another cigarette, crumpled the empty pack, tossed it into the corner
with a covey of other crumpled packs, and again wiped
his hands on his shirt. He mouse-clicked to another of his
"friends," Frank Worth of Anaconda, Montana.

Frank commenting:

I know that the goverment puts spy cameras inot
the eyes of wild birds in order to spy on remote
outposts, it sounds incredible but its a fact. The
technology comes from Area 51, a highly secret
operation.

Frank's friend adding:

Your right, Frank. People laugh at this like it's
some kind of 007 shitbut it's real. You can berry
your head in the sand, freinds or wake up and
realize that the govenment is not your freind.

Frank elaborating:

Where I live there is a buzzard that lives around
here with one wierd eye and I always thought

that something wasn't right about the whole thing because nobody ever saw this bird before and all of a sudden its here with this strange eye and I will be out cutting wood or soemthing and all of a sudden I'll get this creeped out feeling and look up and there it is, staring at me. So you tell me.

To which the Skipper wrote on Frank's wall:

Frankie: After careful consideration I herein declare you the dumbest shitkicker I've ever had the misfortune to forbear. And, no, *forbear* does not mean more than three bears, you dumb dick-sucker.

My guess is, you raise pit bulls and have sex with your sister, and your children resemble possums.

Good luck, jackoff.
John

He clicked the send button and sighed with airy satisfaction. Feeling better—despite his still-sore knee—he stood up and stretched, his large fists nearly reaching the sagging ceiling. He gazed around the room, whose dimness he had gotten used to, having hardly stepped outside since returning from that nasty gig off the Malecón. On a wood plank suspended between stacks of cinder blocks, sat the transmitter he had used to blow up the Iranian president's translator, along with a jumble of wires, batteries, two volt-ohm meters, printed circuit boards, miscellaneous loose electronics—capacitors, transistors, resistors—and hand tools: two pair of jeweler's pliers, soldering gun, magnifying glass, roll of solder, jar of flux, various-size screwdrivers, clamps, and a Windex bottle now filled with cloudy water. And, at the foot of a cinder block, half a dozen orange-colored bricks of Semtex plastic explosive.

He blew Marlboro smoke from his nostrils, coughed, and reached under his bare, filthy mattress. From a dilapidated manila envelope, whose clasp had long ago broken off, he emptied out his entire remaining bankroll—fifty-five dollars and eleven cents.

He limped to the broken window, bent down, brushed the pillowcase aside, and, squinting, peered out. He checked the time on his computer. His guest was late. He was worried. What if (through no fault of his, of course) the plan fell apart? Shit. His heart raced. He counted his money again, but it hadn't reproduced itself over the last two minutes. Still fifty-five and eleven. Shit shit. How the fuck was he supposed to live without money or any way of making it?

Where the fuck is Thurston?

He tried to calm down. He wondered if he could still make a living from his boat, maybe still offering dive or fishing trips. Well, not in Florida, certainly—not after the little "misunderstanding" with that bitch last year in Key West that had gotten him busted and thanks to which he had become a bail-skipping fugitive and much looked for on open water.

He'd have to create a whole new identity for himself and *Key Stroke*—and even that might not be enough, not after having choked the court-appointed shrink and jumping bond. Now, if he so much as got boarded for a fucking fishing-license check, he'd never again see the light of day. He couldn't survive being locked-up. Indians were made for open air, not suffocating prison cells.

So Florida was definitely a no-go, and in this Internet age, the whole U.S. of A. was probably the same story. Maine, California, Hawaii—arrest-warrant information was only a click away. That left trying to set up shop off-shore—some quiet tourist island whose jerkwater police wouldn't ask too many questions (as long as the kickbacks were adequate). Easier said than done, though. All he'd have to do is hand his passport to one wrong official, and that would be that. For the rest of his life he'd be looking over his shoulder—another kind of prison cell.

Defecting to Cuba was an option, then, even if Castaways' Revenge failed. Obviously, he knew important people there now. But the truth was, the post-mission plan notwithstanding, he didn't want to live in fucking Cuba. In Cuba you had to stand in line for a scrawny drumstick or a rancid pat of butter, no matter who the fuck you were. He hated standing in line. He recognized his limitations. Even before that wicked fall on *Key Stroke*, his knees weren't that great. Tall guys had bad knees. Seminole Indians had genetically bad knees—probably from that motherfucker Andrew Jackson making them walk to fucking Oklahoma. Cubans were short; they could stand in line. He couldn't, period.

Anyhow, he needed his Twinkies. Marlboros, okay, he could always substitute a European brand, although they were shit. Even Cuban tobacco was shit these days, since, after the Russians quit subsidizing them in '89, they had to plant it in substandard soil and rush it to market. But what are you supposed to substitute for Twinkies?

Where the fuck is Thurston?!

Finally, finally, tires crackled on gravel. He peeked out the broken window again. A rusted pickup truck with a cracked windshield and gimpy front spring squeaked up the drive. "What fresh hell is this?" the Skipper grumbled, thinking this must be someone lost or some redneck coming to ask for a church donation. He had to quickly decide whether or not to open the door, and figured since there wasn't a lock on it anyhow and these snake-kissers didn't respect private property, there would be no point pretending he wasn't home.

So when the knock came, he answered.

A hefty, tanned hick in bib overalls, construction boots, and plaid flannel shirt with cutoff sleeves stood holding a rolled-up catalog. He wore a Florida Marlins baseball cap and sported a full, gray, ZZ Top beard.

"What's up, bub?" asked the Skipper.

"Would you be interested in some excellent nutritional supplements, mister?"

Pause.

The visitor unrolled a Wow-tality Nutritional Supplements catalog. "Right here you will find every vitamin and mineral to ensure your ongoing good health and vibrant energy." He ran his eyes over his prospect. "And, frankly, from the looks of it, you could use some of both."

"Go away, or I'll kick your ass," the Skipper snarled.

"I can see you're a little on edge, neighbor. A nice supply of herbal tea would be just the thing to calm your disposition. Very reasonably priced." He flipped a business card from his bib pocket and handed it over. "If you're not interested now, you can always call me later, when you're really, *really* broke."

Huh? The Skipper angled the card to the light. It read,

PRESIDENT FOR LIFE, VENEZUELA

ADVISORY BOARD, NITCO OIL

BOARD OF DIRECTORS, NATIONAL TELEVISION
(OVER)

He flipped the card over.

(FROM OTHER SIDE)
HEAD HONCHO, EVERYTHING ELSE
FUTURE TOP-PRODUCING DISTRIBUTOR,
WOW-TALITY MINS AND VITS

"*Thurston?*"

The salesman handed him the catalog. "At your service. Always just a phone call away."

"Jesus H. Christ."

"I assure you, had the Wow-tality company existed in *those* days, the fellow would have gone door to door dispensing mins and vits, not that turn-the-other-cheek horseshit."

The Skipper yanked him inside.

"You like my disguise?" the Venezuelan president laughed, tugging his whiskers.

"Amazing. I'm not easy to fool."

"You were my big test."

"You got the accent down. The beard's perfect."

"Glued on. Not some cheap hook-on job from China."

"I was beginning to worry you got sidetracked."

Thurston looked around the dim room and grimaced. "Everything is still a go. We only have to hope the weak links in the operation don't drag us down."

"You want something to eat? How about a Twinkie?"

The visitor sniffed the air. His nostrils caved in. "No thanks. I've got a cooler in the truck. Had a little something on the way over."

"Sit, sit," the Skipper insisted, brushing off his chair.

Instead Thurston shuffled to his host's makeshift work-bench, almost kicking the plastic explosives.

"Watch it!" the Skipper exclaimed, yanking him back. "You want to blow us to hell?"

The Venezuelan president stepped back in horror. "You're kidding?"

"Not kidding."

"You leave this stuff lying around? Are you crazy, man?"

"It's the only patch of sunlight in this hellhole. I'm trying to bleach out the ethylene glycol."

"The what?"

"A chemical that customs dogs and electronic apparatus can detect."

The Venezuelan sat.

The Skipper sat on the edge of his mattress, facing his guest. "What weak links?"

"Pretty much everyone except you and me. Lovey is beyond demented, Little Buddy is crazy as a chicken, and that bootlicking Professor gets so much on everyone's nerves, we're trying to figure out some way to kill him when this is over. I hope you don't mind."

"He's no friend of mine," the Skipper assured him. "I met him at a Native American Reparations conference. He was hanging around like a wad of snot—inviting himself to parties, getting drinks for people, running out for pizza. Talk about collective fucking guilt. Everyone thought he was a supercilious baboon. He kept griping about getting overlooked for a promotion, how his bosses don't appreciate him. Blaming 'American anti-meritocracy bureaucratic imperialism' or some shit. We couldn't fucking stand his whining. But the guy does know Miami. And his politics are right up your alley. The prick is dying for a monument to himself."

"To give the devil his due, he did come up with the matzo-ball delivery idea. Ideology aside, though, I'd still like to kill him."

"Do what the fuck you want with him, man, just get me the fuck out of here already. Dry land is making me wacky. He's up in Chicago bitching and moaning, collecting his tenured salary, while I'm stuck in this shithole, stone broke."

The president of Venezuela slipped out a notepad and pen from his back pocket and flipped it open. "The Professor is *dying* for a monument," he repeated, smiling. *Dying for monument*, he scribbled. He closed the pad. "Duly noted."

Fat Banana's floundering Mr. Bon lay dead on the floor of the cruise ship *Sterling Star*, his eyes wide, his mouth stretched, his corpse twisted in final agony. The captain was promptly notified, and arrangements were made for a private funeral, in which, because the skiff was of Haitian registry and its occupant had a Haitian accent, the captain, not himself a Catholic, nevertheless read a few words from the appropriate section of his ministerial manual. They then snuggly wrapped Mr. Bon in a pastel-green sheet and stored him in a lower hold, where he would bother no one until they reached the next port, Nassau, where they would unload him on the Bahamians, who, based on the captain's long experience, enjoyed filling out forms anyhow.

Equilibrium seemed restored, although the members of the Midwest Pork Producers Association of America still were not convinced that the appearance of the bedraggled boatman wasn't part of a folklorique. Many of them had remained at the railing for over an hour, spitting cherry stems overboard and gazing around for more of the show. At happy hour they gathered in the aft-deck lounge, where they feasted on pigs-in-blankets and barbecue pork fritters and played bingo (Porky Pig appearing on the center spaces of the cards). On a side table, the ship offered for sale porcine-themed jewelry and sundry souvenirs: pig-earred baseball caps, pink T-shirts, Miss Piggy-headed house slippers, elastic-banded party snouts. Later, at dinner, as they had for the last four nights, they would rip into all kinds of ham-based cuisine—ham being, after all, their bread and butter—and then retire to the casino, temporarily named "The Pig Sty," where drink waitresses would don piggy ears and corkscrew tails and oink when taking orders. On *Sterling Star*, the passenger was king—or, in this case, swine.

By the time the first "eee-eee-eee-oleven" was called out, the MPPAAs had pretty much all forgotten about the floundering Haitian. Someone had heard that the poor guy croaked—he was a Frog, after all!—and a couple of them raised their drinks and shouted, "Restez in peace!" and went back to counting their chips.

Unfortunately, six decks below, in a cool, dark storage hold, the Haitian boatman was not exactly restezing in peace. As the deck hands had carried his corpse through the cargo space, a fresh, even more maniacally mutated brood of recently larvaed, now transmutated, mandibled masticators, bubbling merrily in the (now certainly for-mer-) commerce minister's belly, got a good whiff of what awaited them on the other side of their host's flesh. Not just pork, but pork-imbued human MPPAA sinew—hock and rind, knuckle and snout.

Near the bottom of Charbonnay's ribcage, his shroud began to undulate, something subcutaneous and sinister searching for a way out.

In the quiet darkness of the cargo hold, the tiny ma-rauders, having gotten a taste of the pork slice that Dr. Cummings had dropped into Henri's gullet, and even more blood-thirsty than their preceding generation, goose-stepped out of the former commerce minister's nostrils. Their scouts stood atop the sheet, where, their antennae humming, they GPSed the captivating pork-human-flesh electro-chemical signal six decks above, and, in their murderous-termite language, relayed those coor-dinates to their ravenous brethren, still filing out from the Haitian's sun-blistered nose.

From the back of the pickup truck, the Venezuelan presi-dent fetched Fenwich's ratty canvas knapsack—the one he had lied to Diane about giving to the blind—and brought it into the Skipper's cabin, being careful not to step on the Semtex.

"The Professor's mark thinks there's only one of these," he explained, laying the sack at the Skipper's feet. "It's an old trick, brilliantly simple," he told his cohort. "You'll place one next to the other—when and where to be determined—grab the harmless one, and scram the hell out of there. When you're safely away, do your thing. That's it. Nothing more complicated than the Malecón operation."

"Nothing more complicated! Man!" The Skipper limped to his workbench, grabbed a Semtex brick and held it in front of Thurston's nose. "You want to try working with this shit all fucking day?! How about in a Force-9 gale! Fifteen-foot waves! How about when you're about to smash into fucking boulders! You think it's so 'simple,' you fucking do it!"

Frightened, the Venezuelan president held up his hands and backed into a corner. Clearly, the Skipper was a madman. "Relax, relax, *muchacho*. I was only making the point that next time you won't have killer surf to contend with, that's all."

"That's all you meant?"

"I swear."

"You're not implying that I'm fulfilling only a minor role?"

"Certainly not."

"Or that my work is easy? That I'm expendable."

"Get serious, man. Put that down, will you please?"

The Skipper, snapping out of his rage, realizing he was squeezing enough explosives to kill them and a dozen alligators, gently placed the Semtex on the floor. "Hey, sorry, dude. You sort of hurt my feelings."

"I won't do it again."

The Skipper hefted the knapsack. "What about the 'deli'?"

"Little Buddy is delivering those himself. Says he doesn't trust anyone else. Anyhow, he says it's his nuclear program, so he's entitled to be the one to bring them. I thought the pipsqueak was going to hold his breath and turn purple."

"Where will you be?"

"Combining business with pleasure. Once the chaos starts, no one at Wow-tality International will be in any mood to award distribution franchises. I have to get my contract beforehand. Anyhow, while I'm there, I may as well look in on a few gas stations."

"You're not serious about these mins and vits."

The Venezuelan drilled him a stare. "You have a problem with that?"

"No problem."

The future Wow-tality king ran his eyes over his host. "Like I said, you yourself could benefit from supplements. You look like you were exhumed. You been getting enough sunshine and exercise?" Referring to the Skipper's limp, he asked, "What's wrong with your leg?"

"I wounded my knee on the fucking job. Except I don't get fucking workers' compensation."

"You been eating right?"

The Skipper held up a Twinkies wrapper.

Thurston winced.

"What do you expect? I've got no fucking money. I've been stuck here waiting for instructions. Did you bring money?"

Thurston plucked out a wad of cash from his overalls and, as his host's eyes watered, peeled off twenty one-hundred-dollar bills. "I can't force you, of course, but in my opinion you'd do well to spend some of this on fiber powder. I'll bet your bowels are a train wreck. As long as the catalog is here anyhow, why not take a peek?"

The Skipper stuffed the bills into his waistband. "You

know what I really need, '*muchacho*'? McRibs, fries, and a chocolate shake. There's your fucking mins and vits. I have an idea. Why not drive that rust bucket of yours to Mickey D's? It's just north on U.S. 1. I can browse your catalog on the way. It's only a few miles. What do you say?"

"What time you got?"

"Five-fifteen."

"I suppose I can spare an hour or so, if you're not jerking me around about the catalog. I need to get to the mainland before dark. My night vision isn't what it used to be. Driving that damn bus ruined me."

The Skipper shut down his computer. "Let's roll."

"Say, have you ever considered being a distributor yourself? I'll show you the chart over dinner. It's a very rewarding career, financially and emotionally. Seems to me like you're ready for a little of both."

"Who am I suppose to sell supplements to—pelicans?"

"That's the point. It'll force you to get out more, socialize, meet new people, make new friends. If you don't mind my saying so"—he cast a glance at the Semtex—"this holing-up business isn't doing your spirits much good. Okay, you're not the sociable type, fine. You're tech savvy—so create your own Web presence. You'd be your own boss. No office hours, no jerk-off telling you he doesn't like the length of your hair—which could use a trimming, by the way. No getting fired for no reason. No more burning down the judge's house to teach him a lesson. Plus, I'm telling you"—he winked—"it's a great way to meet the ladies."

"We'll talk on the way."

"Your inventory requirements would be quite minimal, very affordable, especially with the money you're going to make on this operation."

They climbed into the pickup. While he barked directions, the Skipper leafed through the Wow-tality catalog, pretending to be interested. But the truth was, he couldn't stop thinking about those McRibs, fries, and shake. And maybe afterward he could talk Thurston into stopping at Dunkin' Donuts for some holes.

As the Skipper licked his lips thinking about that heavenly powdered sugar, Thurston, glancing at his co-conspirator's lap, where his Wow-tality catalog touted the nutritional and spiritual benefits of carrot powder and beet capsules, mistook his associate's lip-smacks for nutritional-supplemental craving. The Venezuelan president grinned, convinced that carotene and calcium would soon be bringing more revenue to his national and private coffers than crude. Some day oil reserves would be depleted. But vits and mins are forever.

Eleven

MATZO BALL SOUP

Chicken-soup dumplings are made with the finely crushed crumbs of unleavened kosher-for-Passover crackers. They have a light, succulent, soft texture and are considered Jewish "comfort food."

Beat until thick and well blended:
    2 egg yolks
    3 tbsp soft chicken fat

Pour into mixture and beat well:
    ½ cup hot chicken stock

Stir in gently a mixture of:
    ¾ cup matzo meal or cracker meal
      (Manischewitz)
    ½ tsp salt
    ¼ tsp ginger
    ¼ tsp nutmeg

1 tbsp finely chopped parsley
1 tbsp finely grated onion

Beat until stiff:
2 egg whites

Fold the egg whites into the cracker mixture and chill, covered, for ½ to one hour, then form this dough lightly into small balls★. If you wet your hands with cold water, the job will be easier. Drop them into:
6 cups boiling chicken stock

Reduce heat at once to a simmer and cook, covered, for about 15 minutes.

You may refrigerate or freeze finished balls and soup.

★ Balls may range in size from (in diameter) ½ inch (minis) to two inches (standard) to three inches (jumbo). The bigger the ball, the denser and chewier the center. Standard size is recommended.

With a pot of chicken stock steaming on the stove, her shoulders dipping and swaying, Diane softly sang "deedle deedle bubba bubba deedle deedle dum," as, with wet hands, she first molded, then rolled the matzo dough into two-inch balls, the slightly-chewy size Karma preferred, pressing her thumb to render them a tad off-round.

For some reason Karma had an aversion to them spinning freely in her soup—as a youngster she would flail ferociously at the sight of it—so her mother had more or less solved the problem by making them a bit oblong with slight indentations. It wasn't a perfect fix, but, after some discussion with her daughter, apparently good enough, provided mother understood that she had essentially failed.

"Deedle deedle deedle."

This was Diane's second batch, the first already in the freezer. These six balls she now plunked into the near-boiling soup (she ignored the recipe's "boiling" directive, believing that boiling the stock depleted it of vitamins and risking the negligible chance that under-heating would pose a bacteria risk), covered the pot, and, tugging her double chin, continued to sing.

"Oy, what a goofy mood I'm in!"

A rhombus of dusty sunlight stretched across the counter-top. On the porch railing five fledgling barn swallows—Eenie, Meenie, Miney, Mo, and No Mo'—lined up waiting for their parents to return with bugs. Diane washed and wiped her hands, went to the refrigerator for the third batch of dough, retrieved a bottle of V8 for herself, poured a glass, drank it all in one toss-back, licked her lips, and got a terrific idea.

"Didle doodle doodle didle duuum."

She hip-swayed down the hall, deedle-deedling. She came to the master bedroom door and knocked tentatively.

No answer. But she thought she heard something. She pressed her ear to the wood and listened. There it was again—an airy whistle. Then she smelled it...or thought she did. She looked down at the crack under the door, took two short whiffs, looked back up, thoroughly con-fused. "Les?" she whispered. "Are you awake?"

He called back, "Awake and happy as a happy clam—pardon the tautology."

She smiled and opened the door. "Honey, I have this great idea. I thought maybe *you* could roll one batch of…" She stopped.

Professor Fenwich lay naked on the bed, sitting up against the headboard, his legs outspread, blowing giddy-smoke rings at his feet, trying to snatch them with his big toes.

It took her a moment to figure it out. "What the heck is this?" she asked, sniffing harder.

"What?"

She nodded at the smoky air. "*This?*"

"What?"

She went to the side of the bed and saw that he had taken her night-school diploma off the wall and put it on his crotch to use as an ashtray. She gazed at it in disbelief.

"What?" he asked again.

"Les?"

He reached over, grabbed a zip-lock baggie from the nightstand and offered it to her. "Here, baby, treat yourself. Pure Venezuela—the *best*, most *far out* goddamn weed you'll ever suck, bar none." He jiggled the baggie. "Don't ask me where I got it, that's all. Ask no questions, I tell no lies. Don't ask, don't tell. Come on, baby. You've been working hard doing, you know, whatever it is you do. Indulge."

She stared at her diploma, the glass smudged with ash, the oak frame burned. She stared at him grinning at her. She stared at the dangling baggie. Her carotid artery throbbed. Her ankles pulsed.

"You wouldn't think in a million years they grow this kind of shit in *Venezuela*, of all places. Ha! Learn something every day. Colombia, for sure. Mexico, why not? Honduras, Nicaragua, Belize, Chile, Peru—"

She ripped her diploma off his lap, under which his penis gazed up at her, grublike.

"Hey, what's up, doll baby?"

"How could you?!"

"I didn't want to mess up the bed. Hey, you're not freaking on me, are you?"

"I worked hard for this. Seven years part-time!"

"You're kidding, right? You're really bent out of shape?"

She shook the ashes off the glass, clutched the frame to her chest, and choked back a sob.

"Chill out. It's only a symbol. It's not the *thing*. Haven't you ever read Claude Lévi-Strauss—the post-structural theorist, not the guy who invented jeans. Derrida? Bakhtin? Walter Benjamin? Frederic Jameson? What *did* you read in night school?"

"I don't care about *theory*. This isn't theory. This is *real*, and it's *mine*."

"Maybe if you had gone to regular college, instead of loser school, you'd have read them"—he screwed his eyes toward the diploma—"and that would actually be worth something."

"*Actually?*"

"Lighten up, babycakes. You're blowing my mind."

She snatched the baggie out of his grip.

"Hey!"

She strode to the door and, voice cracking, called over her shoulder, "Maybe if you hadn't been a cheapskate, you wouldn't have used a defective condom, and I wouldn't have *had* to go to night school!" She slammed the door behind her, staggered, wobble-kneed, toward the kitchen, stopped, retraced her steps to the bedroom door, and shouted, "This is a no-smoking household, Les. No shirt, no shoes, no service. Leave!"

"It's *Doctor* Les to you, you…dropout!"

"Leave. Now!"

"I'm going! Give me back my grass!"

She sat hunched at her kitchen table, face in hands, chicken soup boiling over onto the burner with hisses that drowned out her sobs, her diploma lying between her elbows, Les's baggie tucked between the salt and pepper shakers. She heard him hurling things around the bedroom—shoes thudding against walls, bed frame banging against floor, dresser doors slamming, more shoe thudding, more bed banging, lots of swearing, screams of "I'm not a cheapskate!" and "I want my weed back! Venezuelan pot!" and "You should've taken birth control pills!" and "Whore!" and "Give me back my grass!" and "It wasn't my fault!" and "You have no right to take away my treat!" and "Cunt! Whory cunt! Cunty whore! Bitch! Bitchy cunty whore!"

She lifted her face from her hands. She tilted her head at his ranting. Something occurred to her—something extraordinary.

After delivering a fiery speech to the United Nations General Assembly, during which the ambassadors of the U.S., Great Britain, Israel, Germany, France (Sarkozy was president), Japan, and three other sensible nations had stormed out in protest, the president of Iran, Akhmed, returned exhausted to his Manhattan on Green hotel room and collapsed, cruciformed, onto his bed. He tried taking a little late-morning nap, in vain. Thoughts crisscrossed his mind like Jet Skis. He got up and checked his minicooler of nuclear matzo balls in the bar fridge. Satisfied they had been undisturbed, he returned them to the fridge and shuffled to the window, where, arms akimbo, he gazed down at Central Park and the streets on either side. He tried to imagine how exciting it was down there, but he couldn't seem to get his blood going. Perhaps it was just post-speech letdown, but maybe it was something more profound. He gazed around the room, detesting the color scheme. Was that the problem? Palette dissonance?

No, it went even deeper. The truth was, he missed Hazeem. Having had him blown to smithereens certainly seemed like a good idea at the time, but now he wondered. Sometimes he would find himself reaching for the phone to call him, only to remind himself that the man wasn't going to answer—ever. Other times he would be in his room watching videos and thinking to invite Hazeem over, only to stop midthought. Without question, he felt his absence. Hazeem was a good man to bully. He was a great sounding board to rant against the Zionists and sundry other enemies of the true faith. He was usually willing to get schlepped around to different nightclubs. Whom did the president have now? No one, that's who. And for this unfortunate turn of events, he blamed Hazeem, the ungrateful dog.

"I don't need you to be happy," Akhmed declared to his murdered friend, shaking his fist. He decided to slap himself out of his malaise by diving into the profligate life of this decadent city. There it was, spread beneath him, smorgasbord-like, waiting to be grazed, sampled, gourmandised, digested, pooped. He clapped and rubbed his hands. That was it, all right. He was going to do the town! Who needed Hazeem!

He undressed, took a hot shower, wiped the steam off his bathroom mirror, inspected from all angles his bristly mug, and made another exciting decision. He would shave! Shave his stubble! These wimpy American men didn't know a manly look, for sure, but why should that prevent him from maximizing his enjoyment while tripping the light fantastic? When in Rome, baby! If these evil, carnal, venal, libertine American women dug smooth-cheeked males—*yuck!*—so be it. He could grow it back in a couple of…well, never mind. Besides, after having made his incendiary speech—which would surely be broadcast worldwide—being recognized on the street would only cramp his style. And if it was one thing Akhmed had, baby, it was *style*.

He unwrapped the hotel disposable razor, inspected it, tried to figure out how to use it, thought he could muddle through, and wound up slicing his face to shreds. After the bleeding more or less stopped, he gazed into the mirror blissfully. He hadn't seen his actual face for many years, and, in truth, the lacerations notwithstanding, he had forgotten what a handsome fellow he was. He looked positively half his age! If he died today—*ptuh! ptuh!*—those seventy-two virgins would wet their panties.

He ran the bottle of hotel aftershave under his nose, whiffed rapturously, and splashed the entire bottle over his cheeks—*ouch!*—behind and into his ears, under his arms, around his crotch, between his toes. He got dressed—true, he had only brought three of the exact same charcoal-gray suits, but who said he couldn't do a little shopping on such a glorious day?—combed his hair, primped his collar, gave his face one last wound-dabbing, cast a perfunctory glance at the bar fridge, and headed out, hanging the DO NOT DISTURB sign on his doorknob, in case the maid was effronterous enough to want his autograph.

As he began his exciting day plying the avenues, he was a little disappointed that no one seemed to recognize him, before convincing himself that New Yorkers, by nature polite, knew who he was but were too shy to ask to have their pictures taken with him. He walked without a firm route but with a vague idea of a sightseeing itinerary: Central Park Zoo; Hello Deli; Carnegie Hall; Macy's; Broadway; Trump Tower; Michael's Pub (maybe that Zionist dog Woody would be playing!); Chinatown; Washington Square; Little Italy; and, naturally, the pièce de résistance—he wouldn't have time to see it and the Statue of Liberty, too—the gaping World Trade Center Ground Zero site. Glorious!

First things first. His stomach was growling, and he had learned to ignore its low protestations at high peril. He had always wanted to try one of those Nathan's Famous Frankfurters, and now that, clean-shaven—again, notwithstanding the wounds—he resembled every other garden-variety New Yorker, he with confidence lolled up near a vendor, listened as several native-seeming pedestrians placed their orders, then watched with fascination as they unwrapped their treats and nibbled, chomped, gobbled, gnawed. What a strange people were Americans! Walking and eating at the same time! Finally, when his stomach could bear it no longer, he approached the cart, pretended to be as self-assured as any lifelong resident, cleared his throat, and asked if these franks were all beef, no pork.

The vendor, a middle-aged immigrant Greek, detonated. "You think I could make living in this fucking city if franks got fucking pig inside, you motherfucking sonbitch! Who you think you are, insulting Gus with bullshit, eh?! Get the fuck out of my sight, you sonbitch motherfucking sonbitch Arab diaper-head motherfuck sonbitch!" He hurled a tub of sweet relish at Akhmed's head, knocking him to the sidewalk. The vendor strode around to the front of the cart with a hotdog, stood over his customer, pitched that, too, at his face, dug out his tub of mustard, turned it upside down and emptied it onto his client while screaming, "On the house, you cocksucking sonbitch! Pork my Greek ass! Fuck you! Welcome to New York!" He turned scarlet-faced to three people waiting in line. "Next!"

"Let me have two with the works," said a young businesswoman, as she stepped over her supine predecessor. "And a cream soda."

"Here you go, lady. Have nice day."

"You too." She glanced down at Akhmed and smiled. "You too, Arab motherfucker."

She recognizes me, the president thought—not unhappily. He hauled himself to his feet, cleaned ants off his hotdog, scraped the condiments off his clothes, hair, and skin, and, like other New Yorkers, tried to eat and walk at the same time. It was not as easy as it looked, and, concentrating on the lunch, he smashed into a light pole, which, like the vendor, knocked him to the sidewalk. This time, though, a friendly hand reached down to help him up. A brown hand.

"Hey, my foreign brother, you seem to be a stranger to our fair city. I can see you need a little cheering up, dude, am I right on?"

"Maybe a little," Akhmed, getting to his feet, agreed. "I do feel better now that I ate, though. This Nathan fellow, he is a Zionist, you think?"

His rescuer glanced around furtively. "You got to be cool, brother, cool. Come on over here, I want to do you a big favor."

A big favor, huh. Well, well, that could only mean that this Negro chap—who, considering he referred to Akhmed as "brother," must be a fellow Muslim—recognized the Iranian president, too. He followed the man around the corner to a small table, behind which another young black man sat doing a trick with cards. Things were looking up, all right. Street entertainment, just as he had heard about!

"You want to have some fun?" asked his new friend.

"Indeed I do, yes, yes. When in Rome, dude man!"

"Yeah, well, I think you made the wrong turn back at Genoa, brother, but never mind. You got ten bucks?"

When Akhmed hesitated, the man said, "Dollars, man. Moola, smackers, gelt."

"Oh, moola!"

"Come on, fork over a sawsky. I'm going to do you something nice. You will thank me."

The president fished his change purse from his inner jacket pocket, peered inside, and frowned. "Oh, I am so sorry, fellow brother. All I have are one-hundred-dollar bills. So sorry."

"What kind of visitor you call yourself?" his new friend scolded. "You tourists expect us to be good hosts, but you never want to extend the same courtesy." He wriggled his finger-bling. "All right, okay, let me see what I can do. I happen to like you. You want to have fun, don't you?"

"Oh, yes. Fun, fun."

"Cool. Okay, dude, dish it over." When Akhmed took a beat too long plucking out a bill, the man snatched the purse. "Come on. I'll show you something."

As the sitting black man was moving three cards around the table agilely, the first black man plunked down one of Akhmed's C-notes and whispered in his ear, "You see that red queen? The motherfucka think we don't know where it is, but watch this." When the cards stopped, he again whispered, "Tell him middle. Go on. Middle."

"Middle," Akhmed called, boldly.

The sitting black man winced, reluctantly turned over the center card, and, lo and behold, it was the red queen! "Shit," exclaimed the card player, "how you guess that, man? You clairvoyant or something?" And he gave Akhmed not only his own hundred back but five twenty-dollar bills besides! Oh, yes, this definitely was fun!

"Go away, man, you gonna ruin me."

"We ain't going nowhere," insisted the black Muslim. "The ACLU say you can't discriminate. Deal the mother-fuckin' cards."

To his glee, Akhmed won three more times in a row. But then his luck turned, and, fifteen minutes later, he had lost all his money and his jacket and belt, too. The first black man said, "Bad vibes, bro, but tomorrow's another day. Say, I got an idea. Follow me."

But as the president started to follow, his beltless trousers slid down, and he tripped and took a header into the gutter. A police officer ran over, stomped on his back a few times, handcuffed his wrists behind his back, Maced him, and dragged him back over the curb, his pants around his ankles. "Pervert, huh?" he barked. "You're under arrest, sicko." He read Akhmed his Miranda rights, more or less.

"I have diplomatic immunity."

"Yeah, and my wife is Queen of the May."

"I'm the president of Iran."

"I don't care if you're Chief Thunderthud. Get in the back of the car. And don't sit on my Cheetos!"

In a holding cell, Akhmed met a fellow named Artie—he liked the sound of that; it sounded so…yes, arty, and, portentously perhaps, it began with the same letter as his own name—who taught him how to play another card game called kaluki. Since neither of them had money, they played for eyelashes. Artie was an alcoholic and a tollbooth operator, and he wore one latex glove, and every thirty seconds he would stick out his hand and say, "Buck and a quarter." Apparently Artie had something of a temper because when his new cellmate, trying to be cordial, asked him how he liked his important job as a bulwark against the ravages of impersonal Western automation—i.e., being replaced by E-ZPass—Artie got red in the face, hurled the cards around the cell, grabbed Akhmed by his collar, and slammed his head several times against the bars. In a few minutes he calmed down, took a deep breath, collected the cards, and redealt.

"Union's working on it."

"Perhaps we should change the subject."

"You know how to play Hide the Salami?"

"Another game with cards?"

"Not exactly, no."

"I like salami. It's a Middle-Eastern word, you know."

"People should learn to live in peace," Artie said, sticking out his hand. "Buck and a quarter."

"Are you a Zionist?" Akhmed asked.

"What, you mean like a Jew? Nah. They always hand me twenty dollar bills. You have no idea how mad that makes me." His face began to get red again. "My ex-wife was a Jew. She's the one who taught me how to play ka-luki. No one has seen her for thirteen years."

"I'm the president of Iran," the president said quickly and defensively. "You recognize me, I suppose."

"Anyhow," Artie went on, "Jew broads are always talking on their cell phones when they come up to the booth. Yada, yada, blab, blab. Do you have any idea how disrespectful that is?"

"Really, Artie, I don't think you should get yourself all worked—"

"With their Hummers and Mercedes. They can't put their phones down for one freaking second? Who the hell are they talking to, anyhow?"

"Really, Artie—"

"To their jewelers? When will their diamond rings be back from resetting? Or calling the Jaguar dealer to see if the lime-green XJ-12 came in yet?" He started jumping around like a gorilla. "Oh, I know! They must be talking to their Jewish girlfriends, telling each other what disgusting, insensitive, horny husbands they have!"

"Artie, I—"

But the tollbooth operator was already thumping his cellmate, throwing him against the walls like a banana peel, trying to flush his head down the toilet, strumming his nose across the bars guitar-pick-like. Then, as quickly as it had begun, his tantrum ended. Again, he inhaled robustly, dusted off himself and his cellmate, handed Akhmed a wad of toilet tissue to press against his bleeding nose, and dealt the cards. "Forget Hide the Salami…for now," he said. "Got any eyelashes left?"

Diane raised her face from her palms, tilted her ear toward her bedroom, which, in a Venezuelan-pot-withdrawal fit, Les was apparently obliterating, and her brain made a connection. She had always suspected Karma of having been born with latent anger issues, but had expected them, like baby fat, to eventually melt away. Despite Diane's consistent and continual self-denials, though, Karma's hostility had only gotten worse. Diane had known it, had seen it, had been its object, had absorbed its brunt, but had always dismissed it as merely immature and transient. In her rare moments of reflective parental lucidity, she would admit to herself—sort of—that, yes, Karma was a bit high-strung and self-centered, but she, Diane, had always blamed herself. If Karma had grown up with a father figure; if Karma had had a loving male disciplinarian; if Karma had only known the security of a nuclear family; if Karma had not felt different from her friends, rejected by half her parents….

No, her innocent little girl would never have had to suffer those myriad indignities if Diane had not made the selfish, and ultimately wrong-headed—didn't Les turn out to *want* to know his daughter?—decision to not trouble Professor Fenwich but to raise Karma on her own.

So in the end who really sacrificed for Diane's martyrdom? Not Diane: she'd had the privilege of reminding herself daily how "noble" she had been. Not Les: he had been as oblivious to his defective condom as was whichever Third-World nine-year-old had check-marked the quality-inspection sheet. Karma—she was the real victim. Hadn't she been entitled to a little more ego-pampering than the average kid? Hadn't indulging her deep-seated hurt and insecurity been the least her mother could do—considering it was solely, absolutely, totally Diane's fault?

For nearly thirty years Diane had wallowed in guilt and self-reproach, but that was nothing compared to her recriminations of the past few weeks, since Les had shown his eagerness to be a good father and his remorse at having missed raising his only child.

But now, as she sat quavering downrange of his tyrannical rant, his vitriol, his rampage, something changed. She saw the father he would have been, and she realized she had been right all along. But there was more to her epiphany—much more. For, although she wasn't quite at the point of being able to admit it, in her heart she also knew something else wasn't entirely her fault: Karma.

The bedroom fell into ominous silence. Diane glanced at her knife drawer. She was a quick three steps from a turkey carver. She was about to get it, when the bedroom door creaked open, and Les stepped out, wearing pants but no shoes, socks, or shirt.

She got up and glided backward to the drawer, wrapping her hand around the pull. To her relief, though, it appeared the steam was out of him. Curled like a shrimp, he shuffled to the kitchen, eyes downcast, shoulders slumped. He scraped around the chair she had just been sitting on and straddled it.

They were silent. Her hand dropped from the drawer pull. Morosely, he said, "That wasn't me, you know."

She didn't reply.

"The weed talking, I guess," he tried, without looking at her.

Still no response.

"I'm no psychiatrist," he offered, "but I think I know what might have happened there. I'm convinced it was my repressed anger at your having denied me my moral, biological, and probably legal right to have known my daughter. For the past few weeks I've been keeping it all in, and it finally boiled over."

"It's my fault?"

"I've shown restraint, that's all I'm saying. It's about me, not you. I see how much I've been hurt—deeply and ir-reparably. I missed my only offspring's entire childhood."

"*I* made you miss it."

He finally looked up at her. "You understand, then? I mean, the broken things are only *objects*. But how can we fix my broken heart?"

Their eyes met, but she didn't know what to say. She saw him, the real him, for the first time. Yes, something had changed.

"Can I still go to the wedding?" he whimpered.

"Let me think about it, Les." She already knew she wouldn't deny her daughter's wishes, even if she could. She knew that father and daughter were one; that she, Diane, was the outsider—not Les. She had a frightening premonition. Like two smaller weather systems coalescing into a terrible storm, Karma and her father were about to unite into a ferocious, destructive force.

"Fair enough," he said. "That's all I ask." He cleared his throat. "I guess I should leave now, huh?"

"It would be a good idea."

"Do you want me to undeconstruct the bedroom?"

"Just leave."

He got up and disappeared into the maw of hallway darkness. She hardly breathed until, ten minutes later, the front door opened and closed. Only then did she find the courage to move, and her first motion was to turn to see, on her porch railing, a hawk holding down one of her baby barn swallows, plucking out its eyes.

After the Iranian leader spent three hours in the slammer with Artie, the desk sergeant came back to the holding cell and told him he was free to go—once he signed a couple of forms. "You must be a popular guy out there," the sergeant said. "You got yourself two."

"Two what?" Akhmed asked.

"Yeah, two what?" Artie demanded.

The sergeant cut Artie a stare. "Is this your business? Sit down. You ain't going nowhere."

"Goodbye, Artie," said the president, waving. "Thanks for teaching me kaluki."

"Keep your change loose, bud."

The sergeant nudged the Iranian to the front desk, where he shoved a clipboard into his gut. As Akhmed signed, the sergeant retrieved a manila envelope with his personal effects. Not understanding the concept of bond-posting, the president assumed he was being released because someone of authority had finally realized who he was, and so as he started walking out, he was already formulating the wording of the written apology he would demand from the American consulate.

"Where you off to, little man?" came a female voice from behind. He turned without stopping, and although he saw the woman, he assumed she was addressing someone else and kept going, not spotting the other woman in front of him and crashing into her. She didn't budge, but he reeled backward, staggered, and fell on his bottom.

Both women stood over him—one with hands on hips, the other, arms folded and chewing gum. The chubby, gum-chewing one smiled, but the skinny, hands-on-hips one looked glum.

"I think you owe us something, tiger," said the skinny one, holding out her hand to help him up. He grabbed it, rattling her bracelets.

"I owe you my thanks," he said, letting her help him to his feet. Again he started to walk away, but again the gum-chewing one blocked him.

"Nooo," said the other one, hands on hips again. "I think you owe us…oh, a thousand bucks, with interest accruing by the second."

"What?"

"You know, Bev," said the chub, cracking her gum, "I don't think he gets it. I think the guy is densed out."

"You think you got sprung because of your looks, turtle nose? Want to look in a mirror and guess again?"

"Turtle nose?" No one had talked to him that nicely all day.

The skinny one—Bev—explained about posting bail.

"But why would you do that for me? You recognize me, even without my beard?"

"Beard, schmeard. We're here because Reggie told us. Him and cop stations don't exactly get along, and he didn't trust neither one of us by ourselves." She glanced saucily at the fatty. "Although Felice and I get along just fine."

Felice winked back.

"Reggie?"

"Reggie G. Said to tell you he's the one showed you the red queen."

It took Akhmed a second. "Oh, the fellow who took my change purse."

Both women exclaimed in unison, "That would be Reggie."

He looked the women over again. They, clearly unlike Reggie, were white. Was it possible they were Muslim, too? "Reggie got me out of jail?"

"A thousand bucks"—Felice glanced at a tattoo watch on her wrist—"plus interest."

"He saved me again!"

The ladies traded glances. "Glad to see you have such a good attitude about it," Bev said. She pressed, "Reggie said you wouldn't give us no trouble."

"Trouble? Oh, today's been nothing but trouble."

"It's almost over, little boy—and me and Felice intend to make it worth your while...don't we, honey girl?"

"You can't imagine."

"But first you got to pay Reg back for his generosity."

"Oh, yes, yes. Tell Reggie I will be eternally grateful."

"That's swell, but what I think he has in mind is, uh… money?"

"Bail plus interest," Felice repeated.

"He said you probably got a few more shekels tucked away in your hotel room. Is he right?"

Akhmed thought. "Yes, he is. I have quite a lot there. Not shekels"—he made a sour face—"U.S. dollars."

Again the women's eyes locked. "Lead the way."

"It's the Manhattan on Green."

"Come on, we'll grab a cab."

Bev had short, dirty-blond, lusterless hair and a peach-fuzz mustache. Her arms were also covered with fine hair, like a wheat field whose farmer died before he could harvest. From her lobeless ears dangled tiny silver crucifixes. She wore a sleeveless blue-jean blouse that hung straight down her chest, and loose-fit, black Levis. Her eyes bulged a little, and her dirty fingernails were polished clear. She propped up her black-canvas, hemp-soled, open-toed platform shoes against the taxi's seat back, so that her ankle bracelets—two on each leg—dangled trapeze-like. She lit a cigarette, despite a sign on the partition saying not to, and dropped the match into the money tray. In the rearview mirror the driver—a turbaned Sikh—scowled at her biliously, and she scowled back. She exhaled the smoke out her nose at the partition.

Felice, on the other hand, radiated jolliness. She wore a brown rayon blouse with a breaching-dolphins pattern and tight beige jeans. Her blouse was knotted under her ample breasts, which wiggled from some inner joy. She had a wide forehead and cheeks like scoops of butterscotch ice cream. She kept looking at that watch tattooed on her wrist as if it were real, creeping out Akhmed. Next to her navel was a birthmark shaped like the Yucatan Peninsula. She wore six turquoise rings, and she alternated cracking her gum and her knuckles.

"You ever had two girls before?" Bev asked.

Affecting a debonair suavity, Akhmed replied, "Too often to recall."

"She means at the same time," Felice guffawed.

"Reggie told us to make sure we show you the best time of your life...*after* we get his dough."

"My whole life?"

"All, what, twelve years of it? Who taught you how to shave?"

"Oh, this? Zionist razor."

They pulled up to the Green, and, as Akhmed and Felice headed inside, Bev dangled a hundred-dollar bill at the driver.

"I have no change for this. Can't you read the sign?"

"I don't read."

"No change for bigger than a twenty."

"Then I guess you're screwed."

"You have to get change."

"I'm American, pal. I don't have to do anything."

"I'll call the police."

Bev started walking away. "You do that."

"Wait!"

She turned.

"I found change."

"A Hindu fucking miracle."

She stiffed him a tip, and he whooshed away, cursing.

She met her companions in the lobby. "Where's Giuliani when you need him?"

"Those Pakis don't smell so good," Akhmed said, curling his nose.

"Guess what, little boy? Right now you're not exactly wafting like a spring meadow. Before you get the time of your life, you're definitely headed for a hot shower. Have you people ever heard of soap?"

"Oh, yes, we have soap in Iran. We make it from chicken poopies."

At the elevator, a bellman fluttered his eyebrows at the girls.

"Shove it," Bev suggested.

In the Iranian's room, the girls admired the view, then plopped down on the bed, intertwining ankles. "Not bad," Felice giggled.

"The colors are atrocious," Akhmed apologized. "For this kind of money, wouldn't you think they would hire the best interior designers in the world? I didn't even have formal training, and I still know that earth tones are passé. *Ick!*"

"Let's order room service!" Felice exclaimed. "I'm hungry!"

"Knock yourself out," Bev said. She turned to their host. "You—get yourself into that shower!"

He complied.

"As hot as you can stand it! You smell like cat piss!"

She turned to Felice and said, "There is a God."

"Told you."

From the bathroom, they heard the shower come on, then "Aaaa…llaaah."

"Not bad digs," said Bev.

"You think they get *Andy Griffith*?"

Bev handed Felice the remote. "For three hundred-fifty a night they should get Opie to suck our tits."

"I like Floyd. Who's your favorite?"

"I always wanted to beat the bejeesus out of Aunt Bea."

Felice channel surfed, didn't find Mayberry, but did land *Leave It to Beaver*. Bev, meanwhile, ordered a ton of food from room service. "Get fries," Felice called. "And them sliced potatoes with cheese. And some shrimps and a cheeseburger. And soup and rolls and an omelet. And plenty of dessert. Cheesecake and some ice cream and cookies. Ask if they have SnackWell's."

"Trust me, they don't have SnackWell's."

"Ask anyhow."

Bev read into the phone from the room service menu and, when she got tired of looking for what she wanted, tossed it to the floor and improvised. "I'll tell you what we want," she told the woman, "and you work it out."

"Ask how long," Felice called, checking her wristwatch tattoo.

"How long?" Bev asked the woman. "You're shitting me."

"How long?" asked Felice, worried.

"We're hungry," Bev snapped at the phone. "I know I ordered a lot. I don't need some snotty bitch to tell me I ordered a lot. I just need a snotty bitch to get up here fast with our food. *Comprendo?*" She slammed down the phone.

"You forgot to ask if they have SnackWell's."

"I don't know how to say it in Mexican."

"How long?" Felice, clasping her hands prayerlike, asked.

"Forty minutes."

She pile-drove her heel into the mattress. "Forty minutes!"

Bev handed her the phone. "It's Obama's fucking immigration policy—what d'you want from me?"

Felice looked around desperately. Her gaze fell onto the bar fridge. "Food!" she grunted, lunging. But when she opened it and found only a minicooler, she moaned, "Oh, crumb."

"Maybe that's where he keeps his cold cash," Bev sniggered. She got up and started rummaging through their host's drawers. "We'd better get down to business. Something tells me they're not into long showers where he comes from. Check the closet."

Felice pulled out the minicooler, fiddled with the lid for a moment before figuring out how it opened, and peered inside. She lifted out a food storage container and pried open the lid. Her eyes got big. "Soup!" she yelped. "With big dumplings!"

"Probably camel shit," Bev offered. "Probably got to heat it anyhow. Forget it."

The shower stopped, and the curtain scraped open.

"Come on, help me find the money, quick."

"I don't care if it's cold. I'm starved!" Felice held her nose to the matzo balls, liked what she smelled, glanced around the room for something to eat them with and, seeing nothing, reached in with her fingers, grabbed one, and opened her mouth wide.

Diane bolted out to save her chick, but it was too late. The hawk flew away, dropping the dead fledgling onto the porch. She scooped up its eyeless corpse, cupped it in both hands, and, moaning, brought it into the kitchen. She placed it on a napkin on the table, sat, and wept for it, for herself, for Karma, for the world. She blamed herself for not having been paying enough attention to the porch, for having let herself get distracted by her fear of Les. It was her fault. Everything was her fault.

She let it all out, thirty years' worth of regret. For a half-hour she sobbed over the swallow's lifeless body and the carcasses of mistaken choices. But when at last she was cried out, something unexpected happened. Her mind had exited a dark, suffocating tunnel into a sun-drenched, breezy, open space. She sat up straight and inhaled. She could breathe. She looked outside, beyond the porch. Colors were vibrant, aromas sharp, details clear. Leaves rustled silvery, pigeons cooed, a robin chirped sweetly. The sky was Wyoming's deep, infinite blue, not Chicago's sickly white. Clouds were fluffy and calm, like sleeping sheep.

She wrapped the dead chick in the napkin and told it that she loved it. She decided this was No Mo'. She kissed the napkin and considered burying the baby in the pot of her porch philodendron.

Pot.

Her gaze fell on the salt-and-pepper-shaker set. Les's baggie was gone. He had snatched it unseen while making his half-assed apology. It's what he had wanted all along.

But the funny thing was, she no longer cared. Without much difficulty she put Les out of her mind and went about her business burying her baby.

Twelve

Termites poured out of the former Haiti commerce minister's orifices and torrented over the cruise ship *Sterling Star* in search of more of the same luscious human-basted pork they recently had the orgasmic pleasure of tasting in their late host's gullet. Having sampled nirvana, they were in no mood for less than the most succulent pork-infused man flesh they could find, and their antennae told them with every quiver that nearby lurked not only more of the same but *lots* more of the same—an entire goddamn *convention* of the same.

As if under hydraulic pressure, they rose through heating ducts and drain pipes, electrical chases and elevator shafts, deck after deck, following the scrumptious scent of porkized people meat, hunting it down. Up through luggage holds and cargo bins and equipment lockers and pump rooms and utility sheds and staff quarters they climbed, story upon story, closer and closer, until, at the restaurant level, the ravenous phalanx stopped in its tracks. A buzzing, shimmering brown mass undulated in a return vent running between a preparation kitchen and the

Bounty Buffet, where, through vent registers, the termites watched and listened as, amid a cacophony of clanking dishes and clinking silverware, bus personnel were busy getting the huge room ready for this evening's themed smorgasbord, "Buccaneers' Banquet."

It was going to be a banquet, all right.

"Stop!" Akhmed blared, as he opened the bathroom door and, through billows of steam, spotted Felice about to chomp a nuclear matzo ball. "Stop, I say!!"

She stopped.

He leapt out, his towel flying off his waist, and snatched the ball and container from her chubby fingers. "Are you mad?! You must be mad!" he shouted, sealing the Tupperware, shoving the cooler back into the bar fridge, and blocking it with his naked body. "Get out! Both of you! Out!"

"What the hell is this?" Bev, springing from the bed, demanded.

"I'm hungry," Felice whimpered.

"I don't care! Get out!"

Felice turned to her partner. "I didn't do anything. I was just smelling it."

Bev stared down their host. "We're not going anywhere without Reggie's money." She glanced at his crotch. "And what is that, a packing peanut?"

He realized he had lost his towel. "That's not packing. It's my maleness!"

"Don't worry, little boy, puberty will get here before you know it."

"You insult the manhood of the Iranian president?"

"Where's our dough?"

"You want your money?"

"I thought while we're here, we might get a little of that," she said, pointing to his maleness, "but now that I see it"—she squinted—"I changed my mind. Not enough there to pack a mouse." She turned to Felice. "How about you? Can you even see it without binoculars?"

"I changed my mind, too," she said. "That wouldn't be enough for a flea."

"A flea!" he exclaimed. "You think my penis wouldn't satisfy a flea?! A bug?! I have many girlfriends in Iran!" He pointed. "This penis is renowned!"

Bev laughed. "Where? In the Iranian Flea Circus?"

Felice thought that was a good one.

"You American women are too fresh! In my country you would be stoned."

"I need to get stoned to forget I ever saw *that*."

"Insolence!"

"Give us our money."

He stormed to the closet, threw his suitcase onto the bed, pulled a wad of bills out of a sock, and hurled it at them. "Here!" he yelled. "Here are your filthy American dollars! Filthy American money for filthy American women!"

Bev stuffed the wad—it contained far more than ten one-hundred-dollar bills—into her purse, and waved Felice to the door. Glancing back at the president, she hung her finger from her nose like a mosquito proboscis. "*Bzzz, bzzz.*"

When they were gone, he stood for a moment, still naked, glaring at the door. Finally, he turned to face the dressing mirror. He stared at his penis. They were right, of course. It was teeny. It *wouldn't* satisfy a flea. It was the truth: he had inadequate equipment.

He fell face down on the bed, sobbing, pounding the bedspread with his fists and feet, cursing Allah for having given him a tiny tool, cursing American women for being impudent.

"Why, why, why, *why*?!" he wailed, the mattress muffling his cries. "Hate, hate, hate, hate, *hate*!"

It had been a bad day, no doubt about it. The streets of New York had not been kind to him. He was more determined than ever to destroy America. More than anything else, he wished with fanatical zeal to destroy American women—every last repulsive one of them.

"Why? Why?" he blubbered into his pillow. "Why, why, *why*? Hazeem! Hazeem! How could you leave me like this? Hazeem, *Hazeem*!... Artie! Artie! *Artie*! *ARTIE*!"

At 6:00 PM, the first of the Midwest Pork Producers Association of America conventioneers, dressed as pirates and wenches, carrying mugs and steins and tumblers and goblets and cups, sipping and slurping and sucking and swallowing, began arriving at the Buccaneers' Banquet, eyeballing the buffet, snorting its steamy emissions, gathering its various grogs and cornucopian appetizers and gargantuan entrees and sauces and side dishes and desserts.

What desserts! Creampuffs and cheesecakes and sundaes and layer cakes and pies filled with every imaginable fruit and some they had never even imagined. If only the desserts, like all the other dishes, could have been made with pork!

From the vents, the termites watched and waited, licking their mandibles, coiling with collective carnivorousness, silent, pulsing—HVAC shafts bulging and throbbing, grates rattling.

By 7:00, the room was packed with Porkers, shoveling all-inclusive, mostly hog-based bulk down their corpulent esophagi, squealing with all-inclusive, tips-not-required delight, waiters and waitresses skittering around the Bounty Buffet waterbug-like, delivering round after round of booze.

And still the termite leaders did not give the signal to strike.

By 8:30, the MPPAAs were heavy-lidded, slumped over, and crumpled—languorous from overeating, torpid from too much drink. The room was a symphony of half-moans, snores, belches, and farts. The staff had cleared away the last of the dessert dishes and was bringing the final Kahlúas and Drambuies and Dry Sacks and Pernods.

At 8:45, the Porker who had first sighted the Haitian drifting on the water, pleading for help, lifted his snifter and spotted a weird-looking bug rearing up at him from the tablecloth, bearing fangs. He pounded his fist on it, smashing it to juice. The thump reverberated off steel walls and through sheet-metal vents, startling the sleepy conventioneers.

That was the signal.

PART III

Thirteen

Having traveled separately from Chicago to Florida—Diane flying, Les Amtraking—the two former, now estranged, lovebirds settled into different hotels (he the Diamond Miami, she the Ornamental Majestic). Even after they got to Miami, Diane spoke to Les as little as possible, not feeling the need to tell him that the matzo balls she had originally intended as her part of their "metaphoric" wedding present to Karma were currently rotting in a Chicago garbage bin.

Now, in Florida, unaware that Diane had disposed of said matzo balls (along with her old notions of maternal guilt and any intention of giving Karma a mutual present with Professor Fenwich), Les set out to bring Diane the knapsack. On his way, he made a detour to his old grammar school, Roosevelt Elementary, at Sea Salt Road and Monarch Street in Miramar, just north of Miami. He had not been back since he had been a boy, the memories being so excruciating. But now that he was on the verge of changing the world for the better, he forced himself to return, like MacArthur to the Philippines (only more morally justified), with bittersweet revenge. It wasn't easy. The moment he had made up his mind to go back, something caustic spurted into that part of his brain responsible for second thoughts, and now, the taxi having let him off in his old neighborhood, almost within sight of the school, he stopped walking several times to reconsider, almost changed his mind, but finally soldiered on.

He felt as if he were nine years old again, trudging to that house of torture, slogging toward humiliation and pain. He approached the school's fence, grabbed the bars, and peered at the south playground, at the very spot where he used to regularly get the crap beat out of him. He remembered his primary tormentor, of course—a beefy kid, Tom Lanahan, whose breath reeked of Beeman's Pepsin Chewing Gum, and who taunted Les by, among other indignities, hurling nose hockers at him before pummeling flesh and bone. He recalled the sting of each slap, the crushing shame of every noogie, the hurt of each trip to the gravel, the degradation each time Lanahan sang out the name "Leslie" as he laid into him. Les-lie...*whack.* Les-lie...*whack.* Les-lie...*whack.* He remembered how he would run home to his mother, even while despising her for having given him a girl's name. Oh, how he loathed her, even as she stroked his too-long hair and kissed his too-rosy wet cheeks.

Where was Tom Lanahan now? he wondered, forcing a smile. What would he think of *Dr.* Leslie Fenwich now? *Head* of the university English Department *Professor* Leslie Fenwich? Would he even remember him? Well, he would soon enough, soon enough.

He scuffed around to the back of the school, running his fingers over the fence bars contemplatively, as he used to do as a schoolboy. Before he turned a corner and saw them, he heard the high-pitched calls of boys playing touch football. He stopped. His heart raced. Memories rushed back. He remembered wanting to play ball with his classmates, desperately wanting to fit in. If only they would have picked him, he would have shown them he wasn't such a nerd—not muscular or staminal, no, but speedy, agile, and clever, able to calculate the putative distance between handoff and "tackle"; facilely adept at evaluating an opposing quarterback's psychological impuissance. If only they would have given him a chance.

He closed his eyes and visualized his future monument in Havana's Plaza of the Revolution: an oxidized-copper statue of himself reading from *The Norton Anthology of Theory and Criticism*. And another, in blinding bronze, three times life size, of him riding his bike, towering over the south playground of Roosevelt Elementary School in Miramar, Florida.

He forced himself to go on.

As he turned a corner where tall, flowering bushes had replaced the old fence, a football careened off his head, bounced off a palm tree, and landed at his feet. "Ow! Little pricks!" he yelped, holding his ear.

"Hey, get it!" one of the boys hollered, shoes crunching gravel.

Without thinking, Les scooped up the football and stuffed it into his and Diane's old knapsack. A second later, a kid came running up to the bushes. Between branches, he searched for the ball. "Hey, mister? Did you see a football?"

"I heard something bounce," Les said amiably.

"I can't lose it, no way. That was my grandpa's football. Real old-time pigskin."

"Pigskin, huh?"

"Yeah, mister. Real, authentic pigskin, like in the old days."

"Then you should have been a tad more cautious, *n'est-ce pas?*"

"Do you see it?"

He nodded across the street. "It went that way, I think. I'll go look."

"Thanks, mister."

"You're perfectly welcome. Wait here. I'll find it."

"Thanks. Oh, man."

"Don't trouble yourself. Be patient. I'll throw it back."

"Thanks a lot, mister."

"Doctor."

"Huh?"

"Thanks a lot, *Doctor*. Go on, say it."

"Uh…thanks a lot, *Doctor?*"

"That's better. Stay here, now. I'll find it." Across the street he rustled some bushes and called back, "I think I see it!" But instead of bringing it back, he tucked the knapsack-wrapped football into his mighty, two-armed, fumbleless clench, and sprinted away between houses and onto the next street, imagining the fireplug at the end of the block to be the goal post.

"Bastards," he panted.

He felt euphoric. He had to admit, he loved the rush of being a bully. The adrenaline high of stealing grandpa's authentic-pigskin football, scoring a touchdown, and of the grandson being psychologically scarred for life for losing it, helped gird Les for seeing Diane. It even boosted his spirits for attending tomorrow's wedding rehearsal, during which he would force himself to be charming to those insufferable Culvertdales.

Returning to his old grammar school had been providential, all right. Not providential in the "divine providence" sense of the word, of course, since there was no God (duh-uh), but in the "opportune or fortuitous" sense of the word. So perhaps he had inadvertently ratiocinated the incorrect term. As soon as his heart stopped pounding and his breathing returned to normal, he would come up with something more *précise*.

A couple of good weed hits would certainly help him come up with more accurate verbiage. Reflexively he patted his shorts, only to remember he had left his stash in his room at the Diamond Miami. So he made another little detour, backtracking to the Diamond to celebrate his touchdown and to consult his thesaurus for a better word than *providential*.

Having had a good cry at the end of a miserable day, Akhmed sat up on his Manhattan on Green hotel bed and, realizing that in his sobbing hysteria he had many times called out the name *Artie*, he knew what he had to do. Now that he understood, sort of, how the concept of bail worked, he was going to get his new friend released from jail, just as (but without women!) his other new friend, Reggie G., had freed him.

From his toiletry bag in the bathroom, he pulled a stack of Iranian one-hundred-thousand-rial bills (Did those horrible females think he was so naïve as to not hide *real* money? He certainly was going to report them to Reggie.), stuffed it into his jacket, and headed back to the police station. He plunked the wad down in front of the desk sergeant and boldly demanded Artie's release.

"Wait your turn."

Having just experienced the worst day of his life, the president was in no mood for nonsense. "There's no one else here."

"When I call you, you can state your business."

"But you're not doing anything but eating a stupid sandwich and reading a stupid magazine."

"Since when is that not doing anything?"

"What kind of country is this?"

"Unionized."

"This is maddening."

The sergeant glanced at the wall clock. "I tack this onto your waiting time."

Akhmed sat on a steel bench. He watched the sergeant eat and read, read and eat. Minute by minute he was more and more glad that America would soon go the way of the Babylonian, Roman, Mayan, Aztec, and Assyrian empires.

When he couldn't stand it anymore—knowing that Artie was still in that cell, perhaps playing kaluki by himself, was driving him crazy—he jumped up and shouted, "That good man should not have to spend another moment in there, when here I am with all this money to set him free!" He picked up his rials and slammed the stack onto the sergeant's magazine.

"Wait your turn."

"This is my turn!"

"What kind of dough is this?"

"Iranian dough, that's what! Take whatever you need to liberate Artie!"

The sergeant hefted the wad. He filliped it and saw that all the bills, the whole two-inch sheaf, were nothing but one-hundred-thousand denominations. "This is a lot of money, boyo."

"You bet!"

The sergeant glanced behind the Iranian and furtively watched as one of his patrolmen opened the cell area door and ushered Artie out.

"Whose picture is this?"

"Ayatollah Khomeini, the George Washington of our glorious nation!"

"I like what's going on with the pastels."

"I designed it myself."

"No shit?"

"None."

With a side-glance, the sergeant watched as, behind the Iranian's back, Artie's pro bono lawyer placed a form on top of a trash container for his client to sign.

"What's all this squiggly shit?" the desk sergeant asked, nodding at the money.

"That's not squiggly shit. That's writing. We *invented* writing."

"No lie? What does it say?"

"What difference does it make?"

"Just curious."

Over Akhmed's shoulder, the sergeant watched Artie and his attorney leave the building.

"It says, 'Let Artie Go!'"

"You're kidding me."

"Set Artie free, you…you…unionized poophead, or I vow there will be an international incident!"

The sergeant looked at the clock and burped. "What do you know, coincidentally, my dinner break is now over."

"I thought that would do it!"

The sergeant fanned the bills over his magazine. "You'll have to fill out a couple of forms, naturally."

Akhmed's face flushed purple. "You mean to tell me I could have been filling out papers this whole time?!"

"It won't take long."

"Give me the blasted things! Hurry, hurry, or I'll have you fired!"

The sergeant yawned, dug some forms from his drawer, looked them over desultorily, shook his head, exchanged them for others, spread the fresh ones over the rials, found a manual in another drawer, consulted it, decided these weren't the correct forms either, and recommended foraging through his desk.

"If you weren't already the police," Akhmed snarled, "I'd have you arrested. In my country, your eyeballs would be rat food."

"Here we are," the sergeant declared, tearing off two forms from their pads. "You need a pen?"

"Of course I need a pen, you fool! You think Iranians write with our knuckles?"

"I never been there."

Akhmed grabbed the papers and pen, stormed to the trash container, and filled them out. When he finished, he returned to the sergeant and triumphantly slapped them onto the desk.

The policeman looked them over and said, "Oh, *that* Artie."

"What do you mean *that* Artie?"

"He already got sprung. About ten minutes ago."

"What?!"

The sergeant nodded. "I didn't know you meant *that* Artie. Why didn't you say so?"

Akhmed swiveled. "Which way did he go?"

"Only one way out. Left with that other guy."

"Other guy?" He swung back around and glared bulge-eyed at the policeman. "*What* other guy?"

"How do I know? A guy, what do you want from me? A tall guy."

"Tall!"

"Tall, handsome guy."

"Handsome!"

"Looked kind of Jewish."

"Allah!"

"Hey," the sergeant said, snapping his fingers at the president's twisted and agonized face, "I recognize you now. I saw you on TV this morning. You're that Iranian nut job."

"You did this on purpose!"

The sergeant offered him the rest of his pickle.

"I'm reporting you to the United Nations!"

"Come on. Dill always makes you feel better."

"I hate you! I hate America! Hate, hate, hate!"

The sergeant shrugged and ate the pickle himself. With a *crack* he said, "That's the great thing about this country, boyo. You're free to hate your heart out. We're the greatest melting pot of hate in the history of the Free World. God bless you, brother, and God bless America. Now scram or I'll Taser your ass to kingdom come."

The president of Venezuela arrived at the Ft. Lauderdale offices of Global Boffo, the parent corporation of Wow-tality International, the nutritional supplement multilevel distribution company. A receptionist took his card, called someone on her headset, handed the card back to him, and said that Laura would be with him momentarily to escort him to the chairman's office. So far, so good. He was feeling pretty upbeat about the whole thing. He was not, after all, the same bus-driving lackey as the first time he had applied to Wow-tality. This time, he was the leader of a great Latin-American nation—baby pudge or no.

As promised, in a minute, a business-attired, fashionably spectacled young woman—flat-chested but otherwise not bad—came out through thick-glass doors and beckoned him to follow her inside (gladly). The Venezuelan president himself was dressed in a brown, sharkskin suit with bronze paisley tie, white shirt, khaki-and-red argyle socks, and burgundy wingtip shoes that a salesman at Nordstrom's had talked him into buying and whom the president was going to have assassinated when all this was over. Every step was agonizing. His bunions were throbbing, and his Achilles tendons were raw.

He squeaked behind the young woman, who led him to a double-doored corner office, where she ran a key card through a reader while glancing up at a ceiling camera. The door buzzed, she popped it open, and gestured him in.

"After you," he said gallantly, but she scowled in that bitchy-American-liberated-working-woman-snotty way of theirs, so he went in first, "accidentally" clobbering her knee with his briefcase. She hobbled away, closing the door hard and muttering behind her.

The CEO's anteroom was as big as a funeral home lobby and just as morbid. Five seating clusters coalesced in different corners of a gray marble floor, and three gray mohair sofas pressed against olive-colored walls. The room resembled a kidney with stones. Above the couches hung oil paintings of nineteenth-century British naval battles. At the far end of the room, a secretary with bulging, slightly crossed eyes and an overbite that could open a can sat at a large granite desk, over which leaned a wild-looking but not unattractive woman of about thirty (like himself, a visitor, he surmised), her palms outspread like Horatio Nelson over battle charts in rough seas, bearing her fangs. Her eyes blazed with fury—again, not unattractively—and her red hair stood on end, making her resemble a cross between Little Orphan Annie and a medieval painting of a vengeful Beelzebub. Unlike Laura, this young woman had melonicious breasts.

"I know he's avoiding me!" the visitor flamed. "You think I'm stupid? You think I don't know he's too lilly-livered to face me?! That he's not more afraid of me than of his horse-faced wife, with her prenuptial horseshit?"

"Really, Miss Weinberg," said the secretary, peering over her reading glasses, "there's no reason to get upset. If you'll—"

"Don't tell me what I should get upset about, you dried-up hag. You're not my shrink. When I'm not supposed to get upset, you'll be the first to know. Now you get his weaselly Protestant ass on that fucking phone before I shove it sideways up your spinster crack—"

"I'm afraid that's quite impossible, dear," the secretary replied imperturbably. "He won't be out of his meeting for—"

Little Orphan Lucifer pounded the desk and stomped her foot. "Call him, you scabby twat!"

The Venezuelan leader immediately dug this firecracker.

It was chemistry, plain and simple—love at first sight. He watched her from the door for a few minutes—in truth he was a little afraid of her, and he found that arousing too—before finding enough courage to approach the desk.

"Excuse me for interrupting," he said.

Karma glared at him, nostrils flaring, a low, feral hiss emanating from her tonsils.

He placed his briefcase on the corner of the desk, opened it with a flourish, and plucked out a sample packet of Wow-tality Calming Tea. "May I suggest a cup of the most soothing herbal blend known to man or woman?" He tore open the packet and pulled out a bag. "Go on, take a whiff. You'll never be the same again." He dangled it under her nose.

"It smells like something crawled up an ass and croaked."

"Don't let that deceive you. It's made from a secret and precise mixture of Amazonian rainforest plants. It works faster, less expensively, and more beneficially than *ten years'* worth of psychiatrists or a truckload of anti-anxiety drugs. I can tell you from personal experience, it immediately takes the rough edges off strife and puts troubles into proper perspective. One cup of this and you'll immediately start to focus on all your blessings."

She ran her eyes over him, from greasy head to burgundy wingtips. "Who the fuck are you, the fucking tea fairy?"

He whipped out his card and two retractable pens, handing one to her and one to the secretary. The pens bore the gold-embossed advertising message:

~ COME TO VENEZUELA ~
~ FUTURE HOME OF WOW-TALITY SOUTH ~
~ OUR INFANT MORTALITY RATE IS LOWER THAN
PERU'S! ~

"President of Venezuela," he told this gorgeous female powder keg, "at your vitamin and mineral service.... And you are?"

She screwed him a gaze. "Yeah, I recognize you at that. The Nitco Oil commie motherfucker."

He held out his hand. "Pleased to meet you."

She stared at it and sneered.

"Say, we could use a go-getter like you on the Wow-tality team," he said, withdrawing his hand. "Have you ever considered a career in multilevel marketing? You're your own boss"—he nodded at the secretary, thinking she might be interested too—"no higher-up to yank your chain, initial investment next to nothing, you can invest as much or as little time as you wish—part, full, or anything in between—great for working moms!—and you'd be offering friends and family products that enhance their physical and emotional well-being."

"I don't have friends," the firebrand snorted.

"Maybe I could be your first."

"You wouldn't happen to know how to reach Culvertdale, would you?"

"As a matter of fact, Mr. C. and I are close associates." He smiled at the secretary. "That is, we're about to be associates, *very* good friends, I imagine." He beamed. "I'm about to become Wow-tality's number one distributor in the whole wide world—black, white, yellow, and red; free-market democracies and brutal dictatorships. And I'm guessing if it's one thing Mr. C. appreciates"—he winked at the secretary—"it's the bottom line."

The secretary handed him a sealed envelope. "Mr. Culvertdale said he's sorry he couldn't be here to see you in person, but he wants you to have this, with his thanks."

"His thanks, huh?" the South American said blissfully.

He tore open the letter and started reading it aloud, mostly because he could hardly contain his own joy but also to impress this foxy potential subdistributor.

> Dear Mr. President:
>
> We appreciate the time you recently took with us and the fine presentation you made to the acquisitions committee. There is no doubt in any of our minds that you are a natural born salesman and will be a great success in any venture you take on. You are enthusiastic, curious, intelligent, and sincere—all essential qualities to rise to the top of any sales career. Our board was impressed with your desire and knowledge of our product line, and there was no doubt that you would be dedicated to making a regional distributorship a success…

Here the president stopped to take a breath and to run his eyes again over what he had read, relishing the acknowledgment of his greatness. As his eyes darted between the redhead and the letter, he once more read the phrase "making a regional distributorship a success."

He continued to read aloud:

> …Unfortunately, the committee members agree that, despite your obvious merits, your position as a Marxist tyrant and Western Hemisphere pariah would be detrimental to the reputation of our company. Therefore, it is with great regret that we must deny your application as the South American distributor of our fine Wow-tality products…

He stopped reading aloud. He reread this part to himself several times. He thought he knew English pretty well but was convinced he was misunderstanding something. His lips moved, but no sound came out. He shifted his weight. His feet began to hurt even more. He tightened his grip on the letter. He forced himself to finish reading it—this time silently.

> …We do wish you the very best in any future endeavors, and keep using Wow-tality nutritional supplements. They obviously are doing their job.
>
> Very truly yours,
> Eddward L. Culvertdale, Chairman of the Board
> GLOBAL BOFFO ENTERPRISES
> ELC/mm

He looked down at the secretary with moist eyes. "It's… not…possible," he stammered. "Are you sure he left this for *me*? The president of Venezuela?"

"I'm afraid so," she said. "Bad news?"

He turned to the redhead, who was smirking.

"Fucked you, too, huh?" she said.

He swiveled so she couldn't see his face. He closed his briefcase and, rubber-legged, stumbled to a seating cluster, his attaché case suddenly weighing a thousand pounds. He collapsed into a chair and stared dully into space. He couldn't believe it. It wasn't possible that they would hold something like being a Marxist despot against him. What about the enormous profit potential in his region? Weren't the Latin American countries overpopulated with Catholics, representing a gigantic per-square-mile per-capita market, and therefore a potentially more lucrative customer base even than developed countries? Weren't corporate officers supposed to care about quarterly dividends? Didn't they have an obligation to their shareholders, irrespective of political ideology?

He felt sick. Sick, sick, sick. His life's dream, down the drain. His purpose on earth, annihilated. He wanted to throw up. He choked back a sob. He buried his face in his hands.

Then something happened.

Someone nudged him. He looked up from his palms, and there was the magnificent redhead, holding a trash basket between his knees. "Go on," she said. "Let it go, bunky. Nothing like a good, old-fashioned heave to make you feel worthwhile again. Beats fucking vits and mins every time."

Propped up on his sixteen Diamond Miami pillows sucking giddy, *Dr.* Leslie Fenwich—a.k.a. "the Professor"—couldn't quite take his mind off the five million dollars waiting for him in a Cayman Islands bank account, the money promised him for his invaluable contribution to the project. At first he hadn't wanted monetary remuneration at all—it was beneath him. He had been only too glad to assist in the deconstruction of America's oligarchical underpinnings. But then he got to thinking. Wouldn't this be another form of redistribution of wealth, formerly in the hands of a greedy and arrogant few? Wasn't the history of revolution replete with instances of the former have-nots finally reveling in the legitimate spoils expropriated from the beheaded haves? And because those spoils had been earned on the backs of hopeless laborers, indentured servants, slaves, the indigent, dispossessed, and downtrodden, to whose oppressed voices Dr. Fenwich gave expression, how could his accepting the millions not be considered valid and just?

Then he got to thinking a bit more. After all was said and done, five million seemed sort of paltry, considering: a) the kind of money in the coffers of the operation's principals, mostly oil money from raping the earth; b) his grave personal risk to life and limb; c) the quality of his work (Wasn't *he* the one who thought of the knapsack scheme? Wasn't *he* the Miami maven? Wasn't *he* the one to beguile Diane into unwittingly carrying the pack with the nuclear matzo balls?). The more he thought about it, the more five million seemed a little insulting. Not for himself, mind you, but for the generations of huddled masses who had endured the cruelties and injustices of the hegemonizing ruling class. For African slaves and Chinese railroad workers and slaughtered picket-line marchers and murdered Freedom Riders and legions of homeless and mentally ill. In the name of welfare mothers and laid-off assembly-line workers and immigrant laborers and the discriminated against and disenfranchised and dispossessed. For the sake of millions of indigents without health insurance or the ability to buy three wholesome meals a day for themselves and their children. For these people, not himself, five million dollars was worse than insulting. It was a goddamn outrage.

Still, it wasn't chump change, either. Even in this day and age of draconian war deficits, of speculator-driven oil prices, manipulated to benefit Cheney's pals Exxon Mobil and Conoco Phillips, of inflated food prices due to taxpayer-subsidizing of agricultural mega-conglomerates, five million wasn't exactly lint. Five million was approaching fuck-you money. With five million he could e-mail Leona Beebe and tell her where to shove her deanship and her gigantic ass, too. With five million he could tell literary theory to go screw itself, and Norton too.

The truth was, he couldn't stop thinking about the money. From beneath his underpants at the bottom of his suitcase, he took the last of his Venezuelan grass and a packet of Zig-Zags and rolled himself a plump spliff. He shuffled to the hotel room window and gazed out at the wall of gleaming white condominium monstrosities, and at the Miami deep-water dock, where the *Countess of the Sea* waited imperiously for the Culvertdale honeymoon. He thought about Che Guevara.

He had always thought of himself as Che's reincarnation, an heroic revolutionary who gives up his cushy bourgeois life—Guevara was trained to be a physician—in service of a more noble calling: the rootless, restless, peregrinating, itinerant champion of the underclass, traveling from one oppressed country to another, inspiring peasants to throw off their shackles, decapitate their tormentors, seize their own destinies. He saw a movie once about Che's life, in which the young Argentine abandoned his upper-middle-class privilege to ride a motorcycle around South America, searching for just causes.

He pictured himself riding a Yamaha two-wheeler, speeding over highways and byways, his hair whipping behind him, no one to answer to but himself and destiny. No addlebrained college students, no sour-pussed colleagues insipiently debating literary deconstructionism over peanut butter and jelly sandwiches. No final exams, no student conferences, no research papers to dissolve his brain. Just he and the wind. Leslie Fenwich and the road and sky. Fresh air and social justice. Sunlight and stars.

"Far out," he mumbled.

When the roach was a fleck under his nails, he grabbed the knapsack, wobbled to the elevator, and, downstairs, asked the concierge to locate the nearest Yamaha motorcycle dealer. In a few minutes, address crumpled in hand, he staggered outside and stumbled into a waiting cab. He handed the driver the address.

"No, wait," he said, remembering the knapsack at his feet. "First head to the Ornamental Majestic. When we get there, wait for me."

He called Diane from the lobby, but she wouldn't see him, claiming she was washing her hair. "Leave it at the front desk," she said.

Like he never heard that one before. Well, fine. "Okay, see you tomorrow. Don't forget, we want to give her the present together," he said, meaning both the knapsack and Diane's matzo balls.

"I won't forget," Diane replied, believing he was referring to the backpack only, having forgotten that she never told him about throwing the matzo balls into her alley dumpster in Chicago. "You're her father."

"See you for the rehearsal."

"I really do have to go. I'm getting the carpet wet."

He left the knapsack on the counter and stumbled back into the cab. "Okay, now to that address."

Ironically, Grosvenor Yamaha was only a few blocks from his old grammar school. Passing Roosevelt, he delightfully recalled "grandpa's authentic old-time pigskin" he had expropriated (Robin Hood-like) from the Tom Lanahan counterpart but, still kind of stoned, he couldn't quite recall what he had done with it. He tried to remember, but when the taxi turned onto Miramar Parkway and the huge, looming motorcycle sculpture atop the building came into view, he forgot all about the football, the knapsack, Karma, Diane, the wedding rehearsal, the university, poor working people, predatory corporations, Marx, Engels, Foucault, the Castros, oppressed Palestinians, interned Japanese-Americans, Vietnam, Guantanamo, Abu Ghraib, health care reform, rapacious CEOs, Bill O'Reilly, Hillary Clinton, Barack "No Drama" Obama, Clarence Thomas, Bakke vs. the State of California, women's rights, the ACLU, prayer in school, labor-management relations, creationism, solar power, dog fighting, cockfighting, girl fighting, dwarf tossing, budget deficits, YouTube, strip malls, Keens, Crocs, Tom Lanahan, the U.S. military–industrial complex, the Alaska pipeline, supertankers, coral reefs, bullfighting, freedom of the press, freedom of speech, the right to assemble, the right to bear arms, student research papers, habeas corpus, and the Culvertdales.

At the moment, all Leslie Fenwich thought and cared about was owning a Yamaha motorcycle (Harleys were too American; buying a Yamaha, though, might in some small measure atone for having bombed Hiroshima and Nagasaki, which, truth be told, he also at the moment didn't give a shit about). "Out of sight!" he gasped at the giant bike. "Jee-zus Christopher H. Christ."

The driver crossed himself.

He gave the guy a fifty-dollar tip.

Les was in a giving vein. He handed the nearest Grosvenor Yamaha salesman his credit card and told him he wanted a bike like the one on the roof—smaller, of course. An hour later, the salesman—a guy in his mid-twenties wearing a white shirt with rolled-up sleeves and jeans and reeking of cigarette smoke—was giving him lessons in the parking lot.

"You ever drive one of these bad boys before?" the young man asked.

"I'll figure it out."

"Hang on a second. Do me a favor and don't touch anything 'til I get back."

The salesman went back into his manager's office and got the thumbs-up on Les's plastic. "All clear and fully debited," the manager said. "Goes to show, you can't tell just by looks."

"I think he's stoned."

"Not our problem now. The geetz is in our account."

It turned out to be academic anyhow. When the young man returned to the lot, both his customer and the bike were gone. The only sign of them was a low rumble fading into destiny.

The Coast Guard got the garbled, frantic call for help at 2113 hours. The operator kept repeating, "Say again, say again? Over, over," into his mike. The staticky screams made his flesh tighten and the back of his neck tingle. He bolted up and ran to his supervisor.

"Got a bearing?" asked Warrant Officer Karen Webster.

He handed her a slip of paper. "As far as I could make out, ma'am."

"No coherent message?" she asked incredulously.

"Nothing. Nothing. I don't get it."

"Let's get a couple of units over there." She studied his scribbles. "Notify Bahamas, too. They might have a closer vessel."

"I'm on it."

Within minutes, two Coast Guard speedsters—a sixty-two-foot patrol boat and a forty-seven-foot motor rescue-boat—were thumping toward *Sterling Star's* blood-curdling cries.

While handing over the sheaf of cash—well, half of it—the home girls told Reggie G. about their experience in the Iranian's hotel room.

"There's more where this came from," he declared, with one hand slapping the bankroll on his knee and with the other dangling a jockstrap in front of his pit bull, Reverend Al. "I can smell that muthafucka's green."

They sat around a coffee table in Reggie's apartment on West 82nd Street, a trendy neighborhood a half-block from Central Park. On the table sat a Glock 9mm semi-automatic pistol, Smith & Wesson chrome-plated .357 magnum revolver, crack pipe, two lines of coke, razor blade, candy dish filled with Raisinets, pot of Tazo tea, Taser pistol, and a plate of Italian-lace anisette cookies.

"The guy's off his rocker," said Felice, helping herself to

a fistful of candy. She told Reggie about the matzo balls in the bar fridge.

"Rocker, my black ass," he said. "I'm headed back."

"Be careful, baby," Bev warned. "He's screwy."

"Mind your own business. This ain't a board meeting. You don't get no vote. Now get out there and make some coin. These co-op association fees are killing me."

He lobbed the jockstrap into the kitchen and, while Reverend Al was tearing it to pieces, Reggie slid out the front door. He hailed a cab, regaled the driver with his theory of mutual fund sector investing, gave him a ten-buck tip, and strutted into the Manhattan on Green on the south end of the park.

Without faltering he went for the elevator, as if he had lived in the hotel his whole life. No one bothered him. Upstairs, he went up to the Iranian's door and knocked. No answer. No one home. In a way it was too bad. He sort of felt like slapping the shit out of the little camel-jockey motherfucker.

He glanced up and down the corridor, slipped his five-piece lock-picking set from his pocket, and plucked out the torsion wrench, medium-hook tool, and snake rake pick. He inserted all three picks into the lock at the same time, and with a speedy but smooth series of finger parries, wrist bobs and weaves, and thumb feints and counter-punches, he had the door open in less than a minute.

So, while Akhmed was out searching for his former cellmate and kaluki partner, Reggie was looting his hotel room. Unfortunately all he found was weird-ass-looking money with some bearded dude and squiggly shit on it. It was the color of Monopoly money, so probably it wasn't worth the price of toilet paper, but he took it anyhow. For the real deal, he checked under the mattress, in and behind the dresser drawers, deep inside the nightstand, closet, toiletry bag, suitcase, hanging clothes. He found no more U.S. money, and all that foraging had made him hungry. In the bar fridge he found the minicooler Felice had described. He peeled open the food storage container, smelled the matzo-ball soup, and decided to have himself a gobble.

The door opened. The maid stepped in and stopped, uneasy. "You not belong here," she said in a thick Middle-Eastern accent. "I call manager."

"Chill out, mom," Reggie cooed, tugging her inside and closing the door behind them. She put up a little resistance, until he yanked out the Iranian's sheaf of bills from his pants and waved it in front of her. "I'm on my way out," he said, flashing a golden smile. He fingered two notes from the sheaf, snapped them in front of her nose, making her eyes cross, and, dexterously folding them into kissing origami swans, tucked them into her breast pocket.

"Your secret is safe with Reggie G.," he said, heading for the door. Then he had an afterthought. He looked back and ran his gaze over her, head to toe. He reached into his pants again, slipped out one of his business cards, and tucked that into her pocket, too, behind the swans. "You got possibilities, sistah. I can do something with that disaster you call personal grooming. That's irony for you. You make up all these rooms, and you yourself is a holy damn mess. Don't fret, Reggie G. know potential when he see it. If you ever want to make some real gelt, give me a tinkle. Bleat, buzz, honk, or holler, any time of night or day, Reggie G's a step away. Okay, got to run, momma. Crack don't smoke itself."

And like a gust he was gone, leaving the maid look-ing in the mirror at the kissing swans poking out of her pocket. There was no point taking out his business card; she couldn't read English anyhow. She had come to America less than a year before, an Iraqi refugee, just she and her nine-year-old son, Simtar—her husband, Simtar's beloved father, having been beheaded by a band of Iranian Shiite mercenaries.

She knew very well whose room this was, and if she hadn't so desperately needed this job for Simtar, she would have sliced the Iranian president's throat while he slept. But Simtar did need her. Who else did that good little boy have? Wasn't it hard enough for him to be in this strange land, the other children tormenting him for being differ-ent and blaming him for America's involvement in the war? Poor, sweet Simtar, watching the other children eat their candy and play with their toys while he, himself, had nothing—barely enough money to eat a decent supper with his mother.

She plucked the paper swans from her pocket. Gentle birds, like Simtar. No, she would not notify the manager about the interloper. She would not call hotel security. She was happy the Iranian had been robbed. Her only regret was that he had not been murdered.

Reggie had left the opened food storage container on the dresser, its ungobbled matzo balls bobbing. The maid peered inside and thought of poor Simtar eating leftovers night after night. Watered down soups, skimpy-meated bones, tasteless stews, pasty sandwich spreads, tissue-thin cheese slices, and a few leached vegetables. She decided then and there to use Reggie's tip to buy her son a toy.

A surprise present—a game, perhaps, which for a few minutes might help him forget his unhappiness, forget his father.

This soup she would heat up for dinner that very night. It smelled wonderful—rich and flavorful and nutritious. So she replaced its lid and spirited the Tupperware container to her cart, burying it in a bin of toilet-tissue rolls.

Tonight Simtar would eat like a prince.

Fourteen

FORMER OCCASIONAL-DIVE-AND-FISHING-BOAT CAPTAIN (until the trouble with that slightly seasick babe who chose to stay aboard *Key Stroke* while her boyfriend went skin diving—what the fuck did she think "Stroke" meant in *Key Stroke*, anyhow, and why can't we all just get along, you know, without all this sexual oversensitivity?), now known in a certain nefarious international circle as "the Skipper," stowed all his belongings—including Fenwich's moth-eaten knapsack with the Semtex plastic explosives and satellite receiver that would detonate the Iranian's radioactive matzo balls—onto his mini-trawler. He took a spare can of gasoline back to the shack where he had been holed up for far too long, doused the siding, lit himself a Marlboro, and flicked the match onto the tinder. *Whoosh!* He had no idea how long it had taken to build this rickety piece of shit, but he took quiet satisfaction in knowing it had probably been a lot longer than the time it just took to unbuild it. When he was halfway back to the dock, he turned to see nothing but a few charred timbers, a dying lick of flame, somersaulting cinders, and a final billow of smoke where there had recently stood his landlord's idea of an abode.

"Fuck you," he growled, as he dropped aboard, started the engine, untied, and headed north. "Fuck everyone."

The remainder of the mission seemed straightforward enough—though certainly dangerous, worth every cent of the five million he was to receive. Sneaking the Semtex in by boat was the ticket, all right, but with the country's post-9/11, beefed-up security—bomb-sniffing dogs, handheld explosive detectors, computerized profiling—far from a slam-dunk.

With any luck, though, at least his part of Castaways' Revenge would unfold according to plan. He would tie up, haul the knapsack through cursory visual inspection, meet Little Buddy and his nuclear matzo balls at the rendezvous point, return to the pier with the matzo-balled knapsack, deftly exchange it with the matching one Fenwich would be standing next to on the dock, and head back out to sea with the empty sack. Assuming, of course, Fenwich didn't fuck things up—a big if.

The Skipper couldn't help but think ahead to his future as a multimillionaire. He wondered how much space all that cash would take up in his Caymans safe-deposit box. He wondered in what denominations it would be and if the bills would be new and crisp or old and crummy. He would rather not have crummy bills. He considered what he would do when he had his mitts on the money, how he would spend the remainder of his days on earth. He ran the idea across his brain like a meaty McRib. Which, in turn, reminded him that he was hungry. For the time being he had to content himself with crapola. He un-wrapped a family-size Three Musketeers, tossed the wrap-per overboard, stuffed the bar into his cheek, and resumed contemplating the rest of his wealthy life.

He had been to St. Martin once and decided it would be a good place to retire. On a small island eventually peo-ple had to listen to you; no matter how fast they ran away, sooner or later they wound up back in the same place. On the Dutch side there was a beach bar, Shorty's, with a resi-dent Amazon Green Parrot who, he was quite sure, would listen enraptured as he explained why the real casualties of 9/11 weren't those three thousand complicit World Trade Center capitalist fascists but the many tribes of Native Americans, the victims of white-European genocide—al-though, speaking of Native Americans, he did enjoy a bit of casino craps and blackjack now and then, which, coin-cidentally, the Dutch side of the island happened to offer.

For sure, the thought of whiling away days sipping Johnny Walker Gold, reading on *Key Stroke*'s deck by day, beach-bar hopping by night, and kibitzing with horny Dutch waitresses held a certain appeal. Terrace barbecues; driftwood-fired, broiled lobsters; snorkeling; maybe a little windsurfing. While those Coors-sipping yuppies would be filthying up some other sucker's boat with their fuck-ing aluminum cans and Doritos, he would be lounging in the tropical sunlight, feet propped on gunwale, blowing boogers into the bay, trying to decide at which beachside restaurant he was going to have dinner, what brand of cigar he would smoke afterward, and with which vaca-tioning coed he would wet his dinghy until he got sick of looking at her and kicked her slutty ass off his boat.

Yes, five million sounded fine and dandy. A nice round sum.

And so as he began puttering his way up the Keys, with supreme delight he imagined a life avenging the injustice dealt to him by the judicial system. Why did women get to define sexual harassment anyhow? If a guy happens to put his hands on a woman's bottom, it's not abuse, it's communication. Can't we just be friendly?

The thought of it fried his own butt. To take the edge off, he unstowed a bottle of Chivas Regal and a cooler of ice, and in a plastic cup poured himself a three-finger edge-offer. He opened a bag of potato chips and nibbled one, imagining it a spring-break coed's nipple. He turned on the dashboard radio and found an oldies station.

It took him three Chivas top-offs and a half-bag of chips before the edge began to soften, and he started counting the flying fish gamboling alongside *Key Stroke*.

The Iranian president returned to the Manhattan on Green worn out, bedraggled, and dejected. Artie had disappeared into the night with some Zionist interloper. What a lousy trip this had turned out to be. So much promise when it had started out—speaking at the UN, smuggling in nuclear matzo balls, learning how to play kaluki—only to have it plunge into an abyss of beatings, muggings, insults, and heartbreak. What more could go wrong?

He was asking himself that very question when he opened his hotel room door and saw that he had been ransacked, violated, penetrated, molested, marauded, plundered, pillaged, robbed, and burgled. His dresser drawers were strewn across the room, helter-skelter, higgledy-piggledy, up-and-down, inside-out, hill and dale, here and there, to and fro. The villains had thrown Akhmed's underwear, as casually as if tossing lopped heads, into every corner, crevice, nook, and cranny. Underpants hung from the lampshade, mirror, curtain rod. Against a wall his suitcase leaned, its contents cascading across the floor and under the bed. The wretches had dumped his toiletry articles into the sink and bathtub and toilet bowl, spilling out his Old Spice, stomping on his toothpaste, smushing his deodorant stick upside down on the counter. They had not unturned any stone. Oh, these thieving American Zionist-loving devils! First Artie, now this! What more could they want from a poor, trodden-upon Muslim soul!

Then he remembered his matzo balls.

The Cuban president was sitting in his bedroom of his Vedado home, watching *Gilligan's Island* reruns and listening to a bowl of Rice Krispies, wondering how Operation Castaways' Revenge was going and feeling a bit miffed that everyone else got to go to Miami except him. How come? How come El *Max*imo had to stay in Cuba when everyone else was going to see the wrack and ruin first-hand? Hadn't they made all their plans right here in Havana? Hadn't he been a good host? Hadn't he provided a loyal assassin to kill Little Buddy's translator? Hadn't he been the one to think of all the code names? So what was the gripe?

He had a scummy hunch his brother—whom he named El *Mini*mo—was behind his grounding. God, how he hated that little rat! His *younger* brother telling him what to do—like Michael Corleone bossing around Fredo! Okay, fine, so the stink-pants had been part of the glorious revolution. So he had gotten *slightly* wounded. That was over fifty years ago. Get over yourself! The *older* brother was the one who went to prison, not the spoiled-little-brat brother. Wounding is easier than prison anytime. Let's see how well *he* would do in jail. That crybaby wouldn't last twenty-four hours before he'd be begging for his *madre*. Head of the defense forces—what a laugh! *What* defense forces? Defense against *who*…the mighty St. Barts navy? Forget that baloney about bulwarking the revolution against the United States. What a crock of doo-doo. If the U.S. wanted to take over Cuba, all they'd have to do is lift that embargo and start opening up White Castles and Dairy Queens. After getting a taste of sliders and chocolate dips, the masses would flush out communism like used poopy paper (not that there was any around here). Marx and Lenin wouldn't stand a hen's chance in hell against onion rings and Dilly Bars.

Oh, Lovey knew about American culture, all right. Didn't he have experts from his electronic surveillance military unit arrange satellite pickup of Nick at Nite? Didn't he have covert operatives smuggle in American toys and games: G.I. Joe, Nintendo, Candyland, Pit? He looked around his room. Wasn't his house stuffed to its chops with TV-offer specials, in anticipation that the American economy would soon plunge into chaos: Seal-a-Meal, Veg-O-Matic, George Foreman Grill, Ronco Turkey Rotissserie ("Set it and forget it!"), Oreck Air Cleaner ("You can't clean air if you don't move it!"), Popeil Pocket Fisherman, Inside-the-Egg Scrambler, Dial-O-Matic Food Slicer?

He rubbed his hands gleefully, then stopped and groaned. He looked around again. Had he stocked up on enough Kraft Macaroni and Cheese and Pic-Nik Shoestring Potatoes and Tootsie Rolls? Twizzlers cherry licorice sticks and Good and Plentys and Famous Amoses and Tombstone frozen pizzas? O-Ke-Doke popcorn and Good Humor bars and Mrs. Gorton's fish sticks? Who knew how long it would take American factories to get up and running again. What if he ran out of all this great nutrition first?

But he comforted himself knowing that even if Castaways' Revenge was totally successful, and U.S. industry came to a screeching halt, as it did after 9/11, it would recover soon enough. You simply couldn't stop that train, no *señoree*-Bob. Those Castaway *pendejos* actually believed they could destroy American capitalism with a few lousy radioactive dumplings. What knuckleheads.

Speaking of high-grade retards, his sneaky *younger* brother knocked on the door. "It's me."

"And it's me."

"Can I come in?"

The president flicked off *Gilligan* and turned to the state propaganda station. "No."

"Why not? Let me in."

"Because I'm beating off, that's why."

"Cut it out. I'm coming in." The door opened.

"So much for my presidential authority. Who told you you could remove the lock, anyhow? Just because I had a bowel operation doesn't mean I shouldn't have a lock."

"I told you, it wasn't me. It was the unanimous decision of the Central Committee."

"Here's your Central Committee!" He stuck his tongue out.

"It's for your own safety."

"I think history has proven I can take care of myself."

"It's not only about you, dear brother. You belong to the state now, to posterity."

"Sometimes I just want to be a normal codger, you know? Play putt-putt golf and rubber-ducky in the bath-tub and stuff."

"We have no golf in Cuba, you know that—putt-putt or otherwise."

"Then let's get it! It doesn't cost a lot. Eight holes to start, and we can add the other seven later. We could get the president of Iran to design it for next to nothing. I'm telling you, this place is borrr-ing. I'll bet putt-putt golf would be a big hit."

"It wouldn't look good."

"Okay, how about go-karts? Or a haunted house? You're telling me a haunted house wouldn't go over? We could disguise it as a political prison. Who would know? We could have Freddy Krueger and Jason and Chucky and Barbra Streisand and—"

"Stop it."

The president stomped his foot. "I'm bored!"

"You're recuperating."

"I swear to God…or whatever…I feel fine."

El Minimo handed the president some papers. "Sign these. That should take your mind off yourself."

"Don't use that tone with me. I used to diaper you."

"And now I diaper you."

"That's the tone I'm talking about!"

"Would you just please sign? We've got a trade deal going with China."

The president crossed his arms. "I'm not signing a thing."

"You have to."

"Try to make me."

His brother sighed. "Okay, what do you want?"

"First, you have to apologize for talking to me like that."

"Fine, I'm sorry."

"Sorry about what?"

"I'm sorry I struck that tone with you."

"Why?"

"Because you're my older brother."

"And?"

"And I'm your younger brother. Satisfied?"

"Maybe."

"What else?"

The president pouted. "I'm thinking."

"China is waiting."

The president tugged his upper lip and released it with a slapping sound that he evidently enjoyed, because he kept doing it.

"Will you please stop playing with your face and tell me what else?"

"Let's play soldiers!" He cast a glance at the floor on the other side of the room, where he had set up, in exact detail, an entire miniature set of the Moncada Barracks compound and surrounding terrain.

"We played soldiers yesterday."

"But you were the revolutionaries and I was Batista. You always make me be Batista. Today I want to be the revolutionaries."

"Because you always screw it up. If we did it your way, the revolutionaries would get slaughtered and, ergo, there would never be revolution. Hellooo?"

"But Batista always gets slaughtered," El Maximo protested. "I'm tired of getting slaughtered. How come you don't get slaughtered once in a while?"

"Because it's not who's Batista or not Batista. It's which general's strategy winds up being the best. You could be Attila the Hun and you'd still get slaughtered. You're a military idiot."

"Let me be the revolutionaries this time. If I get slaughtered, okay. I've been thinking about strategy like crazy." He looked around testily. "It's not exactly like I have anything else to do."

El Minimo hesitated. "If I let you be the revolutionaries, will you sign the papers?"

"Fair enough."

"And if you get slaughtered, will you agree to be Batista for the rest of your life...in the name of historical accuracy?"

"Deal."

The president hung a sheet on an overhead wire so they couldn't see each other, and for several minutes, sitting cross-legged on the floor, they positioned their toy soldiers, armored vehicles, and artillery, in tactical anticipation of their adversary's strategy. El Maximo was nervous, but he was confident that this time he would be the slaughterer, not the slaughteree. He held his breath, arched his eyebrows, pumped his fists, and, finally, pulled down the sheet.

They both assessed the other's positions. The younger brother sniggered with satisfaction, but El Max didn't like what he saw.

"What the heck is this?" he whined.

"Batista waiting for you, you military idiot."

"But Batista doesn't know we're coming. We're going to surprise him. The success of our attack depends on complete surprise."

"Here's what happened," El Min explained. He tapped a soldier's helmet. "See this guy, here?"

"What about him?" the president sniped.

"Well, he was reading the newspaper over last night's dinner, and he saw an article saying that one of the revolutionaries defected and told Batista's security forces of your plans to attack the barracks at daybreak. So he showed the article to his commanding officer"—he tapped another soldier—"and the commanding officer thought we'd better be ready for you. So, you see, you've wandered into our trap. You don't stand a chance. May as well give up now and save your men."

It took the Cuban president only a minute to see that his brother, the little worm, was brutally right. The revolutionaries had crept down from the mountains overnight, expecting Batista's soldiers to be sleeping or using the latrines or, at worst, still shaking drowsiness from their heads. El Maximo's offensive was, indeed, supposed to be sudden and unexpected. His men were going to surround, wedge, divide, and overwhelm. With the mountain behind them, there could be no retreat. But now he recognized, with horror, that Batista's troops had flanked them on a forty-five-degree angle. The revolutionaries were cannon fodder. Dead meat.

The president began to cry.

"Told you," his brother said.

"You crummy bastard."

"A deal's a deal. Sign the papers."

"Something doesn't sound right. Why would he defect?"

"He got tired of hearing your five-hour speeches."

"He could have mentioned it."

"You'd have shot him."

"Could I shoot him now?"

"Tell you what. Sign the damn papers, and you can extradite him back to your camp."

"A prisoner exchange?"

"There you go."

"That's good, that's good," El Max exclaimed, pounding fist into palm. "I've negotiated a prisoner exchange. So I'm a military idiot but a good negotiator."

"A negotiating genius."

"Hand me a pen!"

This wasn't funny anymore. It was bad enough everyone involved in Castaways' Revenge thought the Iranian president was short. It was humiliating enough that his numskull scientists couldn't figure out how to make a simple, garden-variety atomic bomb. Not hydrogen. Not neutron. Atomic, atomic, atomic. He wasn't asking for anything that a few Jewboys hadn't invented in a New Mexico desert, what, *sixty-five* years ago? *Sixty-five!* He wasn't asking for something to blow up the entire Western Hemisphere. Not even to blow up the eastern half of the United States. What had he asked for, really? No more havoc than on Hiroshima or Nagasaki—what was the big deal? One crummy atomic bomb to obliterate a neighborhood or two in one lousy, profligate, American city. A few decadent high-rise condominiums, that's all. It's not exactly like they were an endangered species. In the scheme of things, he'd probably be doing Miami a favor.

Okay, fine, so his imbeciles couldn't pull it off. So, instead, they discover radioactive matzo balls. What a joke. No one would have burgled a three-ton *real* atomic bomb from his hotel room, that's for sure. He figured he must have been a child molester in a previous life. Or maybe a financial advisor. Life was shit. It was a bad system. Because seventeen hundred years ago he had recommended his clients buy real estate at the foot of Mt. Vesuvius, today he no longer had his stupid nuclear Jew food to try to impress the world. *Blecch.*

What were Thurston and Lovey—not to mention the Skipper and the Professor—going to think of him now? Here's what they were going to think: that ancient Persia got to be the leading trade, cultural, and merchant center of the world by accident. That Iranians were nincompoops. That their president was *short.* Everyone suspected that short people had small brains, and now they had proof. If this Iranian mental midget couldn't even hang onto a few deadly matzo balls, how in the hell did they ever rule the world, or hope to rule it again? It never occurred to the fig-sucking fool to lock his great discovery up in, say, the frigging hotel safe? Or maybe a frigging bus-station locker, at least while he was out searching for his kaluki partner? Apparently not.

All along they were probably taking bets that it would be him, the short Iranian, who would screw up the mission. They probably got Las Vegas oddsmakers into the act. He could picture a looming tote board in the sports book of Caesars Palace:

NEW YORK KNICKS VS. CLEVELAND CAVALIERS: 6–5

UCLA BRUINS OVER NORTHWESTERN WILDCATS: + 3
POINTS

GREENBAY PACKERS OVER INDIANAPOLIS COLTS: + 6
POINTS

IRANIAN DWARF FUCKS UP MISSION TO DESTROY
AMERICA: ALL IN

And who could blame them? He *was* a little screw-up. He was. Even those bad women, Reggie's bitches, knew he was a joke. Hadn't they laughed at him when his towel dropped? Weren't they laughing at his packing peanut right now?

That was the worst part of it. Short men had teeny penises. Oh, sure, society was willing to overlook that detail as long as the short men in question had big brains and/ or nuclear weapons. Einstein, a short Jew, probably had a small Semitic penis, made even smaller by that barbaric Zionist practice of circumcision, but no one ever mentions the size of his weenie, do they? You could read every biography ever written about Albert Einstein, and you'd never find a single word, not so much as a passing reference, about his penis size. Did they happen to mention it when they awarded him the Nobel Prize? Nope. Did it appear on his curriculum vitae with his application to Princeton University? Highly doubtful. When they wanted to name a street after him in New Jersey, why did they pick a boulevard? For Akhmed, they would have found an unpaved alley!

So, sure, if you were super smart, you got a pass regarding your penis. But if you happened to have had the misfortune of being born short (of course, all newborns are short, and they all have small penises, but Akhmed was thinking futuristically) and not a genius—for example, screwing up the mission to destroy America—no one on the face of the earth was going to overlook your minuscule maleness. Not Reggie's hoes, certainly.

If it had been up to Akhmed—if he, not infidel Christians, ran the world—all tall people with long penises would be sent to "rehabilitation" camps in a horrible place with hellish winters, such as Milwaukee, Wisconsin, where they would have to work outside all day, naked, looking at one another's crotches and contemplating their freakishness. At night they would be forced to eat swill with forks, from buckets tied around their waists, so their long penises would get in the way, and they'd always be trying to shove them aside to get their utensils into play, and they'd wind up exhausted and hungry, and their male organs, that, while the infidels had run things, had served them so well, now would be poked bloody with fork holes.

So, no, Akhmed wasn't about to voluntarily admit to his cohorts that he had fouled up. He wasn't going to report this break-in to hotel management, the police, or the United Nations. Instead he was going to do the manly thing. He was going to handle the problem himself. What he was going to do was, he was going to buy regular non-nuclear matzo balls, substitute them for the deadly ones, and get back to Iran before the assholes figured it out.

With a heavy heart, he tidied up his hotel room—he wouldn't be able to function knowing it was still messy—then headed down to the concierge, who diagrammed directions to the nearest true Zionist deli, not that dopey Hindu one on the David Letterman show. With his diagram hanging from his belt, he hoofed it south and, at Broadway and 43rd, ducked into Larry's Delicatessen, where he took a number and mulled around the glass case astonished at the sundry ways a culture can destroy itself with animal fat. For a supposedly brilliant people, the Jews certainly were clueless as to why they seldom lived beyond fifty (all Hitler had to do was wait it out), though here the answer lay, steaming under an oily sneeze guard. Salami, blintzes, potato latkes, fatty corned beef, brisket, fried matzo, hot dogs, halvah, chocolate-covered mandel bread, knishes, pastrami, kishkes, sour cream, schmaltz, cream cheese, and other assorted hideous-looking greasy crap that, Akhmed also had to admit, tasted divine and was, in fact, his favorite cuisine, life-expectancy be damned.

"Thirty-eight!" the young woman called from behind the counter. His number.

"Two large orders of matzo ball—" He stopped. He stared at the woman. She stared back. Their gazes locked. Was it possible? No, it couldn't be.

"Mr. President?"

"Samreen?"

"Mr. President?"

It was! It was Samreen, Hazeem's niece! "Samreen! It's really you!"

Her gaze fell. She was embarrassed to be seen like this by her leader.

"Come, girl, come around and let me look at you! Come see your 'Uncle' Akhmed!"

Never taking her eyes off the floor, she removed her apron and shuffled around to the front of the counter. He took her by her elbows, almost as if he wanted to hug her, a friendly face at last, but stopped himself. Something occurred to him. His gaze wrapped around her, pythonlike. Under its tightening grip, she finally looked up, girded herself, and stared directly into his serpentine glare.

"What has become of you?" he demanded. "Where's your burqa? Where's your modesty, girl? Why aren't you covered from head to foot in proper, gray, heavyweight, thousand-thread-count polyester? Why do you look like a modern American woman? Why do you have makeup on your face? Have you gone mad? Have they tortured you into corruption and profligacy? What the devil are you doing working in a Zionist restaurant"—again, he ran his rebuking gaze over her—"wearing blue jeans and a…a T-shirt that says I'M WITH STUPID?!"

"I am different now, Mr. President. This is America. Here I have the same rights as any man—maybe even more."

"Don't tell me where I am. You think I don't know where I am, you impudent whelp?" His tone had changed. He was no longer glad to see her. He had a small weenie, true, but he wasn't born yesterday. He saw what was going on with this young woman whose college education had been provided for through the largess of the Iranian government.

"What the devil is going on?" he repeated. "What are you up to? How dare you sully the image of repressed womanhood. I am ashamed of you. Your uncle Hazeem would be ashamed of you. You'd better have a good explanation."

Her spine stiffened. "I no longer need to explain myself," she replied insolently. "I have my own job now. I make my own money. I will pay my own tuition, and I will repay Iran for its previous investment, with interest, if you insist."

He jumped around. "Previous investment! Interest! You talk like a damn Jew!"

"I'm proud to talk like a Jew. My boyfriend is a Jew! Stevie!"

Akhmed hopped and pivoted, rotated, spun like a dervish. "Stevie?! Stevie?! We'll have you stoned to death, right here on Broadway! You'll never escape our agents!"

"Better to die free."

He bore down, as if trying to take a constipated poop, gritted his teeth, scrunched his face, turned as red as lox. His neck veins swelled and throbbed.

"I'll kill Stevie, too!"

The big finger on her T-shirt that said I'M WITH STUPID was pointing directly at him. "No you won't. He's *taller* than you!"

"We'll kill your Uncle Hazeem, then!"

Her demeanor changed. Her backbone turned gelatinous. The resolve on her face melted. "Uncle Hazeem?" she said, the defiance in her voice drained away. "You've seen Uncle Hazeem?"

"Of course I've seen him. He's my translator, for heaven's sake. What do you think?"

"Lately? You've seen him lately?" she asked, desperation in her voice. "He's here, in New York? Now?"

He shook his head. "Back in Tehran. It's a good thing, too, so he wouldn't have to witness his niece's betrayal. It would break his heart. Shame on you. Shame."

"But when did you talk to him last?"

Akhmed instantly saw the potential of this little subterfuge and was determined to play it to the hilt. "Yesterday, of course. I speak to the man every day. He's my best friend, when it comes to that. Don't get me wrong, though. I'll be happy to have him slain if you don't return with me to Iran immediately."

The owner of the deli, Larry, came out from the back, spotted his employee agitated, and strode over to see what was going on. "You okay, Sam?"

"Sam? Sam? Her name is Samreen, you fat pig. Samreen—a good Iranian name."

"He giving you a hard time, Sam? You want me to choke him for you?"

She handed Larry her bundled apron. "I'll be right back, I promise. Watch the counter for just a minute. I'll be right outside."

"Stay where I can see you, okay?" He minced her visitor a glare. "Don't try any funny business."

"Cram it, you Hebrew cow."

"That's it, I'm going to choke him."

But Samreen stepped between them. "Come outside, Mr. President, where we can speak in private."

"That's more like it."

Outside, with Larry's stare bearing down on Akhmed from behind the counter, Samreen said, "I haven't heard from Uncle Hazeem in weeks. I've tried to contact him many times, but he hasn't answered me once. It's not like him. He's never done this before."

The president shrugged. "It's nothing, I assure you."

"Nothing?" she said, piteously. "But it can't be nothing. You know something. I beg you, tell me."

He looked around and lowered his voice. "He's on a confidential government assignment. Top secret. Completely incognito. Persona non grata."

"Secret assignment? You mean like a spy?"

"I can say no more, not even to you, his beloved niece, for whom he would gladly die."

"But is it a dangerous assignment? Will he be all right? When will I hear from him again?"

He sighed. "Frankly, based on your recent attitude, I'm not prepared to say whether it's a dangerous assignment or not, if you get my drift. I mean, really, Samreen, you don't show up your national leader in front of a deli owner. I mean, really."

"All right, Mr. President. I apologize. You're right, and I was wrong."

"That's better, though far from where you need to be."

"You're always right."

"And?"

"And I'm always wrong."

"Now you're talking."

"If you don't reassure me about Uncle Hazeem, I'll go mad. I've been heartsick worrying about him."

"Stevie has provided scant comfort in your time of need?"

"Please, please. All right, if you want me to return with you to Tehran. If you want me to renounce my temporary insanity—"

"I appreciate it, Samreen, I do. But you know I didn't mean all that. You know I have a bit of a temper, but at heart I'm an old softy. The truth is, today is your lucky day. Fortunately I bumped into you before our agents got to you first." He pantomimed slitting her throat. "Vile, crass thugs with no conscience. Good for you, though, that I adore you."

"What do you want me to do?"

"Nothing much, I promise. No danger whatsoever. You know those two orders of matzo ball soup I started to place?"

"Number thirty-eight."

"What I would merely like you to do is personally deliver them for me."

She waited, but he added nothing.

"That's it? Just make a delivery?"

He snapped his fingers. "That's it. See, that wasn't so bad, was it? Make a simple delivery, after which I promise to use all my influence with those infernal mullahs to get you to talk to your Uncle Hazeem. What do you say?"

"I'll do it, of course. I'll do anything to know he's safe. Come back inside, and I'll finish the order." She opened the door for him. "To where do you want it delivered? I know New York very well by now."

He took the door from her, gestured for her to go first, and followed her inside. "That's splendid, but how familiar are you with Miami Beach?"

Fifteen

"She wants to invite *WHO* to the wedding?!" Marybethlehem Culvertdale frothed, her face the color and density of a fireplug.

"She's mad," agreed Eddward, peremptorily. "Completely, irreversibly deranged. It's not my fault."

She bared her fangs and growled.

"It isn't my fault, sweet one," he mewled. "So help me. How the deuce was I supposed to know they'd show up at my office at the same time?"

"If you don't come clean immediately," she warned between clenched teeth, "I'm calling in my stock options."

Backed against their grand piano in the music room of their Key Biscayne home, Eddward, seeing that he had hoisted himself by his own petard, confessed all—repeatedly assuring the Mrs. that he was entirely the victim of fate. Not his fault, not his fault, not his fault.

"She's trying to punish us for the prenup," he averred. "Revenge, plain and simple."

She circled the piano like a fighting cock. "It will be a scandal the likes of which our church has never seen."

He swiveled as she circled, wanting to be ready if she lunged. "Church? What about the corporation? We'll never be able to spend enough money on damage control to save us. We'll be ruined."

"She won't get away with it. We'll call off the wedding."

"The announcements have already appeared in all the papers."

"We'll say Angus died."

"But he's alive."

"Then we'll kill him."

"She'll tell the real reason. Our stock price will plummet. I'm on the board of the American Enterprise League. My CEO reputation will be destroyed."

"And, what? I'm not a Daughter of the American Revolution? A DAR in good standing?"

"My point exactly. We have to protect our acronyms."

"My great, great, great, great grandfather was Caleb Worthington, printer of the Declaration of Independence!"

"I've never doubted it, pumpky."

She leaned over at him, her eyes pulsating, molars clacking. She shook her fist at his nose. "*Think of something!*"

"I'm thinking, I'm thinking."

"Think *faster.*"

"I can't concentrate when I believe you're going to hurt me."

She began pacing again. "First the little Hebrew witch wouldn't let us bring a stitch of pork on board—there went the shaved prosciutto hors d'oeuvres—then she insisted on a 'lay' minister, whatever that is—probably a minister who laid her—then she prohibited the phrase 'Our Lord' from the invitations, then she said no New Testaments, then she said they're going to name their first baby Abe—"

"I'm pretty sure she made that one up just to irritate us—"

"Shut up! This is all your fault!"

"I swear, cuddlekins, I had no way of knowing—"

"I'm not going to have a grandchild named Abe!"

"I'm sure she meant only if it's a boy."

She snarled, "You'd think it was *her* money. She doesn't have two nickels of her own to rub together. Has she ever even had a *job*? If she didn't have that doormat of a mother—" She stopped both talking and pacing.

"What, precious?"

"Don't 'precious' me, you twit. Shut your yap for a minute. I'm thinking for both of us."

"I'm shut—"

She hissed.

He ran his finger across his lips. "Mm-mm, mm-mm."

"Yes, that's it…the *mother*." Her eyes flashed diabolically. She rubbed her hands together, and one corner of her mouth hooked upward. "Why didn't I think of this before?"

She sat on the piano bench, flipped open the keyboard cover, and began tinking out her scheme. "Yes, yes. The *mother*. Something terrible might happen to the dear"… *tink*…"something possibly perpetrated by her daughter's new best friend"…*tink tink*…"something that, once new-best-friend apparent perpetrator is arrested"…*tink*… "would then just happen to prevent him from"…*tink tink*…"being able to attend the wedding"…*tink tink tink*.

"Oh, no," said Eddward. "You mean…. You don't mean—"

"I do indeed," she confirmed. "The daughter's new-best-friend apparent perpetrator being none other than the Frito Bandito himself…El Señor Presidente Fatso." Her face was in full smile now, long and sharp, as she began to play and sing "Mack the Knife."

She stopped playing, looked up at her admiration-overflowing husband, and, with the placidity of an executioner ordering lunch, asked if he happened to know where they might find an unknown actor, aspiring or otherwise, at the last minute. "Price, naturally, being no object," she added, tickling the piano keys with gusto.

Oh, that shark, babe. So many teeth, dear.

"You're not going to do *what*?" Karma asked, one eyebrow arched.

Diane sat with a cup of tea on her lap in her daughter's suite aboard the docked *Countess of the Sea*. "There's no point in getting all upset," she said. She took a quick breath, steeled herself, and added, "My mind is made up, and that's that." Much of the tea had already spilled into the saucer.

Her jaw set pantherlike, Karma stalked. "Don't do this to me, mother," she snorted, crouching. "I'm fighting everyone else, don't make me fight you too. Even I can endure only so much."

"It's not a flippant decision. I've had to think long and hard about it—including the inconvenience it might cause you at the last minute."

"Inconvenience? *Inconvenience?*"

"I can't go into detail…that wouldn't be fair. Maybe someday. You have to trust the fact that I have my good reasons."

"Trust? You want me to trust you, now that you want to fuck everything up?"

"The fact is, I won't stand next to your father. I'm sorry, I truly am, but I just won't."

"*Won't?*"

"If I did, I'd be a hypocrite. I'd be negating everything I ever stood for. Why do you think I couldn't even stay in the same hotel with him?"

"When the hell did you ever stand for anything?"

"Or thought I stood for," Diane said, to herself more than to her daughter. "It's true, maybe I did forget some things for a while…for a long time, actually…yes, that's true. But lately I've reminded myself who I really am…or used to be, at any rate."

"The only explanation I can think of, Mother, is that you've gone insane. The rehearsal is *tomorrow.* The wedding is *Saturday.*"

"On the contrary. I'm beginning to see things more clearly now than I have in thirty years. I'm a slow learner, I guess."

Though hunched to strike, Karma maintained her composure. She sat across the coffee table and clawed her mother's eyes with her own. "So after thirty years, can't you wait another fucking week?"

Diane forced herself to look into her daughter's half-pleading, half-murderous eyes. She sighed. "This isn't easy for me, either, Karm. In some ways, it's probably a lot harder. The thought of inconven—"

"*Ruining?*"

"—inconveniencing you at the last minute is torturing me. But after the wedding you and Angus will go on to have a happy life, and I'll have to keep looking at myself in the mirror."

Karma's eyelid quivered malevolently. "Yet you don't want to tell me why?"

"The procession won't be *ruined*. It'll be just a last-minute switch. Look, if one of us died, you'd—"

Karma jumped up. "Mother! This is not working! This is intolerable! It's infuriating!"

Diane braced.

But, as if realizing that losing her temper would only make things worse, Karma screeched to a stop, dug her nails into the back of her leather club chair, drew a taut breath, and exhaled slowly. "For God's sake, Diane, what happened?!"

"I don't think it's right to tell you."

She shook her red mane. "Right? *Right?!*"

"I'm sorry, Karm, I really am. It's a matter of principle."

"I just can't put you and principle together in the same sentence."

"There's no sense being sarcastic. I won't change my mind. I'm sorry, I truly am."

Karma's fingernails punctured the leather. Mother and daughter were silent for a moment, while Diane sipped her tea, trying hard not to seem afraid.

"Did he rape you or something?"

"Nothing like that, no. Don't blame Les. Blame me for having been blind. If you have to blame anyone."

Daughter began stalking again. "All right, then, let me get this straight. At the last minute you refuse to stand next to my long-lost father, thereby destroying all my hopes and dreams…"

"Don't you think you're being a bit overdramat—"

She raised her finger. "But you won't exactly tell me why, letting me think that he must be some sort of pervert or something. Is that it? Is my father a sexual predator? Was he on that television show?"

"No, nothing like that…that I know of."

"*What then? What?*"

Diane splatted her cup into the saucer and put them on the table. Wringing her hands, she said, "All right, all right. I'll tell you. I promised myself I wouldn't, but I see I have no choice. I'll have to let the chips fall where they may. If you never want to see him again, my conscience is clear."

Again, Karma positioned herself behind the chair.

Diane cleared her throat. "He…he"—she closed her eyes and drew a mournful breath—"broke my diploma."

Silence.

She opened her eyes. Daughter was waiting for more. "*Deliberately*," mother insisted.

Karma stood in stunned petrifaction.

When daughter didn't speak for a full minute, only stirred the air with her eyelashes, mother added, "I worked darn hard for that degree." Still no response. "I was trying to raise you by myself, hold down two jobs, and still manage to go to night school…not that I'm complaining, don't get me wrong."

Finally, daughter spoke. She started low and slow, like burning cordite. "Don't get you wrong?"

"I was grateful for my blessings," Diane explained. "But the thought of someday earning that diploma kept me going." Her gaze fell. "A lot of times, it was the only thing that kept me going."

Karma sat, elbows on knees, chin on fists. "Mother?"

"Yes?"

"Angus will *buy* that fucking night school, and you can have all the diplomas you want. How's that for a quickie solution?"

"I think you're missing the point. Life isn't always about quickie solutions."

"*You're* lecturing *me* about life?"

Diane looked up, into her daughter's soul.

"Mother, you're going to stand next to my father at my wedding, period. Everything can be worked out."

"With money?"

"Of course with money. Your diploma is a piece of paper, for God's sake. That's all it is."

"Piece of paper?"

"You know what I mean. Stop trying to make this into something else."

"You don't understand. He knew what it meant to me. That's *why* he destroyed it. He wasn't damaging my diploma—he was damaging *me*."

Karma sighed. "I guess I have to fix this, too. As if I don't have enough fires to put out. Where is he now?"

"I haven't the faintest idea, nor do I care."

Leaning way over, slicing atmosphere with her finger, Karma said, "Okay, now you listen to me, my dear. A joke's a joke. So you two had a little lovers' spat. Fine, I'll patch it up. But make no mistake, Mother—you and Les *will* be standing side by side at my wedding. You'll be holding hands and smiling, and you'll take lots of pictures together. This is not open to discussion, negotiation, or the risk of further 'inconveniencing' me. Get it through your head: my wedding is going to be the most perfect wedding ever held anywhere, anytime, by anyone—including Prince William and what's-her-name."

"I thought I knew you once."

"No kumbaya riffs, please, not now. This isn't the sixties, and—I hate to be the one to break it to you—the Beatles are never getting back together."

"Then I realized I only knew my *image* of you, never the real you. And that all those times you volunteered at homeless shelters and raised money for liberal candidates, you were being me, not Karma, and subconsciously hating me for it…"

Karma got up again and turned to the door. "This meeting is over."

"I won't do it, and that's that. I'm sorry to disappoint you, but maybe it's time I did. Maybe it's overdue."

Karma spun around. Her pupils flared. Her lips curled. Her jaw rippled. Her nostrils quivered. Pumping her fists, between clenched fangs she snarled, "Yes, you *will*."

Diane got up. Her legs wriggled. "Your whole life has been a product of my guilty conscience. I see now the damage I've done. But you're not a little girl anymore. At long last you have to stop hating me and realize I did the best I could. I made mistakes, but I did the best I could. That's the truth. That's reality. And the truth and reality are…no, *I will not*."

"You will, even if I have to *chain* you to him." She blocked the door. "I'm *not* kidding."

But Diane nudged her aside. Karma grabbed her hand on the knob. "I'm warning you, Mother."

"Warning?"

"I have resources now you can't imagine in your worst nightmares."

Diane stared at her daughter. "My God," she gasped, "you really are a monster." She yanked open the door, whacking Karma.

"I'm telling you! You don't know who you're dealing with, Mother!"

But Diane was already at the stairway. She had no interest in waiting for an elevator. She had to get away while she still had the courage. The stairwell door closed behind her, muffling Karma's shrieking threats.

As the last faint signals of a Miami radio station sputtered over its cockpit radio, Coast Guard patrol boat *46115*, followed by high-speed rescue boat *47623*, sped toward the last known coordinates of cruise ship *Sterling Star*'s desperate, unnerving pleas for help. In the moon-bright sea, cloud shadows skimmed the swells like sharks. Individual palm tree fronds were clearly visible on outer islands, and a half-rainbow bunted the horizon.

At 0436 hours, the patrol boat spotted a dark, small-craft form in the distance, thudded toward it, and, when it didn't try to get away—drug runners plied this passage like spawning barracuda—approached at a putter, megaphone crackling, sidearms cocked. As the patrol boat came alongside, a million-candlepower searchlight sizzled to life. The name *Sterling Star #14* shimmered on the lifeboat's bow.

There were things inside *#14*—human-size carcasses that didn't look quite human—crumpled in the bottom of the hull. The searchlight followed as grappling hooks dragged the lifeboat within inches, then, when it slipped into the shadow of the patrol boat's starboard gunwale and bumped its hull, and the searchlight's angle was useless, three flashlights flicked on, their beams sweeping *#14*'s strange, lumpy figures.

"Mother of mercy."

"Holy crap."

"What the…*fuck*?"

The flashlight beams held fast, each on a different section of exposed bone and masticated flesh and sinew. The second-in-command, Petty Officer Ludwig, made a move to hop into the lifeboat, but his C.O., Lieutenant Whitehurst, held him back. "Better don't."

"Maybe someone's still alive."

Whitehurst's flashlight swept over the bloody mass. "What's your best guess?"

"What happened? Pirates?"

"This is like no pirate attack I've ever seen. Jesus."

"But what if—"

"I'm making a decision here, Mike. If someone is still alive, I'll take full responsibility. In the meantime, secure a hawser."

"What about the *Star*?"

"I'll have Shriver tow the lifeboat back to Miami, and we'll keep going."

"Sir?"

"What?"

"I think we might need help, sir."

As the sailors tied a hawser to *#14*'s bow cleat, Whitehurst radioed Shriver on the rescue boat to come alongside. He explained his plan and ordered him to tow *Sterling Star*'s lifeboat back to Miami. "But keep it a hundred yards astern. No closer."

"Regulation is fifty, sir."

"Forget regulations on this one, Len. I'm working on gut here. If it starts to get choppy, reduce speed. Otherwise, get back to port as soon as you can. If you're in doubt, go slower, but no closer."

Shriver understood. His men took the hawser and secured it to their own tow cleat.

Lieutenant Whitehurst radioed base that the rescue boat was returning—where the hell was Bahamas?—but that *46115* was continuing with the mission, that he felt certain *Sterling Star* was nearby.

He felt it in his bones.

Sixteen

THAT EVENING DIANE PICKED UP THE KNAPSACK FROM THE Ornamental Majestic concierge (something lightweight was inside—Les's old fringed vest, she guessed, not that she gave a damn anymore), took it unopened to her room, cleaned up, watched *Iron Chef*, then went back outside to take a stroll up Collins Avenue. When she was a little girl she and her parents had once stayed at the Surf Motel, but it and its famous Shipshape Bar were now long gone, replaced by a teal-and-white condo high-rise. She recalled that vacation fondly, the nattily dressed old people filling the Eden Roc dining room, the Fontainebleau's grand, floating staircase, the sparkling Deauville. She missed her mother and father very much, and for a long time she thought they would have liked to know their granddaughter, but now she was grateful they never got the chance. She tried to remember exactly where the Surf had been. But it was so long ago, and everything was so different now, and she felt lost.

A little after nine her cell phone rang. Seeing it was Angus, she answered.

"I'd like to talk with you about something super important," he said. "I tried calling you at the hotel."

"I'm walking up Collins. If it's about Les, you're not going to get me to change my mind."

"It's not about that."

"Is Karma okay?" Old habits die hard.

"She's fine. Can you meet us? I mean me. Meet me."

"Now?"

"It's important."

"I won't change my mind."

He mentioned a restaurant on a street she didn't know and started giving her directions. "Hold on," she said, juggling the phone between chin and shoulder while digging out a pen and note pad from her purse. "Okay, start over."

"It's not far."

She hung up, walked a couple of blocks south, then turned west. The streets quickly fell into shadow, ambient neon flickering hazily on art deco façades. Soon she was beyond Collins's residual luminescence, and she was sure she had made a wrong turn. She held the note pad close to her glasses, confirmed her route, and kept going. She turned another corner, peered into the tarry darkness, saw no restaurant or even commercial street, retraced her steps, and headed back east. She stopped, took out her phone and started dialing Angus, when someone ran out of a gangway behind her, covered her mouth, and stuck something pointed into her back.

"No sound or you're a dead broad," came the mugger's raspy voice. "This is a heater here"—he poked her a little harder—"a gun, in case you're not hip to the lingo…a hardened-steel, snub-nosed thirty-eight with matt black finish and rubber Pachmayr grip, loaded with hollow-point, copper-headed, guaranteed-one-shot-kill slugs, get it, sister?" He sounded a little like Humphrey Bogart in *The Big Sleep*. "Hang up the phone, shweetheart."

She folded the phone, and he took his hand off her mouth.

"Take my money. Here—" She hurled her purse, as she had learned in self-defense class.

But he didn't take the bait. "Don't insult me, shweetheart."

She was too terrified to scream or run. "I have an STD," she said, remembering that, too.

"I hate gas-guzzlers," he growled.

"I'm a transvestite."

"Relax, lady. I'm not going to violate you, okay? Actually, I'm not a bad guy, kind of a marshmallow, if you don't count this kind of thing. Everyone has to make a living. Look, just to prove it, I'm putting the rod in my pocket. It's right here. But no funny business, see?" The gun stopped poking her spine, and a second later, he snapped a blindfold over her eyes, the kind you buy at Walgreens for $1.99. "Do what I say and no one will get hurt." He led her away by her upper arm, scooping up her purse along the way.

"Where are you taking me?"

"You'll find out when we get there, toots."

A car door opened, and he nudged her behind the steering wheel. His footsteps scraped around the car. The passenger door opened, and he plopped in. "Okay, drive where I tell you. I've got the gun on you again."

"I can't see."

Silence. After a moment, he said, "I knew that." He got out, ran around again, helped her out and into the passenger seat, and got behind the wheel himself. "I was just testing you," he said. "You know that, right?"

He drove for five minutes, stopped, and pulled away again. She could tell he was driving around the block. He orbited several times and stopped again, this time turning off the ignition. He got out, opened her door, and helped her out. "Watch the curb, sister."

An overhead door clattered open, and, again nudging her with the gun, he led her inside. She was collected enough now to catalog her impressions, in case she had to reconstruct the location for the police. It was a high-ceilinged, concrete-floored warehouse, she was sure. Their footsteps echoed. She walked into a stack of cardboard boxes. He stopped her at a door, which he unlocked and creaked open. He turned on a light—she could see it from under the blindfold—and shut the door behind them. He led her to a metal folding chair and commanded her to sit.

"Stick out your arm," he demanded.

"What for?"

He poked her with the gun. "Just do it."

He snapped a cuff on her right wrist. "Hey!" she cried, but it was too late. She tugged, but at the end of a three-foot chain the companion cuff was anchored to something. Tired of the whole charade, she ripped off the blindfold.

"Hey!" he yelped. "You're not supposed to do that. When the heck did you ever see a hostage do that?"

"Wait a second. You're not Angus." He was a skinny guy with a balding pate, slightly buck teeth, and oversized glasses that accentuated his bulging, crossed eyes. He wore

an untucked madras shirt, tan cargo shorts, and white running shoes.

"Angus? Who's Angus? I'm no cow. I'm a kidnapper."

She gazed at his index finger. "That's some gun."

"Oh, this?" He flexed it. "Broke it playing softball. No
range of motion anymore. Believe me, I've got a real gun
right in my pocket."

"I don't believe you. Let's see it."

"What the heck did you take that off for, anyway?"

"You're as much a kidnapper as I am. You're not even a
good actor, if you want to know. Talk about every cliché."

"Don't get me riled, I'm warning you."

"See?"

"I can't believe you took that off. Just yanked it off
without asking."

"Where's Angus?"

"Now you listen, lady. You're out of bounds. I ask the
questions, see?"

"No, I don't see." She rattled her chain. "Let me go."

"As soon as I get back. In the meantime"—he nodded at two plastic tubs at her feet, full of junk food and
soda—"there's plenty to eat. And if you have to go to the
bathroom"—he glanced at a floor drain—"well, any port
in the storm."

"You expect me to go to the bathroom in the floor?
What am I, French?"

"Look, lady," he pleaded, "you're being kidnapped. This
ain't supposed to be the *QE2*. Be fair. You got everything
you need, it's nice and cool inside on a hot Miami night,
and if it rains, which it's supposed to, you're high and dry.
With any luck, you'll be out of here in a couple hours,

tops." He rummaged through the tubs and pulled out an *Us* magazine. He handed her a pen from his pocket. "Here, do the crossword puzzle. Take a little snooze. I'm telling you, it's great to get away from all the hubbub for a while."

"I have no money. No one will pay a ransom."

"I got to go, lady, please. Tell you what: I'll come by in a little while with a radio, how's that? I shoulda thought of it, but I forgot. I'm not perfect, all right? I'm just trying to make a buck, like everyone else. And after I let you go, you can keep the radio." He tucked her purse under his arm. "I'm sorry I gotta take this, but I promise to bring it back, okay?"

"It's definitely not okay."

"I'm sorry, honest. I promise I'll come back soon to let you go. Two, three hours, tops." He slipped out the door, locked it, and padded away. She felt the vibration from the overhead door open and close, and then the building fell into an eerie silence. She felt a claustrophobia attack coming. But again, recalling her self-defense lessons, she took a deep breath, let it out slowly, and willed herself not to panic. Instead, she got busy assessing her situation, mentally cataloging evidence. She saw now that she was in a windowless sprinkler-riser room, where four, red, eight-inch-diameter pipes—one of which she was cuffed to—fed upward into the warehouse, down into the concrete floor, and horizontally to the outside. Several submarine-type valve wheels, also painted red, were in easy reach. On one hung a metal sign:

BEFORE TESTING SPRINKLER

CALL BELMONT SECURITY, (888) 555-6000

She had no phone now, of course, but wondered if turning one of those wheels would signal the alarm company, who would then call the fire department, who would then rescue her. But when, looking at the ceiling, she spotted a sprinkler head, she thought better of it.

On a wall were three fire alarm control panel boxes. Could she signal the company without activating the sprinkler? But she also momentarily forgot about her tether—until she got up and started to reach for the panels, and the chain twanged taut.

She sat again, drew another deep breath, and continued to try to think calmly. She picked up the guy's pen (a cheapy with some advertising message) and began clicking the retractor while she considered.

Click. Who was this clown? Obviously, not a professional kidnapper. More like one of those bad impersonators on Jay Leno's "Does This Impress Ed Asner?" shtick—too ditzy to think of this enterprise by himself. *Click.* Still, this obviously wasn't a random snatching, and Angus's call and directions were a tad too suspicious. *Click.* But what the heck did Angus get out of having her kidnapped? It made no sense. *Click.* Did Karma put him up to it? Was it possible? At long last, was it possible that her daughter was capable of such a dirty, vicious act of revenge? *Click.* But no, that made no real sense, either. Not that Angus wasn't capable of doing her bidding, no matter how ridiculous it might be, only that the punishment hardly fit the crime. *Click.* If, after their argument, Karma had a temper meltdown and decided that if she, Diane, refused to stand next to Les, she'd rather have her father attend her wedding than her mother, all she had to do was simply disinvite her. *Click.* Why go through all this nonsense? *Click.* Did someone need money? That is, someone besides this Marty Feldman look-alike? Angus? Was he in some kind of financial trouble he was afraid to tell Karma about, for fear of losing her? Or was it Karma herself? *Click.* No, that was silly. Obviously, Angus would give her anything her little heart desired. *Click-click. Click-click. Click-click.* None of it made sense. None, none, none.

Distractedly, while her thumb worked the plunger, she began to rotate the pen between her fingers. Turn, turn, *click-click.* Turn, turn, *click-click.* She read the pen's embossed advertising message, but, with her cerebrum deep into pondering, it didn't register at first. Turn, turn, *click-click.*

Her cerebellum giving her cerebrum a nudge, she began to realize what she had read. She held the pen directly under the light, out of her own shadow. It was hot-stamped in gold:

~ COME TO VENEZUELA ~
~ FUTURE HOME OF WOW–TALITY SOUTH ~
~ OUR INFANT MORTALITY RATE IS LOWER THAN
PERU'S! ~

The president of Venezuela, who, despite having just completed a taxi tour of nearby Nitco gas stations, still found himself depressed about having once again been rejected—completely unfairly—by Wow-tality, sat in his hotel room (unbeknownst to him, across the street from the site where once stood the Surf Motel), watching Jim Cramer's *Mad Money* and brooding. Occasionally he would be buoyed by the thought of that splendid redhead, Karma, having reamed out both her future father-in-law, Wow-tality's CEO, and his bulge-eyed secretary, and further cheered by the fact that she had invited him to her wedding, a pretext to see him again, for he sensed that in reality she sort of dug him—hence her promise to get him his exclusive distributorship "one way or another." Would he rather it have been awarded on his own merits? Of course. But life is short. When it comes to vits and mins, you don't look a gift horse in the mouth, especially a melonicious redheaded one.

Speaking of which, he was in the midst of imagining Karma wearing nothing but gaucho chaps and spurs and riding him like a pampas pony, when the door burst open, and in charged half-a-dozen Miami SWAT cops, armed with assault rifles and riot shields. Before he could twitch, they were straddled over his bed screaming for him to turn over and put his hands on the back of his head. Two of the cops knelt on his back and legs, while another twisted his wrists until he yowled, and still another cuffed him with a blood-stopping *CLACK-CLACK.*

"You're under arrest for kidnapping, holding person or persons against their will, attempted bodily harm, and forcible containment, Section 3, Subsections V, VII, and XI of the Florida Criminal Code! You have the right to remain silent. If you cannot afford an attorney, one will be appointed for you."

The president of Venezuela had absolutely no idea what the guy was babbling about, but if this was Karma's idea of a kinky joke, it wasn't bad…not bad at all.

What a woman!

As dawn began to bleed into the sea, Coast Guard motor rescue-boat *47623*, tugging *Sterling Star*'s lifeboat *#14*, revved up to a Port of Miami dock, having gotten emergency clearance to tie up behind *Countess of the Sea*. Sailors jumped out, grappled *#14*, and tied that up, too, Ensign Shriver ordering them to secure a tarp over the boat's grotesque cargo, protecting the bloody remains from prying eyes and sensitive noses. With any luck, he'd get quick clearance to continue towing the lifeboat to a sequestered slip. Meanwhile, he ordered his crew to stay aboard their own vessel. He gazed up at the looming *Countess* and saw not a single cabin light. He padded across the pier to the Coast Guard station.

As had the shroud of the Haiti commerce minister, the tarpaulin covering *#14* began to quiver and, soon, to undulate. Soundlessly, a new crop of ravenous, pork-loving termites, their DNA now imprinted with the one-generation-removed collective memory of cruise-ship smorgasbord, scurried single file over the towropes to the dock, merged into a parade column, made a military-crisp left turn, and marched toward the *Countess*'s service gangplank. Fifteen minutes later, the regimen was gathered on board, its collective antennae quivering, testing the air for the scent of hog-meat-infused human cargo.

Seventeen

Her kidnapper having fulfilled his promise to set her free, Diane, in Karma's suite on the *Countess*, leaned over her daughter and bared her teeth. "Contrary to popular opinion," she raged, "I am *not* stupid!"

Karma, who had never seen her mother so menacing, had shrunk into the same club chair whose leather she had recently punctured. "I was worried about you. That's the truth," she spluttered.

"Truth, my foot! Truth! Just because I graduated from *night* school doesn't mean I don't know symbolism when I see it! '*Even if I have to chain you to him,*'" she railed, repeating Karma's threat. "'*Chain?!*' I guess you *weren't* kidding, were you?"

"Mother, you can't really believe that *I* was behind it. It's crazy, crazy. I'm telling you, it was the goddamn Culvertdales. They're trying to keep the president of Venezuela from coming to the wedding. And it worked, too. Right now the poor bastard is sitting in jail, waiting for habeas corpus, or whatever the fuck they call it."

"Oh, please. Give me a break. That kidnapper of yours was so transparently phony, you could see what he had for breakfast. I know damn well you were trying to intimidate me."

"Those fuckers *own* the law down here. But they won't get away with it. They won't."

"It's always someone else's fault with you, isn't it?"

"Mother, I understand why you might be upset, but—"

"Here's another flash for you. If it *was* the Culvertdales, which I doubt, I'd think you'd want to have a little tête-à-tête with your future husband."

Karma began to cry. But Diane stood firm, feet planted, jaw set, knapsack wedding gift between her ankles.

"They want me to sign a prenup," Karma sobbed. "They want to reduce my benefits if something happens to Angus. They want to destroy my self-esteem."

"Not much danger of that."

"They want to control my happiness."

"Prenup or not," Diane chuffed, "I'm sure you'll find a way to live like a queen."

"Well, sure," Karma blubbered, face in hands. "That goes without saying. But that's not the point. People get divorced. Husbands die. Then what am I supposed to do? My income will be reduced by thirty-five percent. I can't stand thinking about it."

"Look at it this way," Diane said, picking up the knapsack and tossing it at the club chair. "You'll always have this."

"What is it?"

"Another symbol, since you're so fond of them. A symbol of the sixties, a symbol of freedom—my new freedom from you and your asshole father—a symbol of peace and the Beatles and…it grieves me to say it…parenthood. That

I now symbolically pass on to you, dear, with my love and best wishes. May you live long enough to find the joys of motherhood yourself. The Culvertdales may deprive you a third of the family fortune, but you can always deprive them a hundred percent of their grandchildren."

"Asshole father?" Karma mumbled. She had never heard her mother talk like that.

"You deserve each other." She started for the door.

"Mom, wait, please—"

"At least you can be sure of one thing. You can never doubt who your father really is. That's my other going away present to you, *shweetheart*—"

"Going away? But you're still coming to the—"

"I'll be sure to send you my matzo ball recipe. But don't be surprised if there's no return address. And, by the way... I'm sorry I didn't abort you when I had the chance."

"Wha...what do you mean? *Abort? Mother?*"

"Oh, that's right. It was the sixties...not yet *legal*. I wonder what generation of starry-eyed idealists changed *that* inconvenience for you self-absorbed, snot-nosed brats."

As Diane stepped out into the hall, Angus was turning the corner from the elevators. When he saw her, he tried ducking back around, but it was too late—she had already spotted him. "Good luck," she told him. And, as she stepped into the elevator, "You'll need it."

And as the doors were closing, she heard her daughter, not weeping anymore, scream from down the hall, "Angus! Get the fuck in here! You and I are going to have a little talk, you filthy shitfaced Culvertdale!"

The termites couldn't find a single morsel of pork on board *Countess of the Sea*. Not one. Collective memory had let them down. Not familiar with the concept of kosher, let alone the wrath of Karma, they were mystified and not a little miffed. DNA had promised them an embarrassment of cruise-ship hog-meat riches, but, apparently, genetics had stuck it up their exoskeletal butts. Deck after deck they searched, antennae vibrating, duct after duct, chase after chase, shaft after shaft. They were getting the shaft, all right. Cargo holds—nothing. Kitchen storage areas—nada. Commissaries—bupkis. Meat lockers, coolers, freezers, pantries, cabinets, refrigerators, shelves, bags, boxes, crates, pockets, cartons, purses. Zero, zero, zero. They couldn't even detect the damn *scent* of pig anywhere on this ship from hell. It defied the logic of nature. It made no sense. Their chromosomes had built up their expectations only to flip them the chromosomal bird.

They were getting hungrier by the minute. Hungrier and more pissed off.

"What do you mean she left and isn't coming back?" Les asked his daughter over the phone.

Karma, weepy once more, explained, sort of, leaving out any hint that it might have been her fault.

Les panicked. He instantly assumed his plan had gone awry, that *his* plan would be the cause of the mission's failure, that they would no longer erect a statue in his honor in Plaza of the Revolution, that his likeness wouldn't grace Roosevelt Elementary School's playground. He'd be lucky if his co-conspirators didn't have him assassinated for screwing everything up. Oh, how he despised Diane and Karma! Why did the world have to be peopled by such intellectual inferiors? Why, why, why?

"She just left some ratty old backpack," his daughter sobbed. "Yuck."

"Backpack?"

"As my *wedding* present. That proves she had a mental breakdown."

"You still have it? It's still there?"

"She was delirious. Something about her matzo ball recipe…"

"I'll be right over!"

"I couldn't bear it if you're not both at my wedding," she choked. "It wouldn't *look* right." But she was already speaking to a dead line. Popsie was on his way.

At ten-thirty, two hours before the wedding rehearsal, *Key Stroke* sputtered to the Port of Miami dock, waited in a short security queue, and, when it was his turn, the Skipper jumped out, tied up, approached the agent's booth, and flipped out his driver's license.

"Where you been, sailor?" the agent, an African American woman, asked, a little flirtatiously, he thought. She was on the hefty side, which reminded him of his current craving for McRibs.

"Key West for a little partying," he answered, flirting back.

"Partying is good." She tapped something into her computer. "Been outside the country or territorial waters?"

"Not that I recall."

She laughed, her face jiggling. "Mind if we have a quick look-see?"

"You're picking on me, aren't you? It's my good looks, isn't it?"

"You bet. I like that streak of gray down the center. Kind of skunky looking." She clacked her keyboard again, then called someone on her phone. Although they couldn't possibly have known where he had been—even in Cuban waters—he still didn't like the feel of it. Had someone ratted him out? He suspected Fenwich, that namby-pamby dipshit.

"Follow him," the agent said, nodding to an inspector, a white guy this time, holding a clipboard and waiting for him on the dock.

The Skipper led him to *Key Stroke* and pulled the mooring ropes to the pier bumpers so they could hop aboard. The inspector dropped on and, clipboard poised, asked to see the life preservers, checked that there were enough to comply with the law, fingered their buckles, eyeballed the boat's registration, rummaged the stowage bins. He made his way into the pilothouse.

"What's up, brother?"

"Checking for foreign agricultural products," the inspector replied, snooping around the galley. "Strictly routine."

The Skipper knew he was lying. But he could only hope the worst he was really searching for was dope.

"What's in here?" the guy wanted to know, toeing a plump Hefty garbage bag, which held Fenwich's knapsack—now packed with Semtex plastic explosives.

"Just some toys for my kids."

"How about a peek?"

"No problem, officer." He picked up the Hefty, out of kicking range, untied it, removed the knapsack and unzipped it.

"Take that out, please," the inspector said, nodding to one of the orange bricks.

"Really, officer—"

"All the way out."

The Skipper complied. Silently he prepared himself to grab the guy's vocal chords, peeplessly choke him to death, and steal away to open water before the desk agent figured anything was amiss.

"Play-Doh, huh?" said the inspector. "I used to love this stuff."

The Skipper's tendons loosened a little.

The inspector squeezed the Semtex, feeling for something inside. "Mind if I break it apart?"

The Skipper winced. "My kid likes the full bricks." He tried to gently take it back, but the inspector held tight.

"I wasn't so much asking as telling." Holding his clipboard between his knees, with a quick and violent motion, he broke the brick in half, the Skipper bracing—not that it would have helped. When they didn't get blown to smithereens, he opened one eye to see the inspector fingering the inside of the brick.

"I guess you're okay," he declared. "Been a shitload of cocaine lately. You're clear." He began to mold the Semtex. "I love this stuff. Check this out. What is it?"

"Looks like a cat."

"It's a dog, man. Okay, fine, I can see where you might think it's a cat. If I had more time…" He squished it and started over. "Okay, here, try this."

"Turtle."

"It's a bird. Come on, you can see it's a bird. Right here, here's the beak…"

"My boy lives in an iron lung."

"What do you mean?"

"He's never even seen himself from the waist down. All he can do is model clay all day."

"That's pitiful, man."

"He probably won't live to be five, and it will be a blessing."

"Oh, man."

The Skipper nodded to the Semtex. "He really loves to tear into new blocks. One of his few joys in life."

The inspector mashed the two halves of the brick back together. "There, good as new." He handed it back.

"Almost."

"Tell your kid it was a mistake." He tore the checklist from his clipboard. "Sign here."

"You bet."

The inspector took a twenty-dollar bill from his wallet and handed that over, too. "Here, buy him some more clay. Tell him it's from a friend."

He took the money. "I'll do that."

Ten minutes later, the Skipper, sweating profusely, knapsack over his shoulder, beat a hasty retreat from the quay. He checked his watch. He had just enough time to grab a cab and get over to the McDonald's on SE 2nd Avenue, to rendezvous with the Iranian twerp. That spot was the Skipper's idea, of course. There, he'd woof down a couple of orders of McRibs, large fries, and a shake. After what he had just been through, he definitely needed a pick-me-up. He patted the twenty-dollar bill in his pocket. Nothing like lunch, compliments of the U.S. government (it was the least they could do). Besides, he'd need to fortify himself before meeting up with that cootie Fenwich, with his moronic secret signal.

God, how he wanted to kill Fenwich with his own two hands. Strangle him, skin him, blow him up, set him on fire, remove his ribs, smoke them, baste them with barbecue sauce, slow-cook them, serve them with coleslaw, baked potato, and corn. The problem was, after Castaways' Revenge the Skipper expected never to see him or hear his ass-kissing, holier-than-thou Ph. fucking D. voice ever again. Which would make killing him problematic.

Oh well, sometimes you just can't have everything.

"You've got to do something," Karma, sitting on the back of the sofa, pleaded. She stuck her thumbnail between her lower front teeth (risking nicking her fresh manicure). "Dad."

Les panned the suite. "Where is it?"

"She's not coming. I just know it. I've never seen her like that, ever."

"Where's the backpack?"

"She flipped out. I mean, like totally went berserk. Oh, Les, I have to have my mother at my wedding. I don't care anymore if she stands with you or not. You have to help me get her back."

"Where is it?" he demanded, sure that Diane had put her matzo balls into the knapsack before giving their present to Karma.

"She told me"—she covered her face—"she wished I had never been born."

He started searching behind furniture.

"She told me...she wished she had aborted me when she had the chance. *Aborted me.*"

"Never too late," he mumbled.

She cocked her ear. "What? What did you say?"

"Where the hell is it?"

"Where's what?"

"The goddamn backpack."

"Oh, that grungy old thing. I didn't even want to touch it."

"Where is it, for Christ's sake?"

"I put it out for the steward, naturally. It was, like, moth-eaten and cruddy. I held it with a towel, and I put that out, too."

"The steward?!" He ran to the door, in case he had missed something coming in. But, no, it was gone. "Who's the steward?" he demanded.

"Huh?"

"Give me a name! *Prénom, surnom, sobriquet,* I don't care!"

She shrugged. "It's a girl, I think. What's the big deal? Why are you acting like this? Why aren't you giving me your undivided attention? Don't you care about my sadness? Don't you want to comfort me?"

"It *was* your wedding present, from the both of us. Our old knapsack and your mother's matzo balls."

"Oh, come on, Les." She wrinkled her nose. "You couldn't expect me to put that old thing in the same room as my real gifts." She shivered. "I know it was just a mean joke."

"They had sentimental value—look it up."

"You're kidding, right? That was your actual wedding present? To your *daughter*? Your *only* child?"

He ran into the hall, calling for the steward.

She ran after him. "Les? Les? I'm not finished. You're coming to the rehearsal, aren't you?" She checked her watch. "Two hours?"

He disappeared into the stairwell. "Les? You're going to find Mom for me? Dad?"

But he was gone. She returned to the suite, collapsed onto the couch, folded into herself. She had to start getting ready. She didn't have much time. But she couldn't. She couldn't seem to move. What good would it be without Diane? She had no idea her mother's breakdown would make her feel so rotten. Why should it? If Diane went insane, why should that spoil the most important day of Karma's life?

Then she fell into bizarre, disturbing thoughts...memories long forgotten. The more she tried to squeeze them out of her brain, the more stubbornly they clung. She remembered the first time her mother took her to Lincoln Park Zoo. She recalled being afraid of the chimpanzees, of jumping into Diane's arms, crying, of Diane clutching her, telling her she was safe, that Mommy would always, always keep her safe. Mom wiped Karma's cheeks with her fingertips. She bought her a small stuffed gorilla. Karma remembered. A furry gorilla. She had never thought about that toy in all these years—was it even possible to remember a detail like that?—but now she was certain. She remembered how the gorilla instantly made her feel better. Then she recalled something else—that after handing her the gorilla, Diane looked into her purse and said, "Uh, oh. Oh, baby, I think we have to give him back."

She remembered her mother that night making another "gorilla" out of a dishtowel stuffed with Kleenex, tucking it under Karma's arm in bed.

Now, with only two hours to go before her wedding rehearsal, she sat sobbing into the crook of her elbow. She couldn't get married without her mother. She couldn't have a life without her. It wasn't possible. She had to get her back.

Then she thought of something that cheered her a little. What if Diane did miss the rehearsal? It's true, Karma had been a little stressed-out lately; maybe she had been a bit testy. Okay, fine, so Diane wanted to teach her a lesson. That's how mothers are—selfish like that. But there was no way, absolutely no way, she would miss her daughter's wedding. She couldn't have freaked out that much. Not Diane. She wouldn't crush the feelings of her baby, her Karma, even if she had gone temporarily wacko. No, Mom would be at the wedding all right, even if—she winced at the thought of it—Karma had to apologize to get her there.

That was it! She'd apologize! She'd be sincere, she'd whimper in front of her. If she had to she…she'd *beg!*

She fell glum again. What if she didn't know how, exactly, to beg? She chewed her lip and tried to imagine being sincere. What, exactly, did humility look like? She went to the foyer mirror and practiced some expressions. She cast her eyes down but, realizing she couldn't then see herself, stomped her foot. She tried again, frowning with contrition, turning one cheek to the mirror, then the other, unable to decide which profile was best, finally deciding that, to hell with contrition, the left side of her hair definitely looked fuller than the right, for which she'd give that bitch hairdresser a piece of her mind.

Gratitude, humility, sincerity—oh, it was all so confusing! How was she supposed to think of all this on her rehearsal day? Didn't she have enough to do? Wasn't she exhausted from running around the fucking ship, making sure there was no pork on board?

Still, she tried calling Diane on her cell phone. No answer. She called the Ornamental Majestic. One more stinking fire to put out. Life was one fire after another. God, how she hated people.

"Ms. Weinberg checked out an hour ago," said the reception bitch.

"That's not possible."

"I'm afraid so. The bill's been paid."

"Maybe she's still in the hotel—having breakfast or something."

"I'm afraid not. I helped her make reservations at the airport. She had to hurry. I saw her leave."

Karma slammed down the phone and, pacing, tried Diane's cell phone again. Still no answer. "Mother," she whimpered. "Mom."

And then she thought of her mother's matzo balls. She imagined them melting in her mouth. She could almost taste them, warm and delicious, slightly asymmetrical and soothing.

She didn't know what to do. For the first time in her life, she didn't know what to do.

The termites were getting more famished by the second, and with each porkless deck, each section, each storage area and cabin and cabinet, they grew more desperate, at once weaker and more fierce, more ready to pounce and destroy at the mere scent of pig molecules. Their hopes soared as they spilled out of a heating vent into a kitchen prep area, only, inexplicably, to find it, too, devoid of hog meat, scrubbed of pork juice, vanquished of oinker smell. Dry storage, ditto. Cold storage, ditto. Cargo hold, ditto, ditto, ditto. Where was the termite God?

Finally, in a last, desperate surge, they staggered into a trash area, deep in the ship's viscera. The scouts stopped, and the others halted behind them. Antennae jumped to attention and began to quiver. The insects turned to one another in querulous wonder. What was this? They turned back to home in on the scent—a weak vapor, yes, so weak they couldn't quite be certain, but an aura that carried promise.

The scouts scanned their antennae 270 degrees, back and forth. Oh, that this wasn't a false alarm! But they couldn't quite get a fix on it, so meager was the signal— no more than that of thin, dried out, old pigskin leather. While the regiment waited hopefully, a few vanguards advanced, tentatively, falteringly, stopping frequently to get a new fix or reaffirm the last. Eventually the signal brought them into a garbage-filled dumpster and a cloth container, a strapped, canvas sack, easy to bore a small hole into even in their weakened state.

A minute later, one of the scouts stuck his head back out of the hole, made a gleeful termite buzz—authentic pigskin, yes!—and the rest of the ravenous, whooping hoard rushed forward.

Les rifled through the *Countess of the Sea*'s corridors, frantically searching for the room steward, the maid, anyone who might have picked up the knapsack. There were very few staff on board—the honeymoon cruise itself not being for another week. He finally found a brown, wispy fellow, a French North African, dressed in rumpled civvies, wandering three decks below Karma's suite. He didn't speak English, so Les pantomimed carrying a backpack, charaded zipping and unzipping it and slipping his shoulders under its straps.

The man shrugged.

"Backpack! Backpack, you foreign nimrod. Speak fucking English!"

He shrugged again.

"Why can't you people learn to speak basic English? Is that asking too much? I speak French, a little German, some Latin of course, a smattering of Portuguese and Romanian, and a modicum of Mandarin. But you can't understand one fucking, simple English word? *Backpack!*"

Shrug.

"Wait a second. Hold on." He tried to remember the word in French. *Valise pour le back*. No, that wasn't right. What, what? Wait! *Sac*, that was it. Back, what was the word for back? *Dos!* Yes, yes. "*Sac à dos!*"

The man grinned. "*Oui, oui. Havresac.*"

"That's it. *Havresac!* Where?! *Où?*"

"*En bas, monsieur. Ci-dessus.*"

Les thought, thought, thought. What did that mean in English? Okay, so maybe he was a little rusty on his

Francophonetics. It wasn't his fault. There had been no one else in the damn English Department he could talk to in French. Americans were so xenophobic. None worse than Chicagoans, with their loser Cubs and Bears and white-trash tailgate parties and food fests and air-and-water shows and fat-assed Oprah. God, how he hated Oprah! How he wished it could be Chicago destroyed by radiation!

"*En bas, dans salles des ordures,*" the little man kept repeating, pointing down. And then, finally, throwing his hands up, "*Eh bien, alors. Suivez-m*oi."

Chauvinistic French motherfucker.

"*Suivez-moi?*" Les repeated. "*Suivez-moi….* Follow me! That's it, follow me." He turned to the fellow. "Yes, *oui*, go, *allez*. Ha! Am I bilingual, or what?!"

He followed the Moroccan (or whatever) through a labyrinth of service corridors, under pipes clacking and clanking and dripping, down steel stairs, down, down, getting colder deck after deck, until they debouched the stairwell into a dim, metal-echoing area, then through aisles of empty corrugated boxes, around piles of discarded plastic jugs, food cartons, lumpy trash bags. The Algerian (or whatever) stopped at an eight-foot-tall dumping bin sitting under a four-foot-diameter garbage chute. "*Voilà!*" he declared with an arm sweep.

"*Voilà?* What the hell is this?" Les thought hard again. "*Qu'est-ce que c'est que ça?…Qu'est-ce qui se passe?…* What gives? *Où est le backpack? Le havresac?*"

"*Voici, monsieur,*" he assured him, pointing to the dumpster.

Les pointed back. "Well, go in there and get it! Don't you pretend not to understand, you pusillanimous little kabab-eater." He pointed with more zest. "*Voici* your ass up there!"

The man shrugged and walked away.

"Back here! I'll report you!"

"*Fou Américain*," the man laughed, rolling a finger around his skull. "*Fou, fou.*"

"I heard that! I know what that means! I speak French fluently!"

Nevertheless, notwithstanding his multilingual dexterity, Leslie Fenwich, Ph.D. found himself alone at the base of a towering dumpster—which had, apparently, swallowed the knapsack with which he had brilliantly planned to free the world of trickle-down prosperity—muttering obscenities in good old American English.

He quickly considered alternatives to retrieving the sack. His brain fell into its 007 mode. Their—his—original plan called for split-second timing and super-agent courage, complete insouciance to the forces of evil and death. He was to meet Diane on the quay before boarding the *Countess*, so that they could present the knapsack and matzo balls together—another of her idiotically sentimental symbolic gestures. But unbeknownst to her, the Skipper would be hanging around, admiring the ship, carrying a black jumbo Hefty bag over his shoulder. At the prearranged signal—Les patting his rump three times in rapid succession, slapping his forehead four times, removing his wallet, covering his right eye with it, shaking his left leg as if it had fallen asleep, hopping three times while making one full rotation, and adjusting his baseball cap (not Cubs!) backwards—Les would momentarily distract Diane while the Skipper slipped the nuclear-balled knapsack from the Hefty and surreptitiously exchanged it with the benign *havresac*, after which Les would claim he had to walk the circulation back into his leg, excuse himself for a moment, disappear around a corner, and get as much distance between himself and matzo-ball Armageddon as possible.

But now, with his satanic daughter in an uproar, hysterical with wanting to have her mother back in her miserable life, he began to get nervous about the rehearsal starting on time. In fact, Karma was probably stalling, waiting for him to notify her that he had found Diane, talked some sense into her, that all was well, and that they were on their way to the practice ceremony. Karma was perfectly capable of screwing up everything he had worked his whole life for, the rotten little cunt. God, how he despised her and the intolerance that wealth spawned! And now, the thought that she stood between him and his statue in Plaza of the Revolution…his tooth nerves ached thinking about it. Somehow, he had to make sure she was in the direct path of the radiation when the matzo balls exploded…she and her rapacious, benighted, labor-exploiting, bloodsucking in-laws.

Even if Les did show up at the dock with the knapsack, but the rehearsal didn't take place because Karma was off somewhere searching for her mother; or if he didn't show up and the Skipper got tired of standing around waiting for Les and a secret signal that wouldn't come because—like Les at that point—the innocuous knapsack was MIA, and the Skipper left in disgust, and Les's plan blew up in their faces—figuratively speaking, one hoped—his revolutionary hero days would be over before they had begun.

On the other hand, even though he was a genius, he couldn't quite conceive, especially under this time pressure, of an alternative plan that wouldn't involve rooting around in a ton of putrefying garbage for the son-of-a-bitching knapsack with, apparently, Diane's matzo balls. If he showed up at the dock without it, the Skipper would be understandably befuddled—not to mention homicidal— and no secret signal in the wide world would unbefuddle him—again, endangering the mission and possibly Les's corporeal self. Yet, because of their precautionary ground rules (checking with the Skipper over cell phone, leaving an electronic trail, had been strictly proscribed), he dare not call the Skipper in advance to explain.

He sucked his teeth. He checked his watch. He gazed up at the garbage monolith. He stared at the steel rungs up its side. He quoted Shakespeare: "There's nothing either bad or good but thinking makes it so."

He climbed aboard, teetered on the edge, held his nose, and jumped in.

With the lumpy Hefty bag at his side, the Skipper, licking his fingers, wiping his chin with the back of his hand, sat at the rendezvous McDonald's, scarfing down his second order of McRibs, fantasizing that the meat had come from Fenwich's thorax.

He checked his watch. The Iranian doofus was already late. He wasn't surprised. They were all a bunch of retards. The whole world was retarded. Fine, they could all die and go to hell, as long as he got his five mill. If they stiffed him out of his hard-earned money, he'd personally blow the fuck out of each of them. He was the last guy on planet earth they wanted to fuck with. He did his part, he expected his money. And even after he got paid, he might still blow them up. Fenwich, absolutely. Thurston, probably. Lovey…well, he might play toy soldiers with him first, and then blow him *and* his asshole brother to smithereens.

A female throat cleared. He looked up from his McRibs and his pleasantly murderous ruminations. A beautiful, olive-skinned young woman, wearing Levis and a Spot Marley Rastadog T-shirt, stood cradling a minicooler. His eyes widened. She was very pretty indeed.

"The Skipper?" she asked.

He glanced around. "I think you must have the wrong person."

"It's all right," she assured him. "Little Buddy sent me. I am Mary Ann."

He looked around again. "Mary Ann?"

"He said to tell you I am delivering the pearls." She held out the cooler. When he didn't take it, she hauled it onto the table.

"May I go now, please?"

He didn't want her to go. He was smitten. Her voice was as sweet as a dove's, her face as fresh as a bud. "For the sake of discussion," he said, "where is this Little Buddy guy? Why didn't he come himself?" He ran his gaze over her. "Not that I'm complaining, mind you."

"He instructed me to say nothing more. I'm sorry. May I go now, please? I am very anxious about my uncle Hazeem."

"Hazeem?"

"Please, I can say no more."

"Hazeem was your uncle?"

Her face drained of color. "What do you mean *was*?"

"Oh, Lordy."

The way he said it made her legs give out. He caught her as she collapsed. One of the counter goofs looked over, but the Skipper waved him off. "It's fine," he called, hoping he understood at least that much English. He propped Mary Ann up in his booth. He offered her a sip of his Coke, and she drank. A minute later, she was nibbling a fry, then another, and another.

"When did you eat last?" he wanted to know.

"I haven't been hungry worrying about Uncle Hazeem. Please, if you know something, for the love of heaven, please tell me." She grasped his hand with both of hers. They were soft, quivering hands, finch bones. "No matter what it is, tell me. I can stand almost anything except not knowing."

He thought of the five million bucks waiting for him in the Caymans when he completed his part of the mission. One part of his brain knew, just knew, that this young woman could somehow come between him and his money. But he couldn't help it—another part of his brain (the between-his-legs part) believed he could have his way with her and have his money, too. A bonus for a job well done.

So he told her what had happened to her beloved uncle, leaving out the part that it was he who flipped the switch that had blown him across the Malecón.

A half-hour later, as she hunched over, quietly sobbing into a wad of napkins, the Skipper, hugging her, nuzzling the nape of her neck, stroking her back, comforting her, silently constructed his scheme to get her aboard *Key Stroke*, where, on the open sea to the Caymans, her cries—ecstatic or otherwise—would fall on jellyfish ears.

His cell phone rang—a straightforward, no-nonsense tone, not like those "hey-listen-to-my-phone-aren't-I-the-most-adorably-creative-person-in-whose-presence-you've-ever-had-the-privilege-of-being?" tones you usually hear at fast-food restaurants spilling from the phones of pimply teenagers you want to beat the shit out of. At first he assumed it must be a wrong number. But he pulled away from Samreen and checked anyhow. Diamond Miami hotel. He let it ring out. A minute later, it rang again. This time, after it stopped, he checked his voice mail.

"The Professor here," came the whiny, conspiratorial murmur. "The excursion has been rescheduled. Check departure hotline for more information."

Fenwich! He knew it. He knew he'd fuck everything up! Goddamn over-educated, useless college teacher!

"Wait here a minute," the Skipper told Samreen. "Don't move. I'll be right back. Watch this stuff. Don't move." He rushed outside, found a quiet spot in some bushes, and called the cocksucker.

"This fucking better be good," he hissed.

"Ornamental Majestic in fifteen minutes. Ten-four, over and out."

"Wait!"

No reply. He shook his phone. "Can you hear me now?" But the Professor had hung up.

The Skipper went back inside. The Hefty bag and minicooler were still in the booth, but Samreen was gone. He checked the women's bathroom, but the only person there was a Puerto Rican transvestite preening himself in the mirror. "Hey! You can't come in here! Can't you read?"

He yanked off the pervert's wig and threw it in the toilet.

He went back to the booth. Samreen was still not there.

Fenwich! Oh, how the Skipper wanted to kill him. Yes, yes, yes. Even if Castaways' Revenge did succeed and he did wind up lounging on *Key Stroke*'s deck in St. Martin's Oyster Bay with his five million, he knew, just knew, he would regret not having risked it all by murdering that Ph.D. fuckup when he'd had the chance.

The Skipper's taxi rolled up the palatial Ornamental Majestic driveway. Fenwich, his clothes crumpled and greasy from having crawled around the *Countess of the Sea*'s garbage dump, waited near the front door, the knapsack between his feet.

So, the Skipper surmised, *Fenwich doesn't know that Little Buddy fucked up*. Those informative few minutes with Hazeem's niece had proven worthwhile indeed. What she herself didn't know, the Skipper deduced. Her glorious president, the twit, had somehow lost the nuclear matzo balls and had coerced Samreen to deliver the deli-bought balls in their, and his, place—no doubt so that once everyone realized they were only garden-variety Jew food, the Iranian president could blame Samreen for having made the switch, for being a Zionist agent, perhaps a Mossad spy. The lousy little worm, taking advantage of Hazeem's emotionally vulnerable niece like that. By the time the Skipper detonated the knapsack, the Iranian leader would probably be safely headed across the Atlantic, back under his Tehran rock.

What was wrong with people? Was there no one dependable left in the world? Okay, fine. Let's see what Fenwich had up his scrawny sleeve. The Skipper wasn't about to kill him quite yet, not while his five million beckoned.

The Hefty bag over his shoulder, he approached the Professor.

"Lobby men's room," Les whispered. "Give me a ten-second head start."

The Skipper was absolutely, totally, completely going to kill him, him and his phony spy drama. Not just kill him, but kill him slowly. Maybe over a spit, like those African savages cooked Cornel Wilde's hunting party in the movie *The Naked Prey*. Or maybe freeze him alive, to conserve his nutrients. Maybe send a carton of frozen steaks to the president of Iran in celebration of the anniversary of their retarded revolution. Maybe grind him up and send him in packets to Thurston to start his own line of vits and mins. *Les-tality*.

A minute later, he moseyed into the men's room, where Fenwich was standing at a urinal, nodding at the one next to him.

"Here," the Professor whispered, motioning with his ear. "Pretend to pee."

"There's no one else here. Talk."

Les flicked a cautionary nod toward the stalls, but the Skipper didn't see any feet there, either. Nevertheless, he took his place at the adjoining urinal but refused to pull down his zipper. He got a good whiff of the garbage festering on Fenwich.

"Make the switch *now*," Les said. "No cameras in restrooms by federal mandate."

"You better fucking know what you're doing."

"*Right now.*"

The Skipper put down the Hefty and slipped out the "hot" knapsack. Quickly Fenwich zipped himself up, catching a wrinkle of skin. "Ouch, ouch, ouch."

In a single, smooth motion, the Skipper stuffed the "cold" knapsack into the Hefty, slung it over his shoulder and, without another word, whooshed out of the room, leaving Fenwich holding his bleeding putz, slapping his forehead four times, shaking his left leg, hopping around and spinning.

So at least he got to use his secret signal.

"Get down to the Ornamental right away," Les instructed Karma over a house phone a few minutes later.

"You found her? Put her on. Let me talk to her. Mother?" she called. "Mom?"

"Just come right now," he insisted. He hung up.

It was a brilliant last-second change of tactics, if Les said so himself. This only proved he had dexterous flexibility of thinking, a trait common to all great military minds—Che, Fidel, Lenin, Mao themselves having effectuated lightning-quick adjustments to their revolutionary maneuvers. His only amazement was that he hadn't thought of this before.

Dirty bombing a massive cruise ship filled with wealthy wedding guests certainly would have propagandistic benefits, yes, and, as the other mission members agreed, would cause such panic in Western financial markets as to make 9/11 look like a day at the beach. But, the Professor decided, what was a paltry cruise ship compared to whacking an entire luxury hotel, chock full of in-season rich bastards, smack-dab in the capitalism-decadent mecca of the world? For sheer blood and guts, nothing beat a landside target. Who knew what anti-radiation and anti-explosion properties a thick-hulled ship held? And anyhow, once the disaster unfolded, all the ship would have to do is sail out of land-harm's way and, at worst, sink itself, sacrificing a few mega-earners and grubby service people, both groups about whom most folks didn't give a flying fuck anyhow. True, everyone aboard every other cruise ship would panic, resulting in high-seas chaos, but those on the mainland would still feel relatively safe, watching events from their cozy, rad-free media rooms.

The real beauty of the Professor's new plan was that now Karma was almost certain to be blown to radioactive dust. With the old scheme, her suffering and death—though delightful the thought of it—would have been iffy. Who knew exactly where she would be on the ship relative to the knapsack when the Semtex detonated?

This new way solved that problem magnificently. The moment he thought of it, he realized it was his subconscious talking, reminding him of how much, for the sake of humanity as well as to fulfill his own sense of moral imperative, he needed to erase Karma Culvertdale from the face of the earth, abrogate every soupçon of evidence that she and her materialistic, avaricious self had ever sullied the planet. Her mother wanted symbolism, she was damn well about to get it.

He left an envelope, marked FOR KARMA, printed in the hotel's business center, at the front desk. Making sure he had all three check-in agents' attention, he said, "A young woman will soon be asking for Diane Weinberg's room. Please, *please* make sure she gets this. It's a matter of life and death."

He walked around to the rear parking lot, where his neon-blue Yamaha awaited. His saddlebags were packed. He didn't need a map. There was only one way to Cuba by bike, and that was through Key West, and there was only one road to Key West, and he already knew the way to U.S. 1. Even stoned he couldn't get lost.

He revved his shiny new motorcycle, headed for the highway, ear buds rocking and rolling, tie-dyed shirt flapping, and never looked back.

Twenty minutes later a Culvertdale black stretch limousine pulled up to the Ornamental. Karma jumped out of the back and sprinted up the steps to the front desk. Heaving for breath, she demanded either Diane Weinberg or Leslie Fenwich, no more bullshit. Instead, the woman handed her an envelope with her name on it.

"What's this?"

"An envelope with your name on it."

She handed it back. "You open it. I just had a manicure."

The check-in woman complied. "Would you like me to take it out and read it for you?"

"Just take it out, bitch. I can read it myself."

The woman plucked out the letter, puffed the envelope apart, saw something, and turned it over. A baggage-claim ticket floated into her palm.

Karma reached over the counter and snatched everything away. She unfolded the letter and read.

> My Darling Daughter,
>
> I needed to get away temporarily to do something for you, but I promise to be with you soon. I'm sure when you see my surprise you will completely understand. In return, dear, you have to promise not to spoil it and to do exactly as I say.
>
> I enclose a claim check for the backpack, which now contains something far more valuable than silly matzo balls—and, for that matter, far more symbolic of my most profound feelings for you, and a wedding present worthy of you and Angus. It's something I wish I could have given you a long time ago, but I didn't have the means. Please claim the knapsack and keep it with you at the hotel at all times until I come back, even if I am slightly late. All will be revealed shortly. Your father will be very happy indeed.
>
> Whatever you do, do not—I repeat emphatically, DO NOT—peek inside until I rejoin you. I trust you, but I put a nylon strap on the zipper to keep out the prying eyes of strangers.
>
> Thinking of you always,
> Diane—"Mom"
>
> P.S. You deserve this, and a lot more of the same—if only that were possible.

O joy! O bliss! Karma pumped her fists to the heavens—at least to the multimillion-dollar Ornamental Majestic frieze—at the news that she had not lost her mother. How could she ever have thought that? How could she have doubted for a single second that Diane was anything but completely devoted to her fabulous daughter? That in the end she would take whatever Karma dished out and like it?

She rushed to the concierge and presented the ticket. He walked her over to the baggage room and, in turn, gave the ticket to the luggage handler. She tipped the concierge a hundred bucks. "And one for you, too," she told the suitcase guy, peeling off a Benjamin.

He returned with the knapsack. Sure enough, a nylon locking strap dangled from a zipper. She could hardly wait. She yelled at him to find her a scissors, "Chop, chop."

What could Diane possibly have thought of…let alone afford…that was "worthy" of her…that she had "always wanted to give her"…that she "deserved" (and if she deserved "a lot more," why not just give her more?). Face it, Diane wasn't very creative. As with most everything else, she was kind of a dud in that department. To her, the high point of humanity's collective creativity was the surprise birthday party. *Ick!* Karma hated surprise birthday parties! Always did, even as a kid. She had always wanted advance notice on everything pertaining to her—which everything did—if for no other reason than that she could practice her facial expressions.

Her phone rang—Wagner's "Flight of the Valkyries." Maybe it was Diane, telling her it was okay to open the backpack before the rehearsal! But no, it was only that halfwit Angus, asking her what to do with the rehearsal guests, who were starting to arrive on the *Countess*.

The luggage handler came back with scissors, which Karma snatched away. "Tell the mooches to keep their shirts on," she told her fiancé. "I can't worry about anyone else's feelings right now. I'm concentrating on my own."

Eighteen

Near the U.S. 1 bridge connecting the mainland to Key Largo, the Skipper cut his engine and checked his watch. The sun was overhead, *Key Stroke*'s shadow dark and blunt. He cast his glance southward, toward his future. To starboard, the bridge shimmered like a spider web thread. He had plenty of fuel to get him to Key West, and, refitting there, on to Havana. But now he was sorry he had already eaten his McRibs to go, had not paced himself. *Self-discipline*—that was the term the judge had used, lecturing him before handing down his verdict. Maybe that fucking judge could now kiss his five-million-dollar, un–self-disciplined ass.

He checked his watch again, and again gazed out at the southern horizon. Key West had a Mickey D's, of course, but after that, what? Cuban food was shit. Maybe he didn't have to go to Havana to lay low. As long as the five mill hit up in his Grand Cayman account, who needed Cuba? Who in his right mind even wanted to live in a country without a McDonald's? Maybe he'd be better off heading straight to George Town, and screw the glorious revolution and hiding out. He never wanted to lay low again. He wanted to lay high. For the rest of his life—high, high, high.

He gazed north, then up at the sky, as if somehow he'd be able to spot the satellite that was soon to relay the signal that would detonate the Semtex putty that would blow up the nuclear matzo balls, fulfilling his part of the bargain. To hell with Samreen. If the other Castaways wound up blaming her for the missing nukes, fine by him.

He checked his watch yet again. Forty-three minutes to go.

He calculated the amount of fuel it would take to go directly to the Caymans, circling Cuba's western coast. He couldn't make it. He'd have to stop in Cuba and put up with that flea-brain Lovey. Then there was always the danger that, once Cuba made him, the Skipper, a so-called hero of the ongoing revolution, they wouldn't even *let* him leave again. Look what happened to Che Guevara. All the poor bastard wanted to do was spread the gospel to other countries, and the Castro boys made damn well sure he wouldn't upstage them. His life wasn't worth a plug centavo once he left Cuban territorial waters.

Decisions, decisions, decisions. He sure wished he had another order of McRibs to help him think.

Former professor Leslie Fenwich weaved down U.S. 1, a log of Venezuelan giddy stuck into the corner of his mouth, happy smoke tickling his sinuses, gnats splattering his goggles, the Beatles pulsing in ear buds under his helmet. His new Yamaha seemed to have been born with an innate knowledge of the way to Havana. It was almost as if he didn't have to steer it himself, as if he could let go of the handlebars, and it would keep going south, south, like a monarch butterfly to its ancestral breeding grounds.

All he could think of was how he would look in bronze, towering over the Plaza of the Revolution on his Yamaha, riding eternally into the trade winds, his gaze frozen onto the glorious proletarian future, an inspiration for future generations of socialists. Lucy in the sky with diamonds—aahh.

He was free, free, free. Free at last, free at last—thank Whatever Almighty, he was free at last. No more kissing Leona Beebe's adipose ass. No more sports jackets and clean shirts; no more syllabi and colloquies; no more pretending to be interested in young minds; no more briefcase; no more symposia; no more research papers to grade; no more telling students to close their laptops; no more motioning for them to put away their iPhones; no more horny eighteen-year-old coeds that (contrary to his Constitutional rights) he wasn't allowed to ogle; no more gender studies; no more CTA buses; no more 'L' trains; no more rancid butter in the staff cafeteria; no more indecipherable undergraduate essays to atrophy his brain cells; no more smiling on the administration building elevator at circus-ugly Professor Liffman; no more queer theory; no more quarterly soirees with cheap white wine; no more automatic deductions for health benefits; no more black studies; no more Jewish studies; no more transsexual studies; no more Foucault; no more Derrida; no more deranged feminists; (speaking of which) no more Hélène Cixous; no more four-part, press-hard supplementary grade forms; no more dissertation committees; no more oral exam committees; no more scrounging for exact change; no more watered-down coffee; no more cheap red wine; no more textbook representatives. No more tax returns; no more 1099s; no more bank statements; no more electric bills; no more telephone bills; no more gas bills; no more answering machines; no more Wal-Marts; no more BK Broilers; no more Banana Republics; no more Great Clips; no more advertising supplements; no more "buy one, get one free." No more, no more, no more, no more.

He accidentally weaved in front of a white Hummer, which honked long and hard. Leslie flipped the driver the bird, like Dennis Hopper in *Easy Rider*. Waving his spliff, he shouted, "Can't you see I'm blowing this popsicle stand?! Blowing this popsicle stand! Fuck you, you materialistic fuckwad! Fuck you!"

The Hummer turned sharply at him, probably just to scare him. But as the Yamaha zigged while the Hummer zagged, and the Venezuelan grass made images appear closer than they really were, Les darted the other way, lost control of the bike, careened off the guardrail, wobbled back into the lane, fishtailed wildly, headed once again for the guardrail, smacked it at a sixty-degree angle, and, with his exhaust pipe skidding on the emergency lane and raising sparks, former English professor Leslie Fenwich, Ph.D. flew head-first off the bridge.

From below the bridge, the Skipper first heard, then watched this crazy motherfucker crash into the guardrail, fly off his bike, somersault several times in midair, belly-flop into the ocean with a resounding *thwop*, and disappear beneath the surface. He figured the bastard had to be deader than calamari. But low and behold, a moment later, up the biker's helmet popped like a purple-flecked buoy, followed by his goggles—slightly crooked—and then his arms, windmilling for help. The helmet must have saved him. Above, a few gapers leaned over the bridge to follow his fate. One was taking a video.

"I'm not a proficient swimmer!" the biker yelled.

His voice sounded vaguely familiar. The ninny started dog-paddling toward the boat, and the Skipper tried to wave him off. "Go away. I'm working. Have to split. Sorry, dude."

But the guy kept coming. The Skipper looked up. More gapers, more cameras. Shit, shit, shit. He couldn't ditch the bastard now if his own life depended on it. The cops would hunt him down like Purvis hunted down Dillinger, and what do you suppose they would think finding all this electronic detonation equipment on board? But he couldn't take him on now, either. He looked around frantically for any other boat within rescuing distance but came up empty.

"Go away," he growled, pretty sure the gapers couldn't hear. But the guy was already at the stern, gasping for breath, belching salt water, grasping for the swimming platform. The Skipper opened the transom door and tried to make it look like he was helping the biker aboard while surreptitiously prying his hands loose from the platform and whispering, "Nothing personal, but get the fuck out of here," but it was useless—some broad on the bridge was frantically pointing out his misdeed to her companions.

The Skipper's thoughts turned heavenward, beyond the gapers. *Dear God, I know I haven't been your biggest booster all my life, but if you do exist, you can prove it once and for all right now by making this asshole drown, and I'll be extremely impressed. Amen.*

"I'm substantially enervated," the biker gasped.

Who the fuck would use a term like *substantially enervated* at a time like this? The Skipper tugged off the guy's seaweed-draped goggles. "You!"

Les looked up at his savior. "You!"

The Skipper gazed skyward again. *Better yet, Lord! Now I can kill the motherfucker with my own two hands! See you in church!*

Fenwich coughed up seawater. "Assistance required, assistance required." He held out one hand, as the other slipped from the platform. "Help."

The gapers gaped.

The Skipper grabbed Fenwich's wrist. "Don't you worry. You're safe now." He hauled him in with a *thump* and a *splat*. The bridge crowd cheered and waved. Two squad cars, lights strobing, had joined the party. Any minute now a police rescue boat would be slicing toward *Key Stroke*. The Skipper turned back to Fenwich, sprawled on the deck like a flounder.

"*Merci beaucoup*," Les choked, coughing up sea spray. "I'm surfeited with gratitude."

The Skipper checked his watch. He leaned over his colleague. "Can you hear me?"

Les's helmet nodded.

"You know who I am?"

Fenwich gurgled yes.

"Is the plan moving forward as discussed?"

"Ten-four."

"Get in the captain's chair."

"Really? Me?"

The Skipper helped him to his feet and behind the helm. "Go!"

"Which way?"

He nodded south. "That way. As far and as fast as you can. Full throttle out. And wave to the Peanut Gallery."

They both waved to let the cops know everyone was fine, and then Les punched it, hurling the Skipper stern-ward.

For now, exactly where he wanted to be. He would deal with the Professor soon enough. Destroying Miami Beach would be a small pleasure compared to murdering *Dr.* Leslie Fenwich.

Nestled in the knapsack in an aft hold, the killer termites were just waking up from an exhausted, full-bellied doze, having recently devoured the authentic-pigskin football, a pork-jerky-gourmet delicacy the likes of which they instinctively knew they'd probably never enjoy again. They rose and stretched, licked their mandibles, flexed their thoraxes, shook their many legs, preened their wings, wiped drowsiness from their bug eyes, sniffed around. The football leather was long gone, and their tiny but insatiable tummies were beginning to rumble again. A splendid scent filled the wind. A scout crawled to a point of light and, where the zipper hadn't completely closed, peeked out. He spied two humans, and—*sniff, sniff*—one of them definitely reeked of barbeque pork ribs! He turned to his troops and, in termite language, buzzed that they would absolutely not believe their continued good luck. "After famine, feast!" he called to the multitude. "People meat!"

The termite soldiers, pincers pincing, micro hairs tingling, sprung into regimental formation. They were no longer sleepy.

Although he had always been reluctant to admit it, Les Fenwich was Jewish. He had felt deeply embarrassed by some of the collective traits of his people—their loudness, money-grubbiness, pushiness—and Israel's unrelenting territorial ambitions and oppression of the Palestinians nearly drove him to convert to Islam himself. He wasn't bigoted; it wasn't individual Jews he had a problem with but the whole race. As a child, his parents had embarrassed him, too, with their infernal Yiddishisms, trying to cut him out of their conversations by talking to each other like Eastern European pushcart sheenies. He had despised his grandmother's chicken soup, with its inch-thick layer of fat. He hated her thick-as-schmaltz accent. He hated Passover, with its tasteless, fatty brisket and greasy latkes and scatological chopped liver and disgusting gefilte fish that resembled barium turds. He loathed Hanukkah get-togethers, clearly a cry for attention at Christmastime (another example of pushiness), with their stupid dreidels and chocolate money—money, money, money—and aunts who wouldn't shut up about their new refrigerators and dishwashers and disposals, and loud-mouthed uncles with their Buicks and Cadillacs, and nerdy cousins with their impossibly high SAT scores. He hated Mogen David wine—what the hell kind of grape could that possibly have come from?—and he despised Jewish lawyers and Jewish accountants, and he hated, hated, *hated* lox.

So from the moment, as a lad, he was able to conceptualize his imposed-against-his-will ethnicity, he went out of his way to flout its rules and regs. He'd wait all week just to spend Saturdays whacking off. He drew swastikas with crayons all over his coloring books. When playing soldier with his friends, he'd always want to play Hermann Goering or Joseph Goebbels or even Hitler himself and sometimes (okay, often) Eva Braun. He ate pork whenever he had the chance. Ribs, ham, pork chops, you name the pig part, he ate it, often in front of his parents, to punish them for excluding him from their sheenie conversations. "Oh, Mom, Dad," he would moan ecstatically, "you people don't know what you're missing."

When he was old enough to buy his first car, he bought a Ford, even though Ford made shitty cars, because the senior Henry had been a virulent anti-Semite. As an undergraduate he had gotten into some trouble with his essay, "Maybe the Nazis Had the Right Idea But Just Weren't Selective Enough," and as a graduate with his paper, "Holocaust Schmolocaust." As a teacher he always automatically deducted a half-grade from his Jewish students and added it to the Muslims' grades, figuring, what the heck, it averaged out. He'd avoid shopping at obviously Jewish merchants, preferring Wiebolt's to Goldblatt's, OshKosh to Levis, Wish-Bone to Newman's Own, John M. Smyth to Wolf Brothers. As a reader he adored Hemingway and Pound, couldn't stomach Bellow and Roth. Painting: Picasso, not Pollock. Music: Wagner, not Mendelssohn. Science: von Braun, not Einstein. Acting: Mel Gibson and Vanessa Redgrave, not Richard Dreyfuss or Goldie Hawn. Comedy: W. C. Fields, not…pretty much everyone else.

If he hadn't been so self-hateful, if he hadn't tried to deny his birthright, if he had only avoided pork, the non-kosher scent of his Yiddish-loathing flesh would not now be mingling with the Skipper's McRibbed pores, streaming down the length of *Key Stroke*'s deck and into an aft hold, through the zipper opening of his old knapsack, and across the collective olfactory synapses of a battalion of mutated, man-eating termites.

In the lobby of the Ornamental Majestic Hotel on Miami's tony Brickell Key Drive, the soon-to-be Karma Culvertdale snipped open the nylon strap seal of her former-hippie parents' old canvas knapsack. With the greedy incredulity of a woman who can't wait to see what her low-self-expectationed mother could possibly imagine would be a worthy wedding present to her overachieving, successful, beautiful, brilliant daughter, Karma unzipped it.

As his boat thudded south, the Skipper unlatched and flipped open an aft hold, took out a gym bag containing his satellite-signal detonator, and, as he had off Havana's Malecón, unwrapped the transmitter from layers of sheet plastic. While sitting on the adjacent hold, he extended the transmitter's antenna and, watching the meter needle, waved it around until he got a good strong signal. A red LED blinked, indicating a sure link. He threw a toggle, and the flashing LED became steady—a signal lock-in. He glanced back at the thinning mainland. *Goodbye America! Goodbye and good riddance!* He glanced over Fenwich's shoulders at open water and, in his mind, Havana beyond, and, beyond that, the Caymans, and, farther still, St. Martin.

His thumb hovered over the red button.

Something stung his foot. *Ow!* Instead of pushing the button, he reflexively reached down and slapped whatever vicious insect had unilaterally declared war on his epidermis. Then another bug leaped onto his slapping hand and bit that, too. *Ow! Ow!*

Now another bite, and another, and another. He dropped the detonator transmitter and jumped up, slapping, hopping, yeowling. In an instant he was covered in murderous insects and shrieking for his life.

When, above the roaring engine, he finally heard his co-conspirator's screams, former head of the English Department *Dr.* Leslie Fenwich turned to see what all the shouting was about, only to have a termite warrior leap onto his eyeball and scoop out a sizeable chunk of cornea. The Professor fell onto the deck howling and writhing,

and in a few short minutes both Castaways sprawled, mangled and flesh-stripped, in a shared pool of blood, where
the termites dived, swam and water-skied.

Meanwhile, with the boat's throttle stuck on full ahead,
the human corpses, whose subcutaneous netherworlds
were already nesting a fresh generation of termite eggs,
raced toward the northern coast of Cuba.

Having opened the backpack, Karma, spotting the wires
leading from the detonating receiver and sticking into the
explosive putty, recalled her mother saying she wished
she had aborted Karma when she had the chance. She
dropped the knapsack, staggered back to the hotel lobby
and swooned onto a baggage cart, propelling it down the
entry stairs—*thump, thump, thump, thump*—where, at the
curb, it crashed into the Culvertdale limousine, hurling
Karma's body through an open window and into the
back seat.

"Where to, M'lady?" asked the driver, remembering to
address her in her preferred fashion.

"Just fucking drive!"

"Very well, M'lady," he said, pulling away.

He could see she was in a hurry.

Epilogue

KARMA WAS SO TRAUMATIZED BY THE REALIZATION THAT her own parents wanted to blow her to hell, she had a nervous breakdown. Her wedding was postponed indefinitely while she recuperated in a sanitarium in the mountains near Asheville, North Carolina. At first Angus came to visit her every day, then every couple of days, then once a week, and eventually not at all. Despite everything, Diane did come to see her, but all her assurances that it wasn't she who had put the bomb in the knapsack fell into whatever cranial abyss currently took the place of Karma's consciousness. All her daughter could do day and night was babble infantilely at the cartoon figures on her wallpaper. Diane had to admit that Karma's regression to toddlerhood suited her well. It reminded her of the last time in her daughter's life she had genuinely liked her.

One day when Diane wasn't there, Karma had an unexpected visitor. She looked over from her wallpaper, saw a wide-headed, dark-skinned man and stopped babbling. "It's me," he said. "The president of Venezuela." At first she thought this was another cartoon character who had come to life and leapt off the wall. But the more he spoke, the more her fog began to lift, and, miraculously, after about an hour, she started to recall her adolescence, college years, young adulthood, and even the Culvertdales. The Venezuelan's voice had had a reverse hypnotic effect, releasing her from her traumatic trance.

He came to see her twice more, then asked the head shrink to have her released to his care. At first the doctor hesitated, but when Karma threatened to shove his clipboard up his fat ass sideways, he figured she was fully cured and signed the release papers.

The president and Karma now own the most successful AirTightWare food-container franchise in Latin America, selling household storage solutions to millions of South and Central Americans through a network of dedicated distributors—some working from the backs of their donkeys. There are many AirTightWare imitators—the Chinese are the worst offenders—but never any duplicators, for only AirTightWare has had over fifty years' experience designing and manufacturing containers guaranteed to keep perishables fresh and crisp with its patented Shush Sealing System™. What's more, AirTightWare isn't just the first name in food-item containment anymore. Now you can call on your local distributor for *all* your storage needs, be they to organize your various beads, gourds, oil-profits cash, or even revolutionary manifestos. AirTightWare has it all. If you're interested in learning more about how you can become financially independent, have fun, meet terrific new people, and provide a valuable service for your friends and community, contact K and H Enterprises LLC at info@airtightware.com and request their full-color brochure describing the wonderful opportunities that await you as a member of the exciting AirTightWare team! This has been a paid advertising message.

Karma soon reverted to her old haranguing, tyrannical, narcissistic, ogress self, which serves her well in the world of multilevel marketing. She insisted on being the corporate president, and she runs the company with an iron fist. But she sure as heck gets results. There are now hundreds of aboriginal Carib Indians living in the Amazon jungles storing their manioc roots and mammee apples in AirTightWare's Cool Smart Modular Mate™ containers. For his part, the Venezuelan president rather enjoys being blustered by a harridan with more steel balls than a pachinko parlor. Evidently having a few mother issues himself, he finds masochistic comfort under the boot heel of this splendid purveyor of spousal brutality.

They have two children, Grendel and Attila, and although they travel frequently, their main home remains in Caracas—a fifty-two-room mansion on the brow of a hill overlooking a hodgepodge of shanty slums and lean-tos, few of which have running water or electricity, but all of which have AirTightWare.

After delivering the matzo balls to the Skipper, Hazeem's niece Samreen, dazed and distracted by the news that her uncle was killed in Cuba, staggered from the McDonald's on SE 2nd Avenue, stepped off a curb, and was almost run over by Angus Culvertdale's limousine. The Global

Boffo heir jumped out to comfort the frightened young woman and, smitten with her innocence and fresh-faced beauty, fell head-over-heels in love. He paid off her then-boyfriend, Stevie, to go away and never come back (enough for law school and a BMW), shortly after which Angus and Samreen tied the knot. They now have three children, whom they are raising Muslim—which resulted in Marybethlehem and Eddward being excommunicated from their country club and church.

Diane now lives in a townhouse in Grayslake, Illinois, with her cat, Golda, her Jack Russell terrier, Barack, and her parakeets, Lyndon and Lady Bird. After the failed terrorist plot, she earned her Ph.D. in English online and now teaches creative writing at the College of Lake County. She bought a used VW Beetle and sputters around town between Tips-To-You Tea Shop, Petco, and Harriet's All Natural Food Market. Three wild-bird feeders hang on her balcony railing, and her mornings are filled with the aroma of chai tea, the chirps of chattering goldfinches, and the burbles of budgies. Last year she invented a combination matzo ball shaper and refrigerator container, the Motherload™, the patent for which she sold to Morton Blitstein—said to be the "Israeli Ron Popeil"—for three million dollars. She finally learned how to use the Internet, built her own Web site, and now spends pleasant evenings—Golda purring in her lap, Barack sprawled nearby enjoying her tummy scratch—answering e-mails from her adoring students and Morty, who recently informed her that the president of Cuba, of all people, placed an order for one hundred thousand Motherloads™.

"Isn't that amazing?!" Mort asked her.

She wears love beads and writes poetry. Her quiet affection for Blitstein notwithstanding, she has found a life of contentment without a man.

A couple of days after the marauding, mutant termites devoured the Professor and the Skipper, *Key Stroke* ran out of fuel and began drifting in the Florida Straits. Two days after that, on a Sunday morning, El Maximo's younger brother, head of the Cuban Revolutionary Armed Forces and a nonchurchgoer, happened to be out fishing off the coast of Cojimar, when his fishing buddy, Luis, spotted the floundering mini-trawler. They pulled up alongside, called *¡hola!*, and, receiving no answer, hooked a towrope to the ghost ship's bow.

"It's an American rig," observed Luis, having noted the Key West registration on the trawler's transom.

"Better yet," declared El Minimo. "Any boat found in our territorial waters belongs to the glorious revolution, of which I am, for all intents and purposes, the big enchilada, so that means me. Anyway, it's a nicer boat than this tub. Maybe we'll switch."

"But what about international maritime law?" Luis asked. "Aren't we obligated to find out what happened to the occupants?"

"To hell with the occupants. They have abandoned their property to the ongoing struggle against the forces of imperialist tyranny and aggression. I'm going aboard to see if they left anything valuable…which will likewise belong to the glorious revolution. Who knows, I might find some American beer. That would be nice, *sí*? Or some Pringles? Mmm. Help me aboard. That's an order."

"But what about the Cuban people? Don't we have a solemn duty to share the bounty with the masses?"

"Do you think if Carlos Marx himself were to climb onto that boat and find a hoard of Sam Adams or Miller MDG, he'd share it with the unwashed proletariat? Get real, comrade. These poor bastards haven't had a whiff of real brew since 1958. The shock would kill them. In the long run, I'd be saving their workers'-paradise heinies."

He stuck out his arm, and Luis helped him hop into the other boat. El Min snooped around, went below, spotted the ugly masses of half-dissolved flesh and bone, pushed the gore around a little with his combat boot, stepped into and over the former humans, and checked the bar fridge. Sure enough, six bottles of Blue Moon Lager! He checked the cabinets, one after another, finding unopened bags of circus peanuts and Jays potato chips and O-Ke-Doke cheese popcorn, an almost-full package of Twizzlers cherry licorice sticks, half a bag of almond M&Ms, a jar of Jiffy peanut butter, a Quaker chewy granola bar, and a six-pack of Coca-Cola Zero.

He poked his head out of the cabin and yelled for Luis to empty one of the duffle bags they had brought with them to hold fishing supplies and toss it over. As he loaded the bag with the American bounty, the Cuban president's brother considered the mini-trawler itself. Yes, it was a beauty and would make a fine addition to his personal fleet—which technically belonged to the revolution, he admitted, but since he was its military and de facto political leader naturally fell into his care, custody, and control. The problem was this human detritus coagulating on the cabin floor. When he gazed at the bloody mess he didn't see the bodies of men with hopes and dreams and heartbreak and joy, maybe with wives and children waiting anxiously at home for their safe return. No, what he saw was bureaucracy. Forms, forms, forms. That was the devilish part of an all-controlling central government—damn paperwork. Stamps and signatures and triplicates and carbon paper and more stamps, more signatures, more copies, more carbon paper. Mother of mercy, how he hated carbon paper! He would no sooner come out of his nice weekly hot shower, fingers all wrinkly clean, don a freshly bleached and creased guayabera, and next thing you knew, some petty functionary would be handing him a damn form in triplicate, with two sheets of carbon paper filthying up his hands and clothes! Did they think detergent grew on trees? (He made a mental note of that phrase, vowing to slip it into his brother's next speech.)

So what he did was, he handed the duffle bag to Luis, jumped back onto his own boat, released the tow line, and let the ghost boat continue to drift. He said nothing about the bodies. "Let fate deliver it where it may," he declared, jiggling the new beer bottles. "Anyhow, we're set, amigo, big time."

They drank only half the American beer that day, because El Minimo wanted to save a few bottles for the roasted pork dinner waiting for him at home that night. How he loved a brewsky with his pig! When he got home, he handed the duffle bag with what remained of his snacks to his wife. As he headed to the bedroom to clean up, she squealed as if she had seen a mouse. He turned and saw her peering into the bag.

"What is it, *gatito*?"

"It's all right now, dear," she assured him. "It was only a few of those flying ants—"

"Flying ants?"

"Four or five only. But they flew away. Everything is fine."

"Don't scare me like that." He shook his head. "I held off Batista's army in the Sierra Madres. I led the charge on the Moncada Barracks! I stared down the barrels of Yanqui guns at the Bay of Pigs without flinching! But a silly woman sees a few flying ants and almost faints! No wonder men rule the world!"

The earnest but inept aspiring actor who kidnapped Diane happened to be the son (and spitting image) of Eddward Culvertdale's bulge-eyed secretary—with whom the President of Venezuela had left his promotional pen. The bumbling abductor later moved to Hollywood, completely failed as a movie star, failed miserably at every other menial job he took to try to pay his rent, wound up homeless, busted out at panhandling, nearly starved to death, became a heroin addict, lost all of his teeth to gum disease, tried being a male prostitute but got beaten to within an inch of his life and suffered extensive brain damage, sold

one of his kidneys for eleven dollars, and eventually became an extremely successful literary agent.

With the failure of Castaways' Revenge, his *Gilligan's Island*
action figures no longer held fascination for Cuba's bored
president. But he soon rediscovered, at the bottom of his
toy box, his Rocky and Bullwinkle action figures. He
played with them for hours at a time, pitting Gidney and
Cloyd (the little green men from the moon armed with
scrootch guns) against Dudley Do-Right of the Mounties,
tucking Boris Badenov under his pillow at night, and
kissing Natasha before turning out his light. Having a
quick and inventive mind, he soon concocted another
of his great plots to kill Miami Cubans, which he called
"Operation Wrongway Peachfuzz," with himself, as maximum leader and brain trust, code-named "Squirrel," and
his revolutionary brother-in-arms and co-conspirator Che
Guevara code-named "Moose" (Squirrel having forgotten
that Moose was dead).

Coast Guard patrol boat *46115*, under the able com-
mand of Lt. Whitehurst, proceeded to scour the area of
Sterling Star's last known coordinates before the cruise
ship's desperate, chilling cries for help faded into the

Bahamian night. Just after dawn they came upon and boarded the ship, discovering its flesh-devoured passengers and crew. Not knowing that the grisly devastation was the work of mutated, pork-crazed termites, the U.S. Defense Department convinced the American president that the havoc wreaked on the *Sterling Star* could only have been perpetrated by some terrorist organization's diabolical weapon of mass destruction: a neutron-bomblike destroyer of living cell tissue, one of the most potentially calamitous weapons ever devised. The United States strongly suspected its number one enemy, Iran, to be behind this attack and, as we speak, is planning a massive counterattack on the terrorist nation to stop its nuclear program, to be followed by an Iraq-Afghanistan-style invasion.

Akhmed, meanwhile, having returned to Tehran for a few months after his team's failed attempt to detonate nuclear matzo balls in Miami but finding himself constantly thinking about his former cellmate, Artie, came back to New York, excited but not hopeful, and set about to find the naughty fellow. He checked with the lead counsel in the county building, a sympathetic and helpful state's attorney by the name of Irwin Mandelbaum. The president had to admit, when it came right down to it, Zionists weren't so bad. He had always suspected his own dentist of secretly being a Jew, and the president had terrific teeth. His gums were very pink, and he admired how the man made him pleasantly suffer during periodic cleanings.

State's Attorney Mandelbaum helped him find his former cellmate and even had one of his assistants drive him to Artie's SRO day-rate hotel on 12th Street. The rascal was sweeping the lobby floor, when the Iranian snuck up from behind, covered his eyes, and exclaimed, "Guess who!" Artie threw up his hands and cried, "It's not mine, I swear! I'm only holding it for a friend!" Akhmed spun him around and gave him a big hug. It took Artie a few minutes to calm down and clear his head, but after several minutes of his old kaluki partner reminding him when and where, he finally claimed to remember, sort of.

That afternoon the Iranian leader took Artie on a Fifth Avenue clothes and jewelry shopping spree and to a hair salon and spa, where they each got a cut, manicure, pedicure, cucumber facial, and a heavenly massage. Akhmed got him a room at his hotel, in which they collapsed at the end of the day, loaded down with bags and boxes, completely but pleasantly exhausted. After a little nap, the president treated Artie to an Italian dinner in Greenwich Village, where, over candlelight and Chianti, they reminisced about their time in lockup, had some good guffaws, and, yawning, decided that tomorrow was another day. That's when Artie offhandedly mentioned that had he not been so tired, he'd love to go dancing.

"Dancing!" Akhmed exclaimed. "You like to dance?!"

"Sure," Artie said. "Any kind of dancing: country western, disco, bump and grind, jitterbug, ballroom, you name it."

"But in jail you never said a word about dancing!"

Artie frowned, looked around cautiously, and whispered, "There's a time and place for everything."

It was then that Akhmed knew he had been put on this earth to live in New York, despite the Jews. In fact, if you ever needed an ambulance-chaser, doctor, aforesaid dentist, or bail bondsman, Yids were the way to go. (Not car repairmen, handymen, plumbers, or barbers, though.) When last seen, the Iranian despot and Artie were rutting the parquet at Simon's Blue Boy Social Club, just west of Washington Square, and, when not dancing, sharing lemon martinis and viewing scenes of Niagara Falls through a 3-D View-Master.

While, in the Havana taxicab, Hazeem waited hornily for Jacobita to come back from (so she had said) searching for the perfect spot on the Malecón to make love, he noticed something odd about her oversized purse. For some strange reason, she had fastened its zipper to a strap hook with a mini-padlock. Odd indeed, for what could there have been so valuable in the junky faux-leather bag that she would want to keep out curious eyes? Not money, surely, as a thief could easily break the flimsy lock. Besides, if something inside was so valuable, why wouldn't she have kept the purse with her? It didn't make sense.

An ordinary horny fellow would have dismissed his suspicions in deference to his erection. But years working for Akhmed had taught Hazeem one thing above all: never trust bad fashion sense. This purse was an abomination. Imitation snakeskin, badly cracked, straps frayed. A six-inch patch of dirty duct tape, curled at the corners, bandaged one end. Very strange, for Jacobita herself was well-dressed, quite sharp, in fact—nothing frayed about her except this ugly handbag.

So as he looked over her purse, he thought, *Hmm*. He gazed beyond the Malecón into the sea's nighttime abyss, spotted Jacobita's empty canvas sack somersaulting toward them, and thought that was quite odd, too.

"Driver," he said, tapping him on the shoulder, "I need to stretch and get some fresh air."

"This is a safe neighborhood, señor. All Cuba is safe."

"Still, I'd like a bit of company. Why not walk with me as we enjoy this good rum?"

"Oh, *sí*, that would be fine, señor."

"Fine, yes," said Hazeem, sipping, as they strode with the bottle down the dark street, Hazeem leading the driver as quickly from the old Chevrolet as possible without raising suspicion.

Leaving Jacobita's purse behind.

After the cab and three abandoned buildings were blown to smithereens, the driver, realizing that Hazeem had saved his life, invited him to stay at his house with his grateful family, which Hazeem did, under strict cover—he dared not even contact Samreen—until Akhmed's atomic matzo ball plot played itself out. He knew that his former boss was such a bumblefuck—he was fairly certain that was the correct term—that Castaways' Revenge would fall apart without a single casualty, except perhaps to the plotters themselves.

Which is how Akhmed's former friend, confidant, and longtime interpreter wound up giving away the bride, his beautiful niece Samreen, at her and Angus's wedding.

The immigrant Iraqi maid, who found the container of matzo balls the con man, pimp, and burglar Reggie G. had left open in Akhmed's hotel room, brought the delicacy home to her young son, Simtar—not knowing, of course, that this was not ordinary deli, but nuclear food. She heated up the soup, tucked a napkin under Simtar's chin, and, after saying a prayer for the soul of their beloved husband and father, recently murdered by Shiite Iranian mercenaries, joined the boy in a scrumptious bowl of the Hebrew delicacy.

A few months later, the maid, desperate for money, took a second job in a New Jersey casino, where, when after work one night she took a chance on the twenty-five-cent Big Bertha slot machine, she won not one but two consecutive $2.5-million jackpots. The slot machine manufacturer claimed the odds of that happening were less than that of a meteor striking the earth and destroying all life. Yet the experts could find nothing defective about that particular machine, one technician declaring it had acted "like it got bombarded with radiation or something." Taking no further chances, the casino encased it in cement and dumped it into Absecon Bay, to sleep with the gefilte fishes.

Acknowledgments

Loving thanks to: Christy Quinto, the best editor on the planet(s); James and Sean O'Reilly, great publishers and friends; Larry Habegger, a writer's pal; my UIC family; and all my friends, here when I needed them—you know who you are (special thanks to Marc Buslik, Steve Rubin, Barbara Ruvel, Lee Buslik, Marv Cohen, Betty Dim, Larry Mayer, Karl Merklein, Nancy Cirillo, David Crawford, Mary and David Whitehurst, Judy and Terry Caldwell, Marilyn and Richard Theobald, Quyen Dang and Chu Lee, Hal Unterberger, Linda Carter, Sonny and Phyllis).

About the Author

Gary Buslik writes essays, short stories, and novels. He teaches literature, creative writing, and travel writing at the University of Illinois at Chicago. You can visit him on Facebook (he needs all the friends he can get), Twitter (ditto), or at www.garybuslik.com and www.arottenperson.com.